# FUKUF...

## Kitten Tales

# 1

## Konami Kanata

# CONTENTS

FUKU FUKU

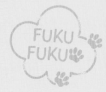

# Kitten FukuFuku

FUKU FUKU

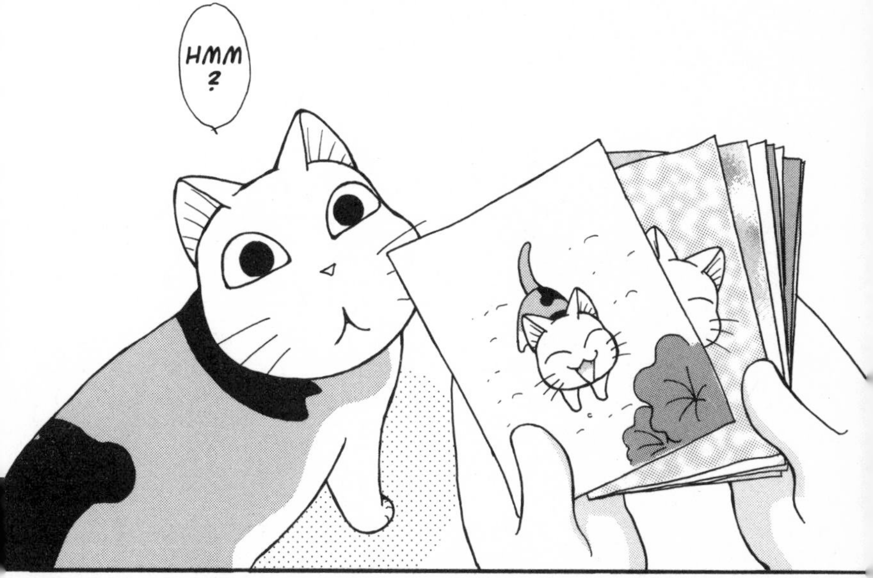
HMM ?

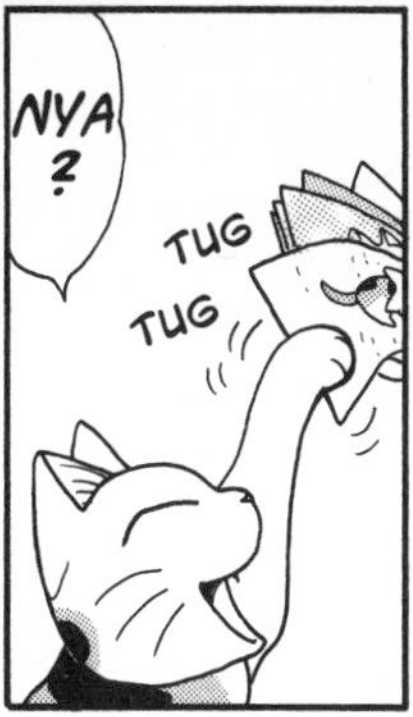
NYA ?
TUG TUG

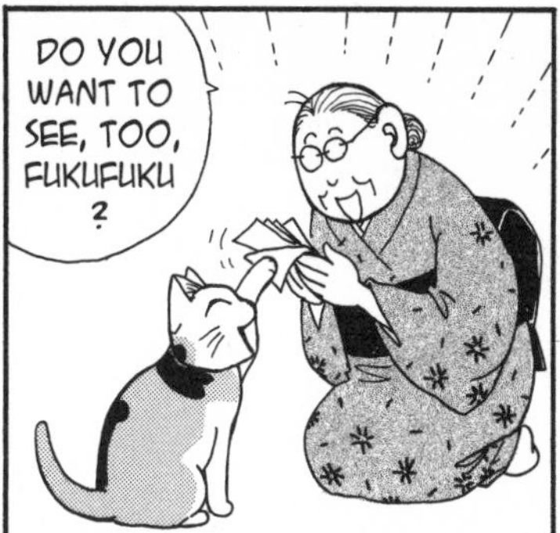
DO YOU WANT TO SEE, TOO, FUKUFUKU ?

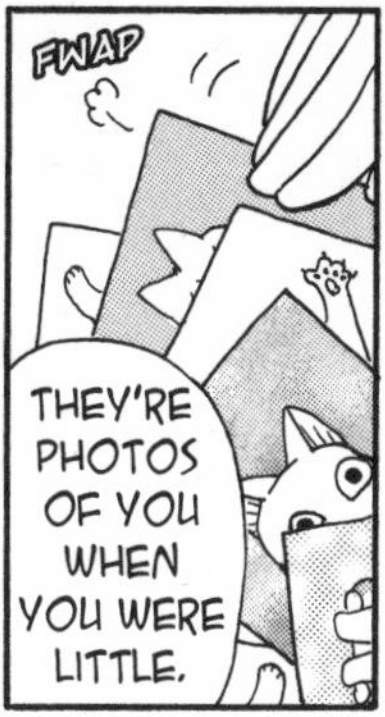
FWAP
THEY'RE PHOTOS OF YOU WHEN YOU WERE LITTLE.

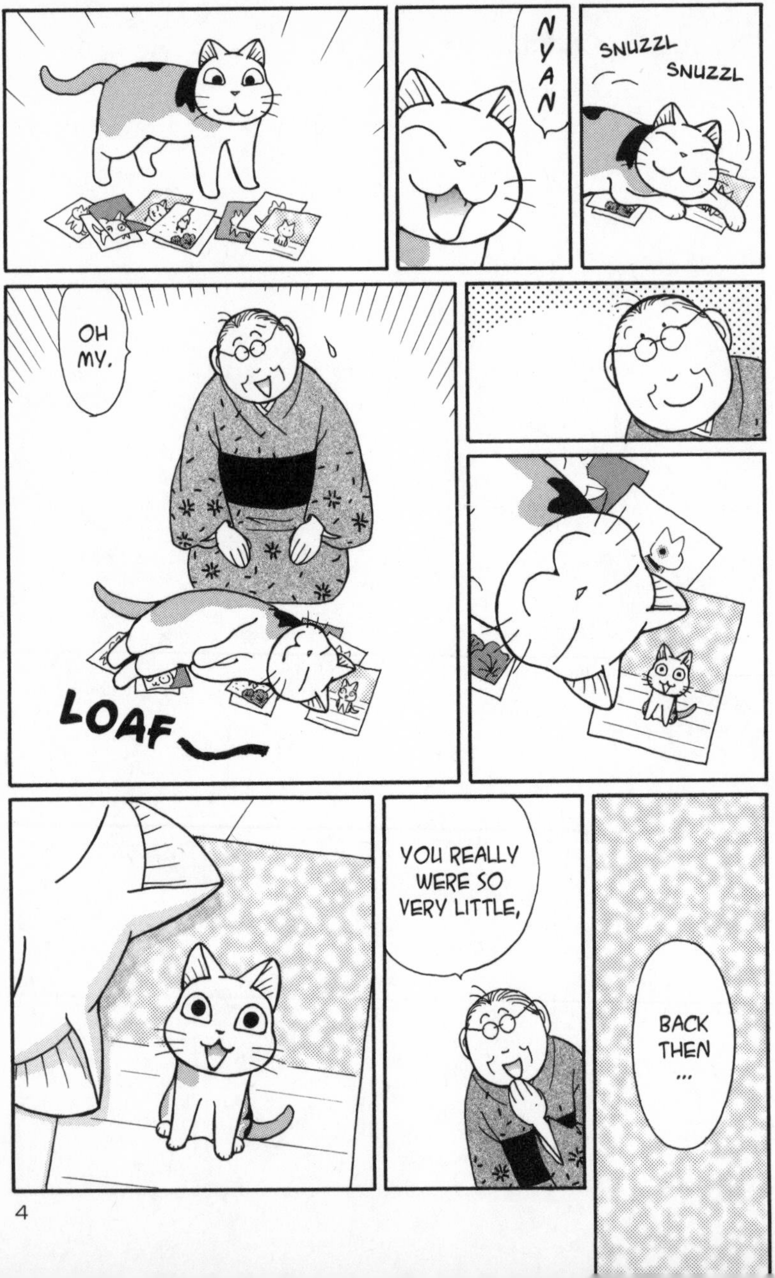

NYAN
SNUZZL SNUZZL
OH MY.
LOAF
YOU REALLY WERE SO VERY LITTLE,
BACK THEN ...

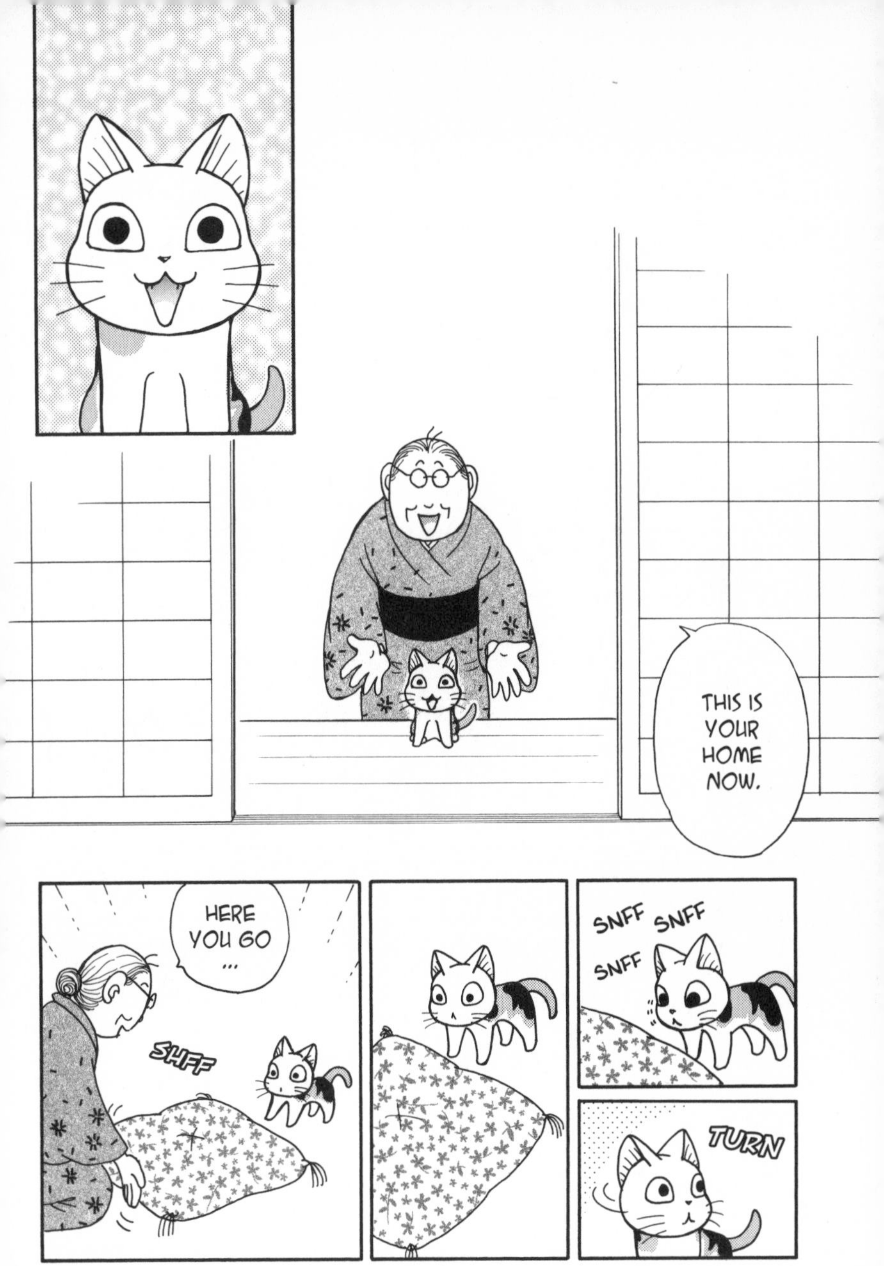
THIS IS YOUR HOME NOW.
HERE YOU GO ...
SHFF
SNFF SNFF
SNFF
TURN

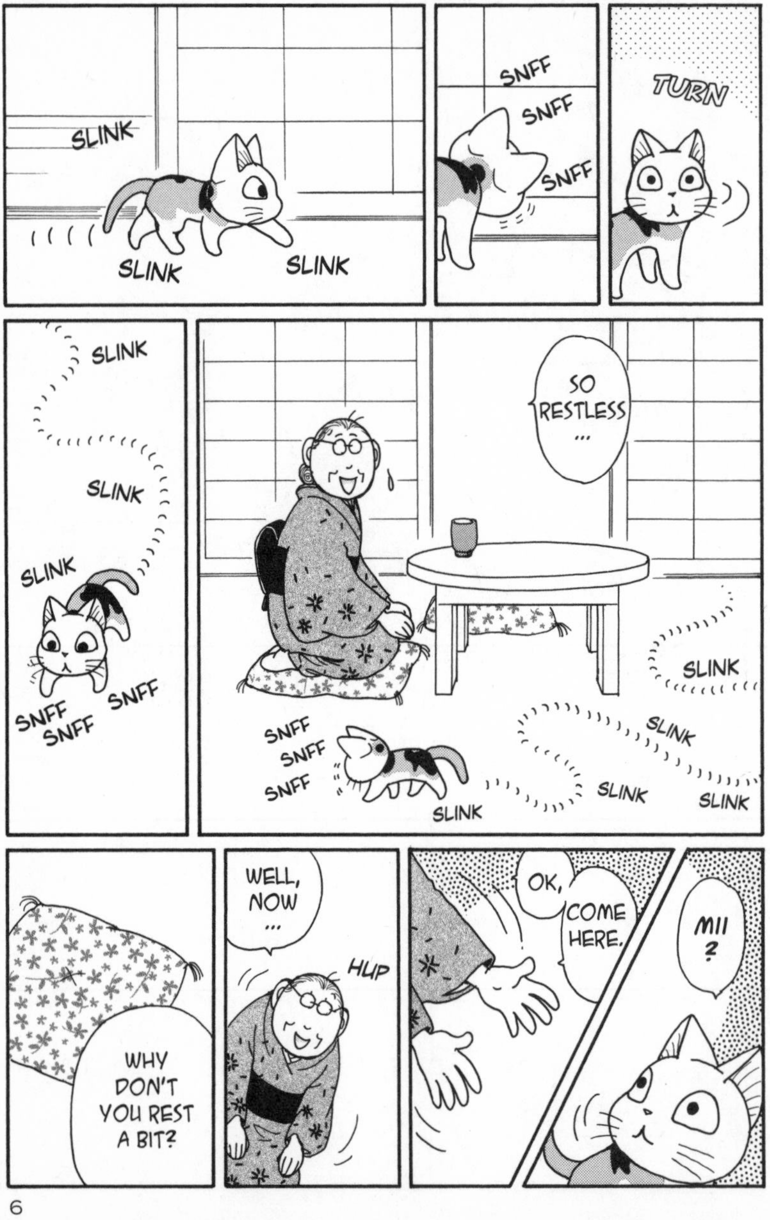
SLINK
SLINK
SLINK
SNFF
SNFF
SNFF
TURN
SLINK
SLINK
SLINK
SNFF
SNFF
SNFF
SO RESTLESS ...
SNFF
SNFF
SNFF
SLINK
SLINK
SLINK
SLINK
SLINK
WHY DON'T YOU REST A BIT?
WELL, NOW ...
HUP
OK,
COME HERE.
MII ?

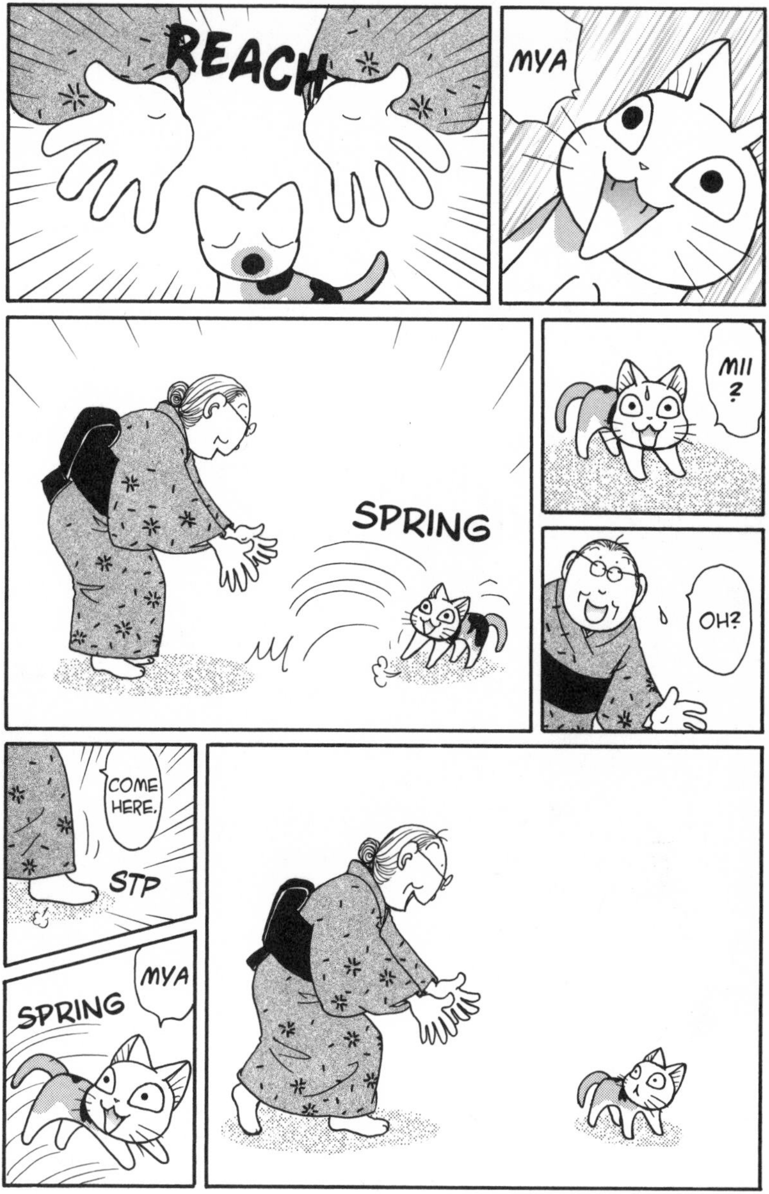
REACH
MYA
SPRING
MII?
OH?
COME HERE.
STP
SPRING
MYA

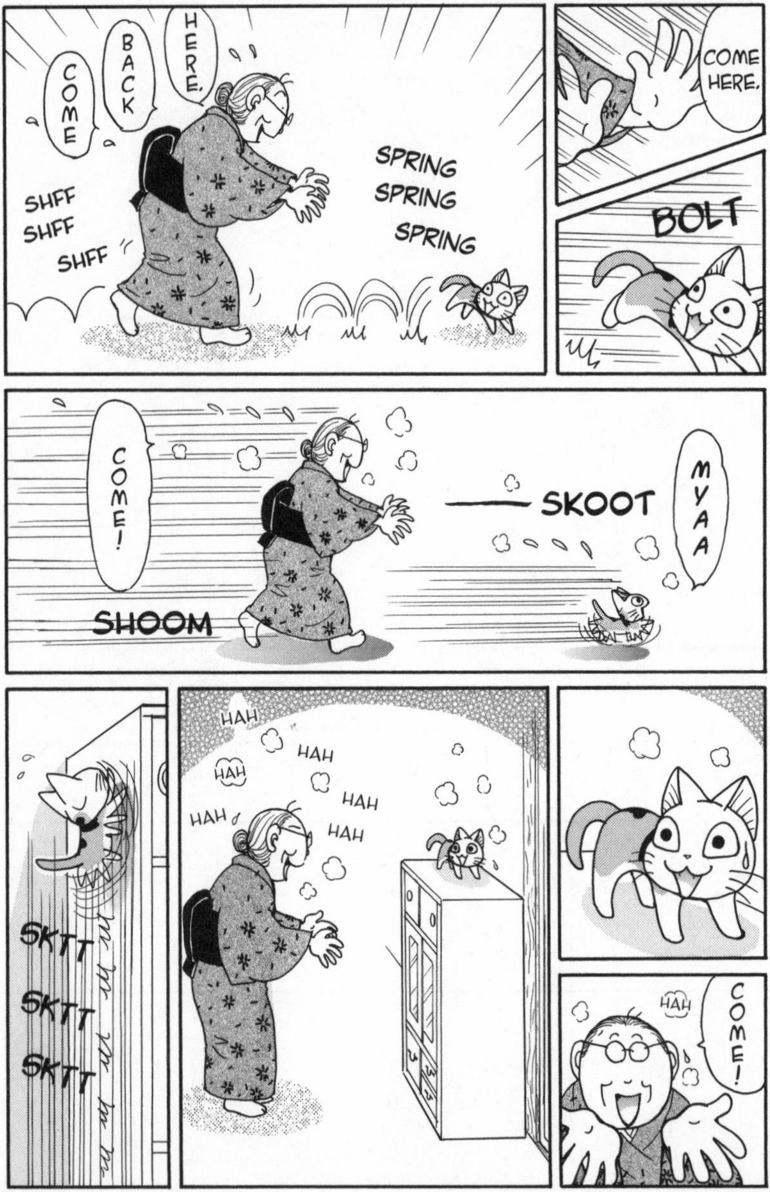
COME BACK HERE.
SHFF SHFF SHFF
SPRING SPRING SPRING
COME HERE.
BOLT
COME!
SHOOM
SKOOT
MYAA
SKTT SKTT SKTT
HAH
HAH
HAH
HAH
HAH
HAH
HAH
COME!

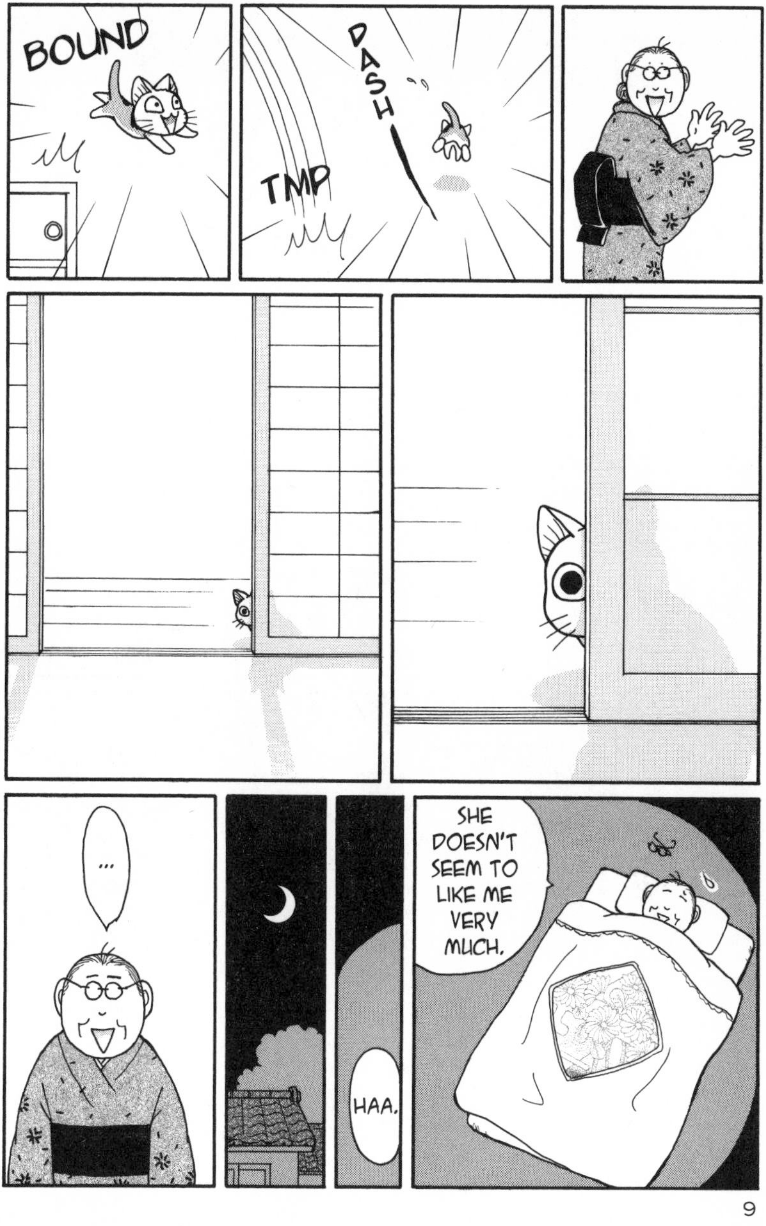
BOUND
DASH
TMP
...
SHE DOESN'T SEEM TO LIKE ME VERY MUCH.
HAA.

I WONDER WHAT SHE'S UP TO NOW.

CREEP CREEP CREEP CREEP

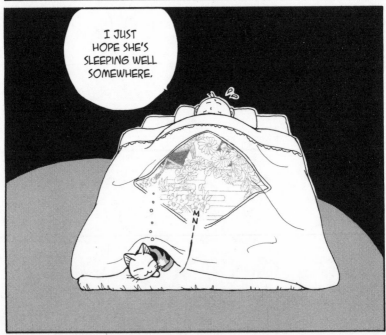

I JUST HOPE SHE'S SLEEPING WELL SOMEWHERE.

the end

# Why She Can't Get Mad

FUKU FUKU

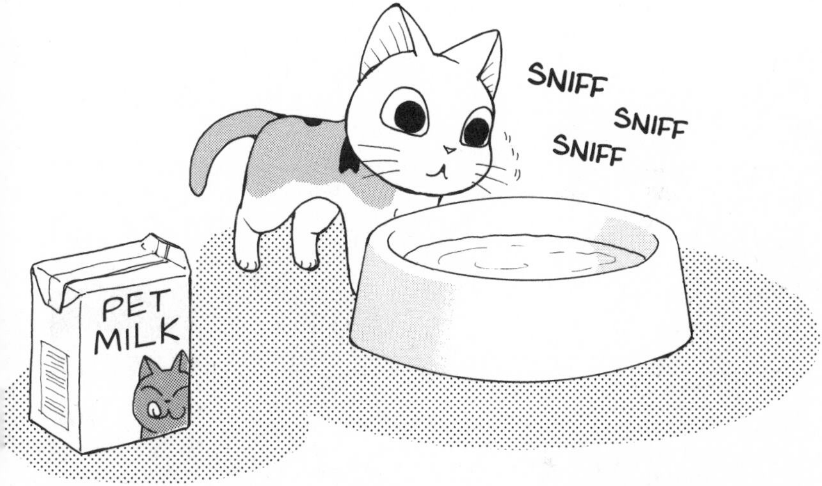
SNIFF
SNIFF
SNIFF
PET MILK

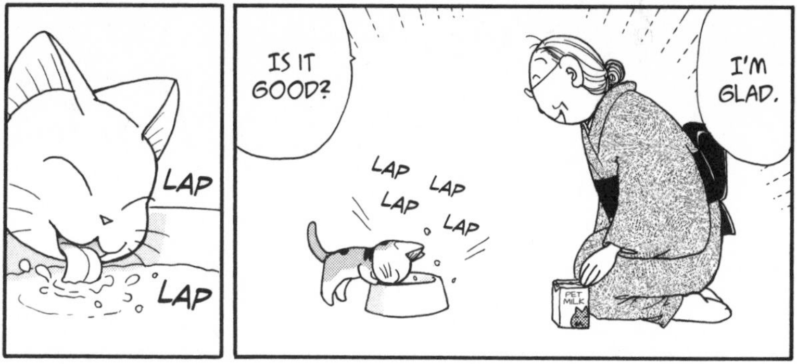
LAP
LAP
IS IT GOOD?
I'M GLAD.
LAP
LAP
LAP
LAP
PET MILK

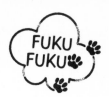

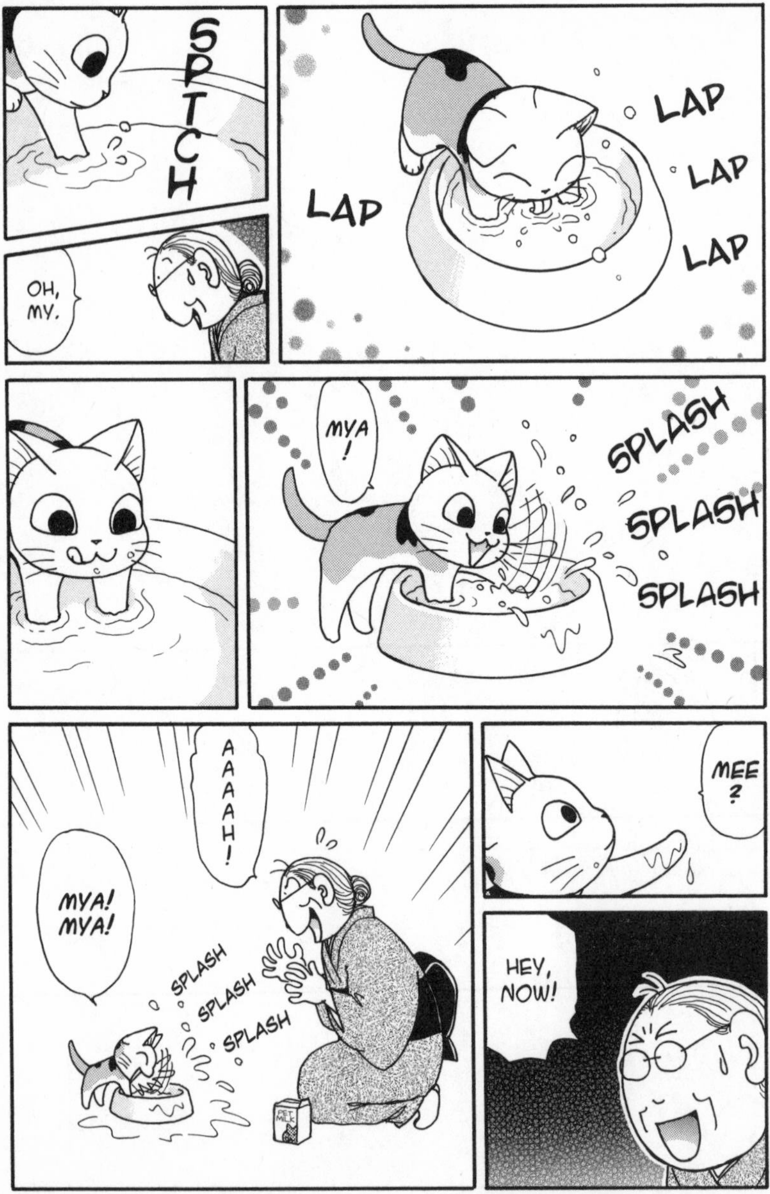
SPTCH
OH, MY.
LAP
LAP
LAP
LAP
MYA!
SPLASH
SPLASH
SPLASH
AAAAAH!
MYA! MYA!
SPLASH
SPLASH
SPLASH
PET MILK
MEE?
HEY, NOW!

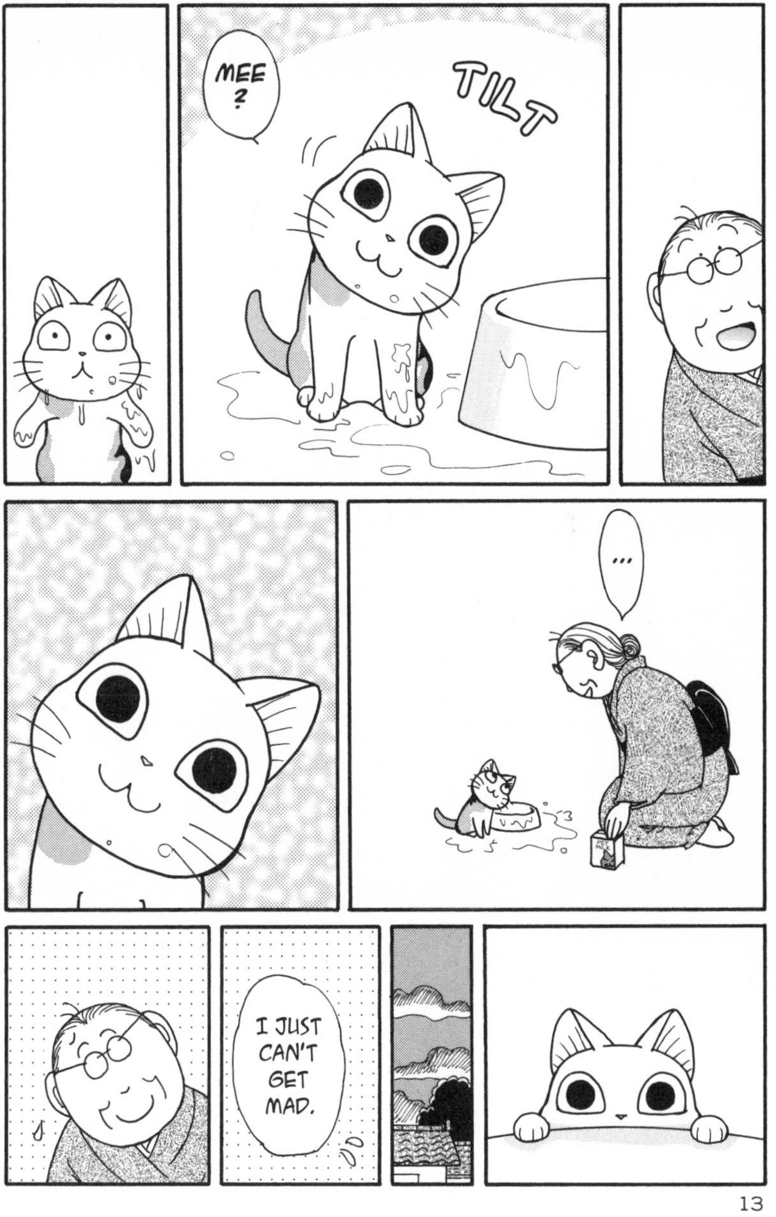
MEE ?
TILT
...
I JUST CAN'T GET MAD.

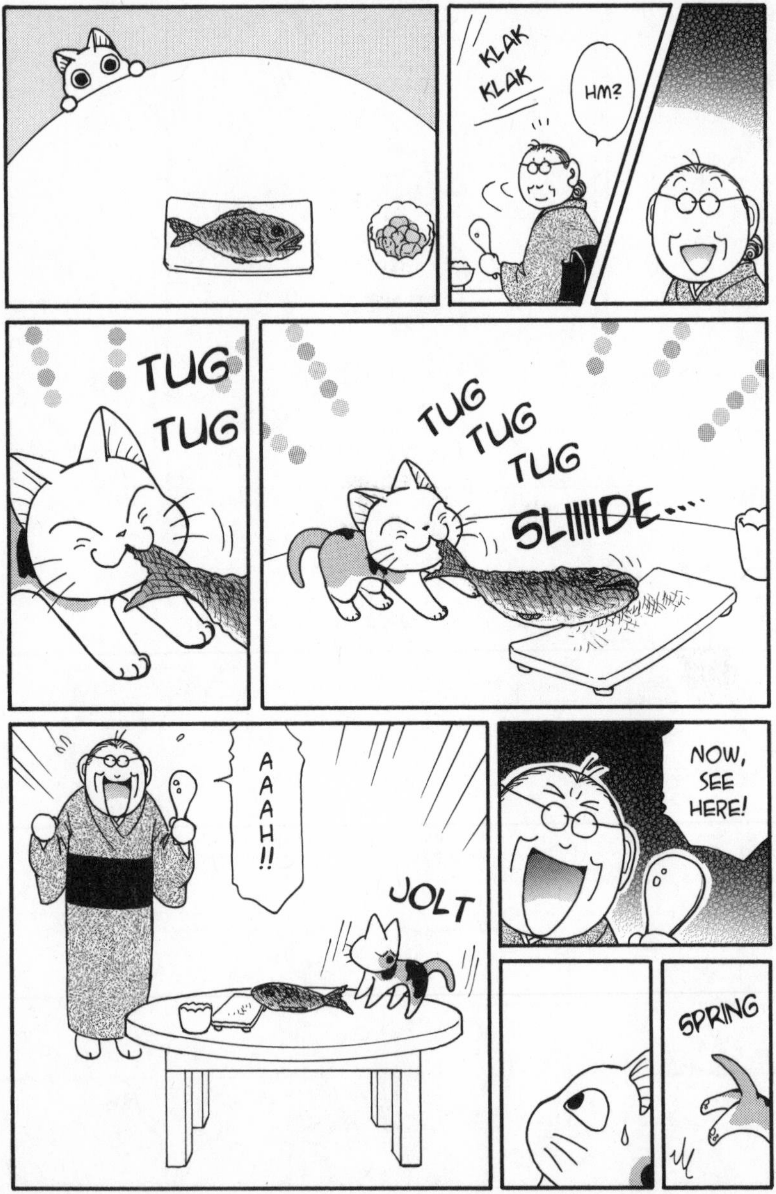
KLAK
KLAK
HM?
TUG
TUG
TUG
TUG
TUG
SLIIIIDE....
AAAAH!!
JOLT
NOW, SEE HERE!
SPRING

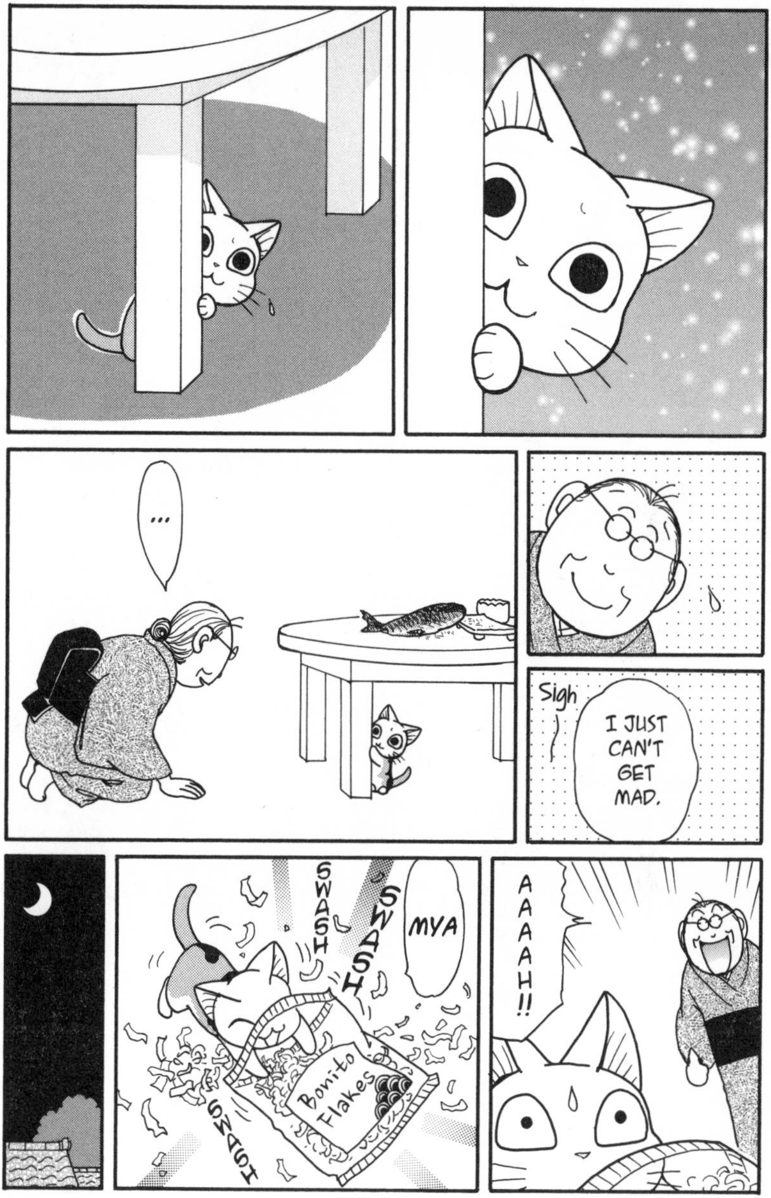
...
Sigh
I JUST CAN'T GET MAD.
SWASH
SWASH
MYA
Bonito Flakes
SWASH
AAAAAH!!

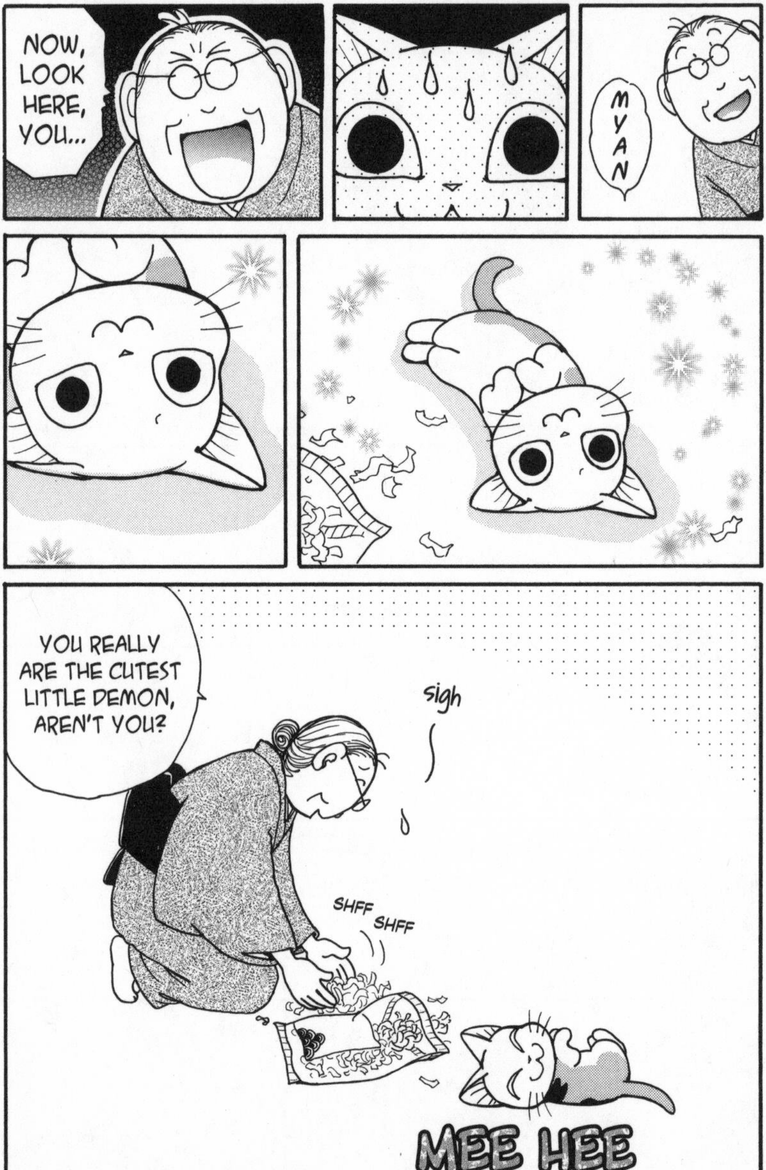
NOW, LOOK HERE, YOU...
MYAN
YOU REALLY ARE THE CUTEST LITTLE DEMON, AREN'T YOU?
sigh
SHFF SHFF
MEE HEE

the end

# Water and Bubbles

FUKU FUKU

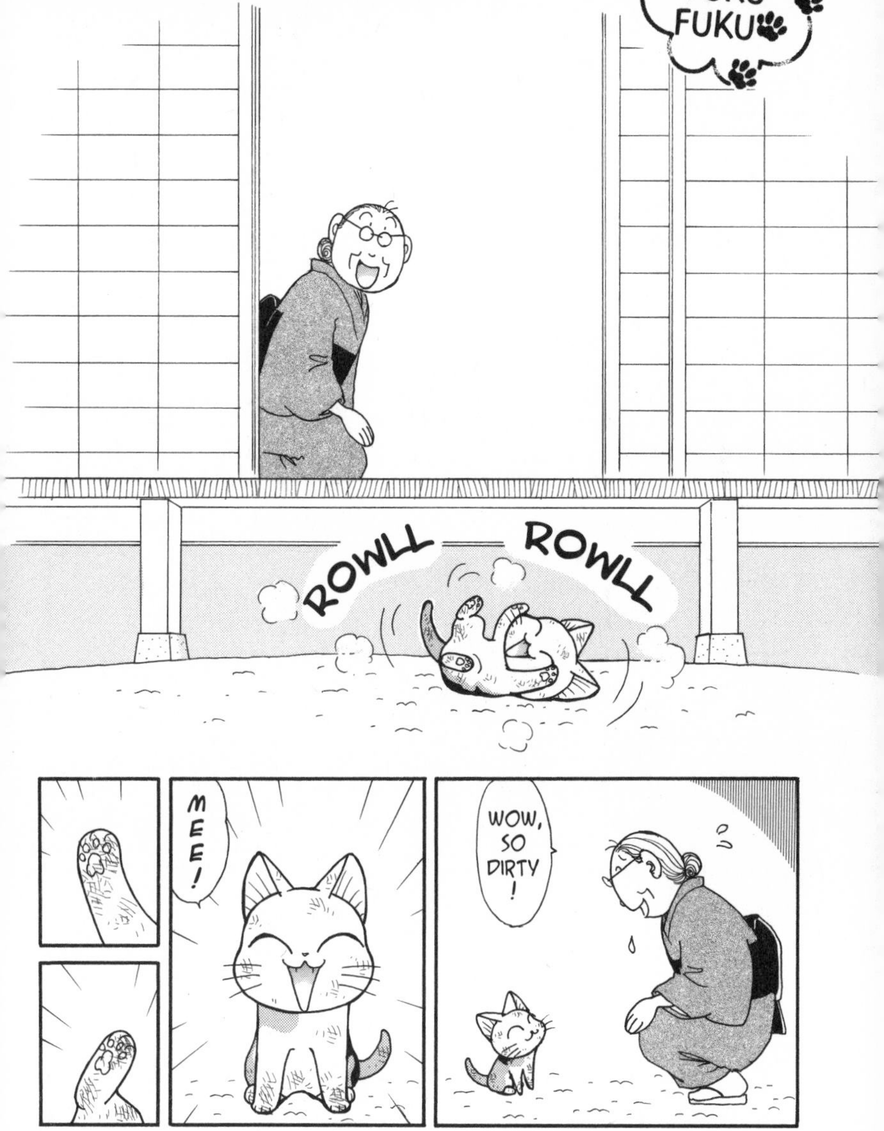

ROWLL ROWLL
MEE!
WOW, SO DIRTY!

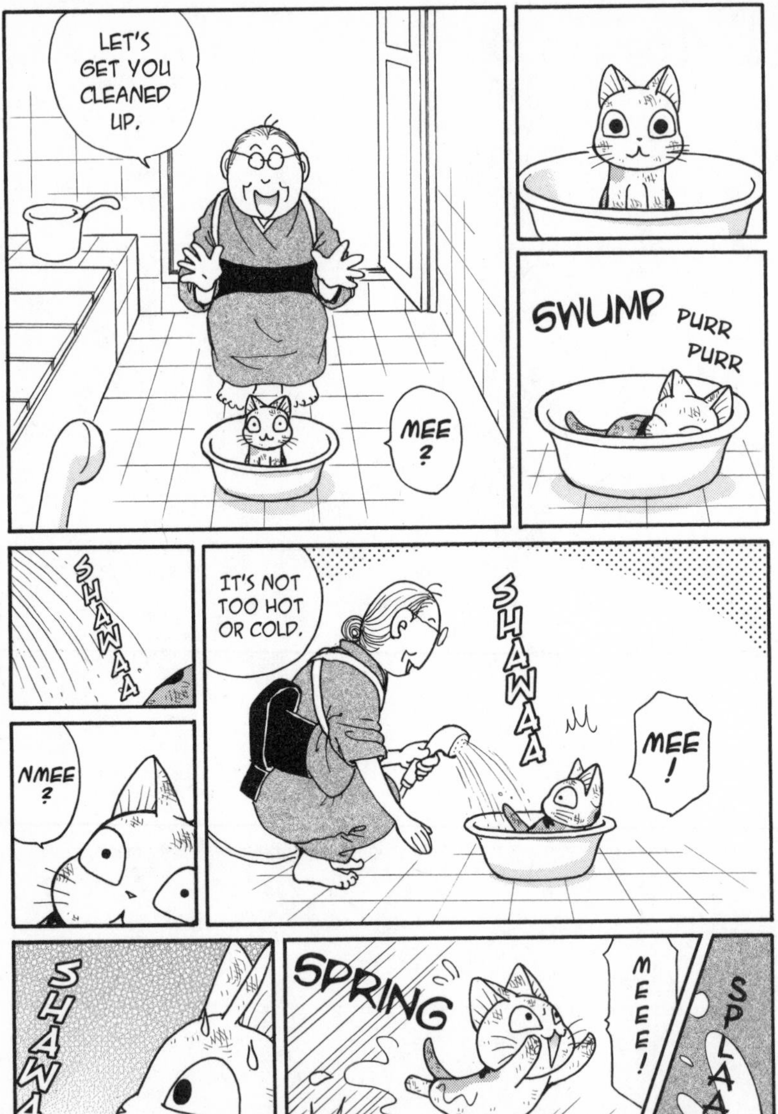
LET'S GET YOU CLEANED UP.
MEE ?
SWUMP
PURR PURR
SHAWAA
IT'S NOT TOO HOT OR COLD.
SHAWAA
MEE !
NMEE ?
SHAWAA
SPRING
MEEE!
SPLAASH

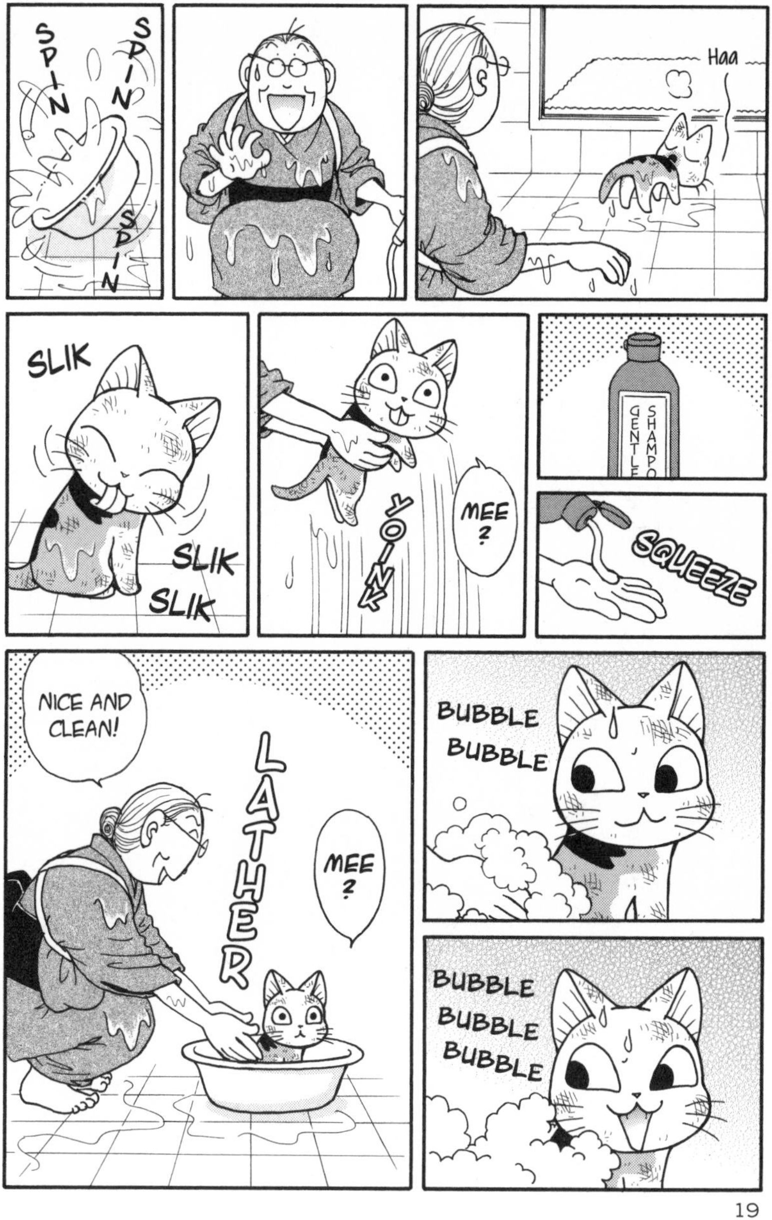

SPIN SPIN SPIN
Haa
SLIK
SLIK
SLIK
MEE?
YOINK
GENTLE SHAMPOO
SQUEEZE
NICE AND CLEAN!
LATHER
MEE?
BUBBLE BUBBLE
BUBBLE BUBBLE BUBBLE

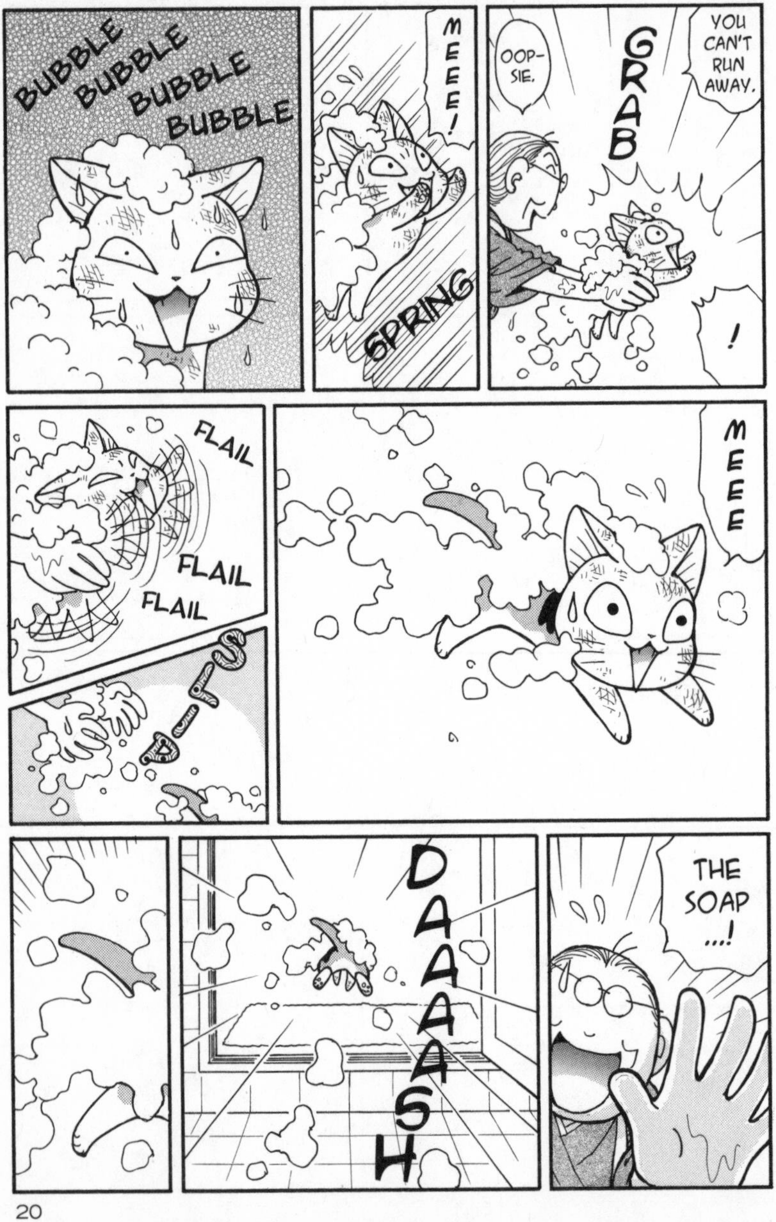
BUBBLE
BUBBLE
BUBBLE
BUBBLE
MEEEE!
SPRING
OOP-SIE.
GRAB
YOU CAN'T RUN AWAY.
!
FLAIL
FLAIL
FLAIL
MEEEE
DAAAASH
THE SOAP ...!

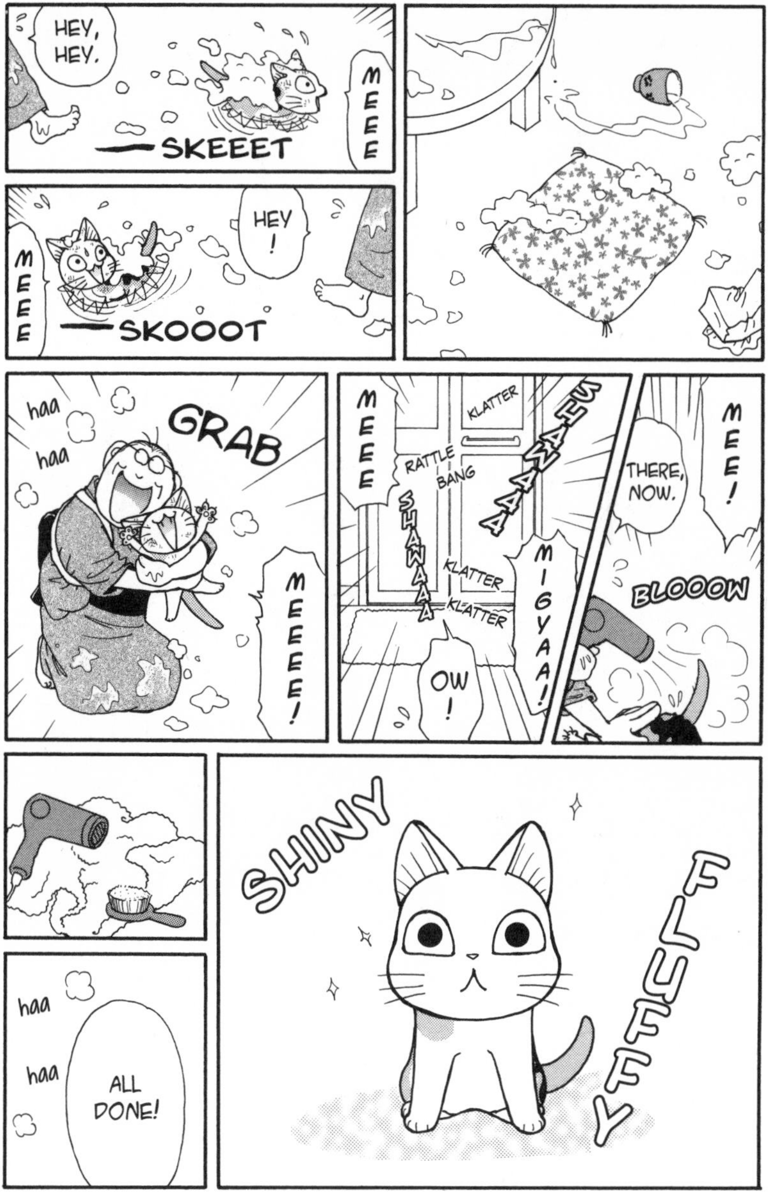
HEY, HEY.
SKEEET
MEEE
MEEE
SKOOOT
HEY!
haa
haa
GRAB
MEEEEE!
MEEE
KLATTER
SHAWAAA
RATTLE
BANG
SHAWAAA
KLATTER
KLATTER
OW!
MIGYAAA!
MEE!
THERE, NOW.
BLOOOW
haa
haa
ALL DONE!
SHINY
FLUFFY

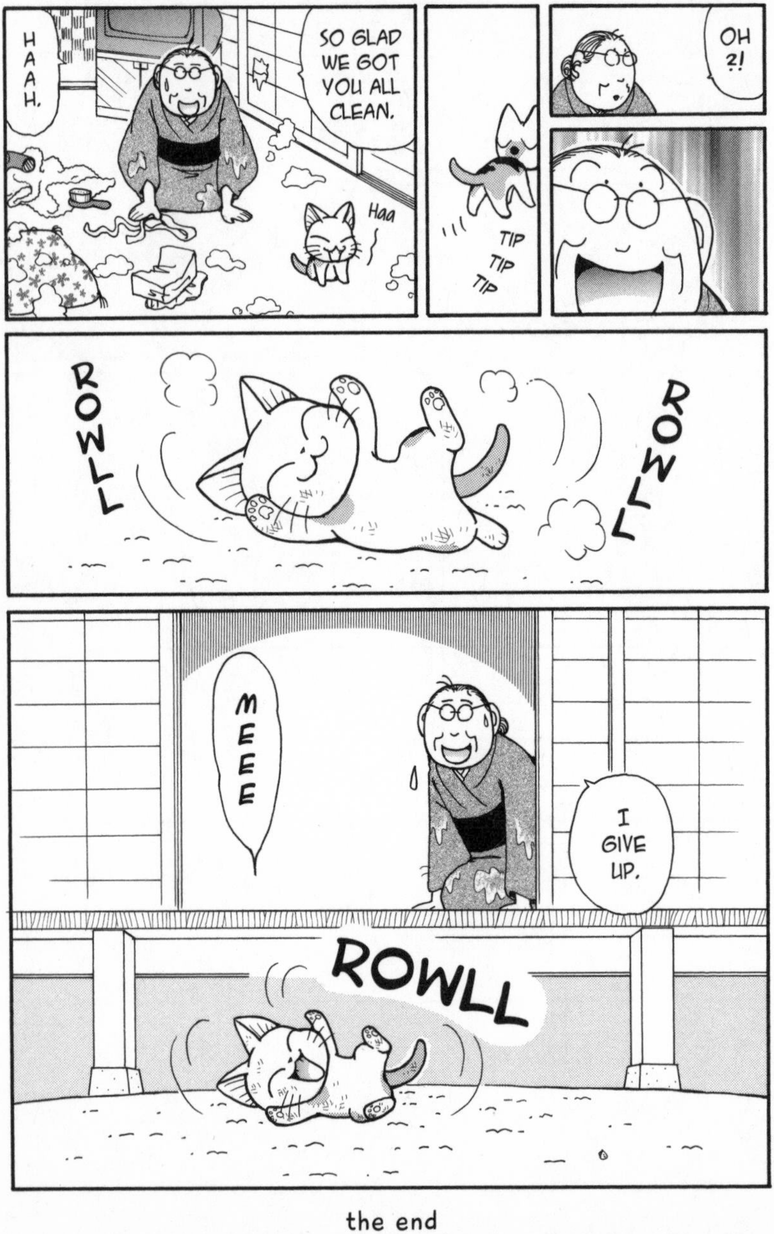
HAAAH.
SO GLAD WE GOT YOU ALL CLEAN.
Haa
TIP TIP TIP
OH ?!
ROWLL
ROWLL
MEEE
I GIVE UP.
ROWLL

the end

# The Key to Friendship

FUKU FUKU

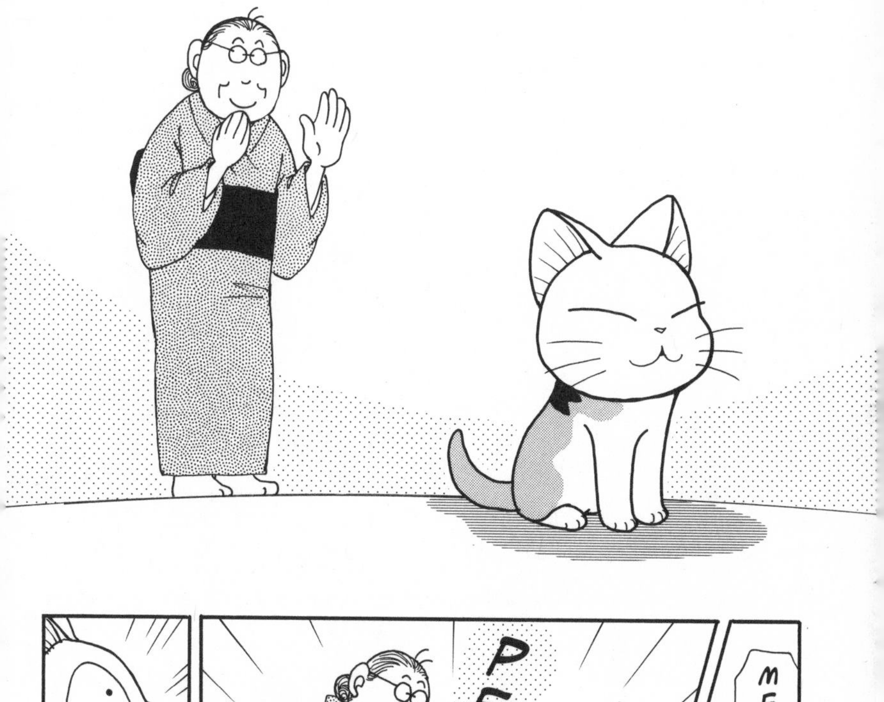

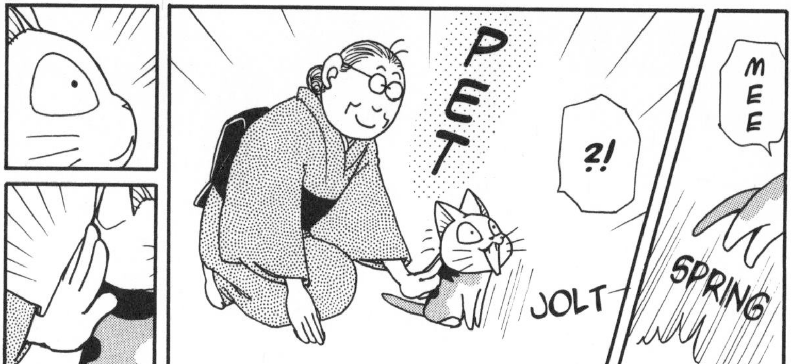
PET
?!
JOLT
MEE
SPRING

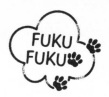

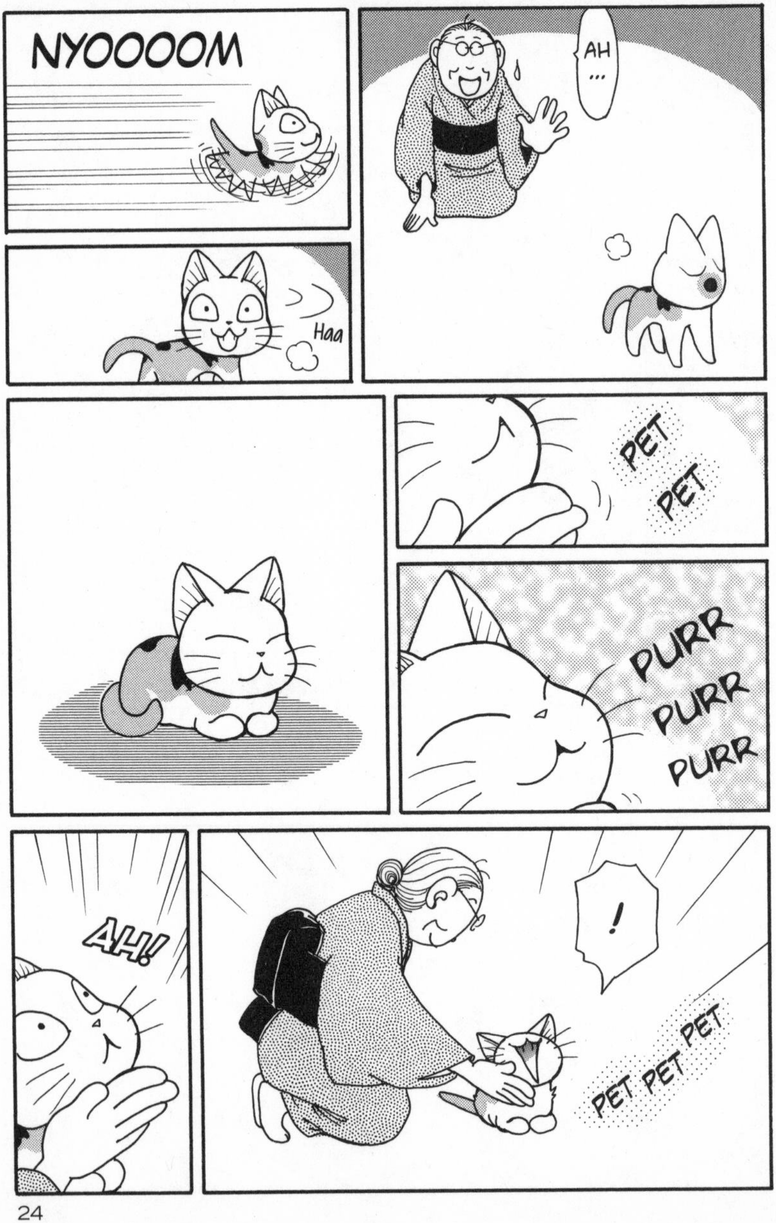
NYOOOOM
Haa
AH ...
PET
PET
PURR
PURR
PURR
AH!
!
PET PET PET

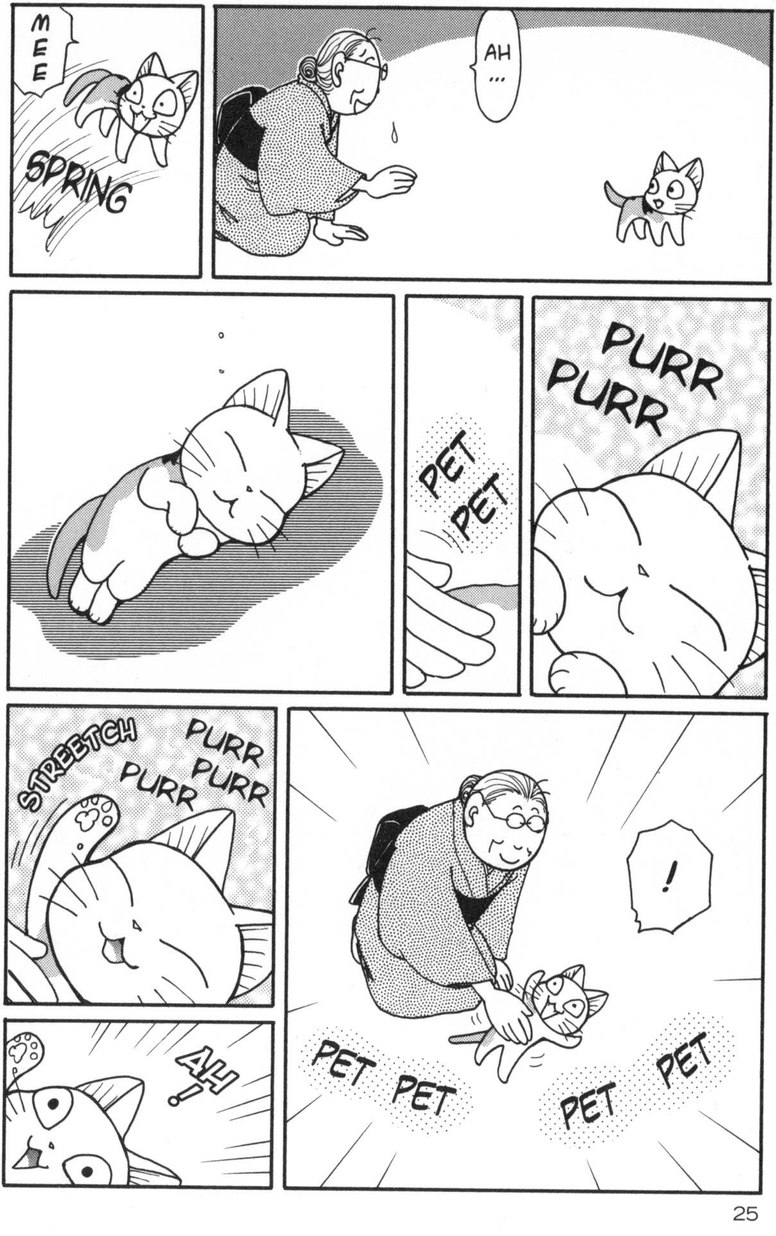
MEE
SPRING
AH ...
PET PET
PURR PURR
STREETCH
PURR PURR
PURR
AH!
!
PET PET
PET PET

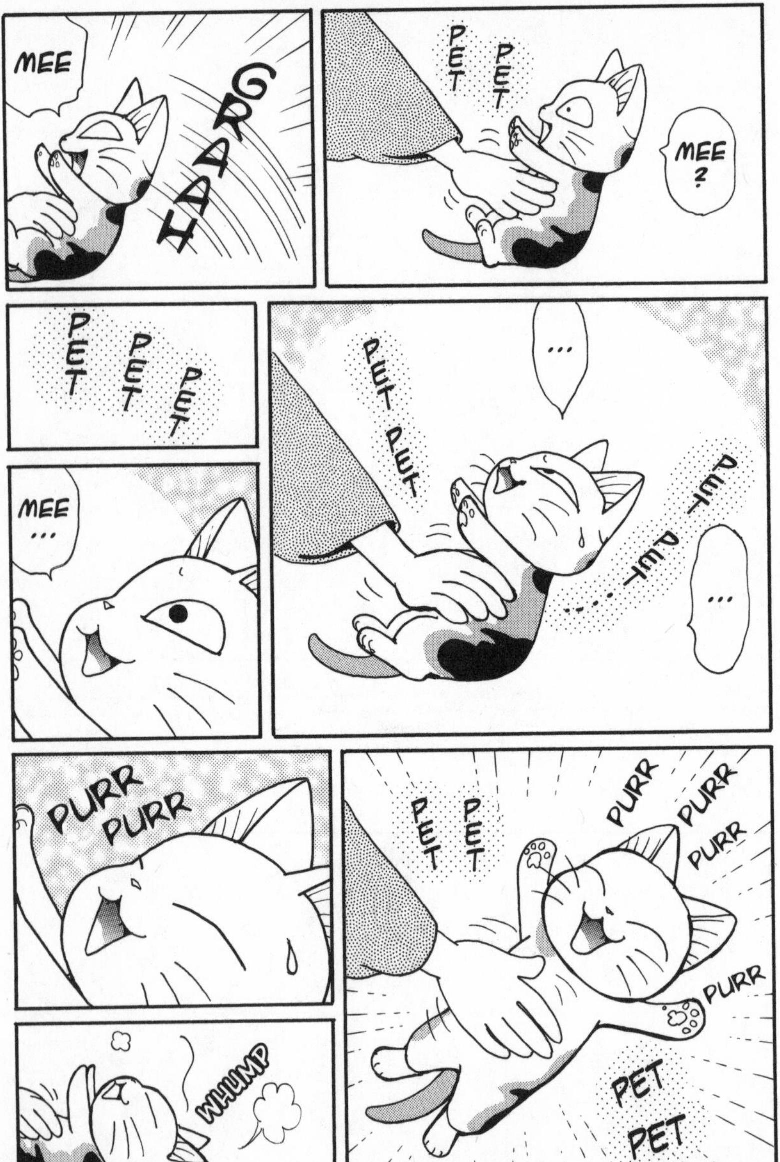
MEE
GRAAH
PET PET
MEE ?
PET PET PET
MEE ...
...
PET PET
PET PET ...
...
PURR PURR
WHUMP
PET PET
PURR PURR PURR
PURR
PET PET

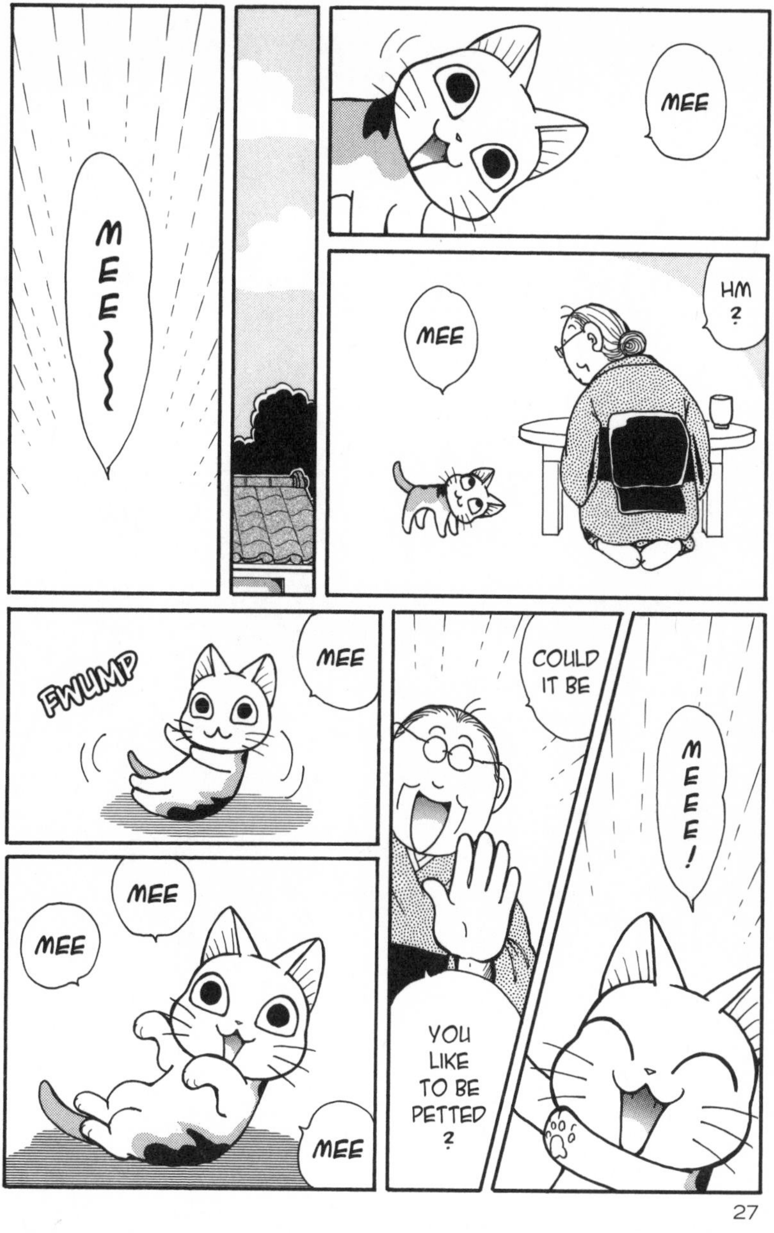
MEE~~
MEE
MEE
HM?
FWUMP
MEE
MEE
MEE
MEE
COULD IT BE
YOU LIKE TO BE PETTED?
MEEE!

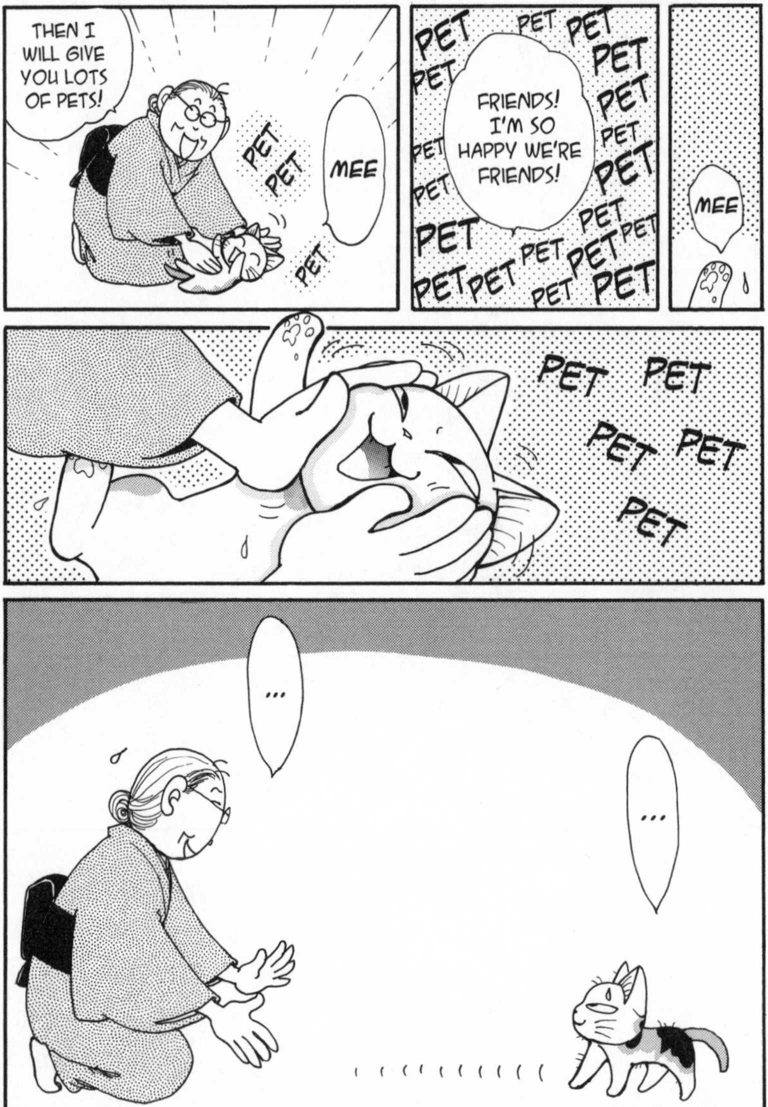
THEN I WILL GIVE YOU LOTS OF PETS!
PET PET
MEE
PET
PET PET PET PET PET PET PET PET PET PET PET PET PET PET PET PET PET PET
FRIENDS! I'M SO HAPPY WE'RE FRIENDS!
MEE
PET PET PET PET PET
...
...

the end

# You Called?

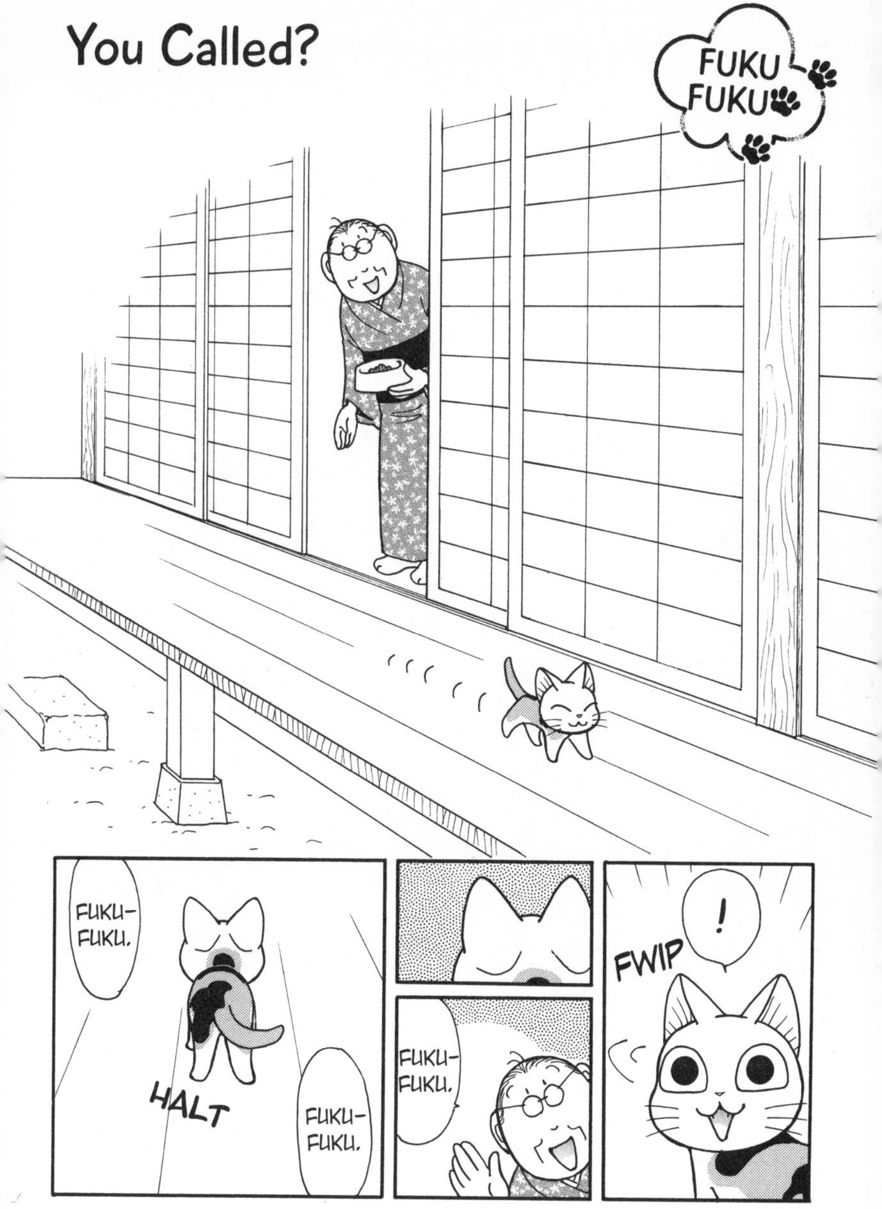
FUKU-FUKU.
HALT
FUKU-FUKU.
FUKU-FUKU.
FWIP
!

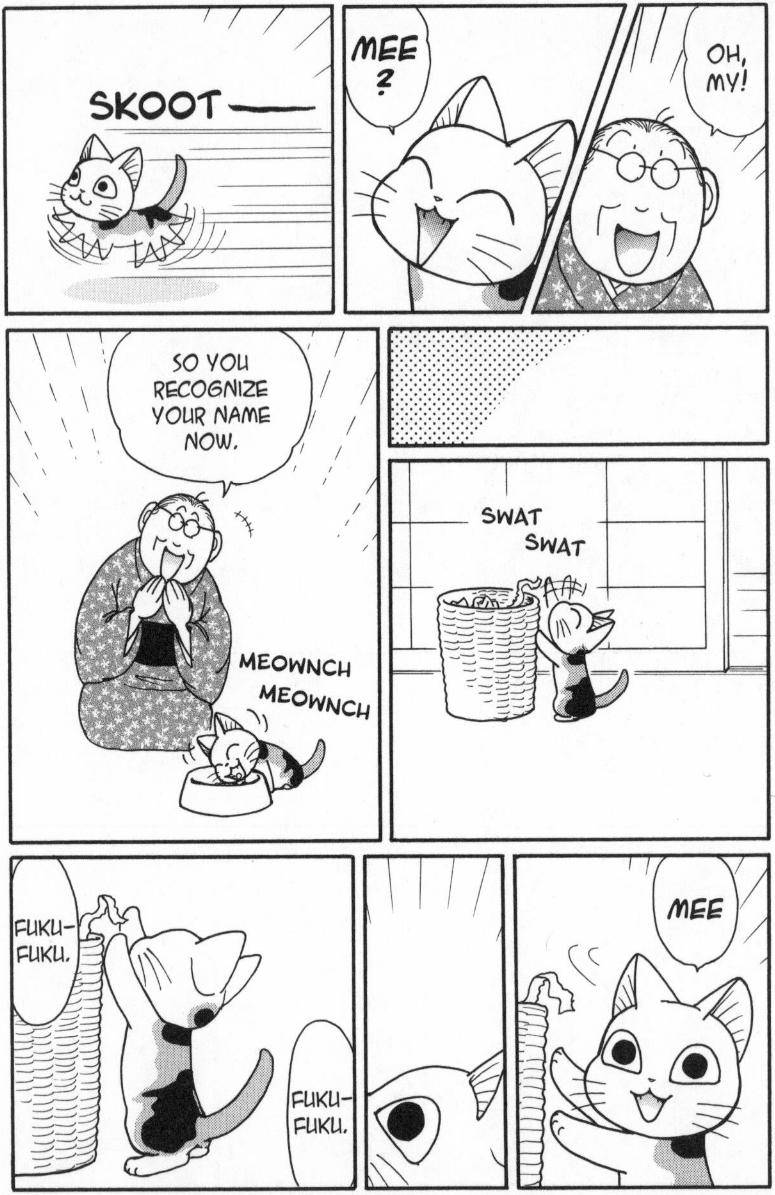
SKOOT——
MEE?
OH, MY!
SO YOU RECOGNIZE YOUR NAME NOW.
MEOWNCH MEOWNCH
SWAT SWAT
FUKU-FUKU.
FUKU-FUKU.
MEE

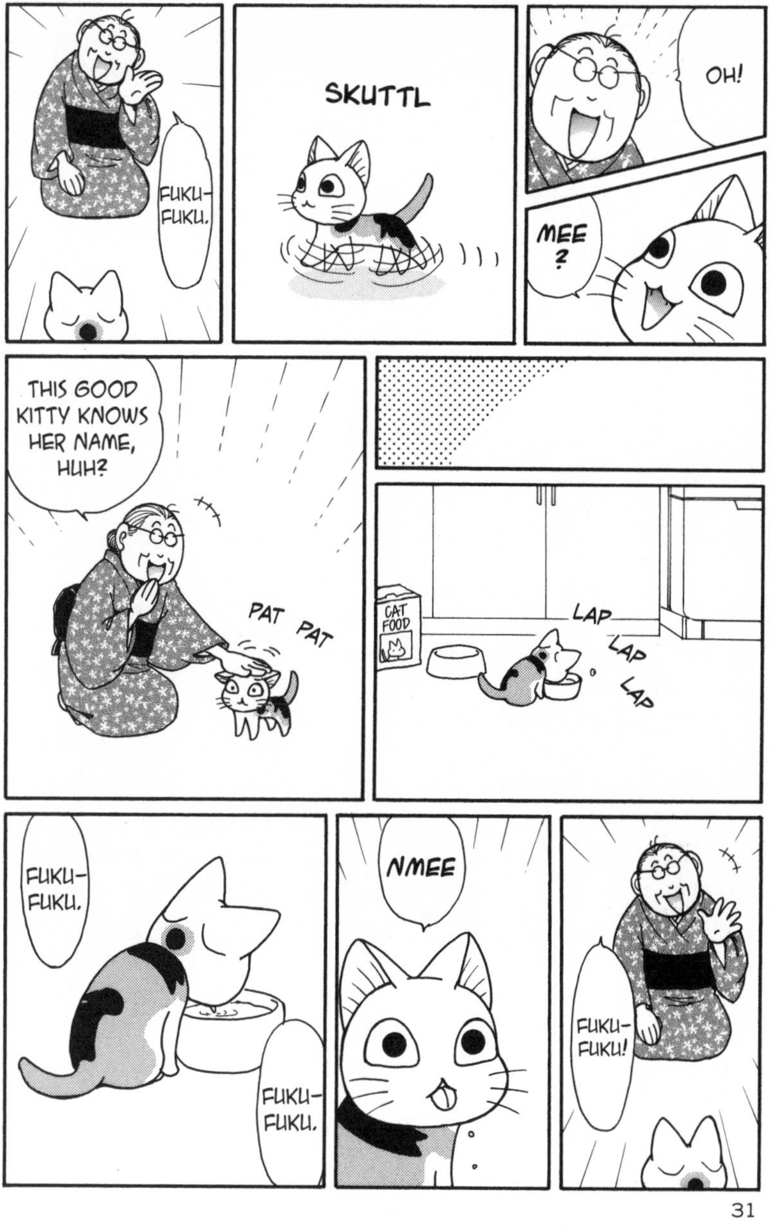
FUKU-FUKU.
SKUTTL
OH!
MEE ?
THIS GOOD KITTY KNOWS HER NAME, HUH?
PAT PAT
CAT FOOD
LAP LAP LAP
FUKU-FUKU.
FUKU-FUKU.
NMEE
FUKU-FUKU!

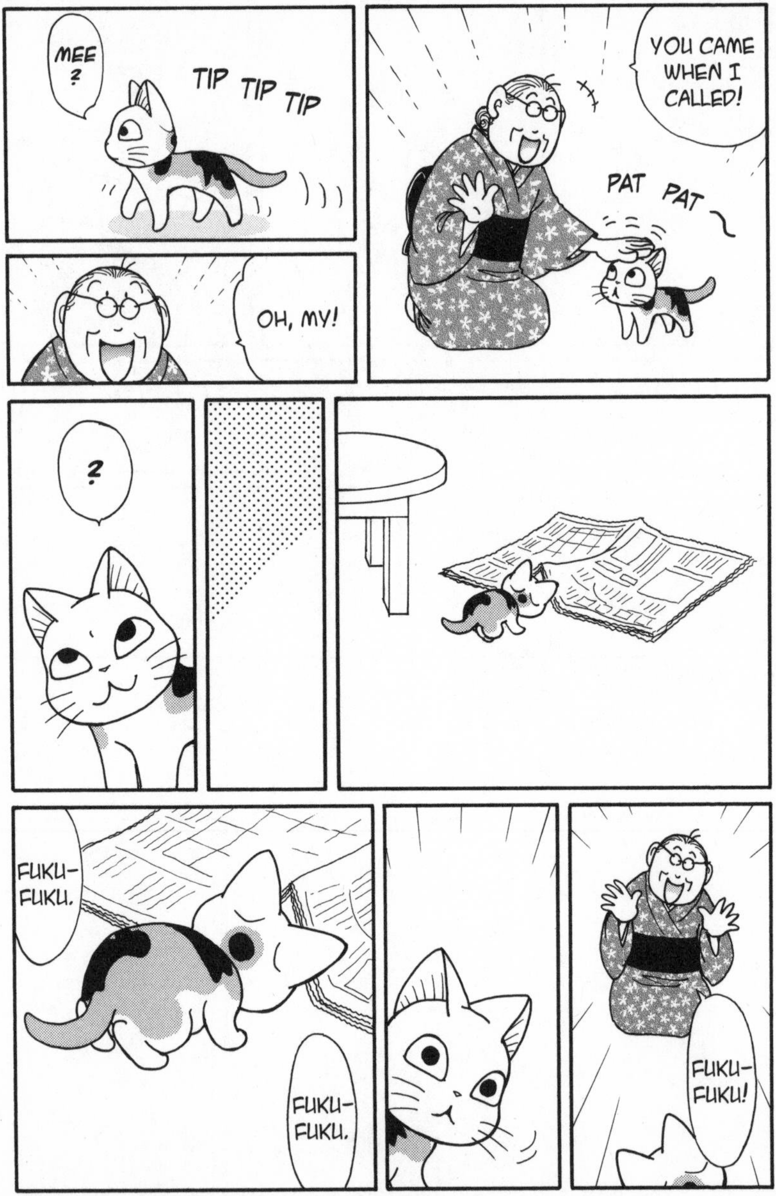
MEE ?
TIP TIP TIP
OH, MY!
YOU CAME WHEN I CALLED!
PAT PAT ~
?
FUKU-FUKU.
FUKU-FUKU.
FUKU-FUKU!

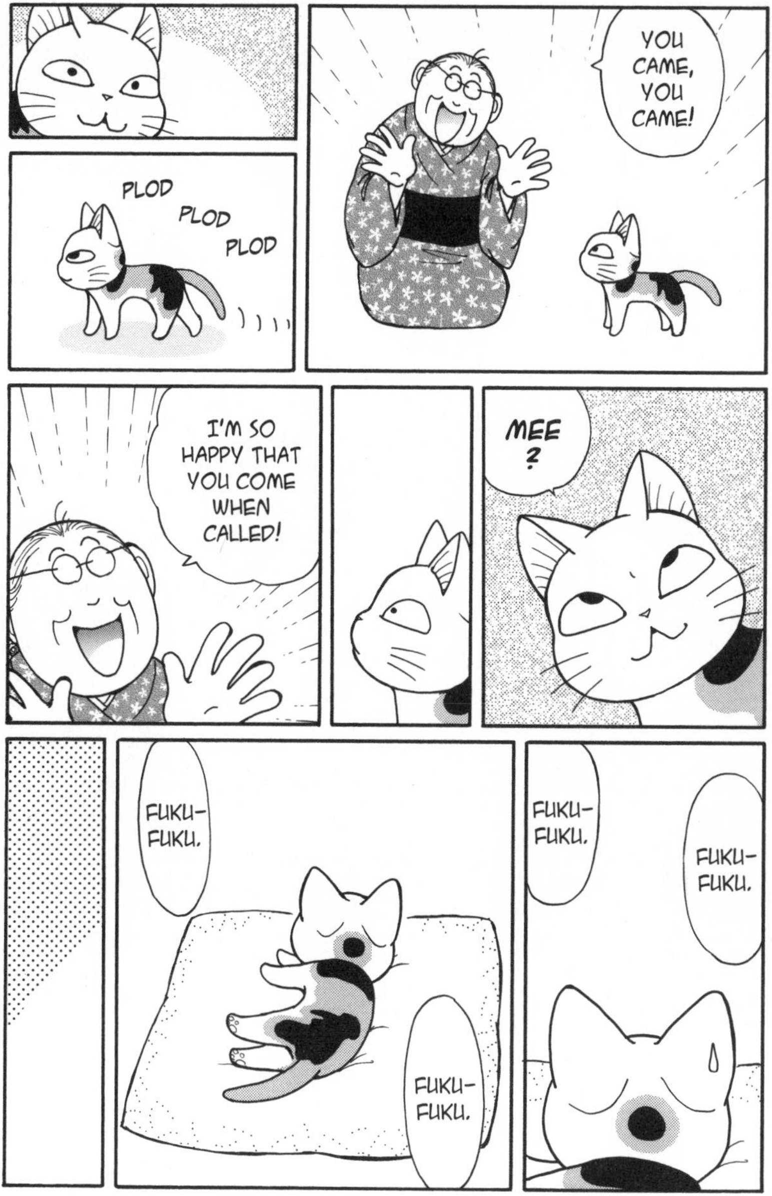
PLOD PLOD PLOD
YOU CAME, YOU CAME!
I'M SO HAPPY THAT YOU COME WHEN CALLED!
MEE ?
FUKU-FUKU.
FUKU-FUKU.
FUKU-FUKU.
FUKU-FUKU.

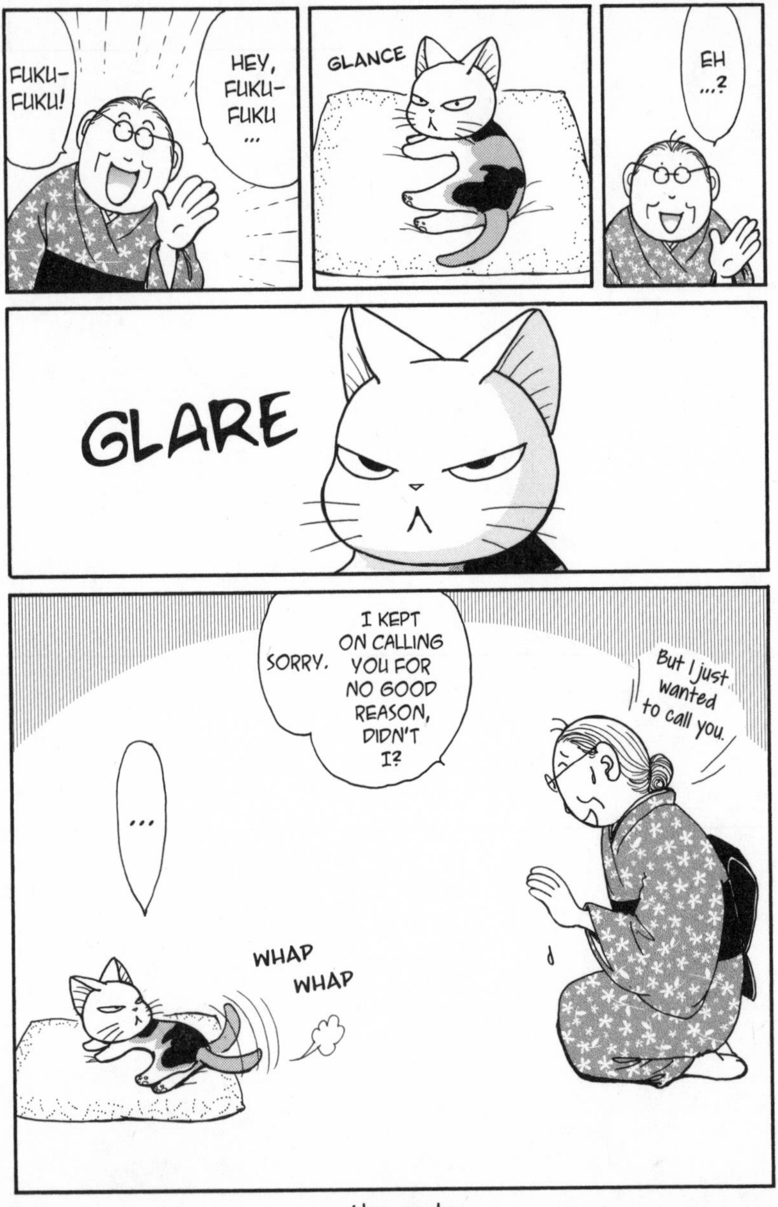
FUKU-FUKU!
HEY, FUKU-FUKU ...
GLANCE
EH ...?
GLARE
SORRY.
I KEPT ON CALLING YOU FOR NO GOOD REASON, DIDN'T I?
But I just wanted to call you.
...
WHAP WHAP

the end

FUKU
FUKU

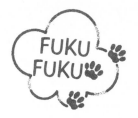

# A Love of Moving Things

FUKU FUKU

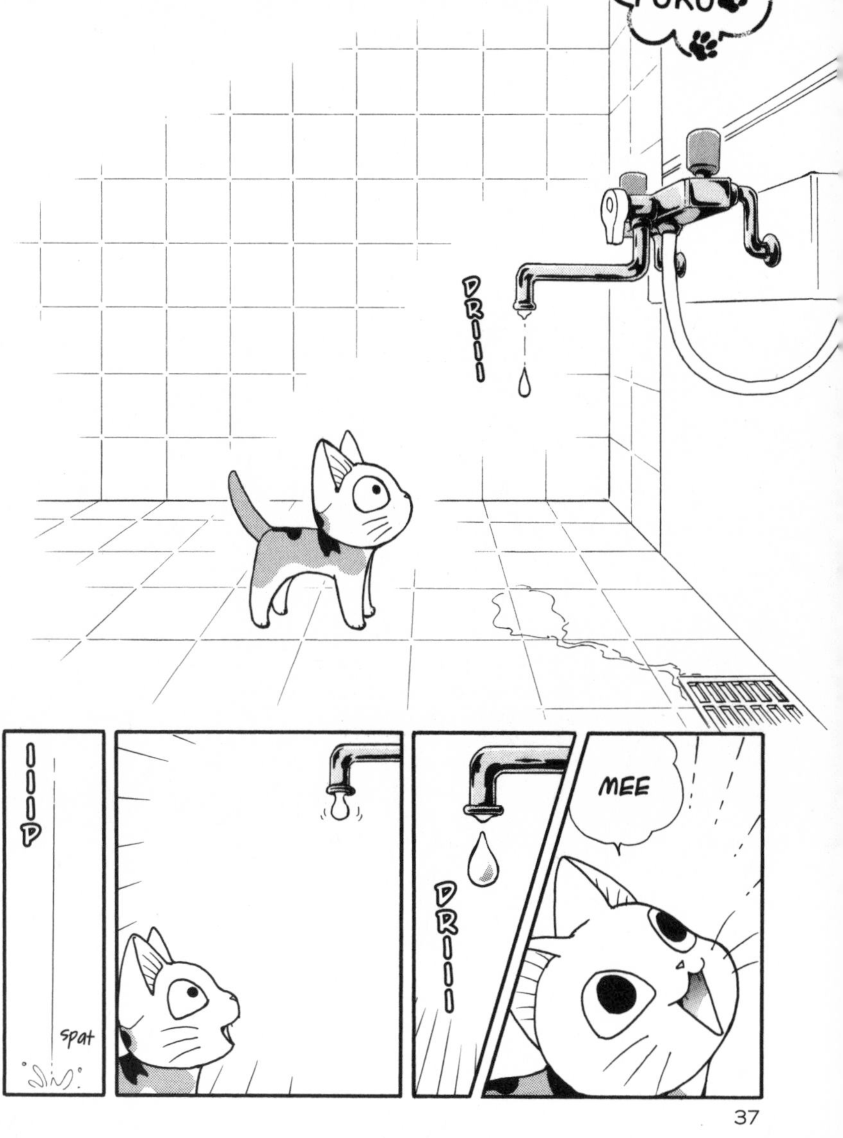
DRIIII
IIIIP
spat
DRIIII
MEE

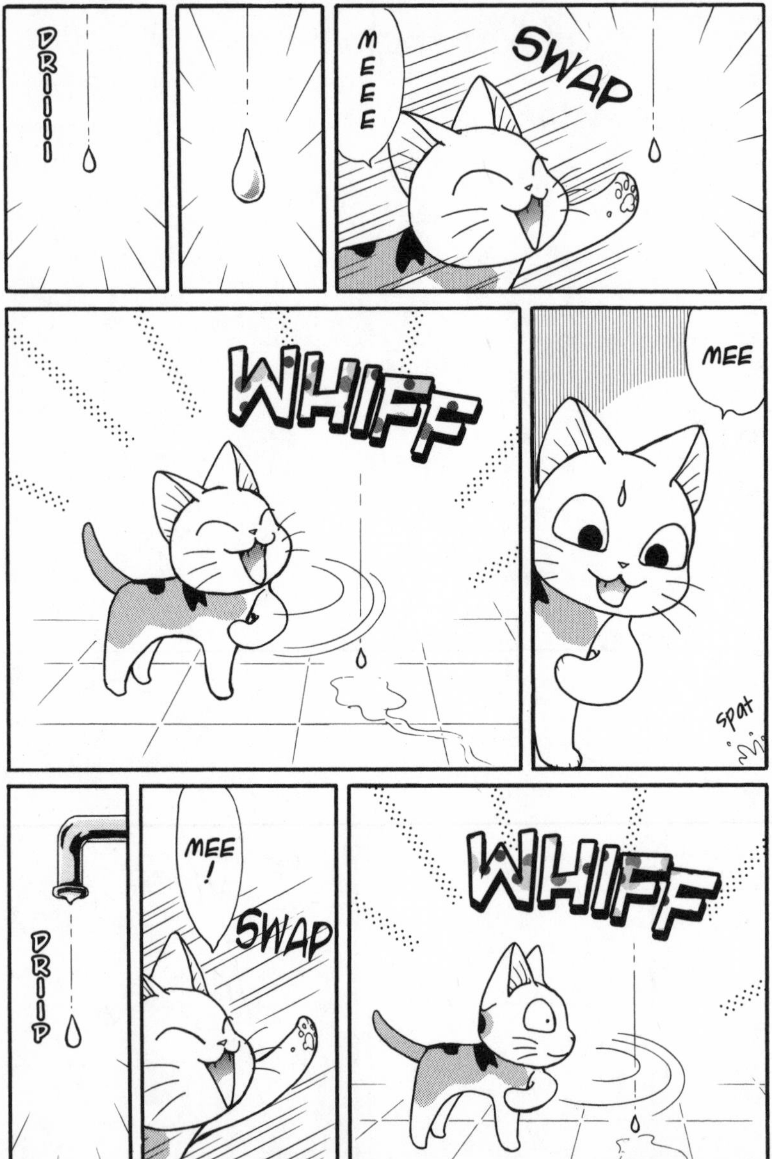
DRIIIII
MEEE
SWAP
WHIFF
MEE
spat
DRIIP
MEE!
SWAP
WHIFF

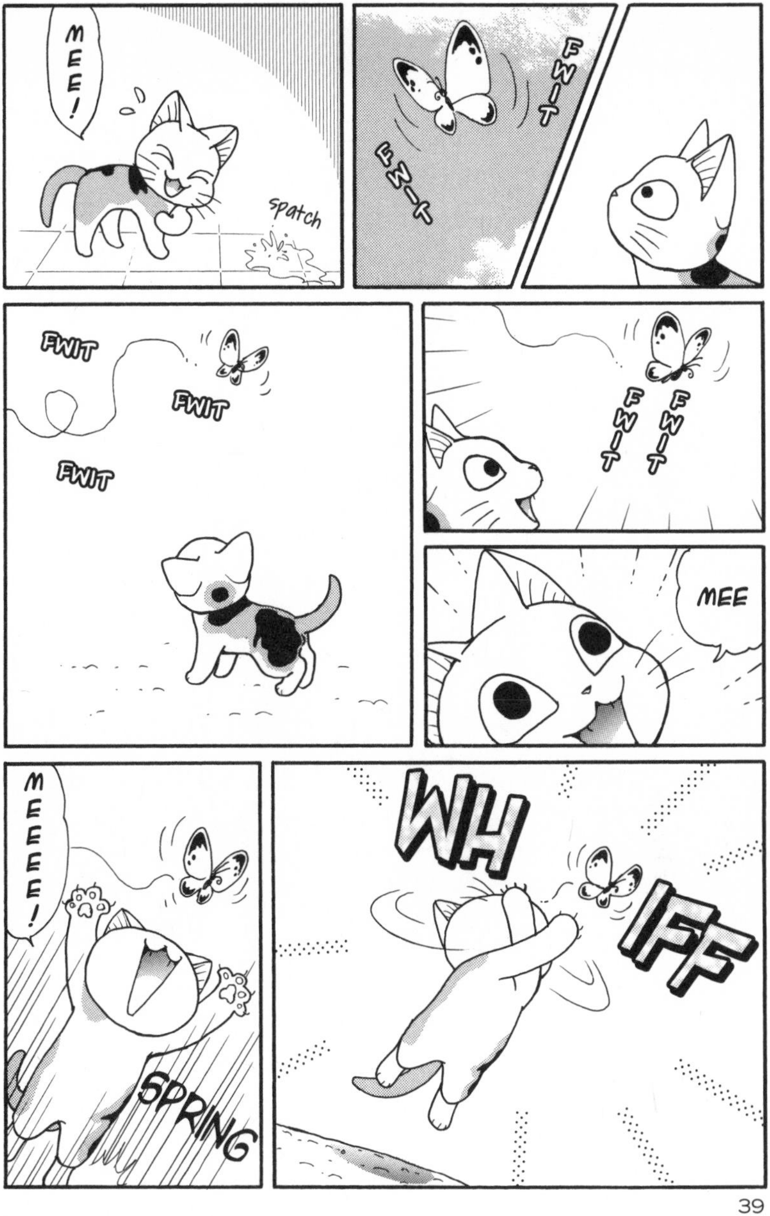
MEE!
spatch
FWIT
FWI-T
FWIT
FWIT
FWIT
FWIT
FWIT
MEE
MEEEEE!
SPRING
WHIFF

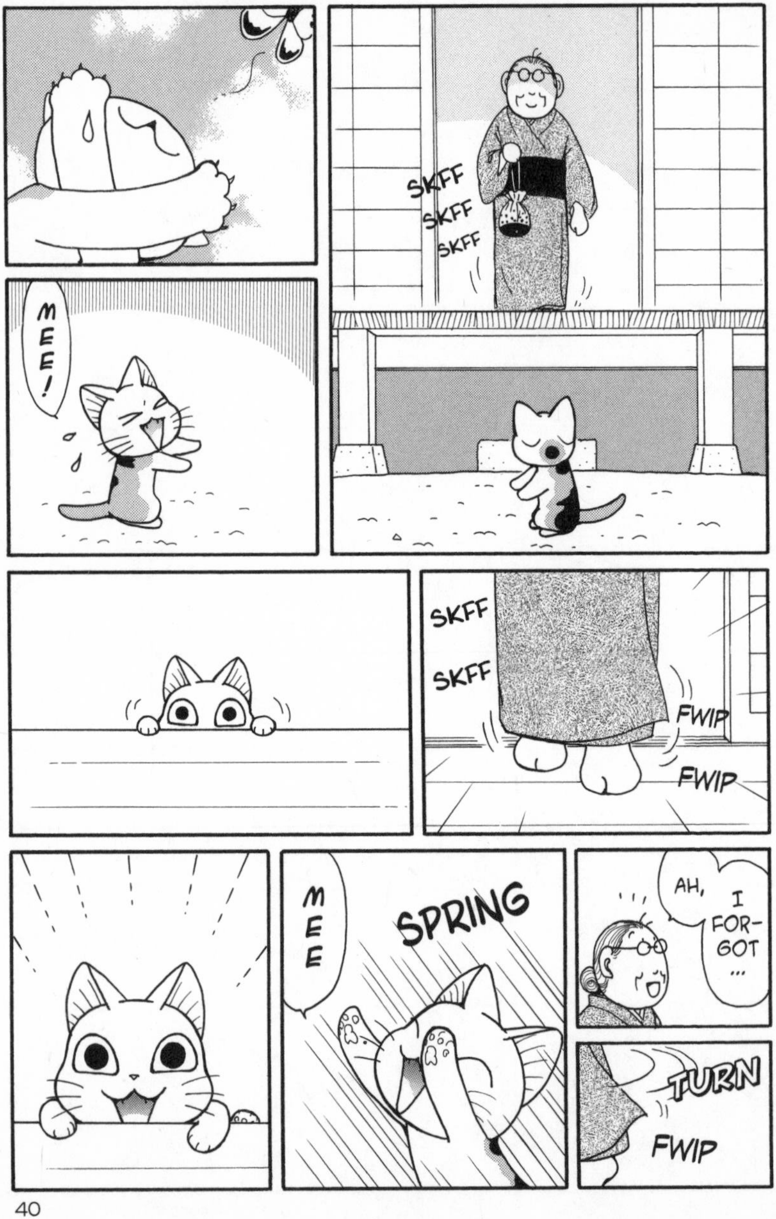

MEE!
SKFF
SKFF
SKFF
SKFF
SKFF
FWIP
FWIP
MEE
SPRING
AH, I FOR-GOT ...
TURN
FWIP

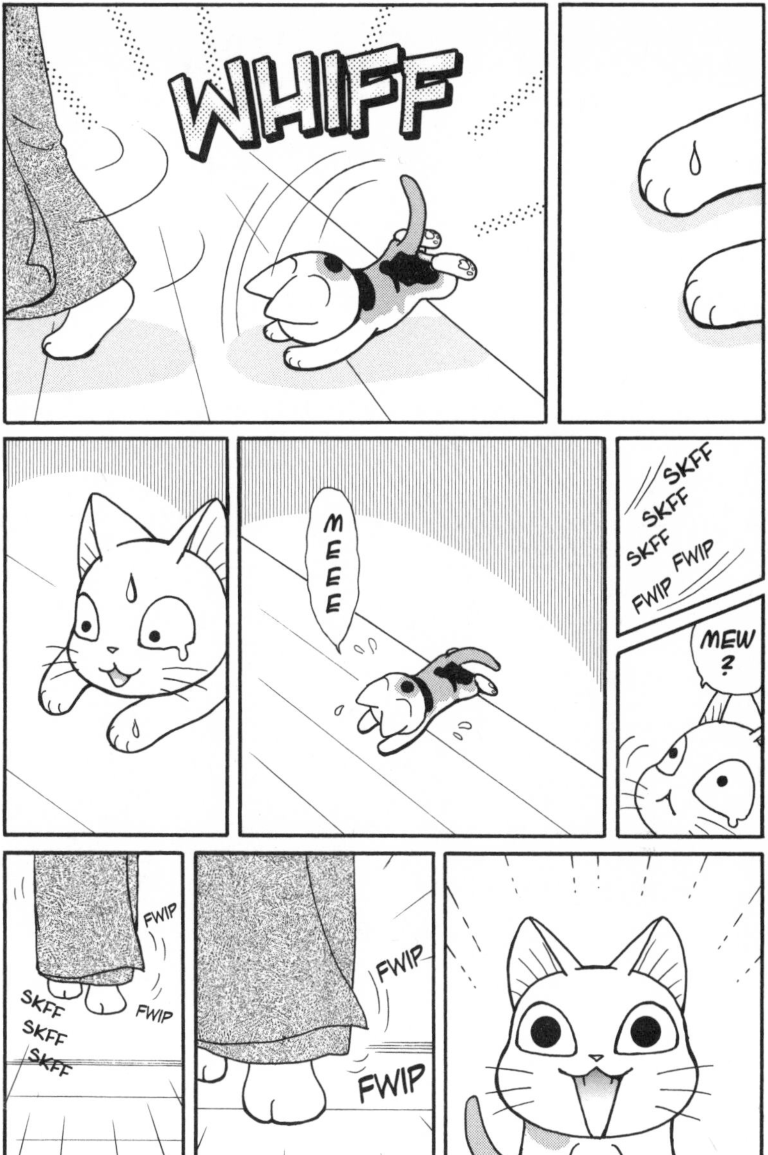
WHIFF
MEEE
SKFF
SKFF
SKFF
FWIP
FWIP
MEW?
FWIP
SKFF
SKFF
SKFF
FWIP
FWIP
FWIP

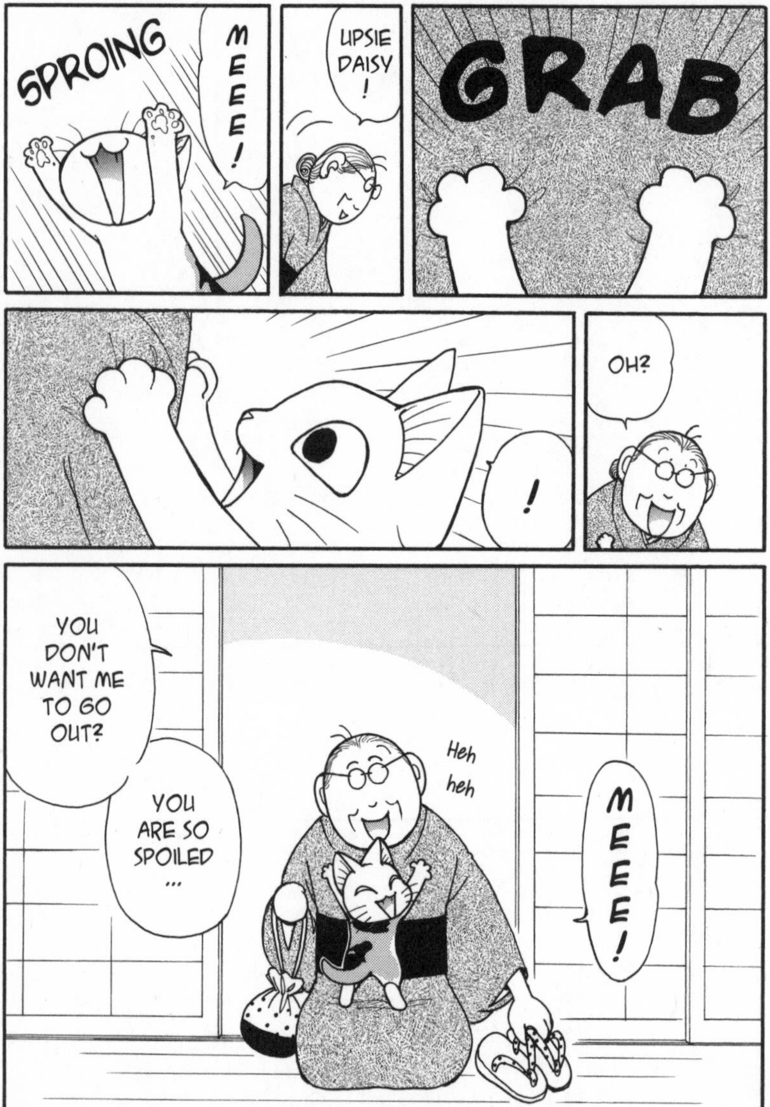
SPROING
MEEE!
UPSIE DAISY!
GRAB
!
OH?
YOU DON'T WANT ME TO GO OUT?
YOU ARE SO SPOILED ...
Heh heh
MEEE!

the end

# The Kitten and Summer

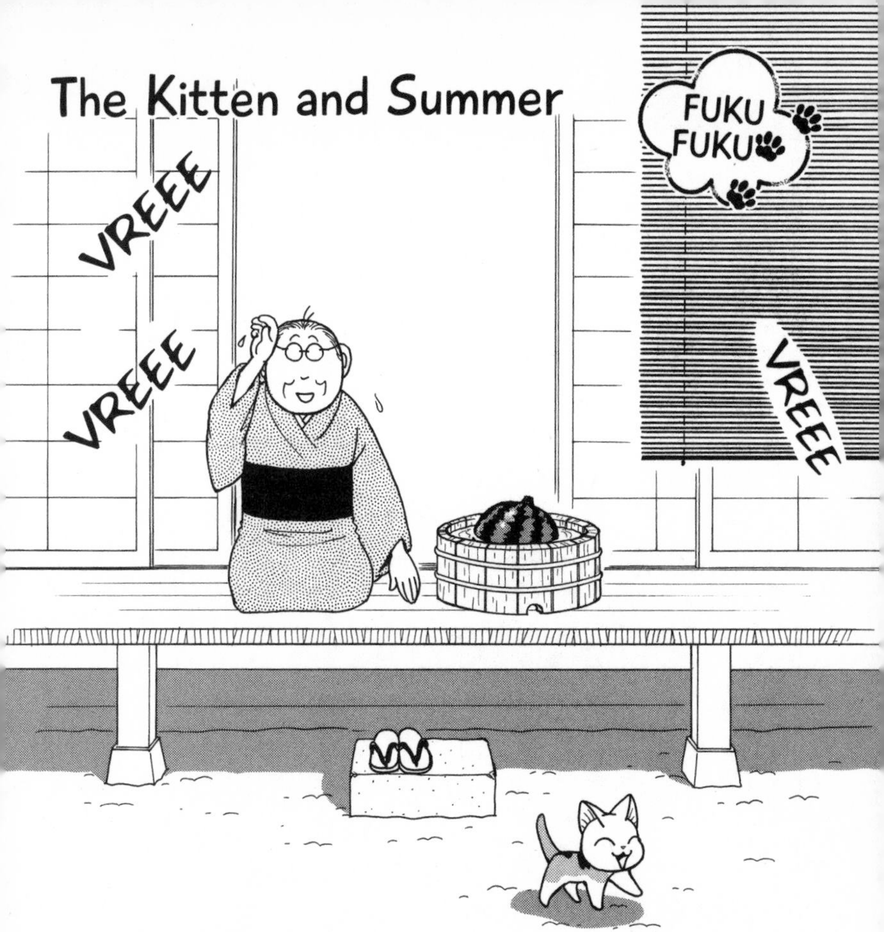
FUKU FUKU
VREEE
VREEE
VREEE

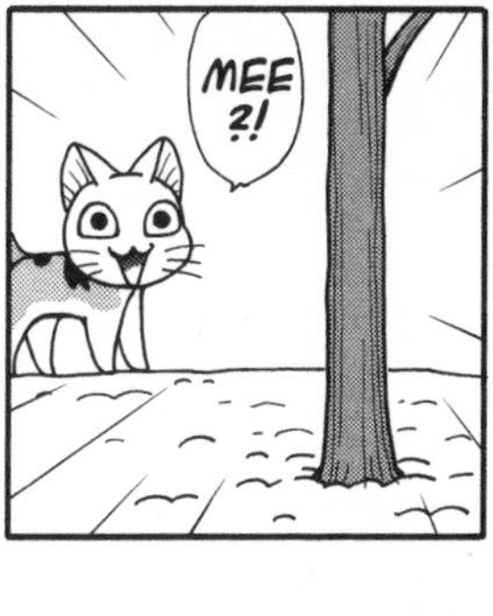
MEE ?!

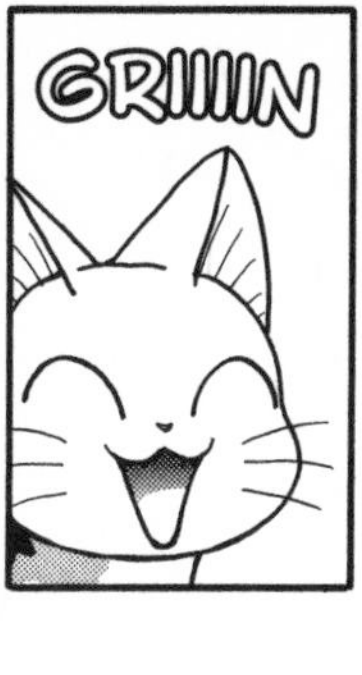
GRIIIIN

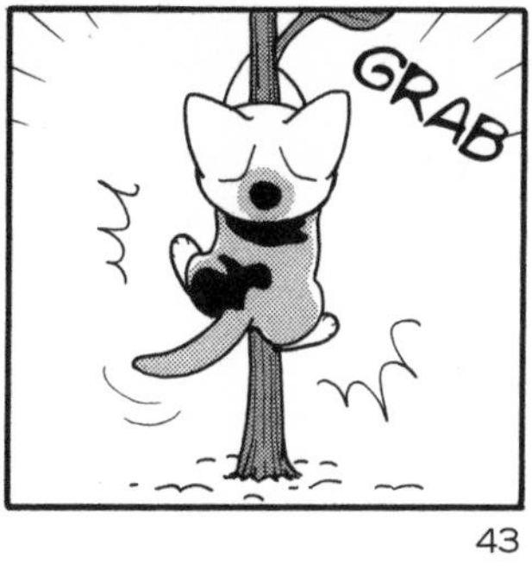
GRAB

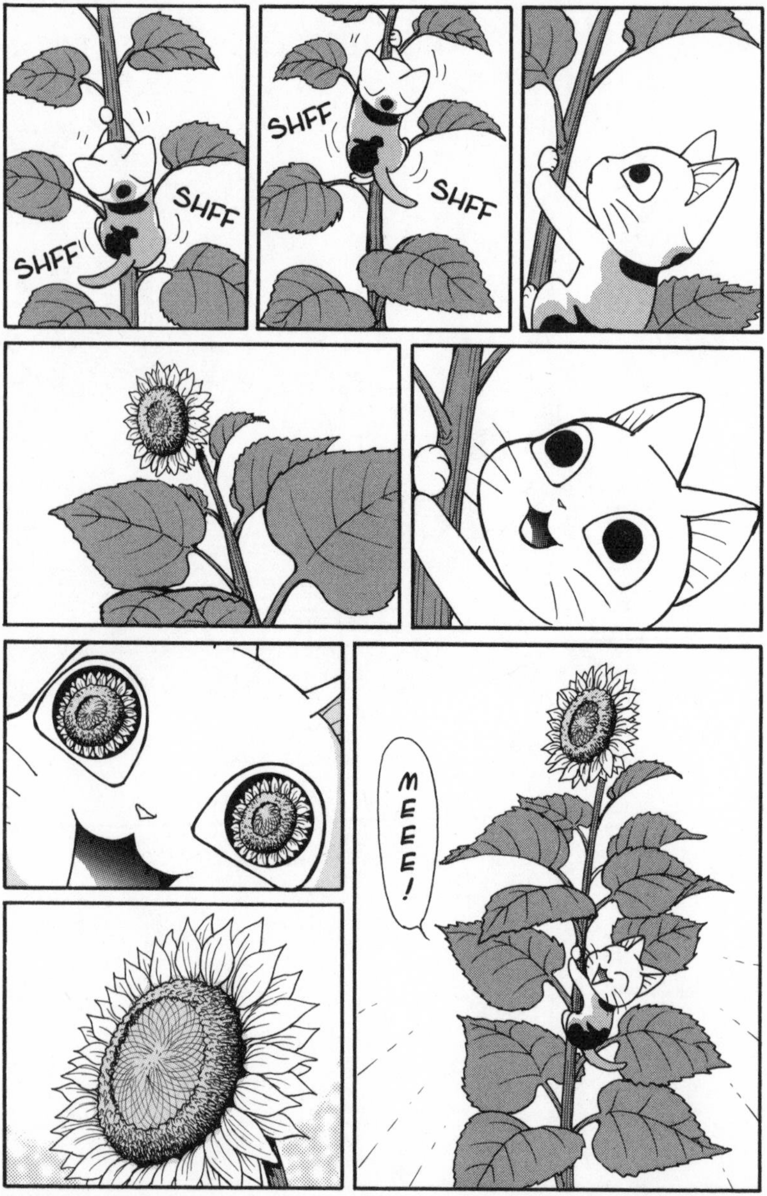
SHFF
SHFF
SHFF
SHFF
MEEE!

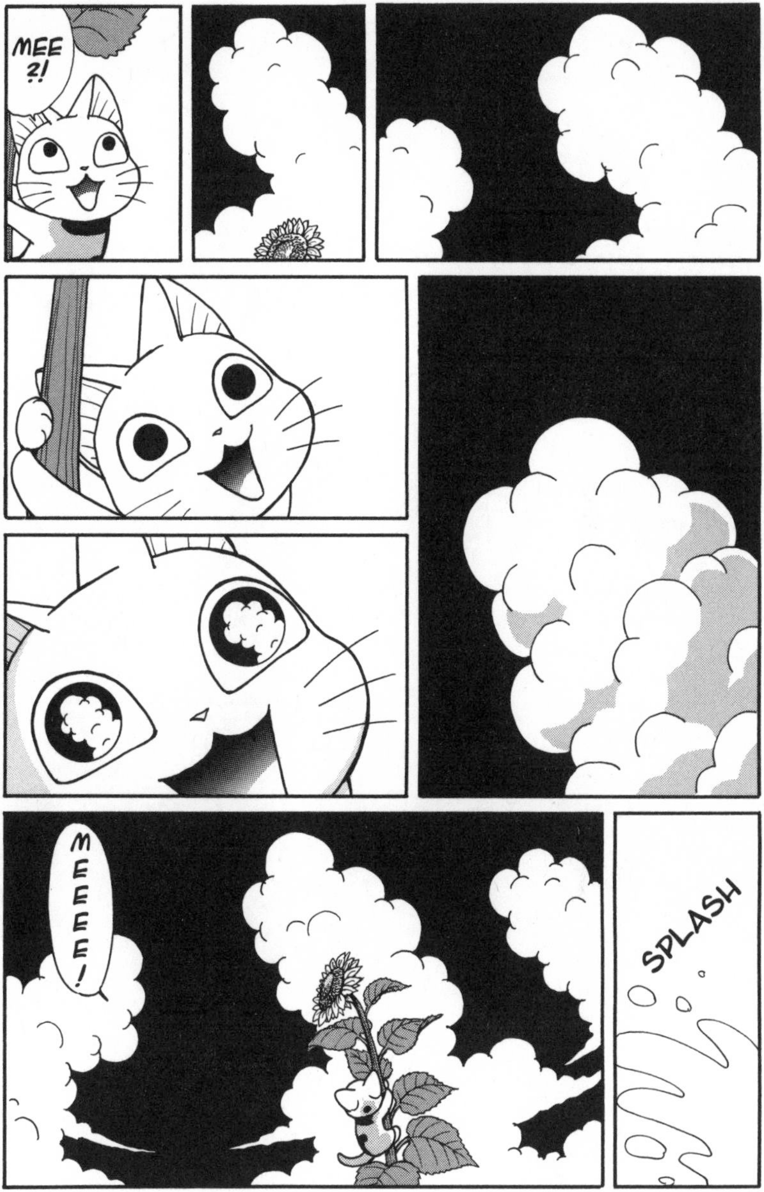
MEE ?!
MEEEE!
SPLASH

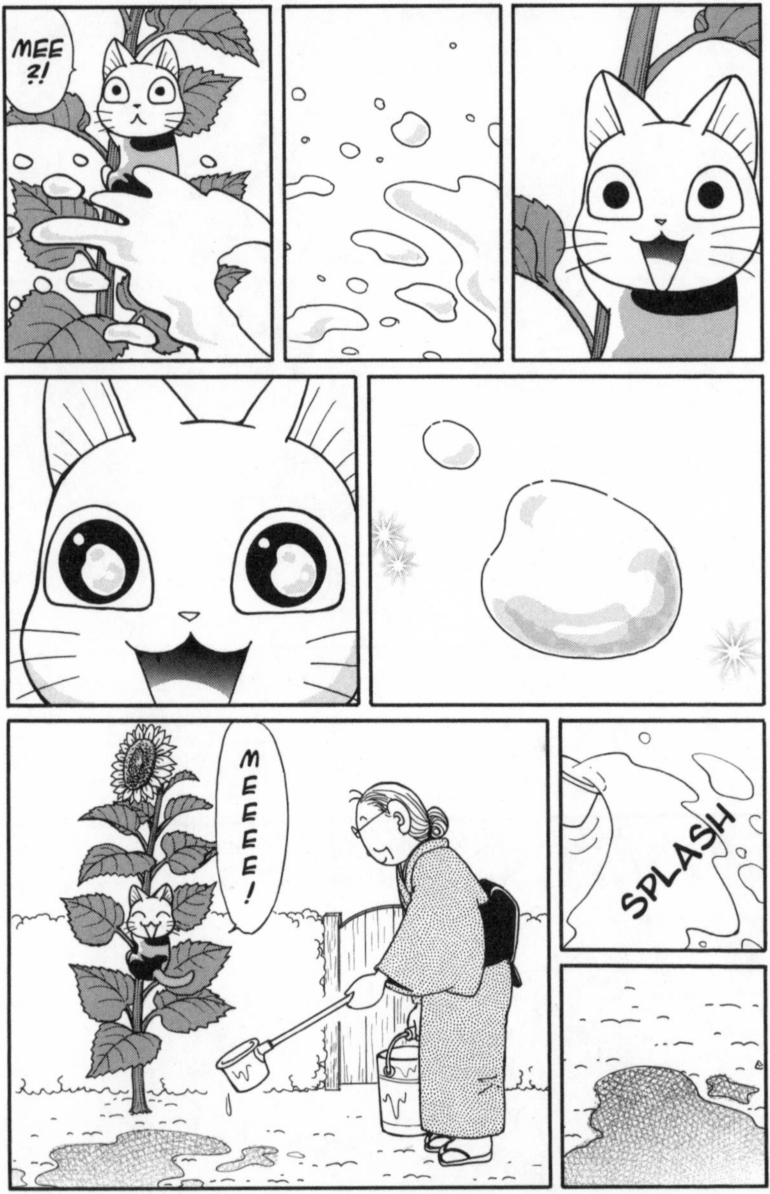
MEE ?!
MEEEEE!
SPLASH

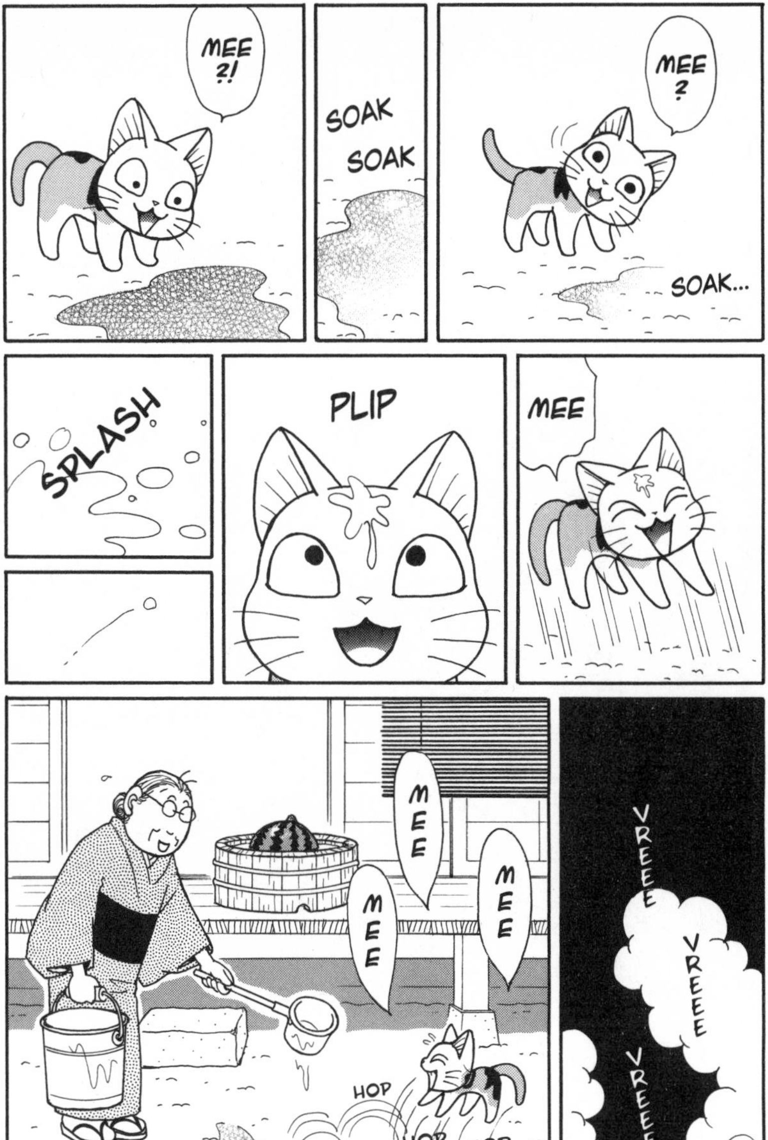
MEE ?!
SOAK
SOAK
MEE ?
SOAK...
SPLASH
PLIP
MEE
MEE
MEE
MEE
HOP
HOP
HOP
VREEE
VREEE
VREEE

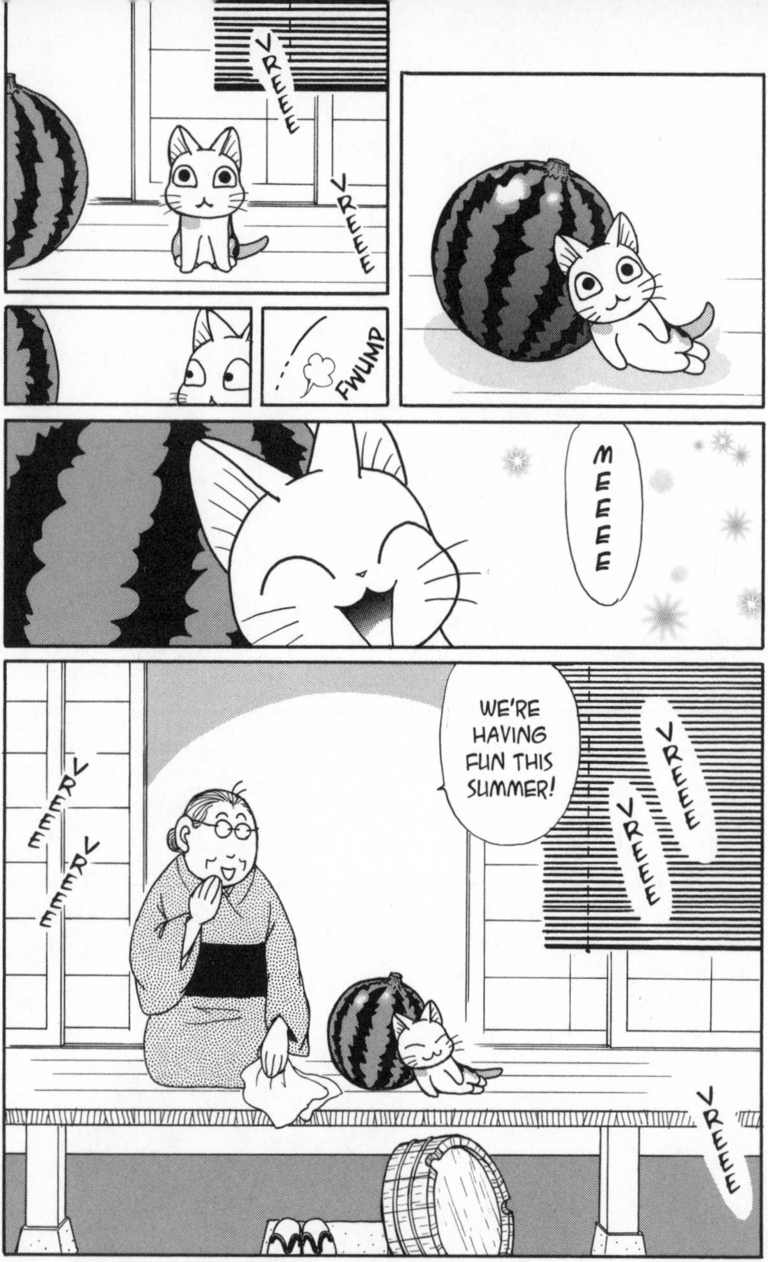
VREEE
VREEE
FWUMP
MEEEE
VREEE
VREEE
WE'RE HAVING FUN THIS SUMMER!
VREEE
VREEE
VREEE

the end

# Napping is the Kitten's Job

FUKU FUKU

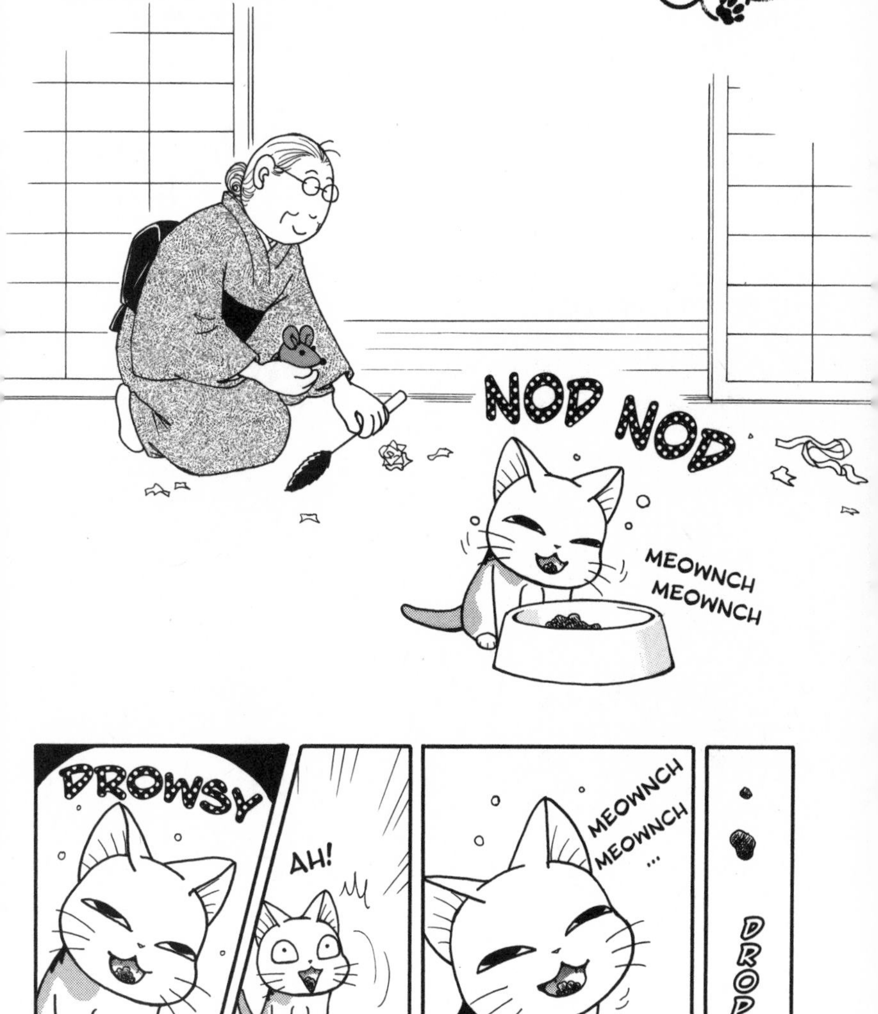
NOD NOD
MEOWNCH MEOWNCH
DROWSY
AH!
MEOWNCH MEOWNCH ...
DROP

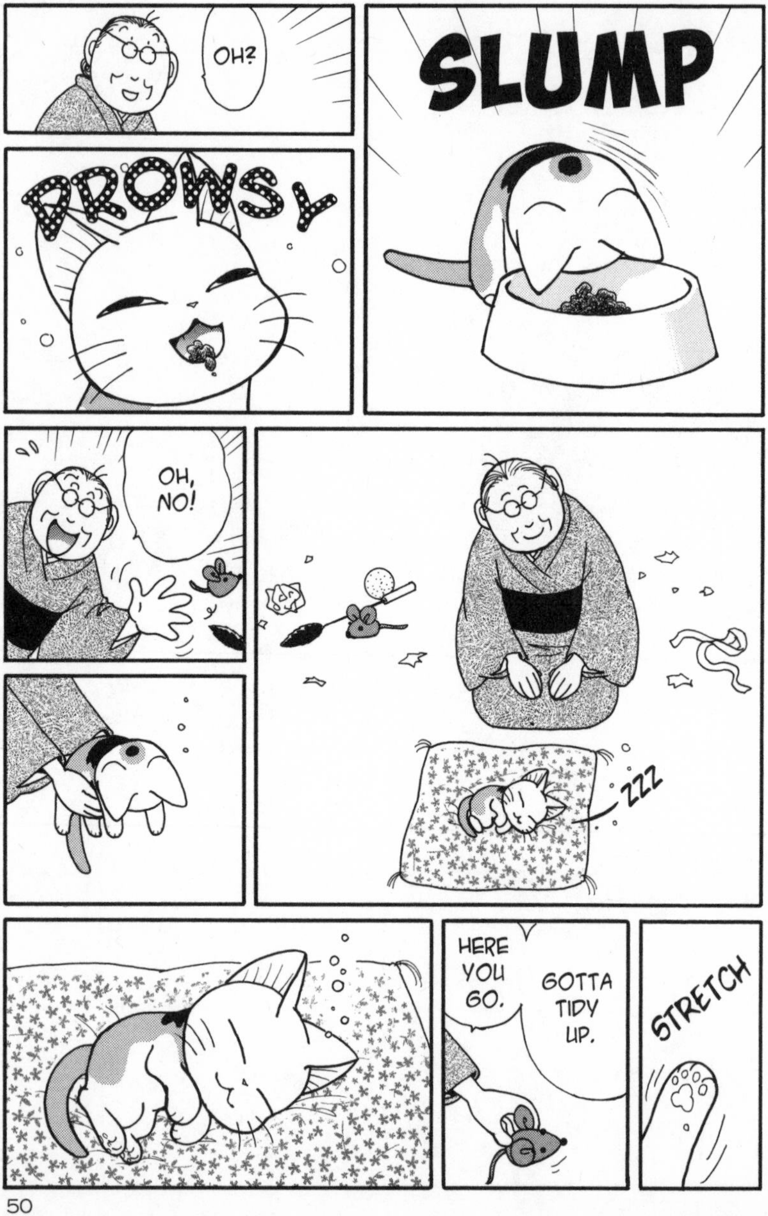
OH?
DROWSY
SLUMP
OH, NO!
ZZZ
HERE YOU GO.
GOTTA TIDY UP.
STRETCH

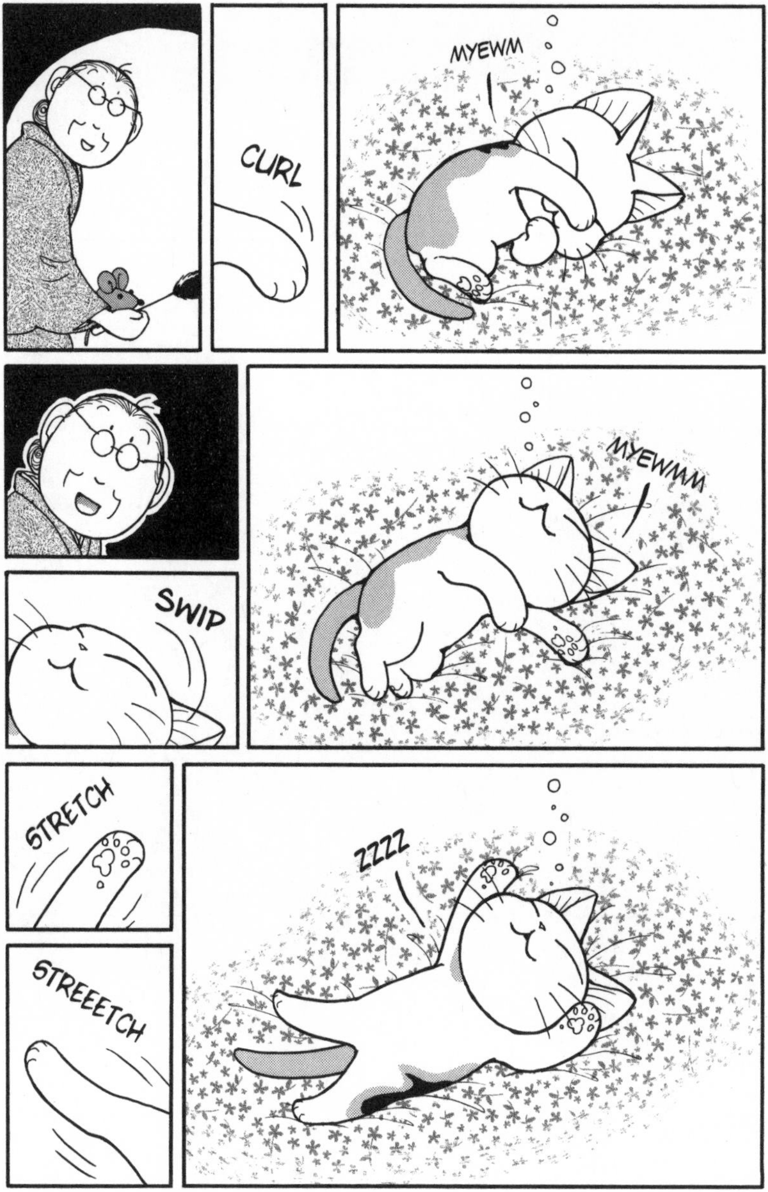
CURL
MYEWM
SWIP
MYEWMM
STRETCH
STREEETCH
ZZZZ

ZZZ

DROWZY

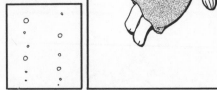

YAWN

KREE
KREE
KREE

STREEEEEETCH

MEE
?!

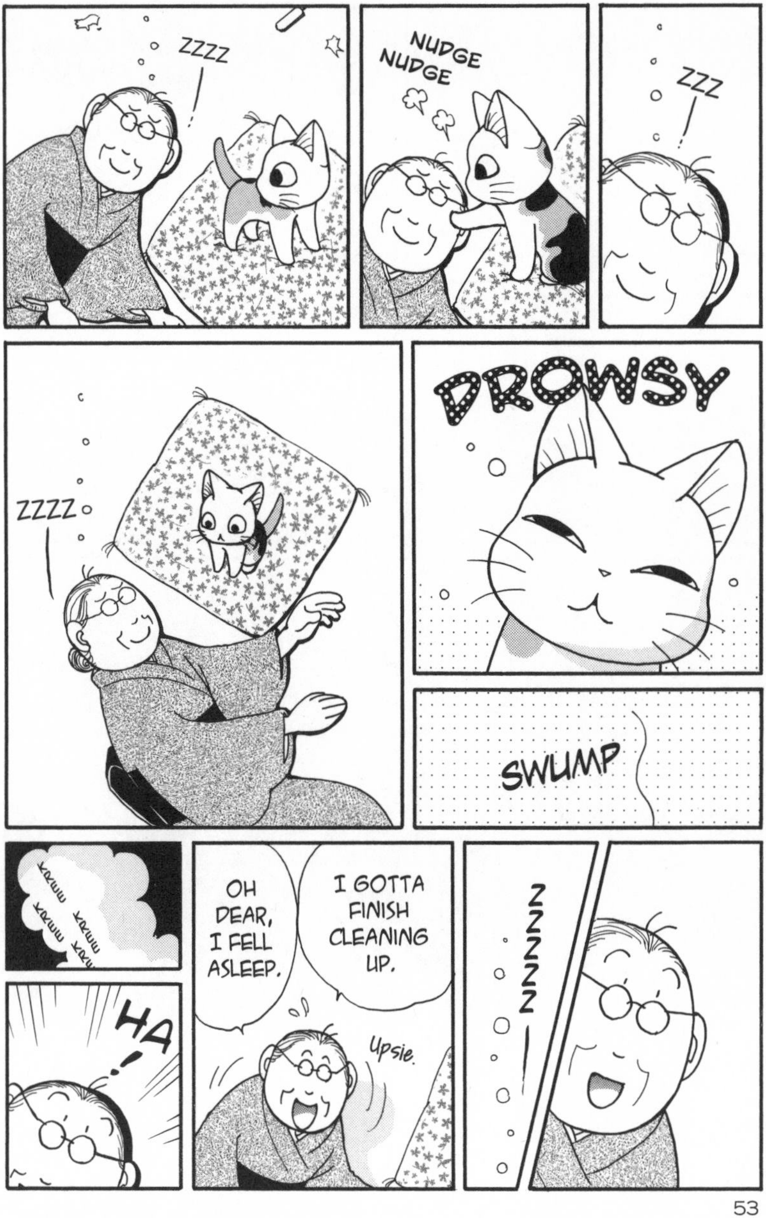
ZZZZ
NUDGE NUDGE
ZZZ
ZZZZ
DROWSY
SWUMP
KRWW
KRWW
KRWW
KRW
HA!
OH DEAR, I FELL ASLEEP.
I GOTTA FINISH CLEANING UP.
Upsie.
ZZZZZ

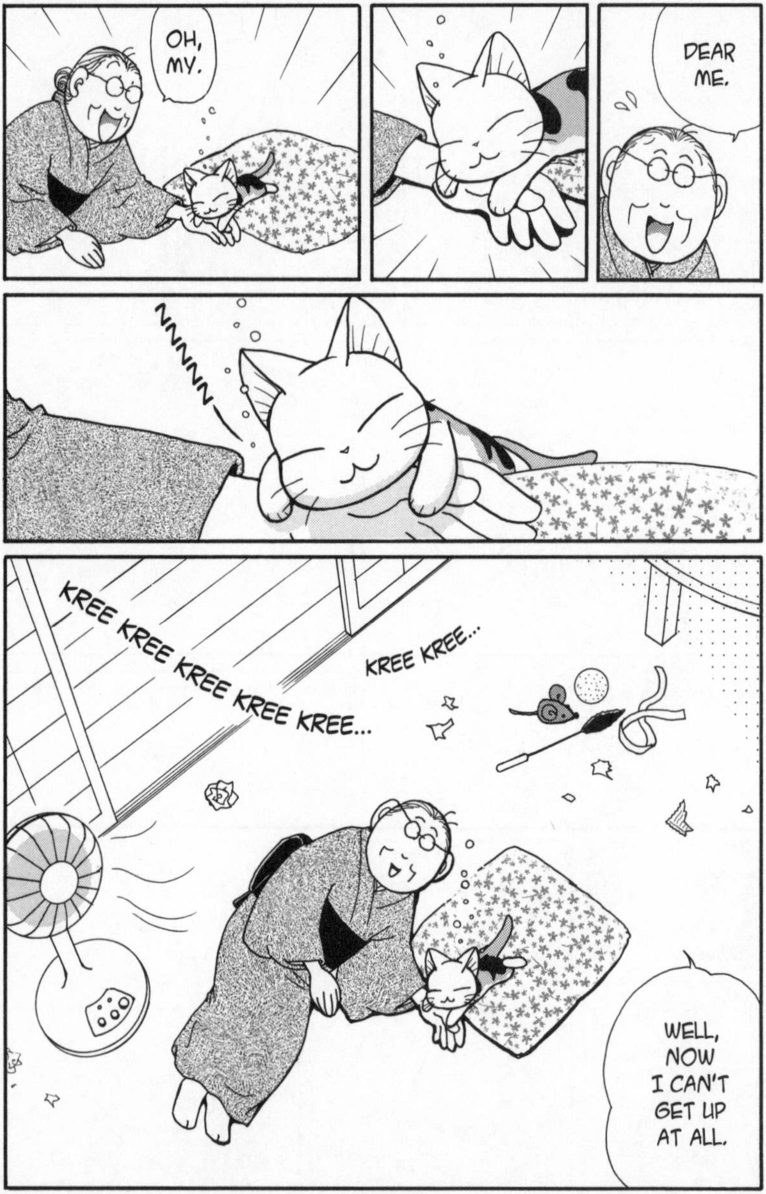
OH, MY.
DEAR ME.
KREE KREE KREE KREE KREE...
KREE KREE...
WELL, NOW I CAN'T GET UP AT ALL.

the end

# Dangerous Heat Wave

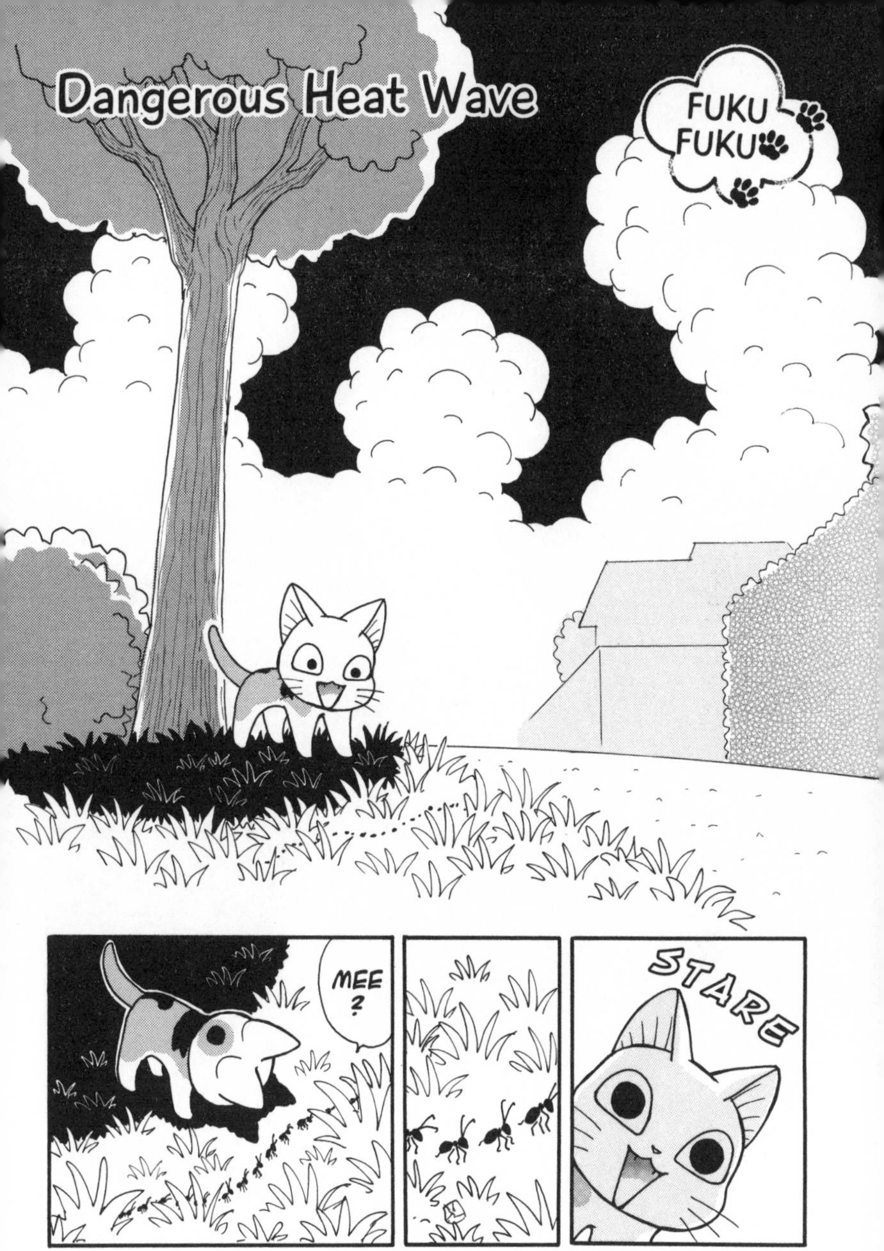
FUKU FUKU
MEE ?
STARE

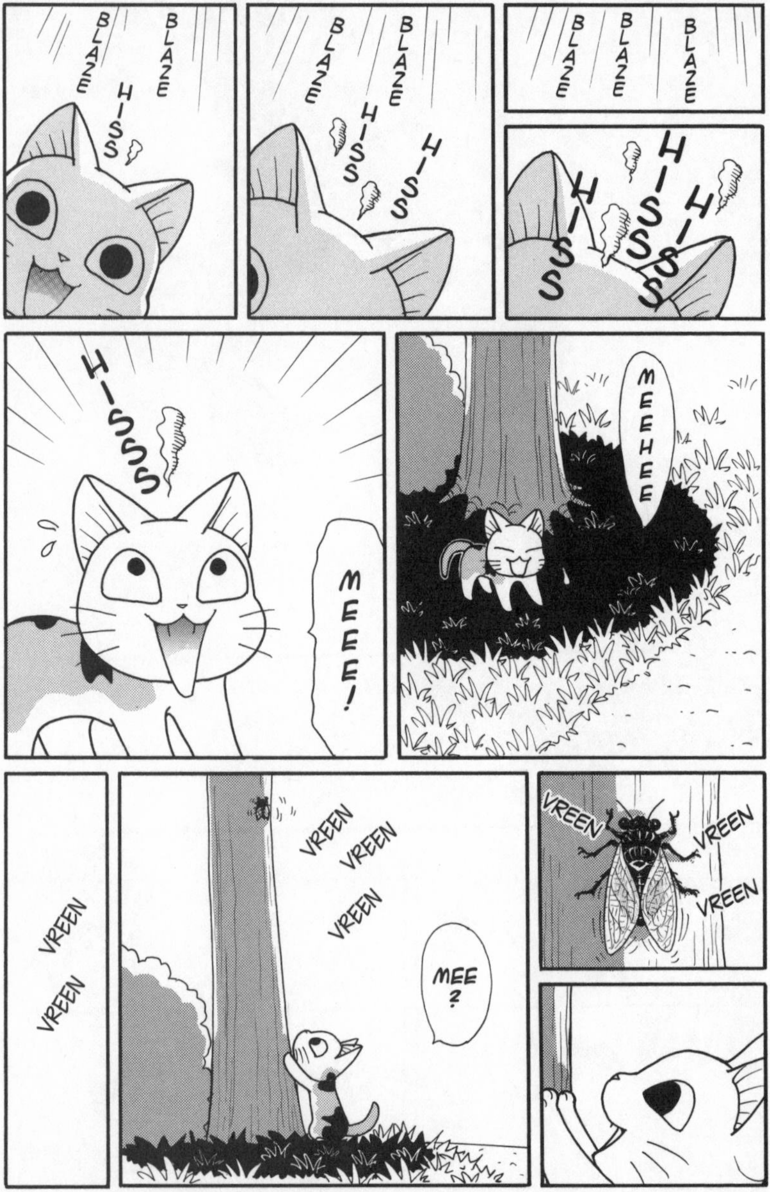
BLAZE
BLAZE
HISS
BLAZE
BLAZE
HISS
HISS
BLAZE
BLAZE
BLAZE
HISS
HISS
HISS
HISS
HISSS
MEEEE!
MEEHEE
VREEN
VREEN
VREEN
VREEN
VREEN
MEE?
VREEN
VREEN
VREEN
VREEN

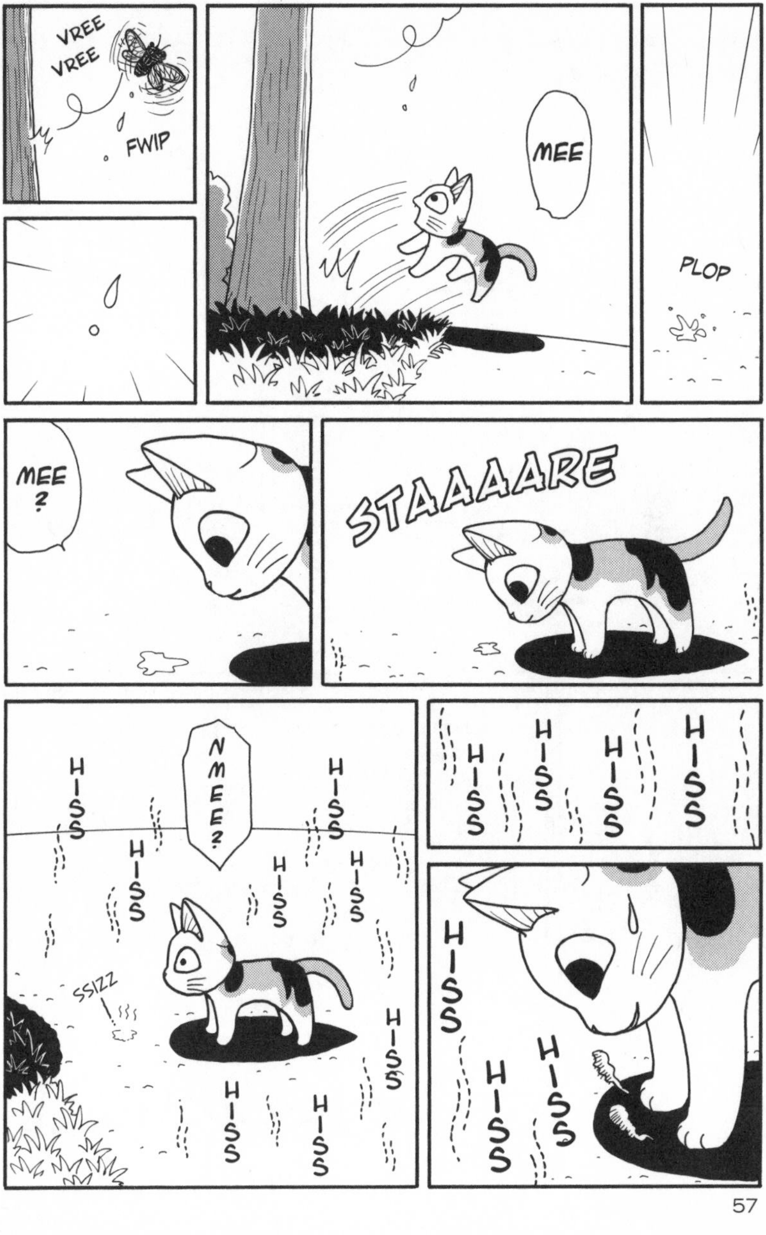

VREE VREE
FWIP
MEE
PLOP
MEE?
STAAAARE
HISS
NMEE?
HISS
HISS
HISS HISS
HISS
SSIZZ
HISS
HISS HISS
HISS HISS HISS HISS
HISS
HISS HISS

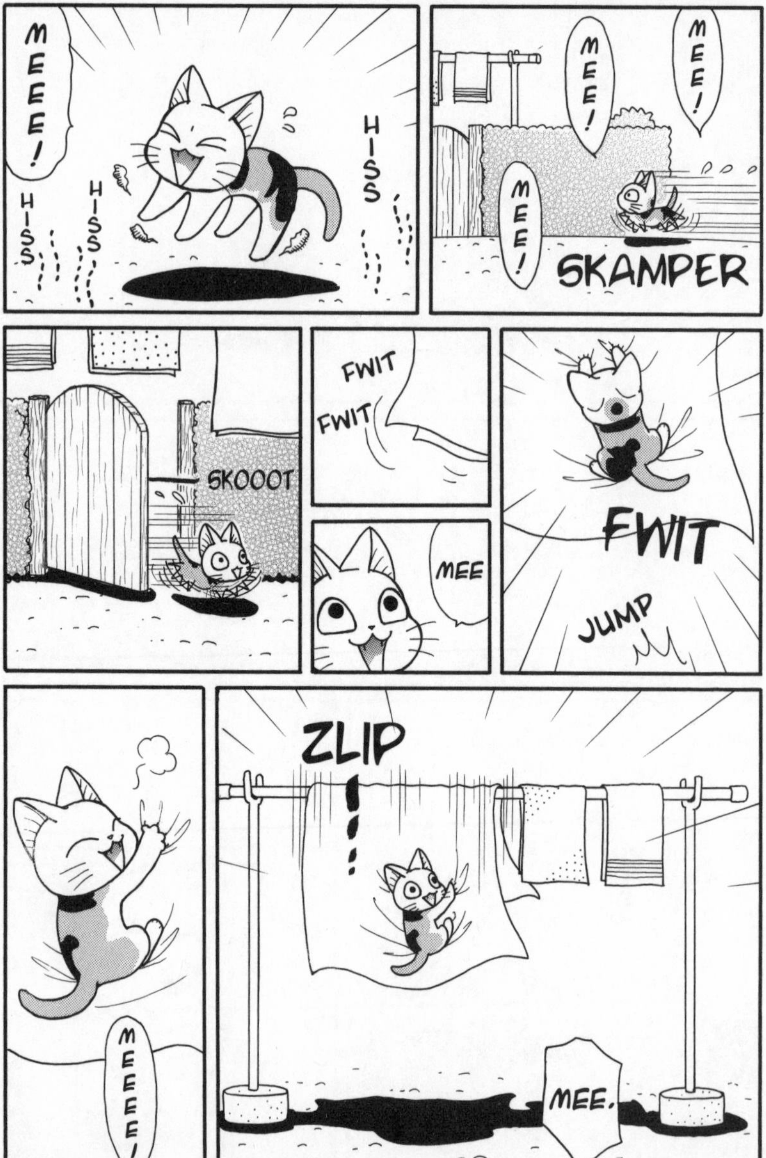
MEEE!
HISS
HISS
HISS
MEE!
MEE!
MEE!
SKAMPER
SKOOOT
FWIT
FWIT
MEE
FWIT
JUMP
MEEEE!
ZLIP
MEE.

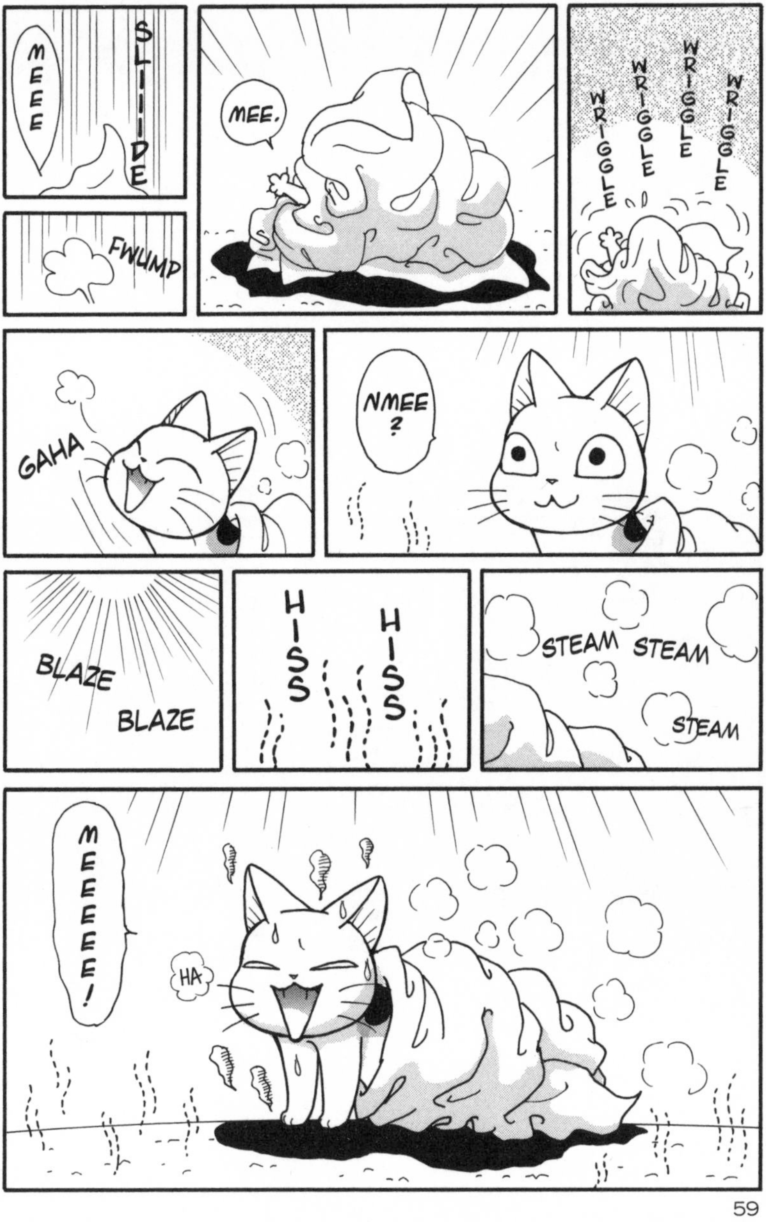
MEEE
SLIIIDE
FWUMP
MEE.
WRIGGLE WRIGGLE WRIGGLE WRIGGLE
GAHA
NMEE?
BLAZE
BLAZE
HISS HISS
STEAM STEAM
STEAM
MEEEEEE!
HA

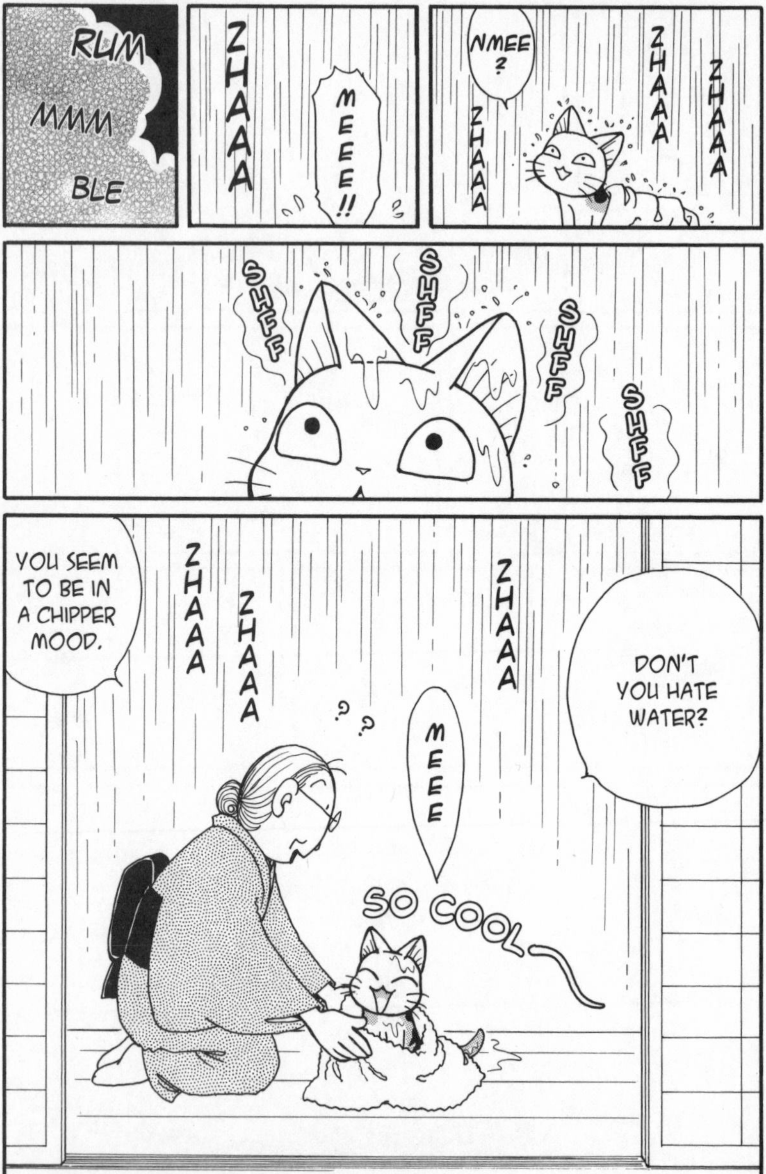
RUM
MMM
BLE
ZHAAA
MEEE!!
NMEE?
ZHAAA
ZHAAA
ZHAAA
SHFF
SHFF
SHFF
SHFF
YOU SEEM TO BE IN A CHIPPER MOOD.
ZHAAA
ZHAAA
ZHAAA
DON'T YOU HATE WATER?
MEEE
SO COOL

the end

# Practicing with the Scratching Post

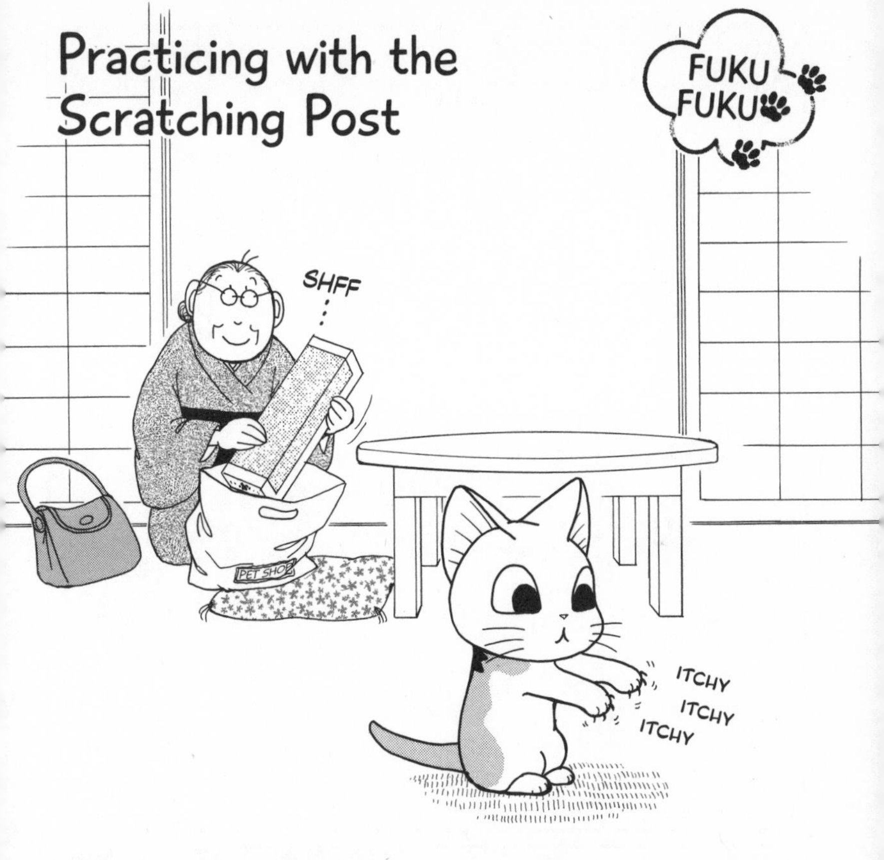
FUKU FUKU
SHFF...
ITCHY
ITCHY
ITCHY

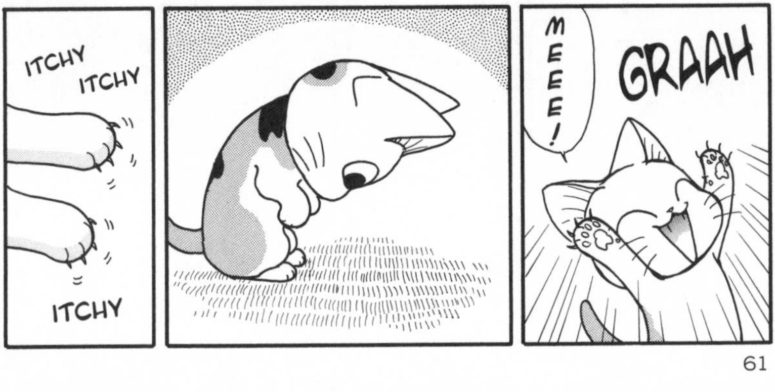
ITCHY
ITCHY
ITCHY
MEEE!
GRAAH

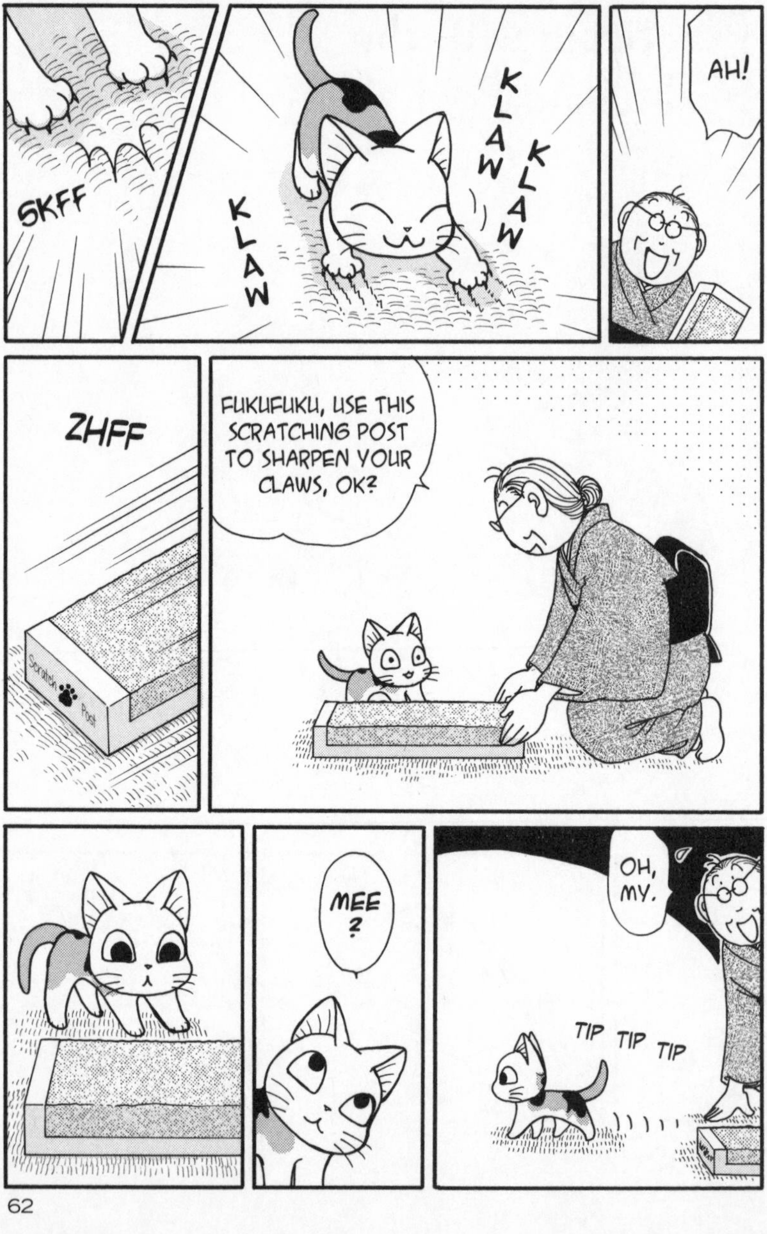
SKFF
KLAW
KLAW
KLAW
AH!
ZHFF
Scratch Post
FUKUFUKU, USE THIS SCRATCHING POST TO SHARPEN YOUR CLAWS, OK?
MEE?
OH, MY.
TIP TIP TIP

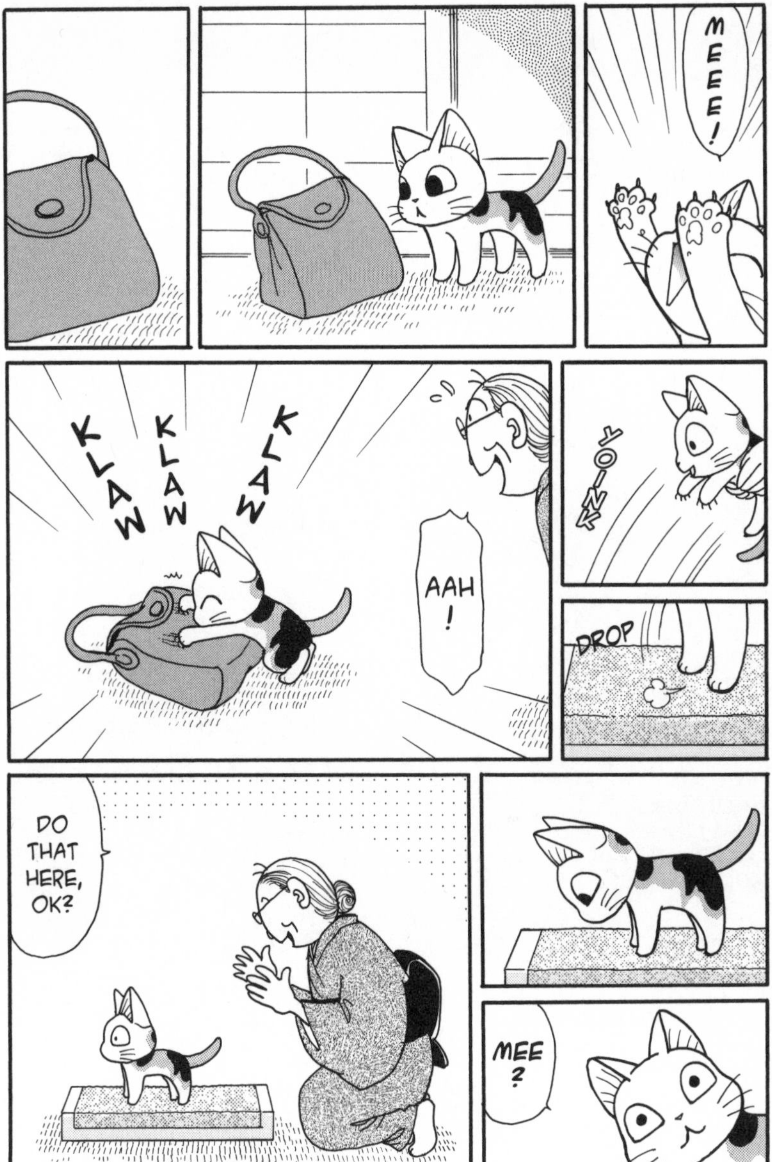

MEEE!
KLAW KLAW KLAW
AAH!
YOINK
DROP
DO THAT HERE, OK?
MEE?

AH...
OH,
DEAR.

TIP TIP TIP

KLAW
KLAW
KLAW

MEE!

NOW,
NOW.

YOINK

DROP

YOUR
CLAWS
GO
HERE...

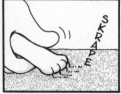

SKRADE

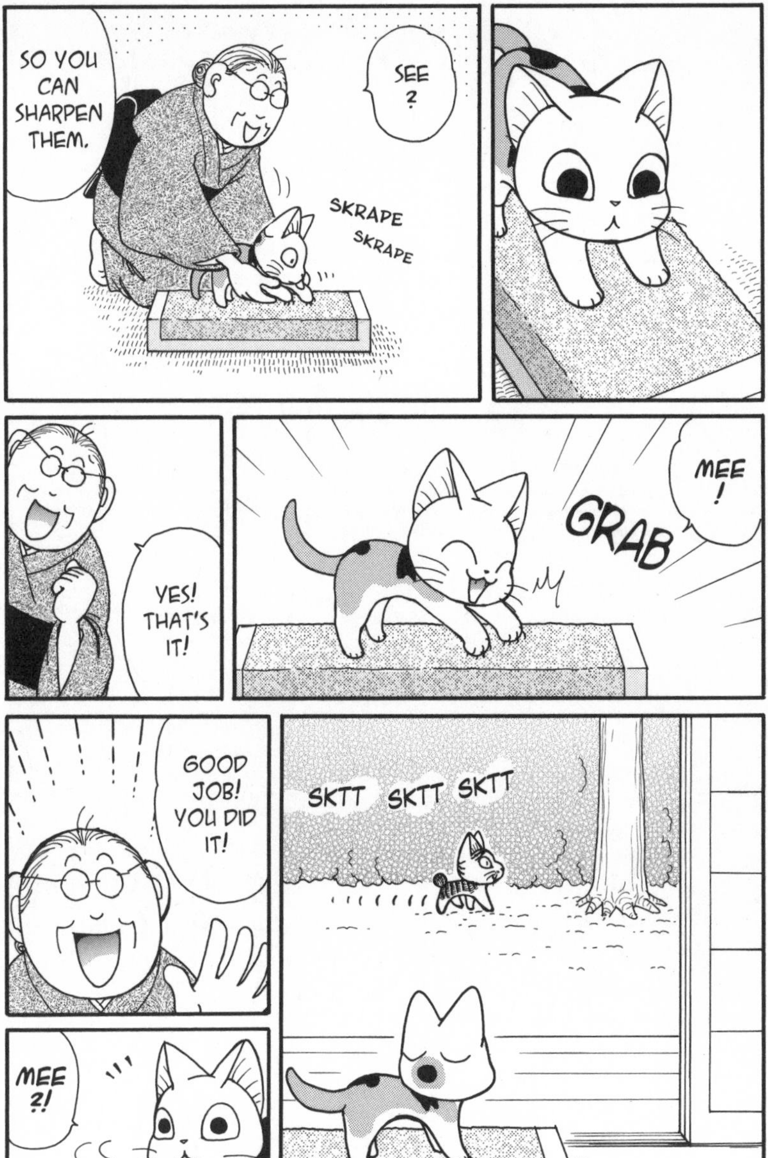
SO YOU CAN SHARPEN THEM.
SEE?
SKRAPE SKRAPE
YES! THAT'S IT!
GRAB
MEE!
GOOD JOB! YOU DID IT!
MEE?!
SKTT SKTT SKTT

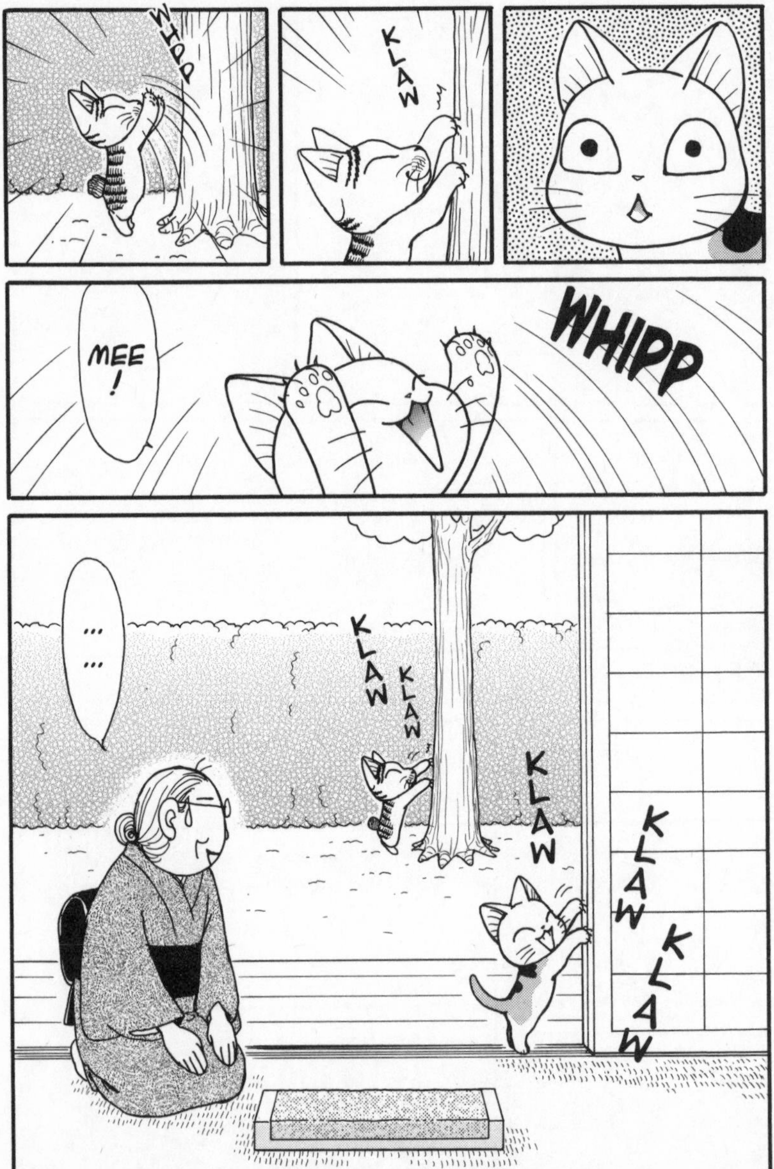
WHIPP
KLAW
MEE!
WHIPP
......
KLAW
KLAW
KLAW
KLAW
KLAW

the end

FUKU
FUKU

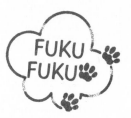

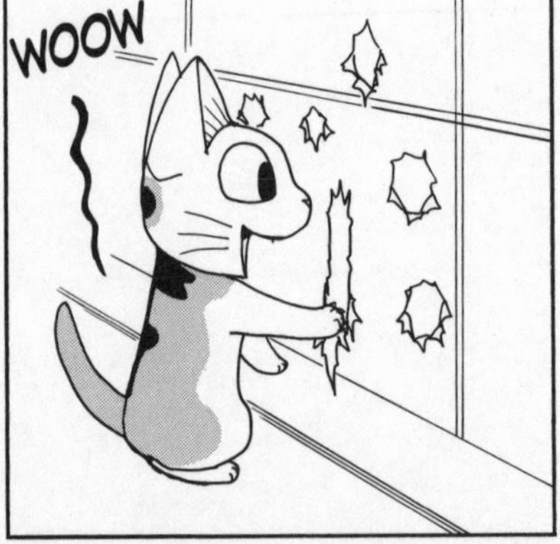
WOOW

# Kitten's Big Adventure

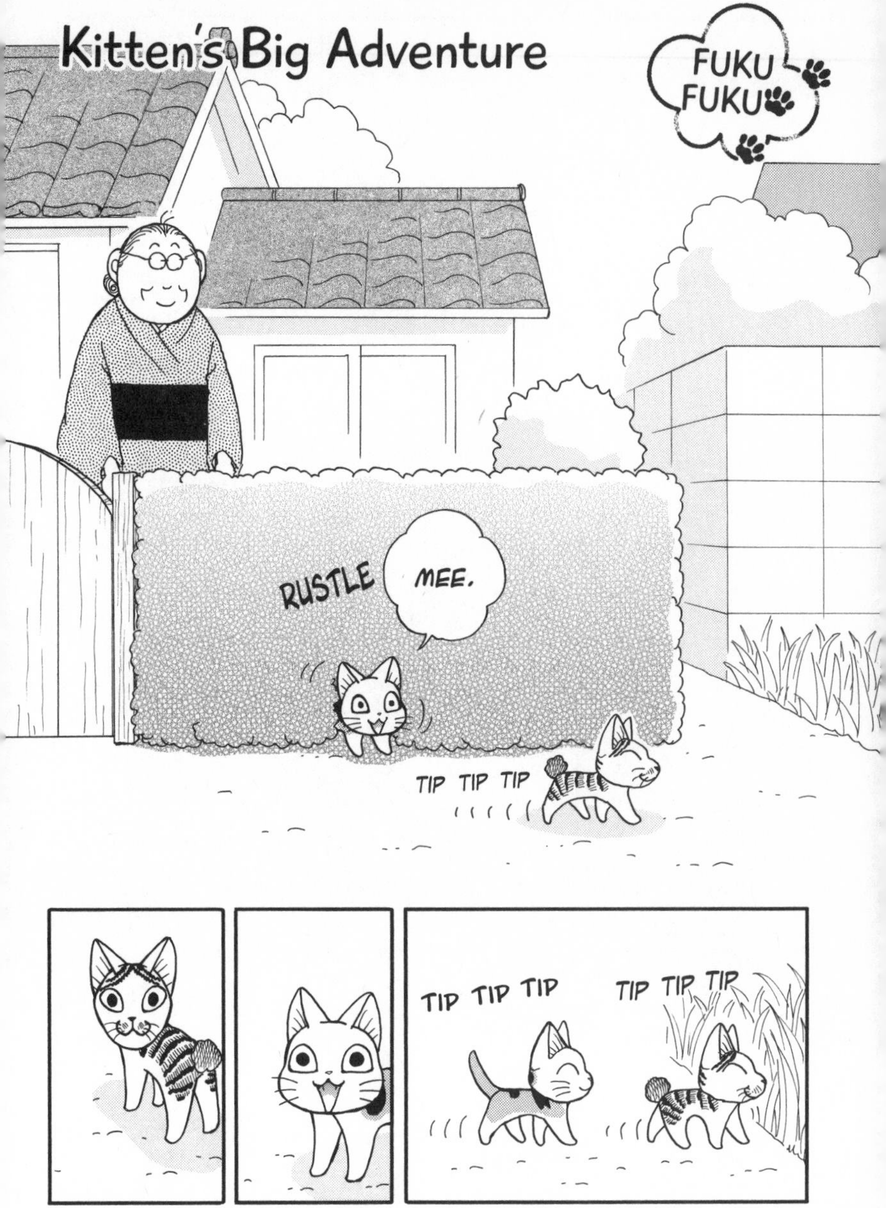
FUKU FUKU
RUSTLE
MEE.
TIP TIP TIP
TIP TIP TIP
TIP TIP TIP

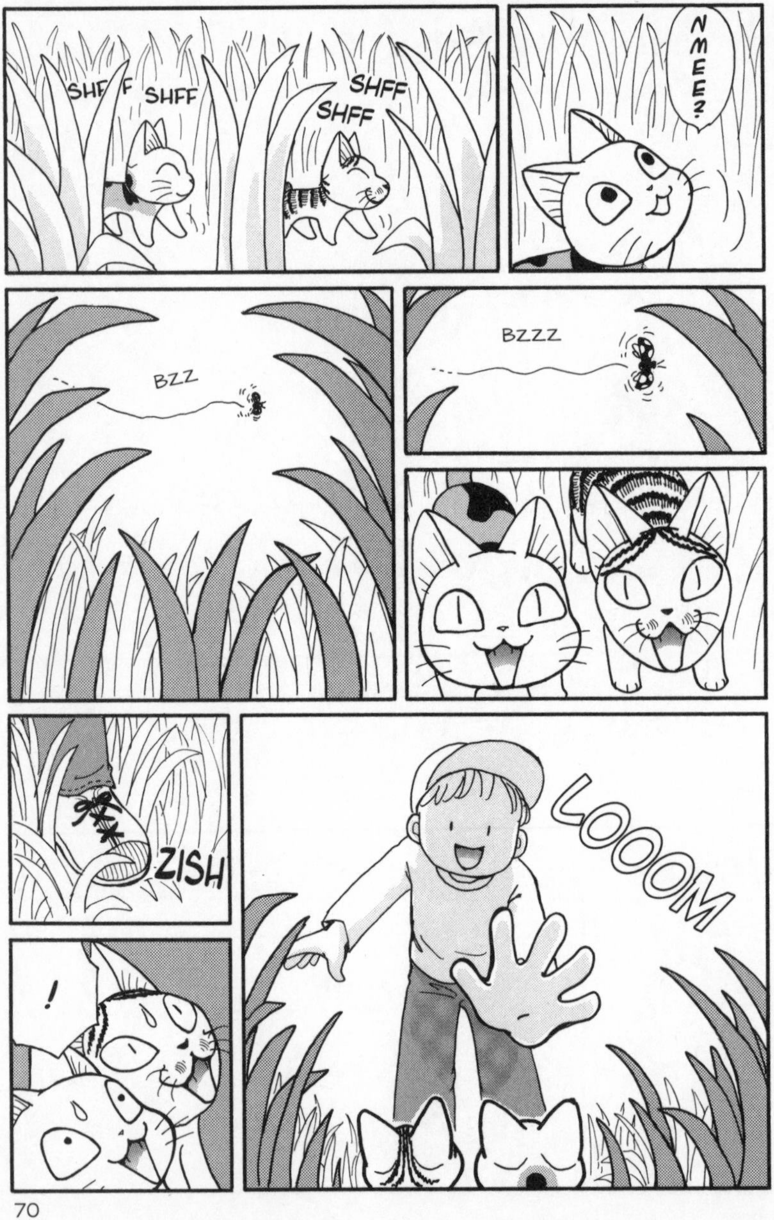
SHFF SHFF
SHFF
SHFF
NMEE?
BZZ
BZZZ
ZISH
LOOOM
!

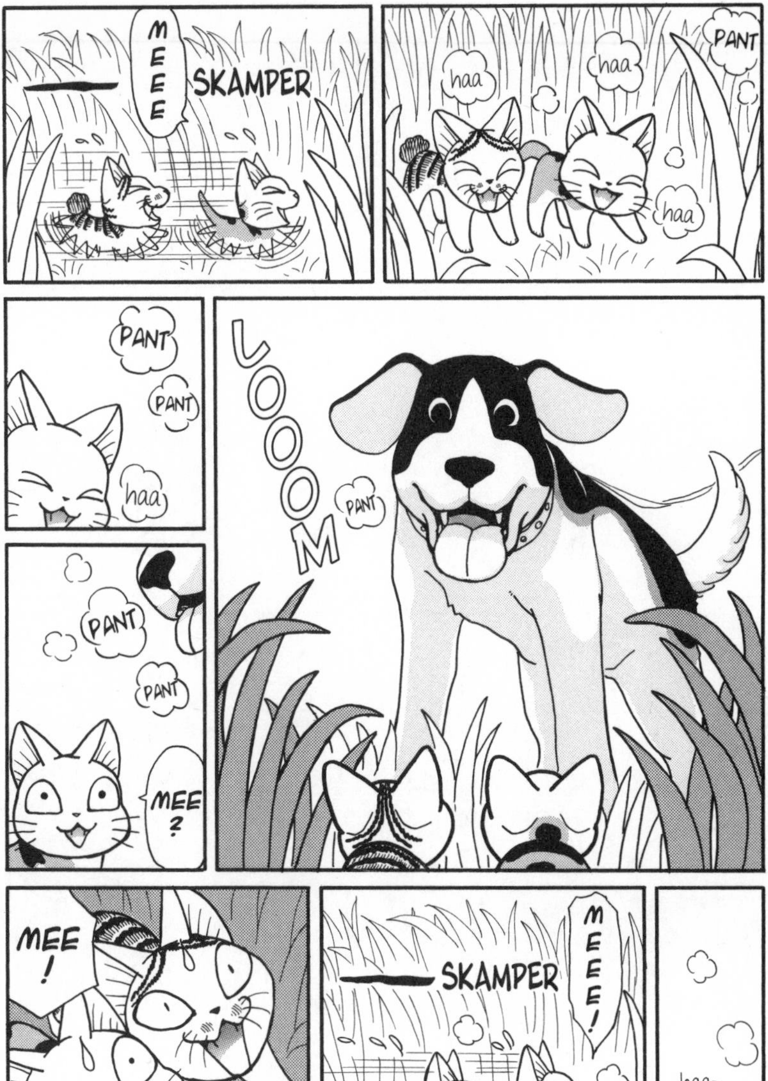
MEEE
SKAMPER
haa
haa
PANT
haa
PANT
PANT
haa
LOOOM
PANT
PANT
PANT
MEE?
MEE!
SKAMPER
MEEE!
haa
haa

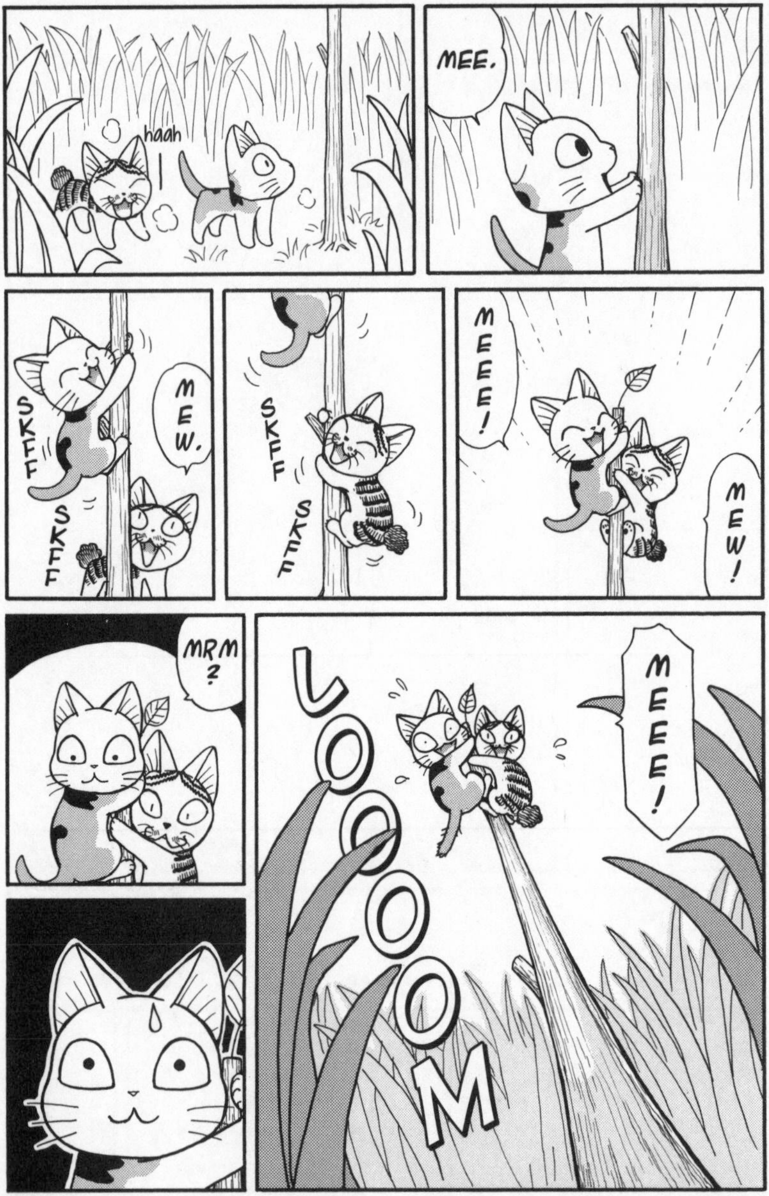
haah
MEE.
SKFF
MEW.
SKFF
SKFF
SKFF
MEEE!
MEW!
MRM?
LOOOOOM
MEEE!

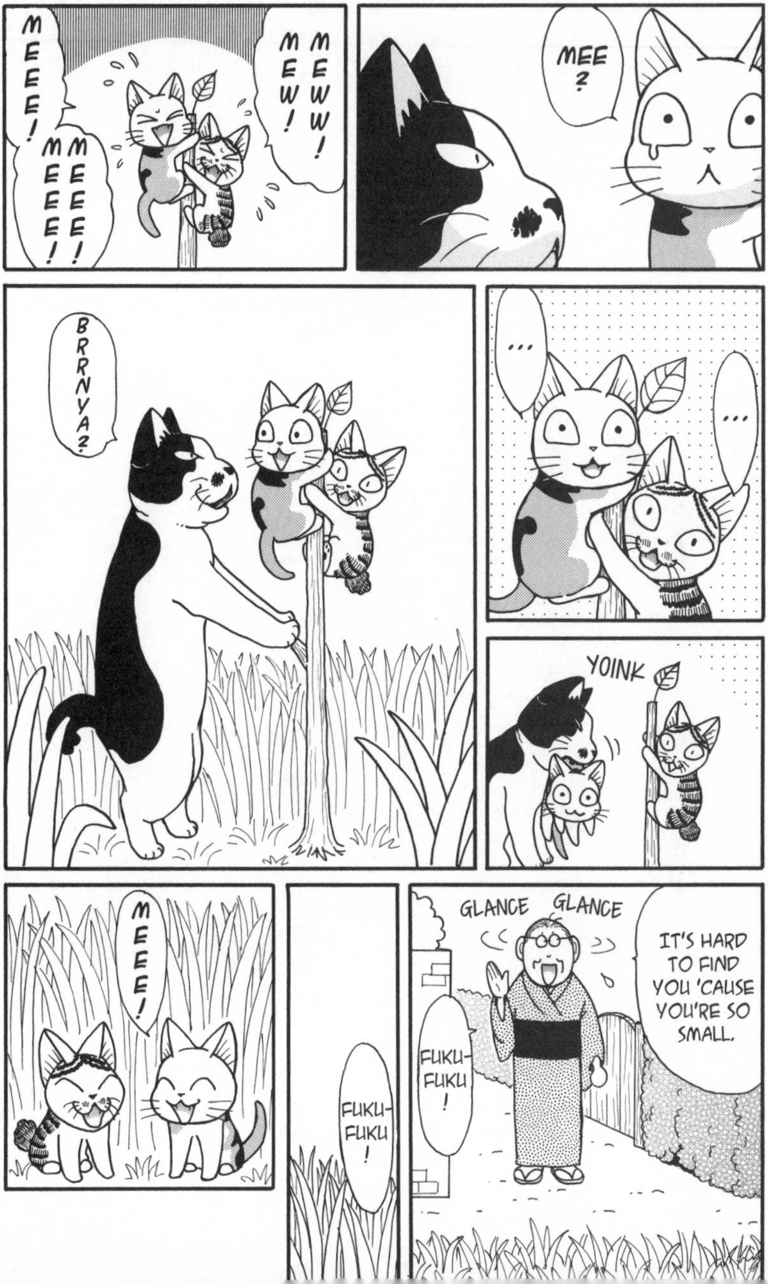
MEEEE!
MEEEE!
MEEEE!
MEWWW!
MEW!
MEE?
BRRNYA?
...
...
YOINK
MEEE!
FUKU-FUKU!
GLANCE GLANCE
FUKU-FUKU!
IT'S HARD TO FIND YOU 'CAUSE YOU'RE SO SMALL.

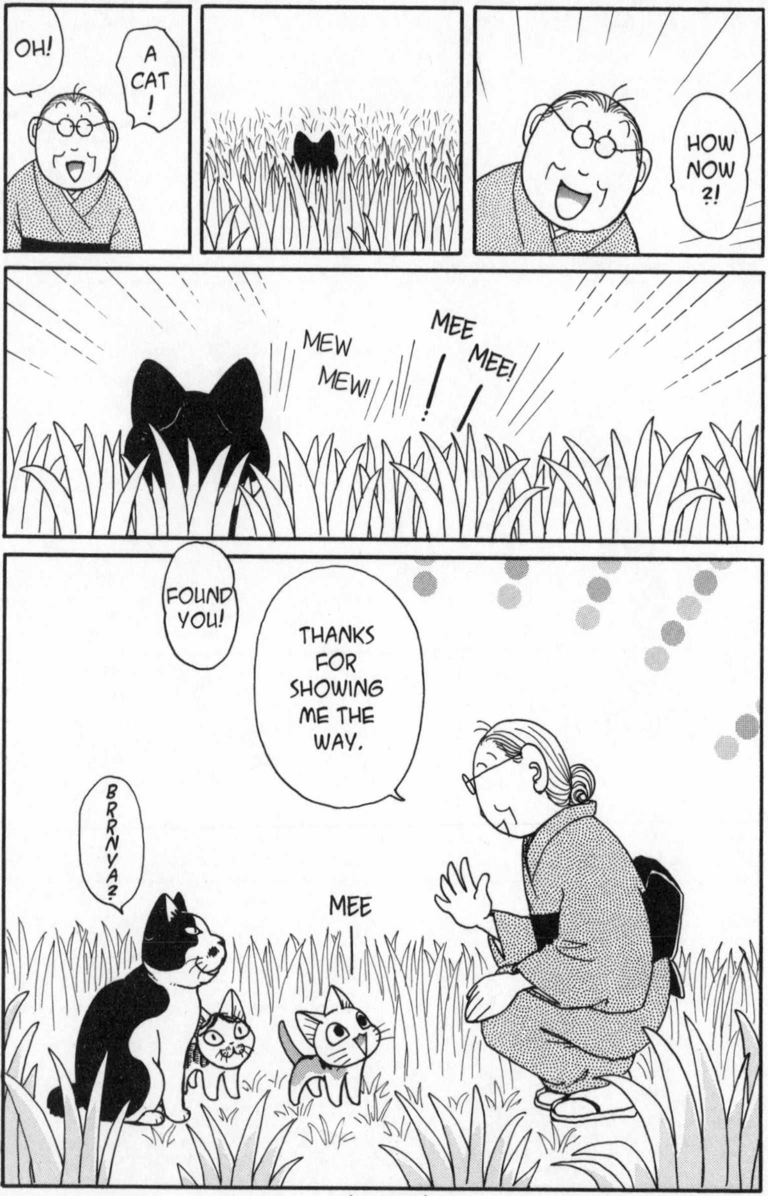
OH!
A CAT!
HOW NOW?!
MEW MEW!
MEE MEE!
FOUND YOU!
THANKS FOR SHOWING ME THE WAY.
BRRNYA?
MEE

the end

# The Kitten and Halloween

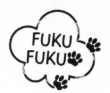

FUKU FUKU

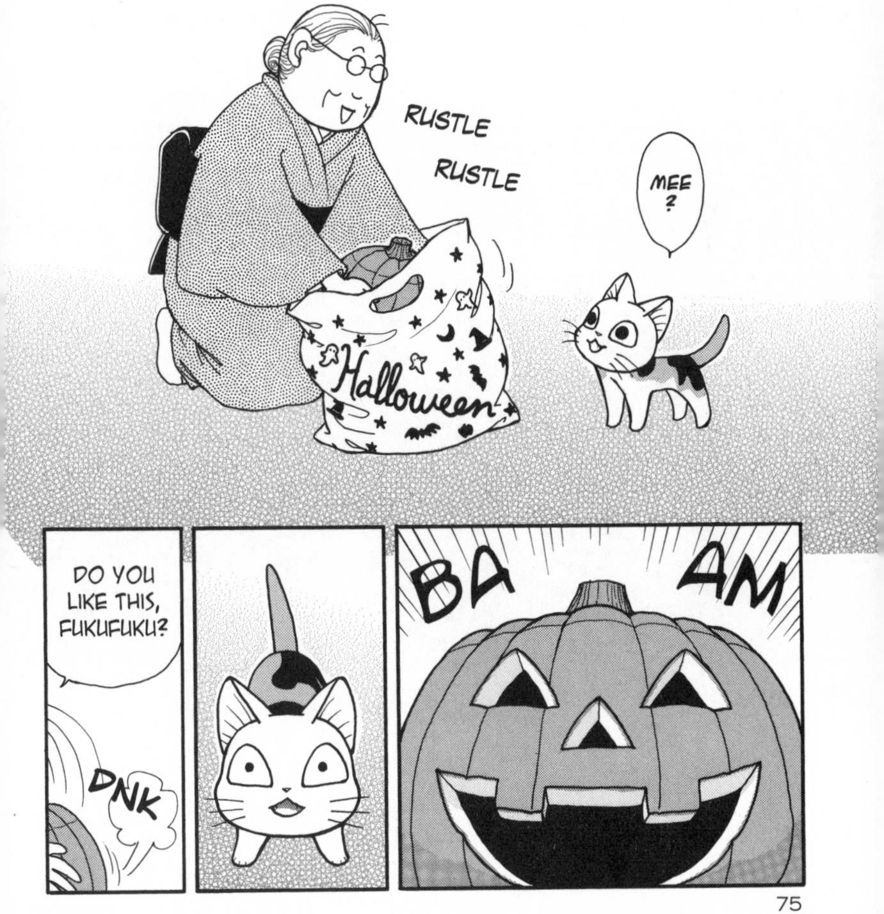

RUSTLE
RUSTLE
MEE?
Halloween
DO YOU LIKE THIS, FUKUFUKU?
DNK
BA AM

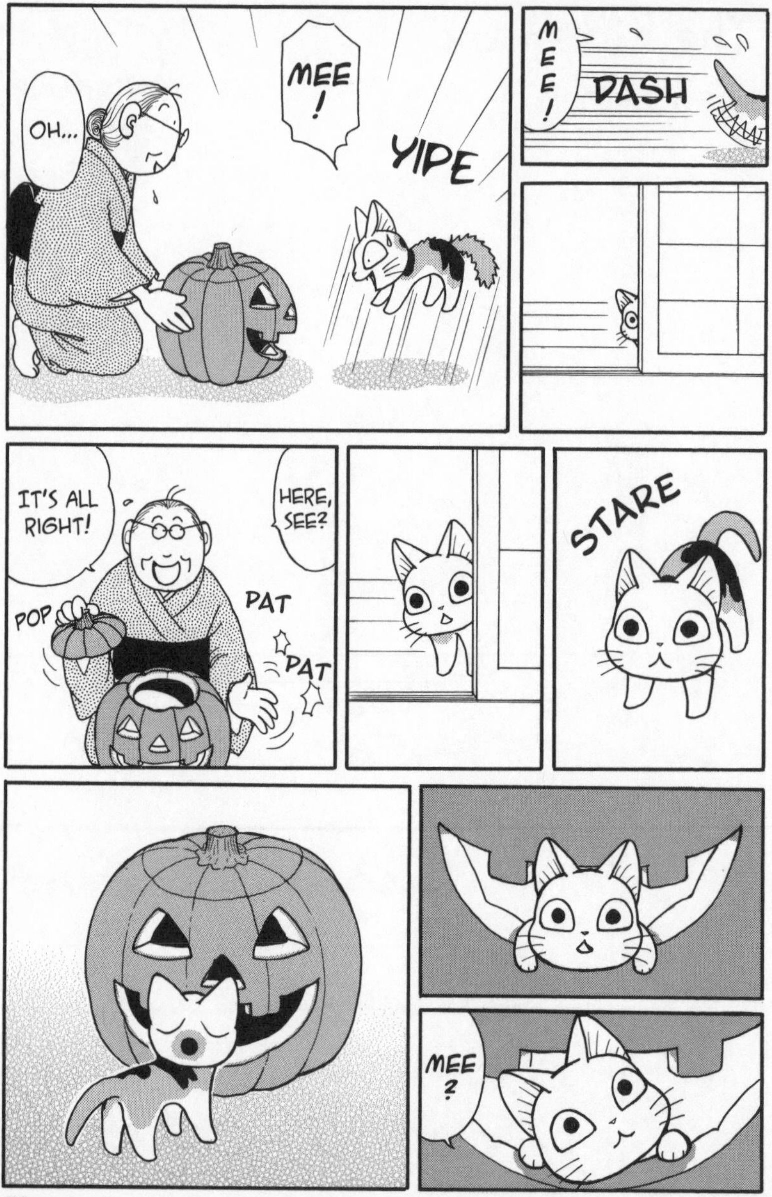
OH...
MEE!
YIPE
MEE!
DASH
IT'S ALL RIGHT!
HERE, SEE?
POP
PAT
PAT
STARE
MEE?

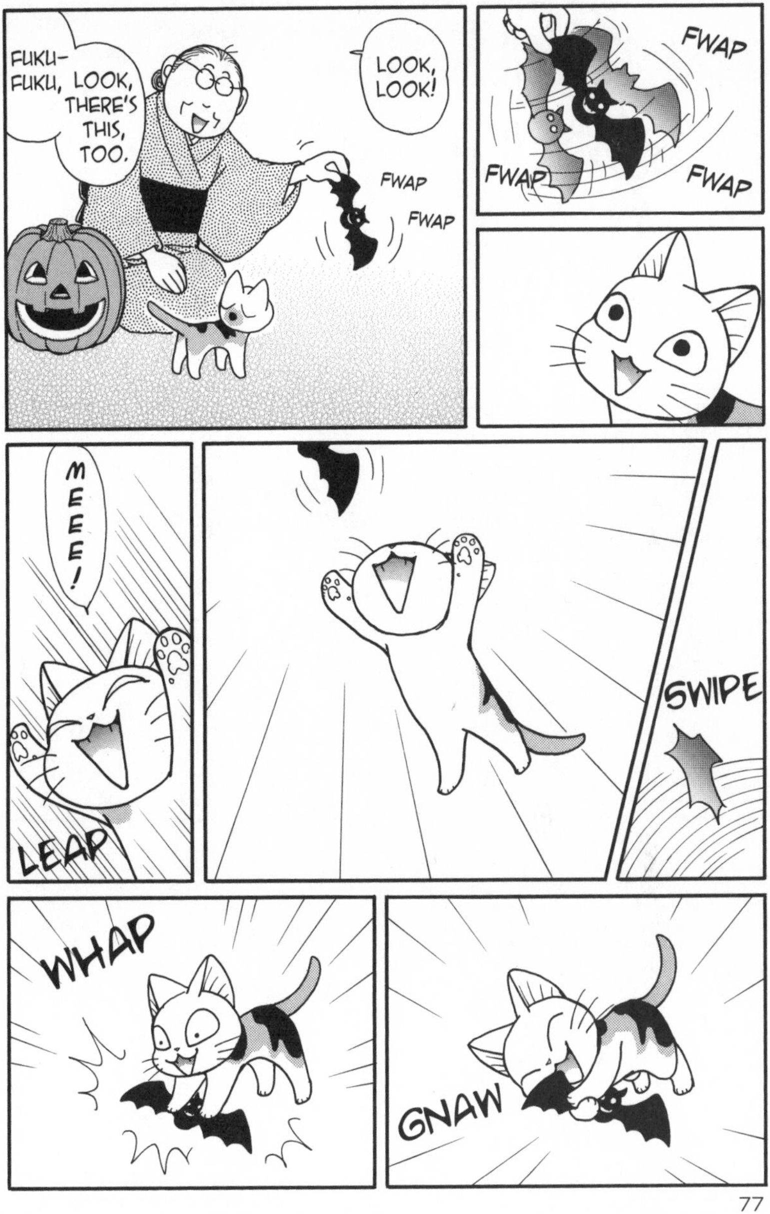
FUKU-FUKU, LOOK, THERE'S THIS, TOO.
LOOK, LOOK!
FWAP
FWAP
FWAP
FWAP
FWAP
MEEEE!
LEAP
SWIPE
WHAP
GNAW

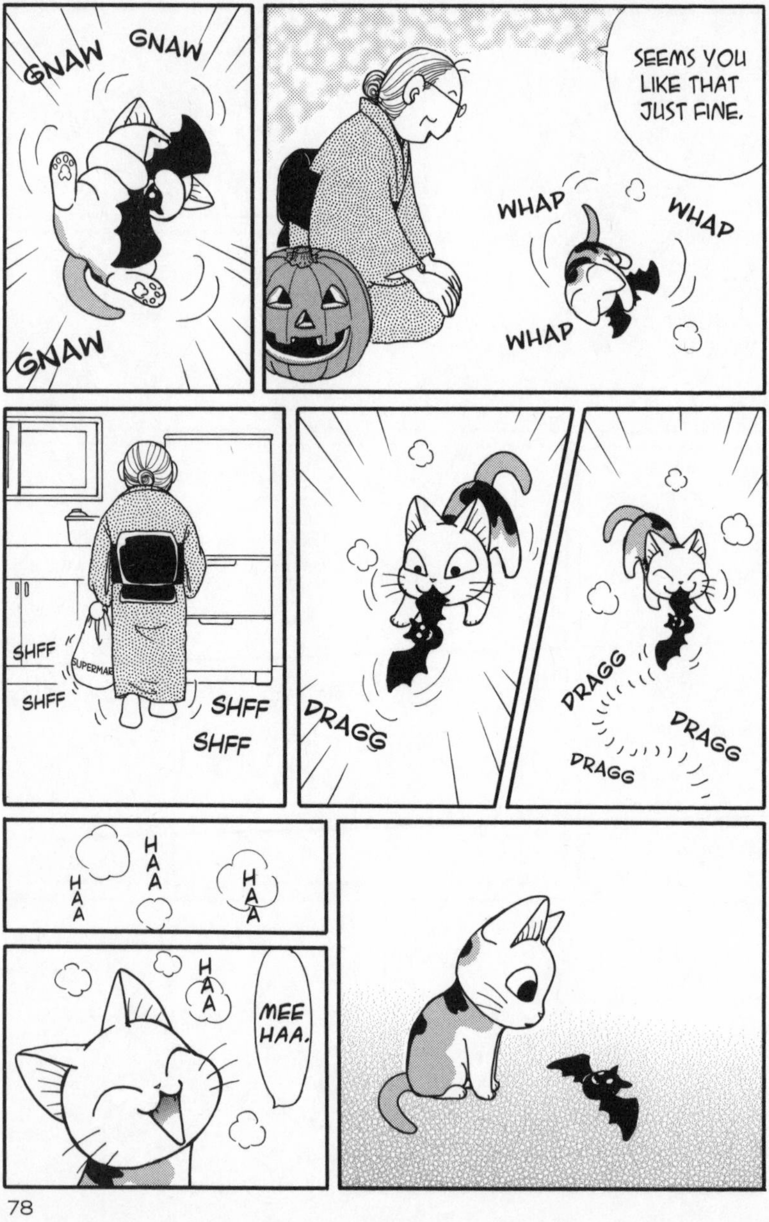
GNAW GNAW
GNAW
SEEMS YOU LIKE THAT JUST FINE.
WHAP
WHAP
WHAP
SHFF
SHFF
SHFF
SHFF
SUPERMAR
DRAGG
DRAGG
DRAGG
DRAGG
HAA
HAA
HAA
HAA
MEE HAA.

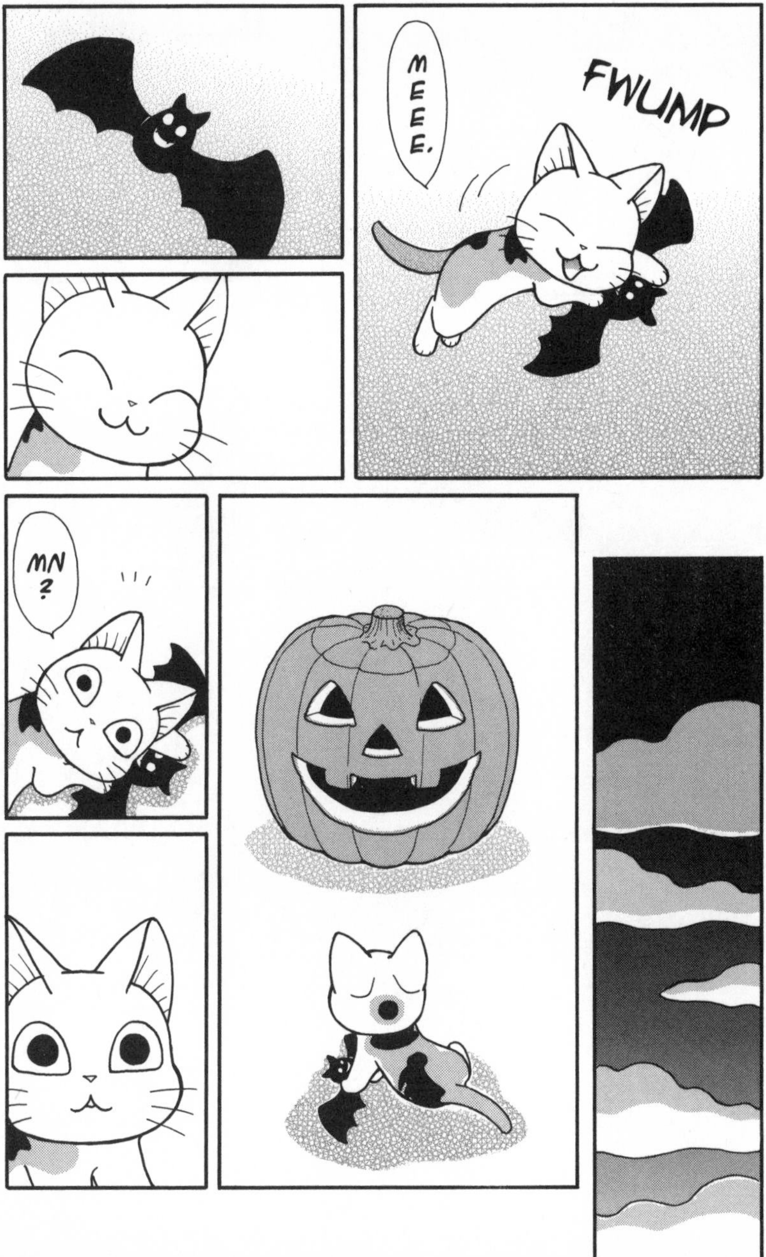

MEEE.
FWUMP
MN?

JUST ABOUT TIME TO LIGHT UP THE JACK-O'-LANTERN.

POP

OH?

AWW.

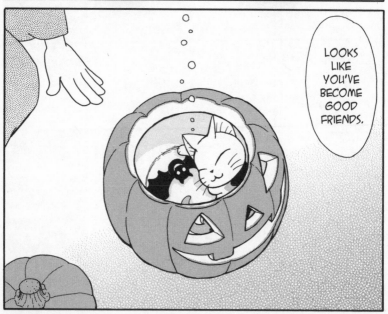

LOOKS LIKE YOU'VE BECOME GOOD FRIENDS.

the end

# The Kitten and Treats

FUKU FUKU

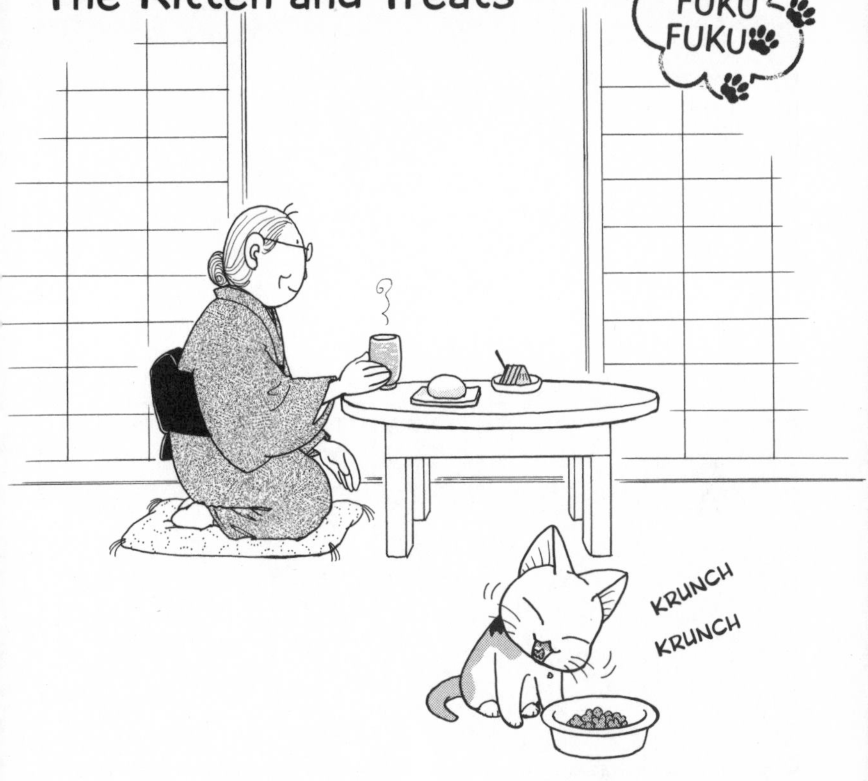
KRUNCH
KRUNCH

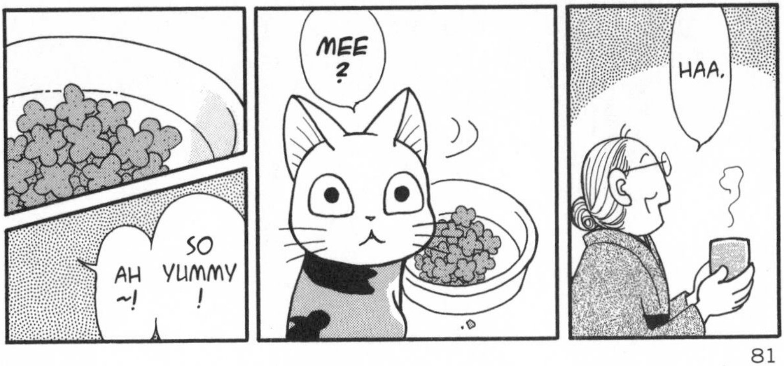
HAA.
MEE ?
SO YUMMY !
AH ~!

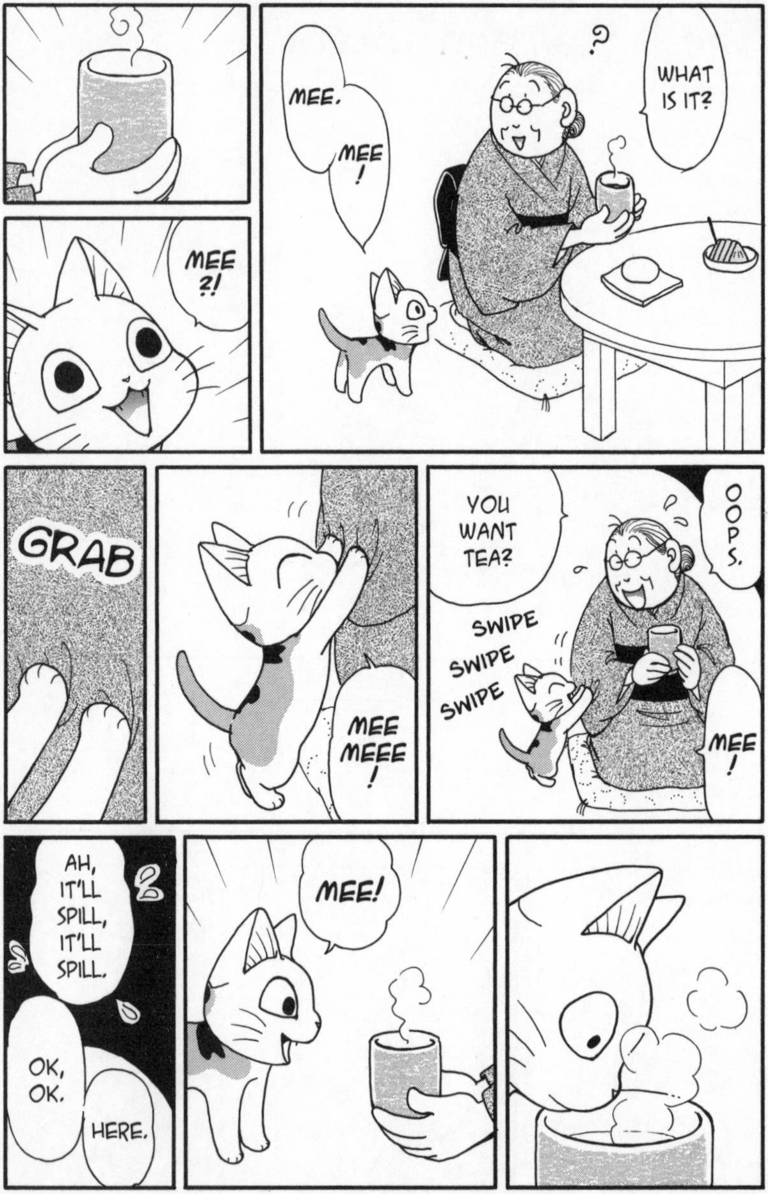
MEE ?!
MEE. MEE!
WHAT IS IT?
GRAB
MEE MEEE!
YOU WANT TEA?
OOPS.
SWIPE SWIPE SWIPE
MEE!
AH, IT'LL SPILL, IT'LL SPILL.
OK, OK.
HERE.
MEE!

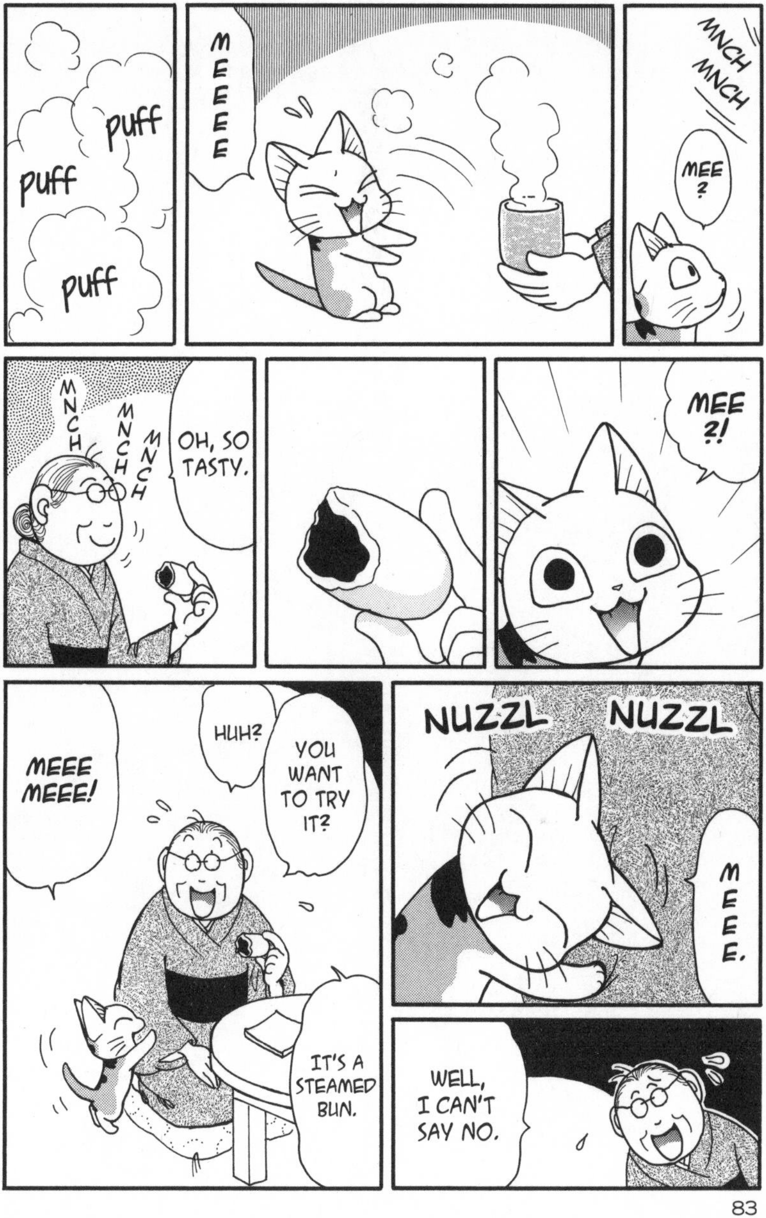
puff
puff
puff
MEEEE
MNCH MNCH
MEE?
MNCH
MNCH
MNCH
OH, SO TASTY.
MEE?!
MEEE MEEE!
HUH?
YOU WANT TO TRY IT?
IT'S A STEAMED BUN.
NUZZL NUZZL
MEEE.
WELL, I CAN'T SAY NO.

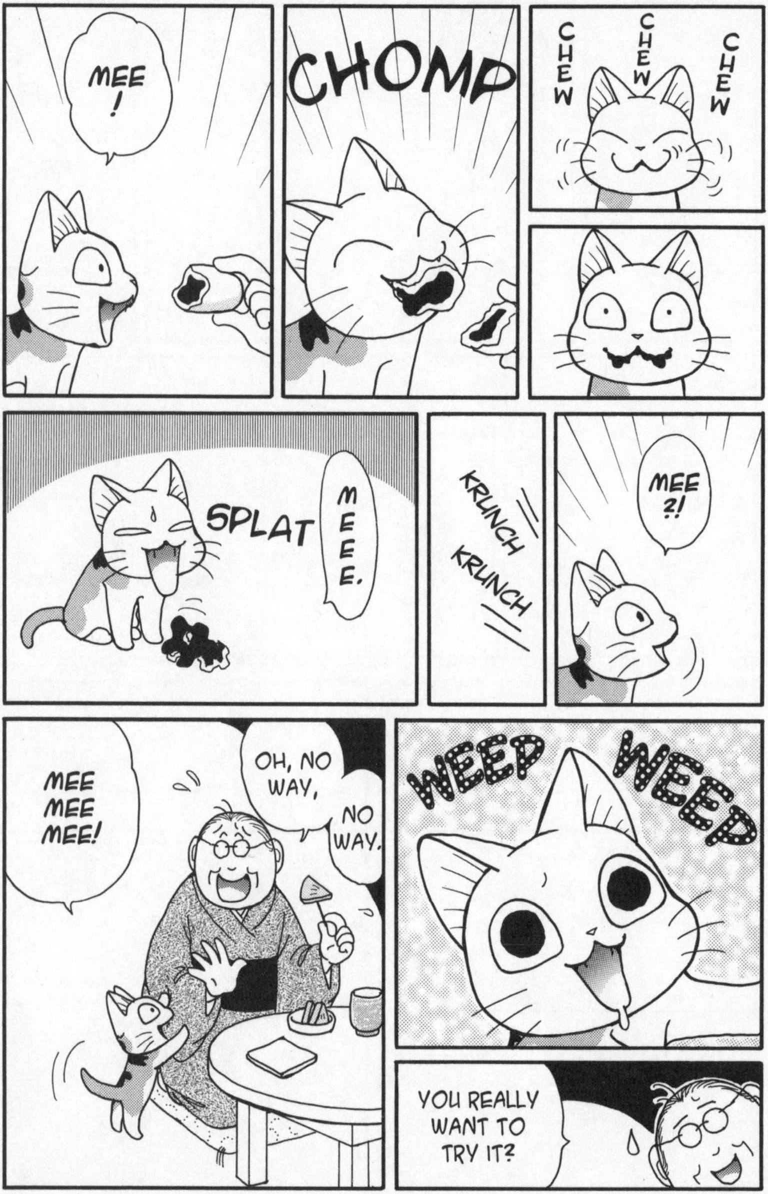
MEE!
CHOMP
CHEW CHEW CHEW
SPLAT
MEEE.
KRUNCH KRUNCH
MEE?!
MEE MEE MEE!
OH, NO WAY,
NO WAY.
WEEP WEEP
YOU REALLY WANT TO TRY IT?

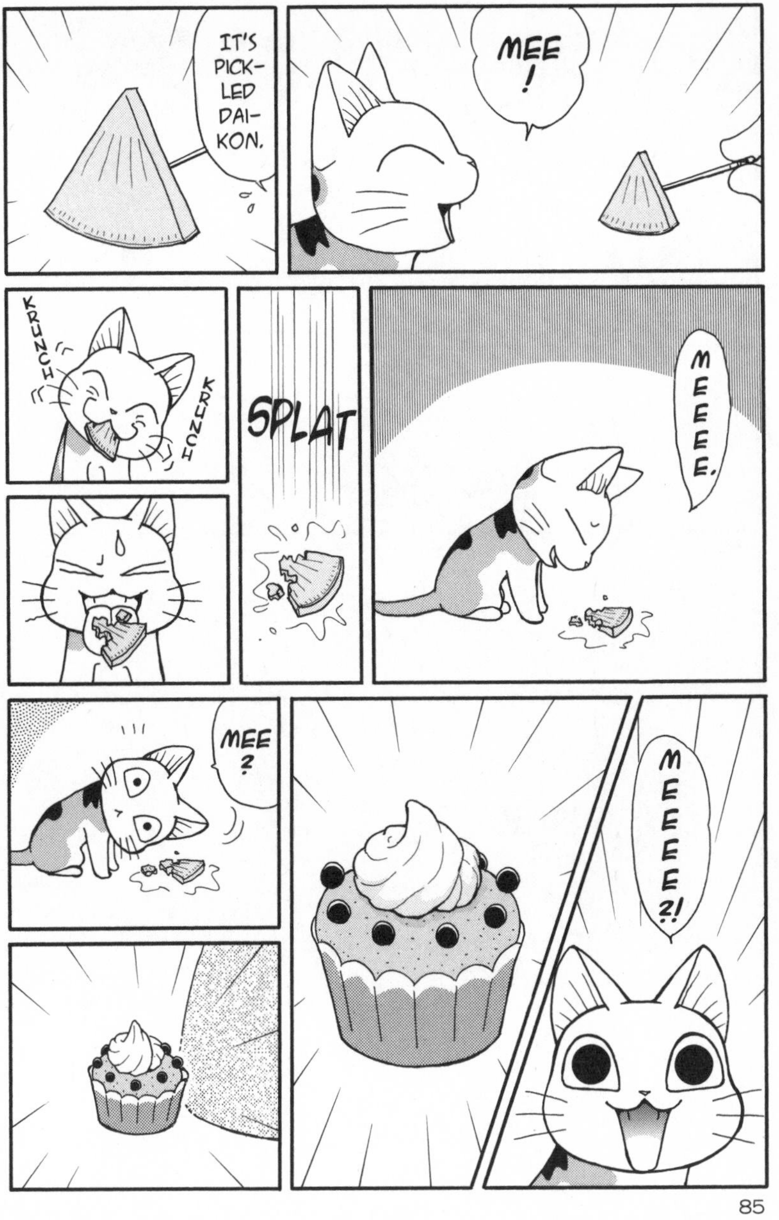
IT'S PICKLED DAIKON.
MEE!
KRUNCH
KRUNCH
SPLAT
MEEEE.
MEE?
MEEEEE?!

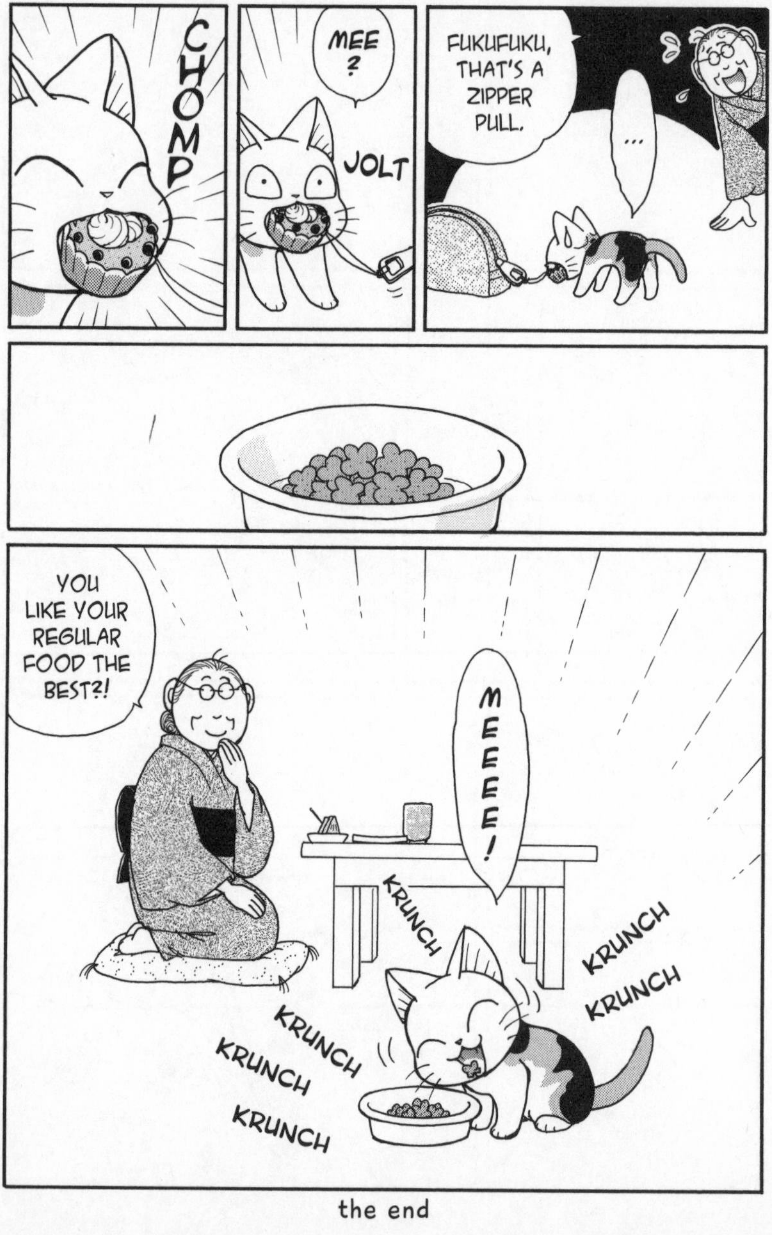
CHOMP
MEE?
JOLT
FUKUFUKU, THAT'S A ZIPPER PULL.
...
YOU LIKE YOUR REGULAR FOOD THE BEST?!
MEEEE!
KRUNCH
KRUNCH
KRUNCH
KRUNCH
KRUNCH
KRUNCH

the end

# The Kotatsu's Debut

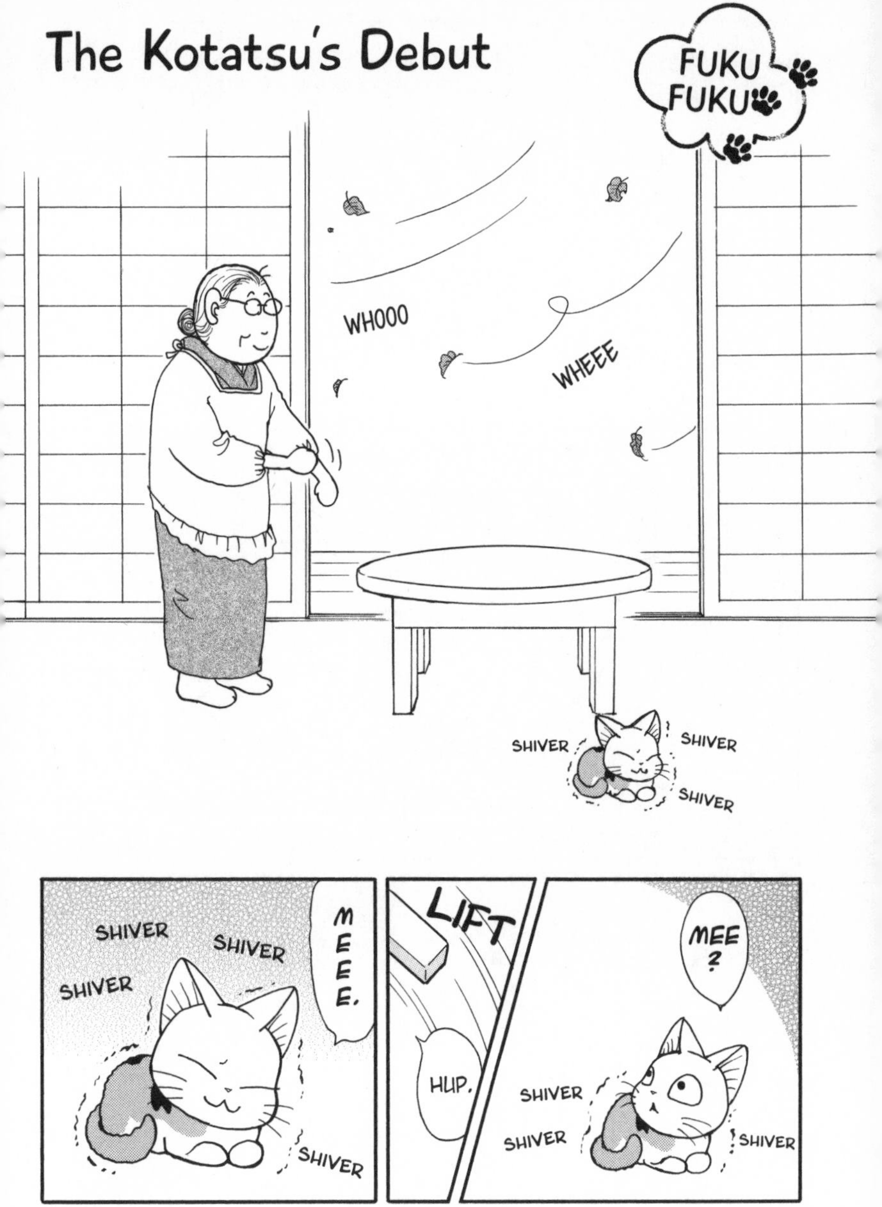
FUKU FUKU
WHOOO
WHEEE
SHIVER
SHIVER
SHIVER
SHIVER
SHIVER
SHIVER
MEEE.
SHIVER
LIFT
HUP.
MEE?
SHIVER
SHIVER
SHIVER

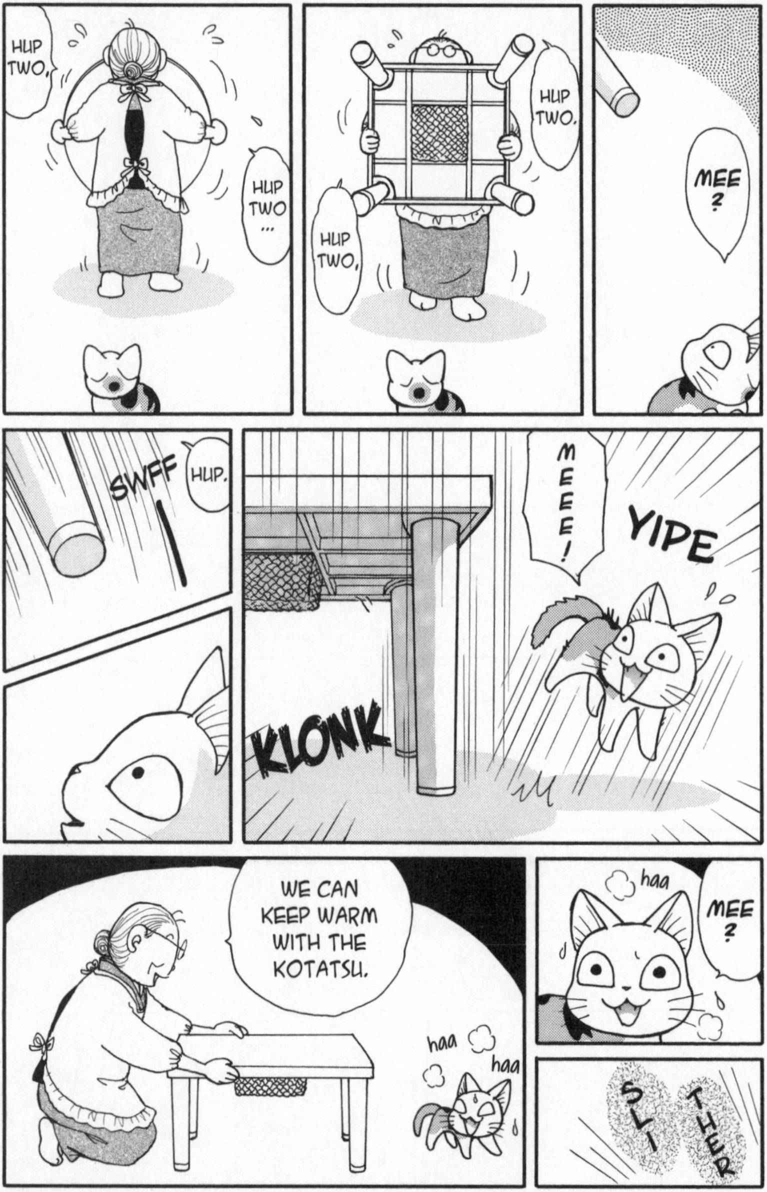

HUP TWO,
HUP TWO ...
HUP TWO,
HUP TWO.
MEE?
SWFF
HUP.
KLONK
MEEE!
YIPE
WE CAN KEEP WARM WITH THE KOTATSU.
haa
haa
haa
MEE?
SLITHER

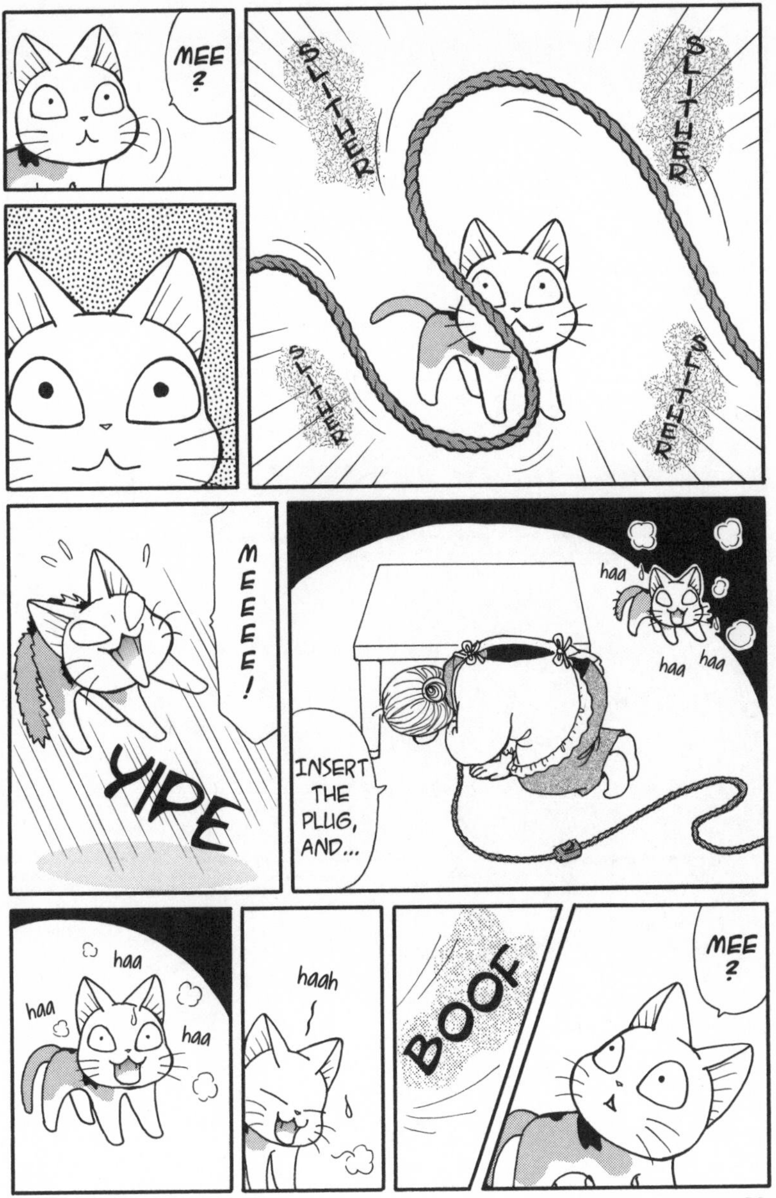
MEE?
SLITHER
SLITHER
SLITHER
SLITHER
MEEEEE!
YIPE
haa
haa
haa
INSERT THE PLUG, AND...
haa
haa
haa
haah
BOOF
MEE?

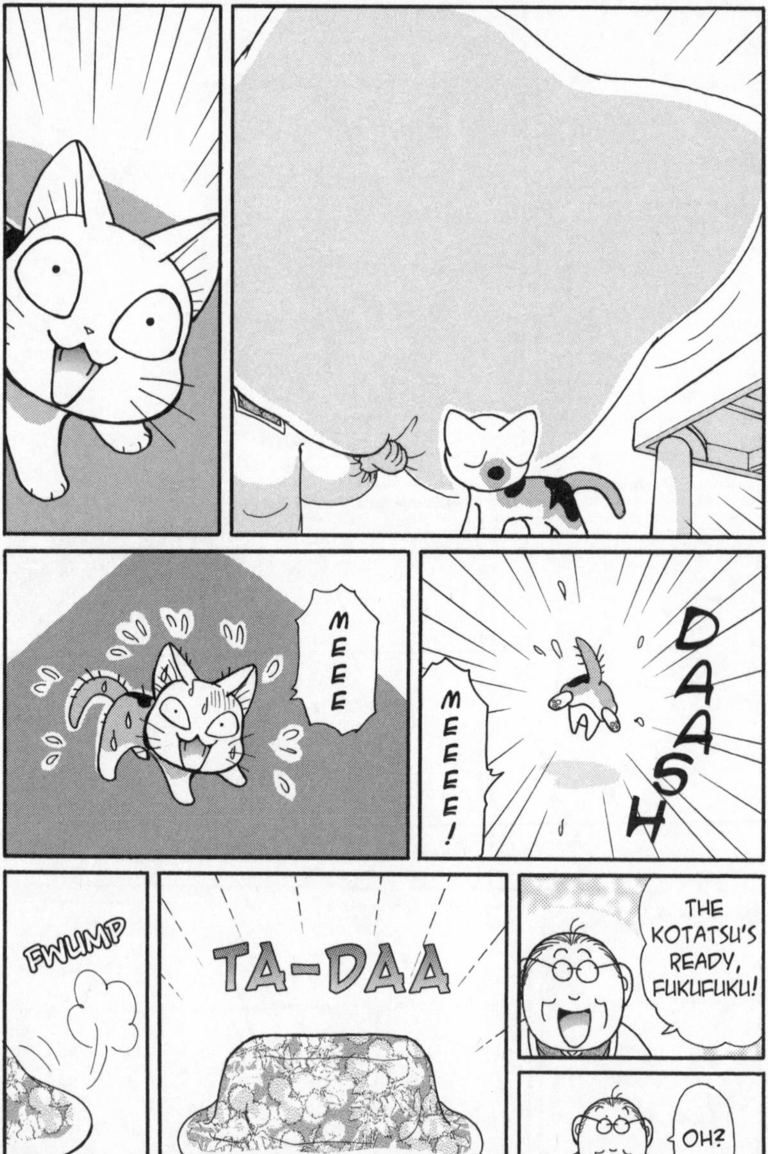
MEEE
MEEEEE!
DAAASH
FWUMP
TA-DAA
THE KOTATSU'S READY, FUKUFUKU!
OH?

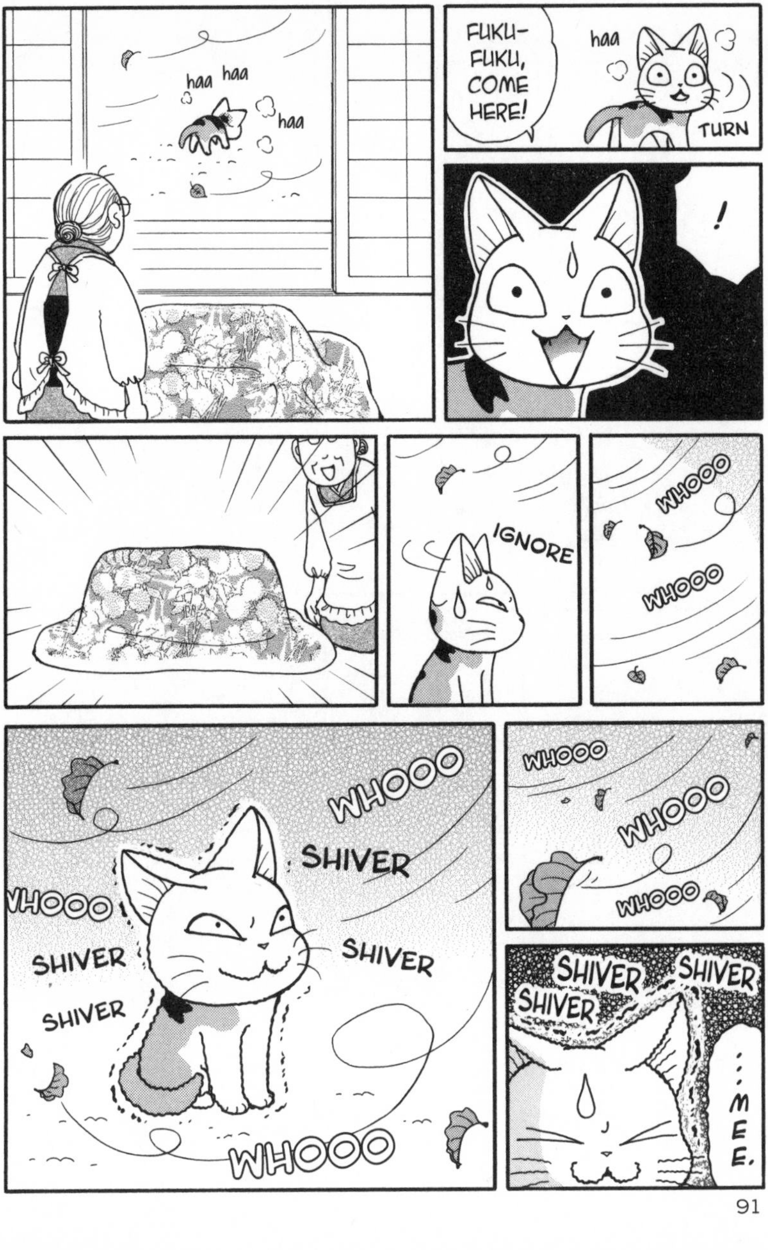
haa haa
haa
FUKU-FUKU, COME HERE!
haa
TURN
!
IGNORE
WHOOO
WHOOO
WHOOO
SHIVER
HOOO
SHIVER
SHIVER
SHIVER
WHOOO
WHOOO
WHOOO
WHOOO
SHIVER
SHIVER
SHIVER
...MEE.

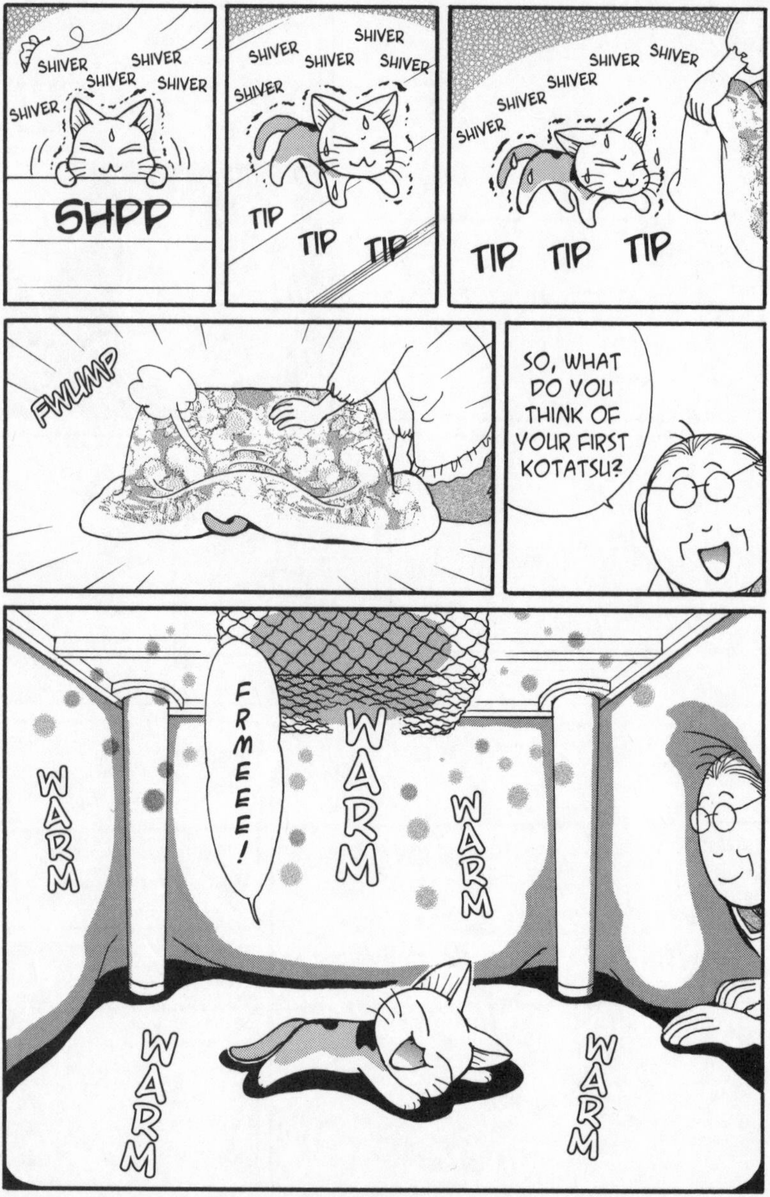
SHIVER
SHIVER
SHIVER
SHIVER
SHIVER
SHPP
SHIVER
SHIVER
SHIVER
SHIVER
SHIVER
TIP
TIP
TIP
SHIVER
SHIVER
SHIVER
SHIVER
SHIVER
TIP
TIP
TIP
FWUMP
SO, WHAT DO YOU THINK OF YOUR FIRST KOTATSU?
FRMEEE!
WARM
WARM
WARM
WARM
WARM

the end

# Fun Ornaments

FUKU FUKU

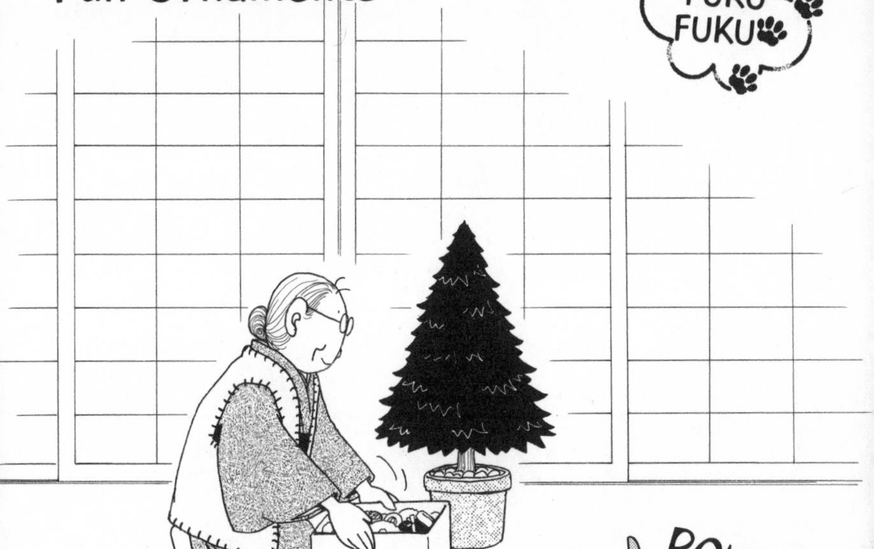
POUNCE

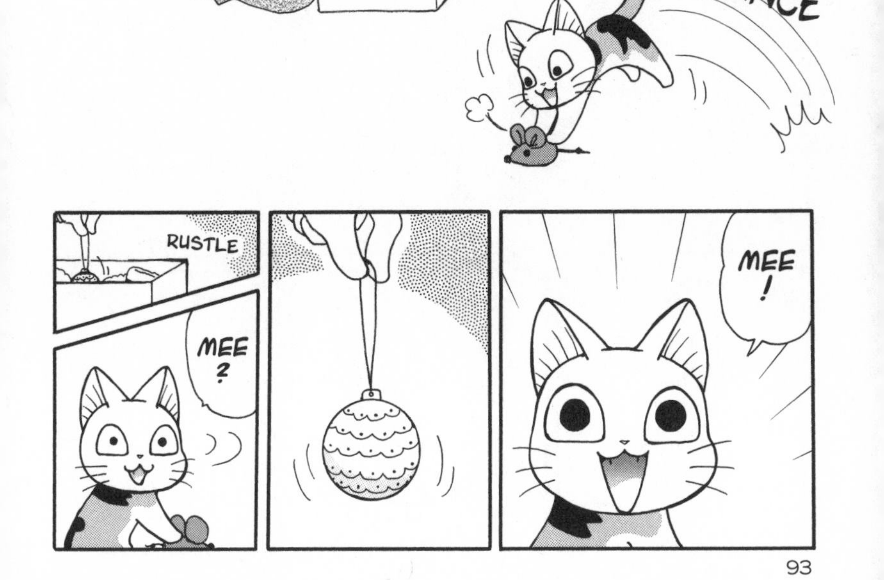
RUSTLE
MEE ?
MEE !

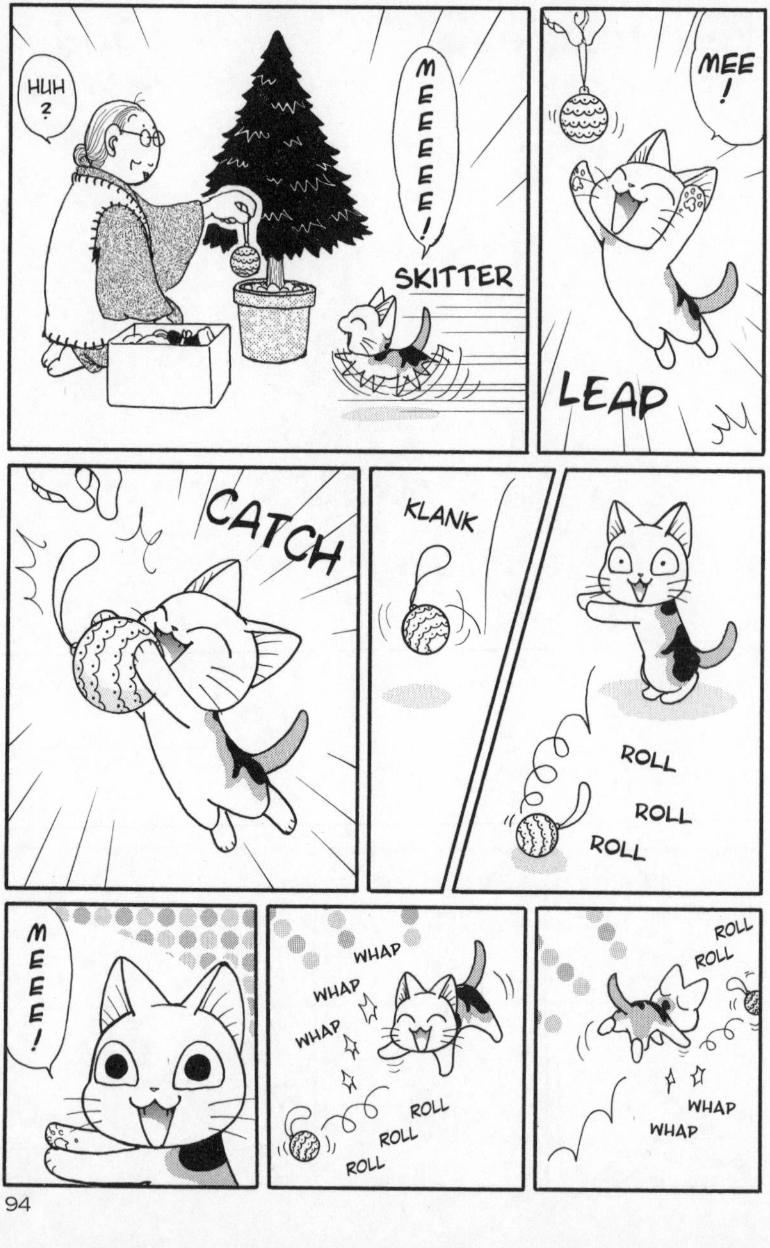
HUH?
MEEEEE!
SKITTER
MEE!
LEAP
CATCH
KLANK
ROLL
ROLL
ROLL
MEEE!
WHAP
WHAP
WHAP
ROLL
ROLL
ROLL
ROLL
ROLL
WHAP
WHAP

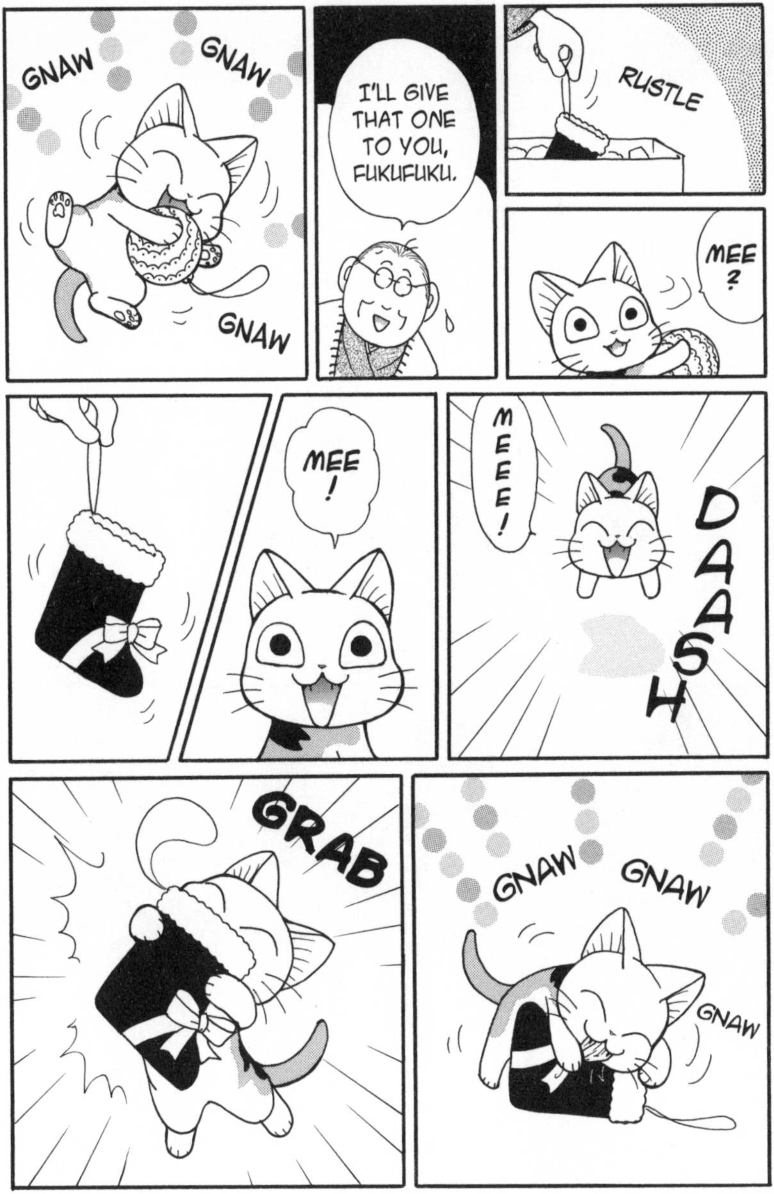
GNAW GNAW
GNAW
I'LL GIVE THAT ONE TO YOU, FUKUFUKU.
RUSTLE
MEE ?
MEE !
MEEEE!
DAASH
GRAB
GNAW GNAW
GNAW

AND NOW THAT'S YOURS, TOO, FUKU-FUKU.

SHFF

MEE?

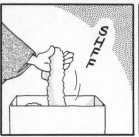

MEEE!

MEEEE!

DAASH

GRABB

YOU JUST JUMP ON EVERYTHING RIGHT AWAY!

SHFF SHFF SHFF

SHFF SHFF SHFF

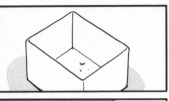

SEEMS WE'RE A LITTLE SHORT, BUT...

THE CHRISTMAS TREE IS ALL DECORATED!

MEE?

MEE!

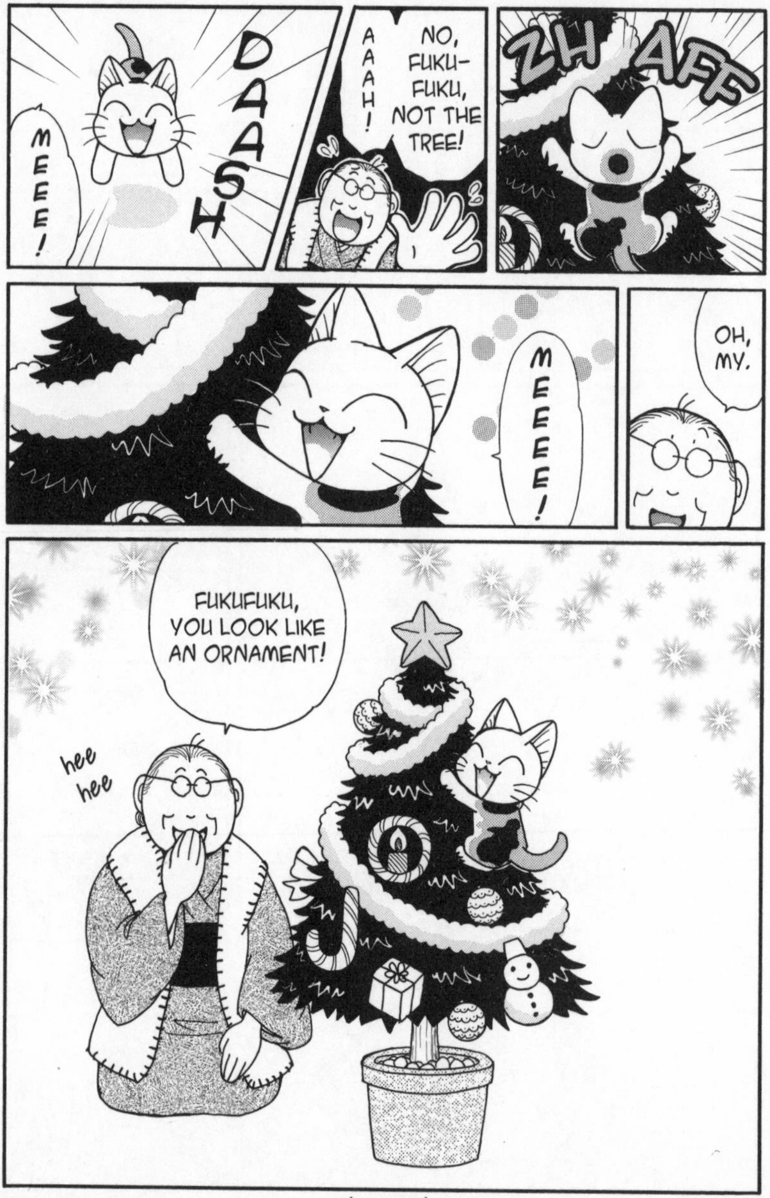
MEEE!
DAAASH
AAAH!
NO, FUKU-FUKU, NOT THE TREE!
ZH AFF
MEEEE!
OH, MY.
FUKUFUKU, YOU LOOK LIKE AN ORNAMENT!
hee hee

the end

FUKU FUKU

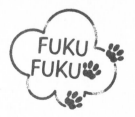

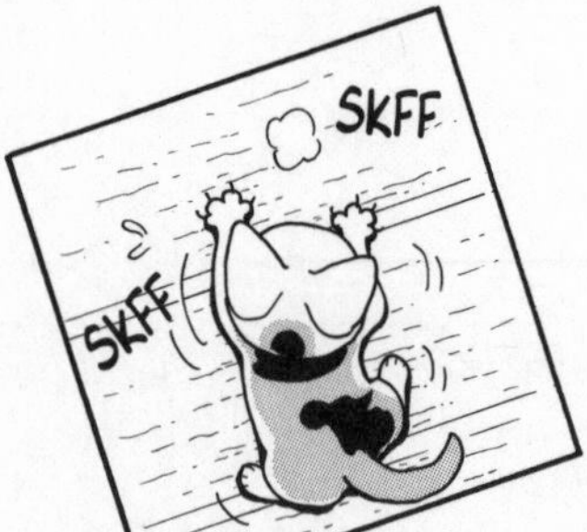
SKFF
SKFF

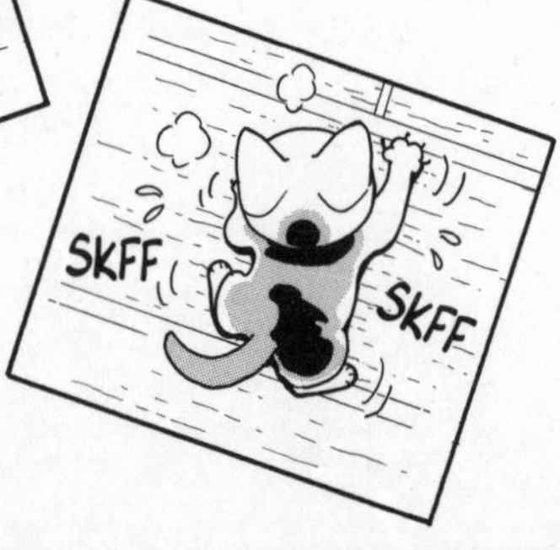
SKFF
SKFF

# A Cold Night

FUKU FUKU

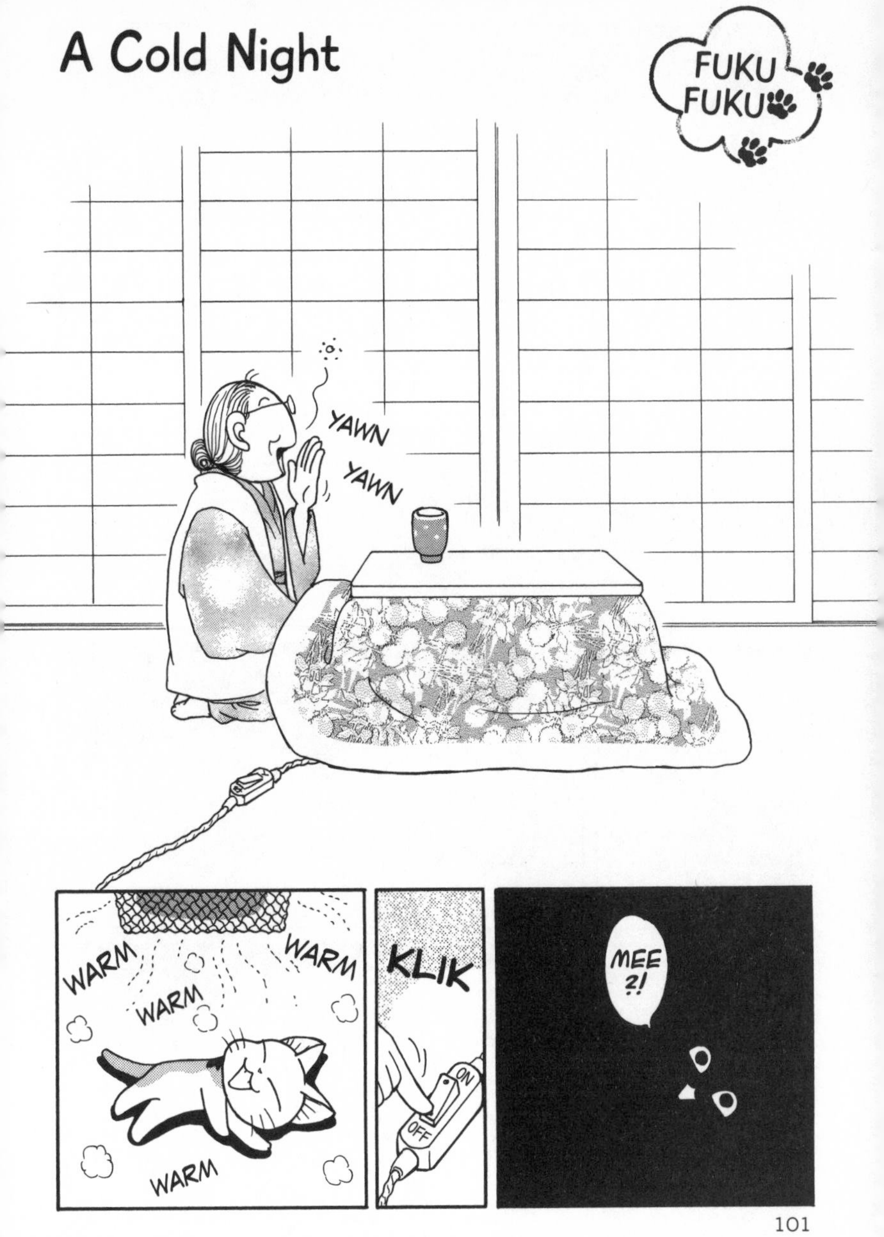
YAWN
YAWN
WARM
WARM
WARM
WARM
KLIK
ON
OFF
MEE?!

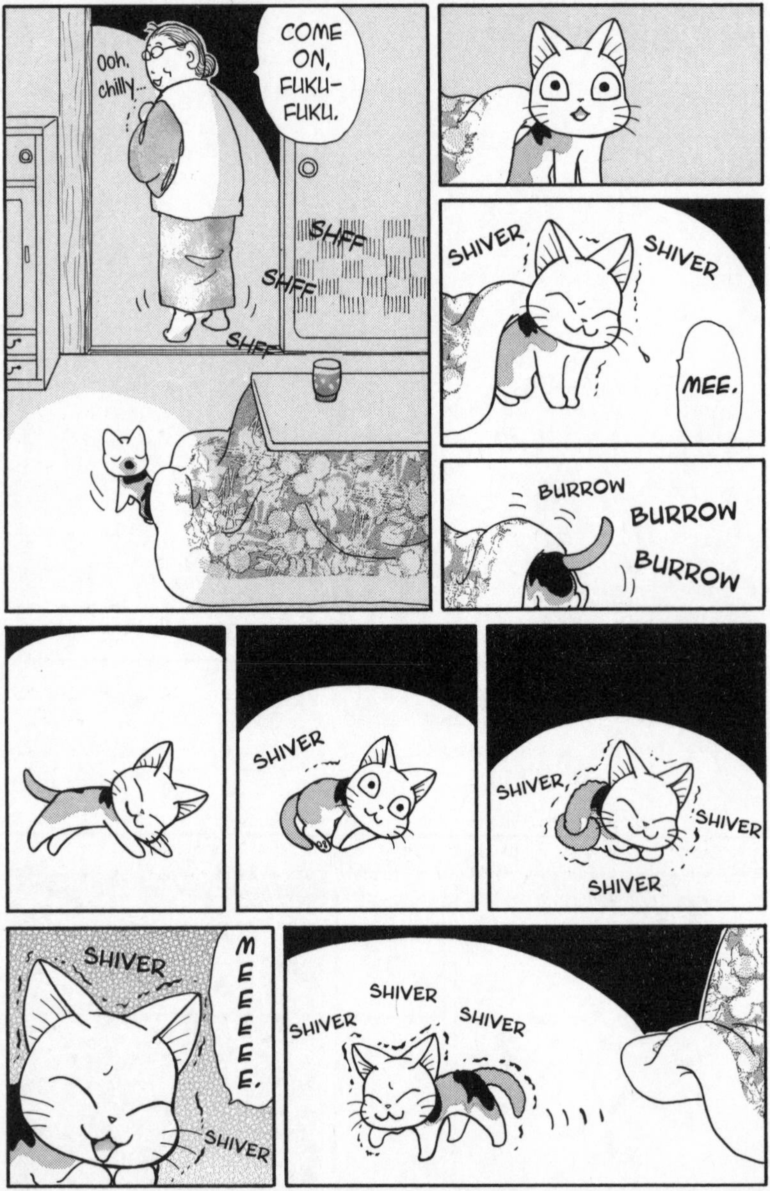
Ooh, chilly...
COME ON, FUKU-FUKU.
SHFF
SHFF
SHFF
SHIVER
SHIVER
MEE.
BURROW
BURROW
BURROW
SHIVER
SHIVER,
SHIVER
SHIVER
SHIVER
MEEEEE.
SHIVER
SHIVER
SHIVER
SHIVER

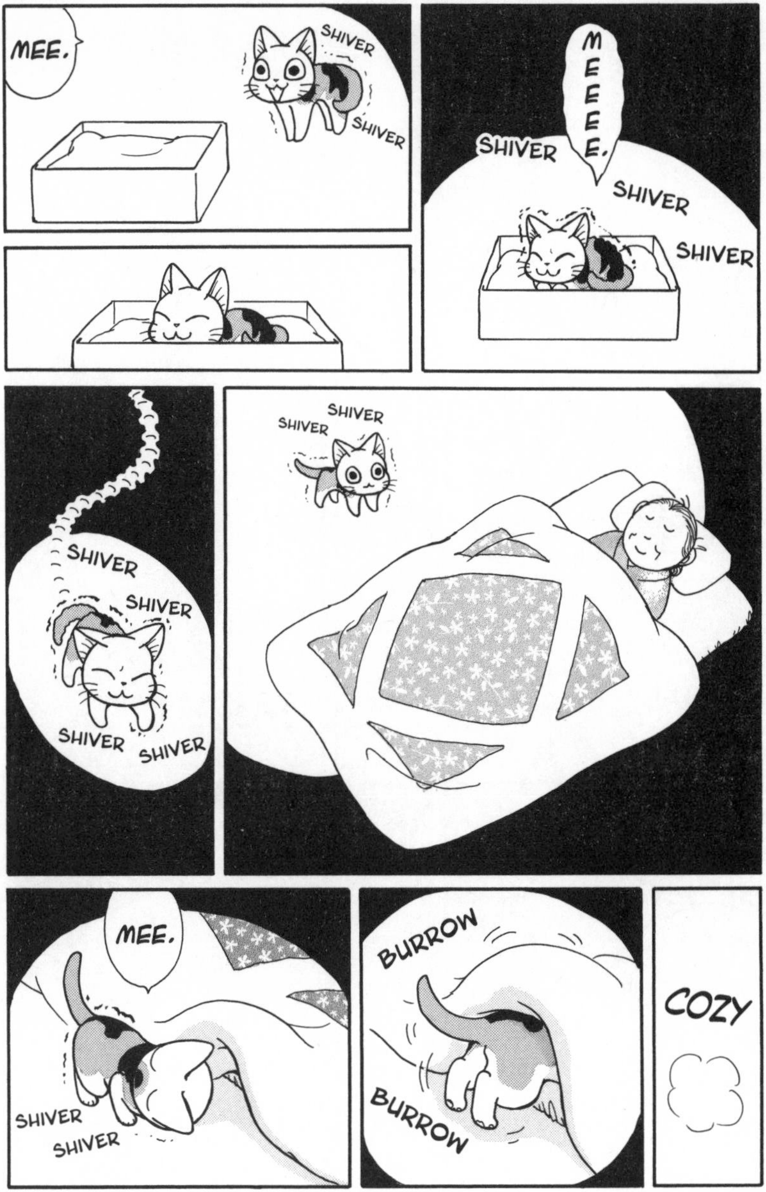
MEE.
SHIVER
SHIVER
MEEEE.
SHIVER
SHIVER
SHIVER
SHIVER
SHIVER
SHIVER
SHIVER
SHIVER
SHIVER
MEE.
SHIVER
SHIVER
BURROW
BURROW
COZY

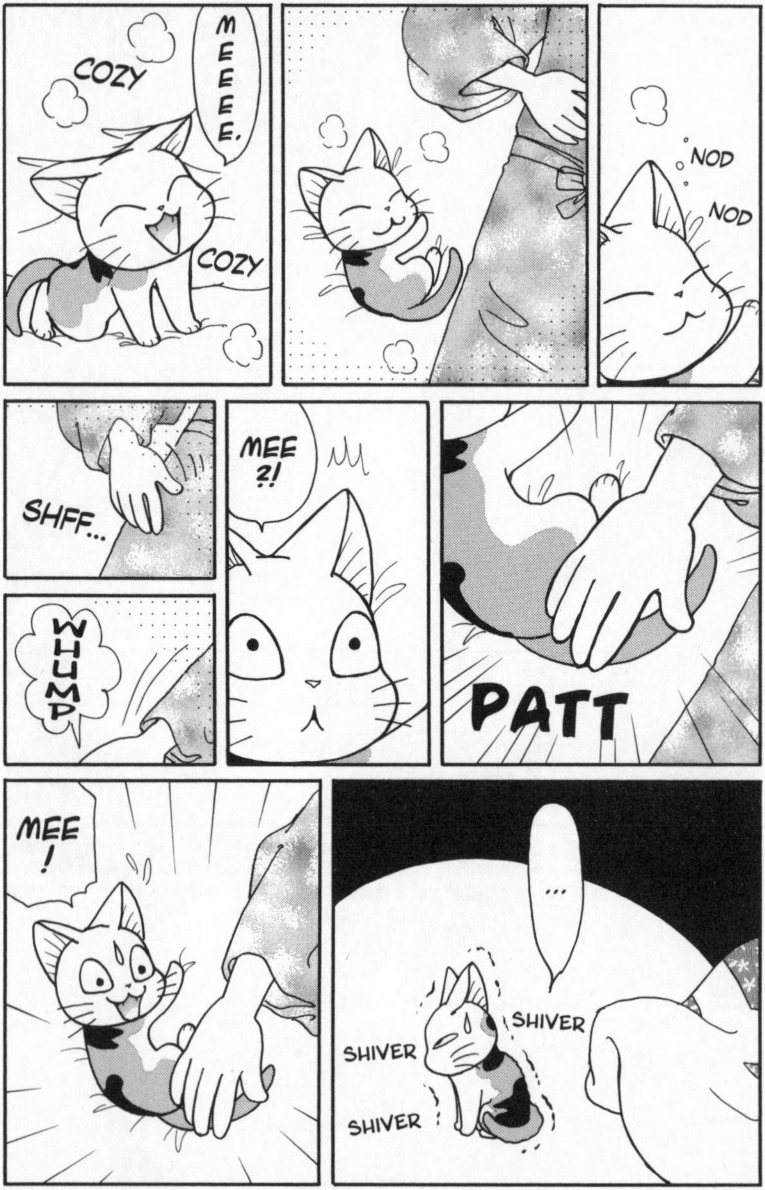
COZY
MEEEE.
COZY
NOD
NOD
SHFF...
WHUMP
MEE ?!
PATT
MEE !
...
SHIVER
SHIVER
SHIVER

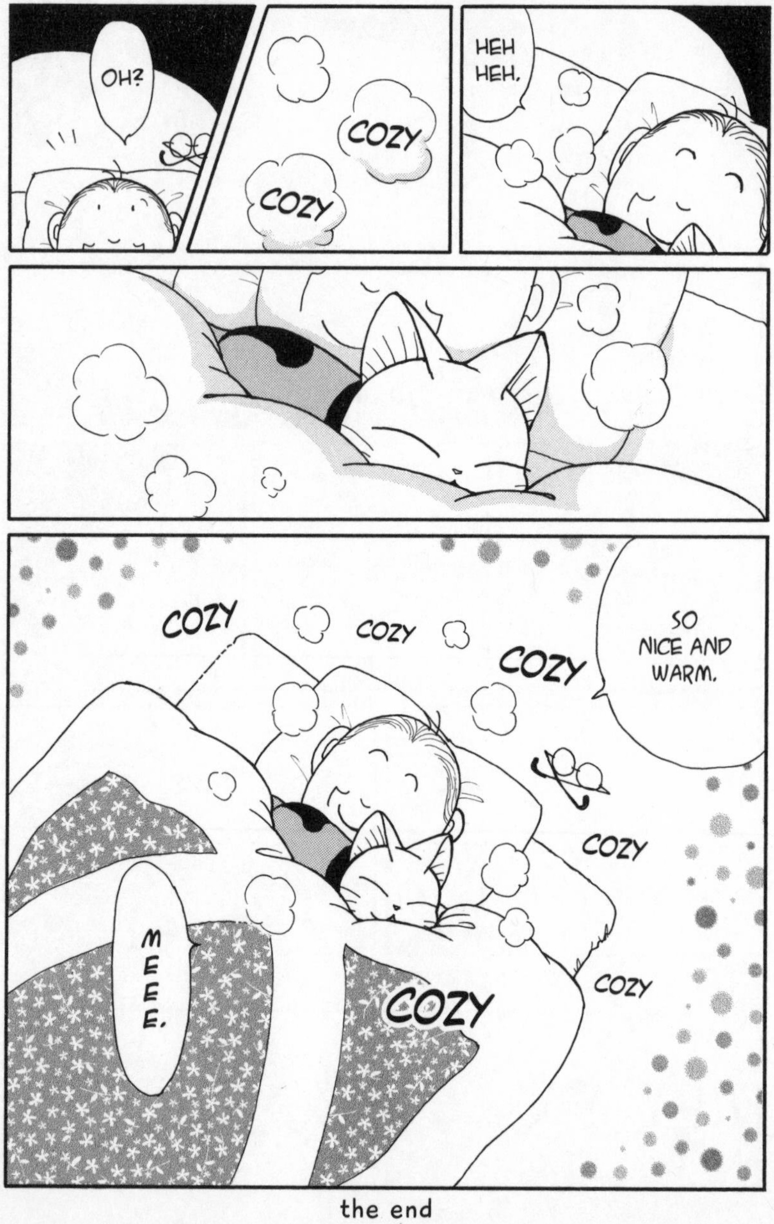
OH?
COZY
COZY
HEH HEH.
COZY
COZY
COZY
SO NICE AND WARM.
COZY
MEEE.
COZY
COZY

the end

# For the New Year...

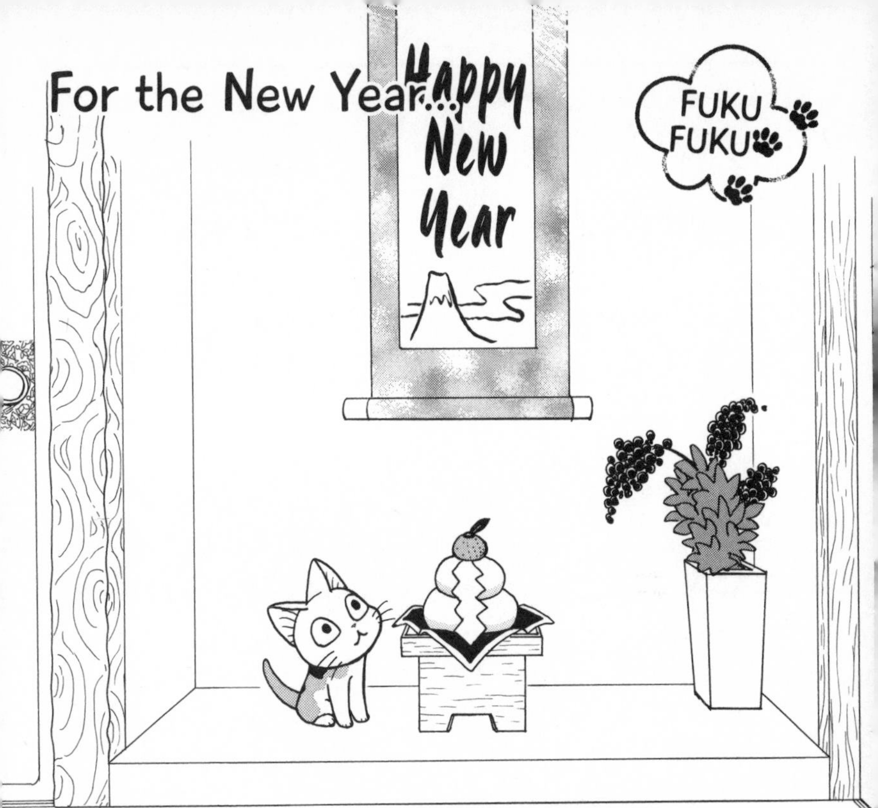
Happy New Year
FUKU FUKU

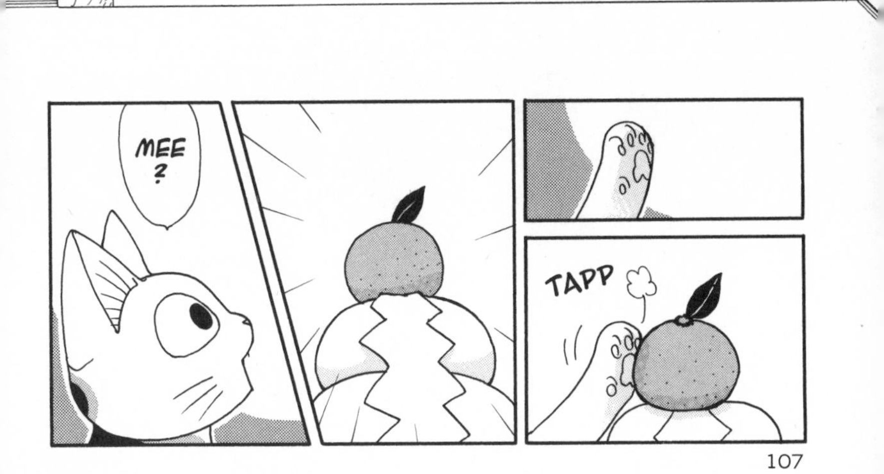
MEE?
TAPP

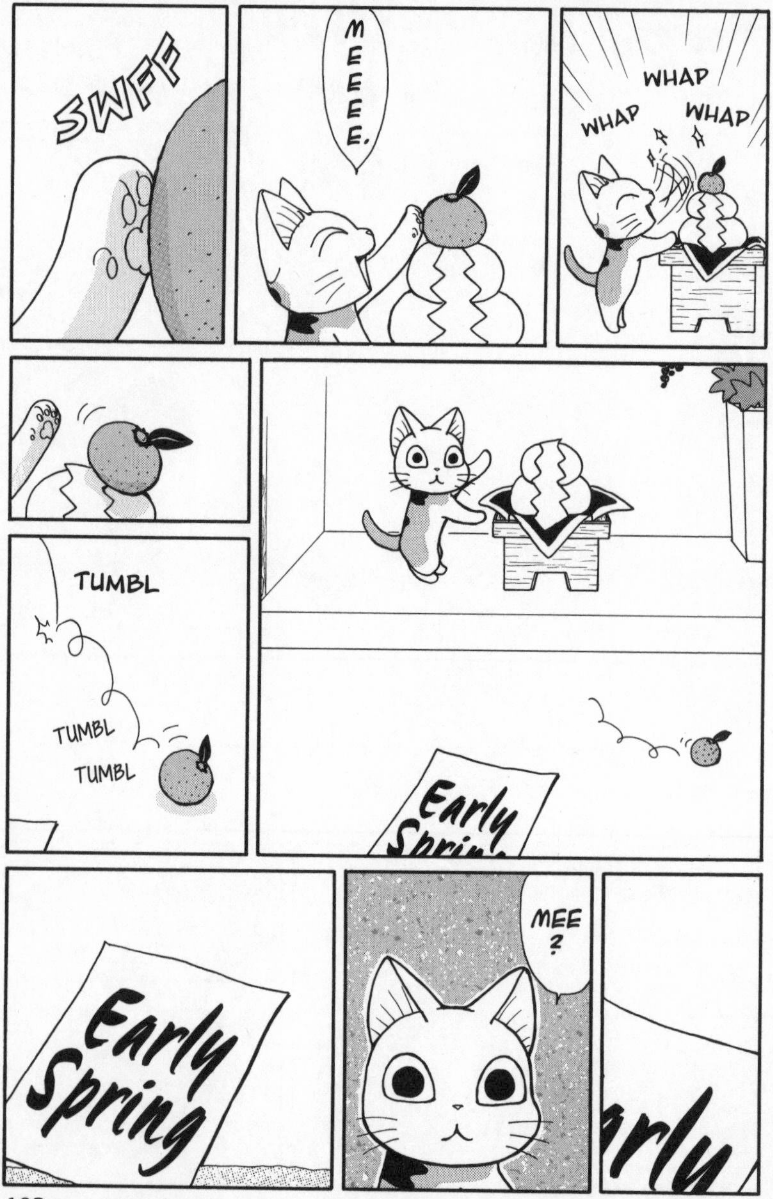
SWFF
MEEEE.
WHAP
WHAP
WHAP
TUMBL
TUMBL
TUMBL
Early Spring
MEE?

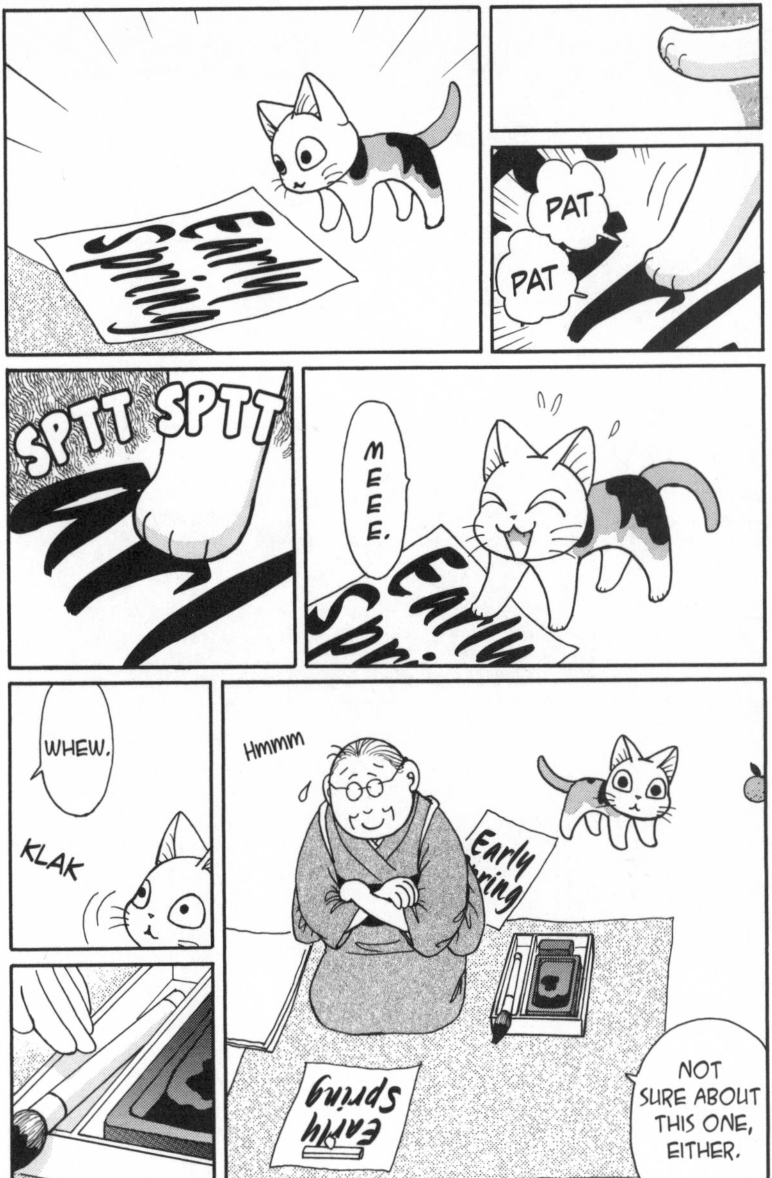
Early Spring
PAT
PAT
SPTT SPTT
MEEE.
WHEW.
KLAK
Hmmm
Early Spring
Early Spring
NOT SURE ABOUT THIS ONE, EITHER.

MEE
?

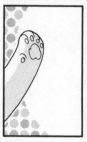

SPSH
SPSH

!

MEEEE!

WHIP

WHIP

WHIP

110

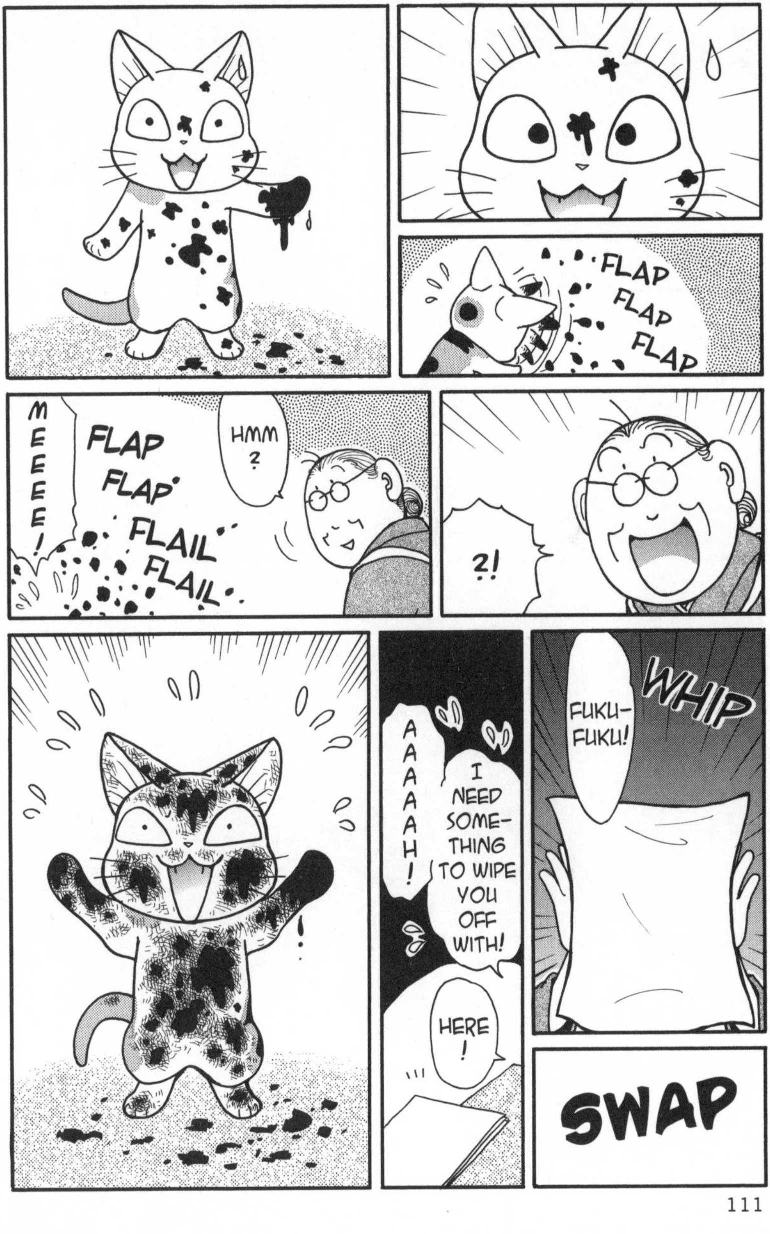
FLAP
FLAP
FLAP
MEEEEE!
FLAP
FLAP
FLAIL
FLAIL
HMM?
?!
AAAAAAH!
I NEED SOME-THING TO WIPE YOU OFF WITH!
HERE!
FUKU-FUKU!
WHIP
SWAP

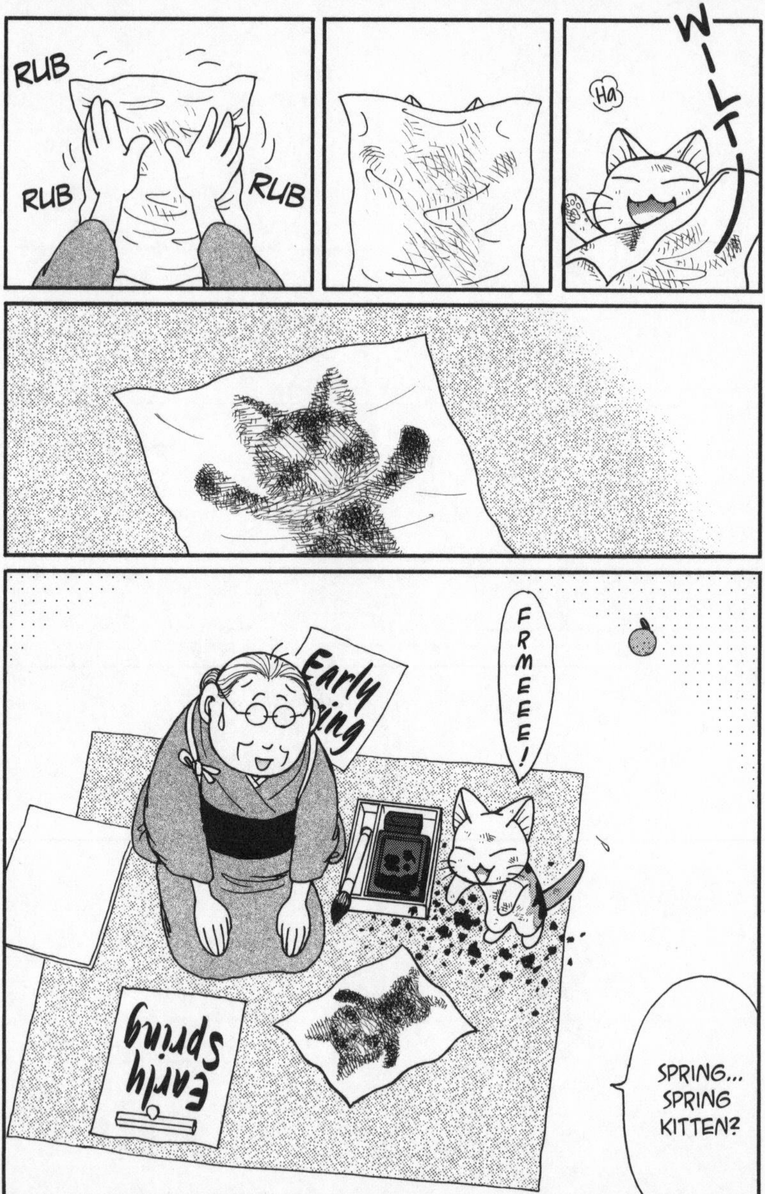
RUB
RUB
RUB
Ha
WILT
FRMEEE!
Early Spring
SPRING... SPRING KITTEN?

the end

# Let's Play!

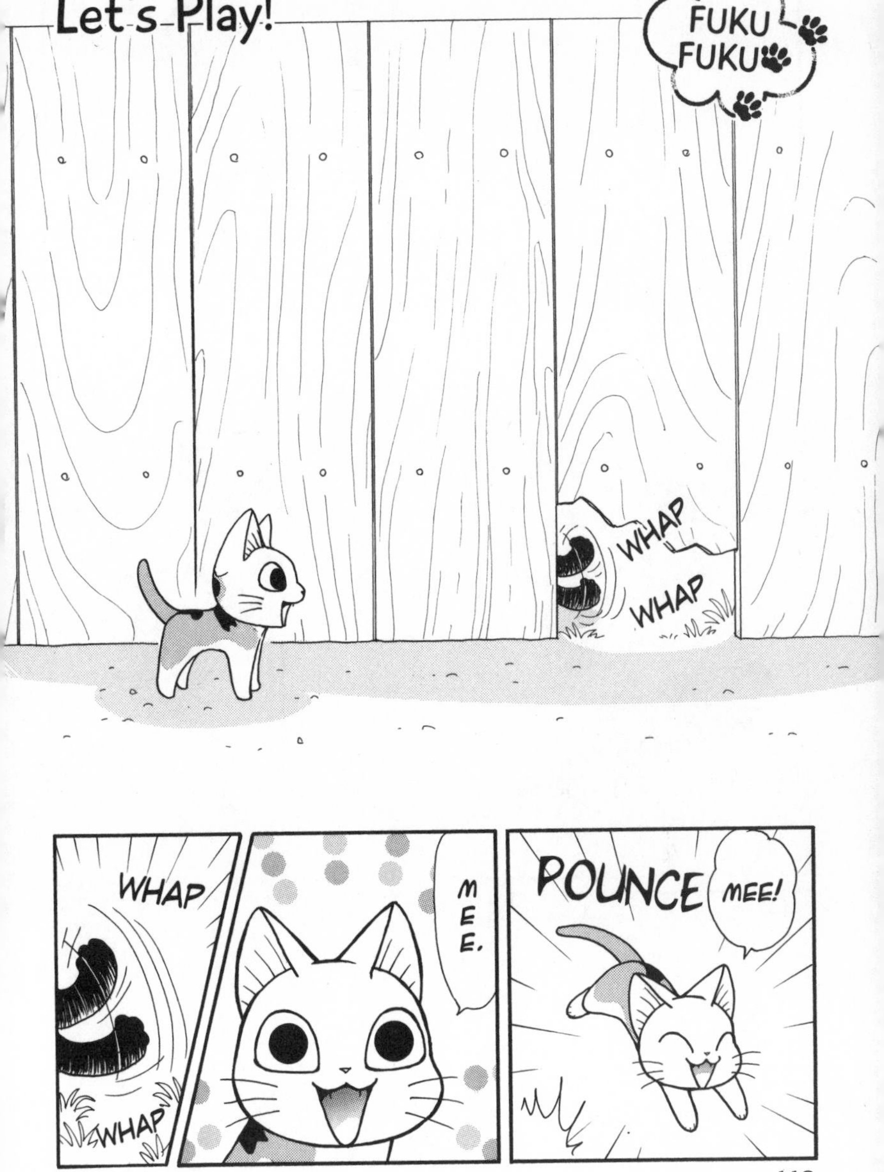
FUKU FUKU
WHAP
WHAP
WHAP
WHAP
MEE.
POUNCE
MEE!

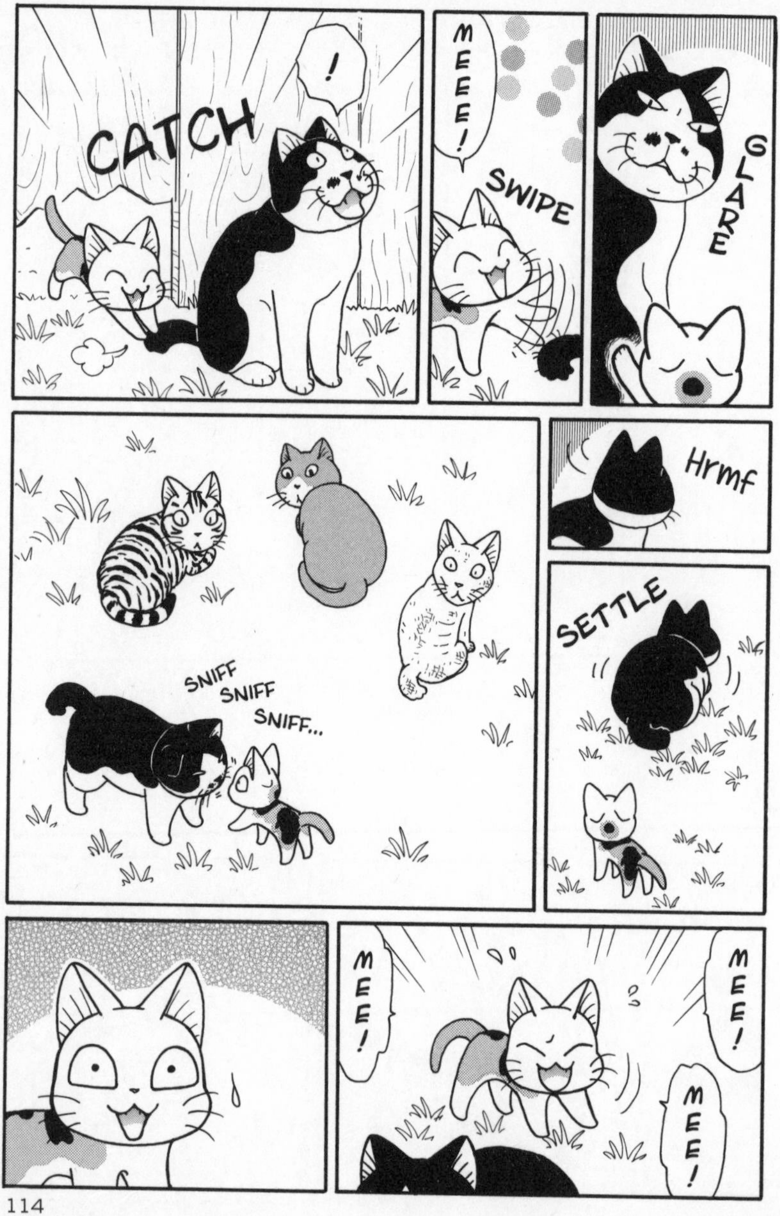
GLARE
MEEE!
SWIPE
!
CATCH
Hrmf
SETTLE
SNIFF
SNIFF
SNIFF...
MEE!
MEE!
MEE!

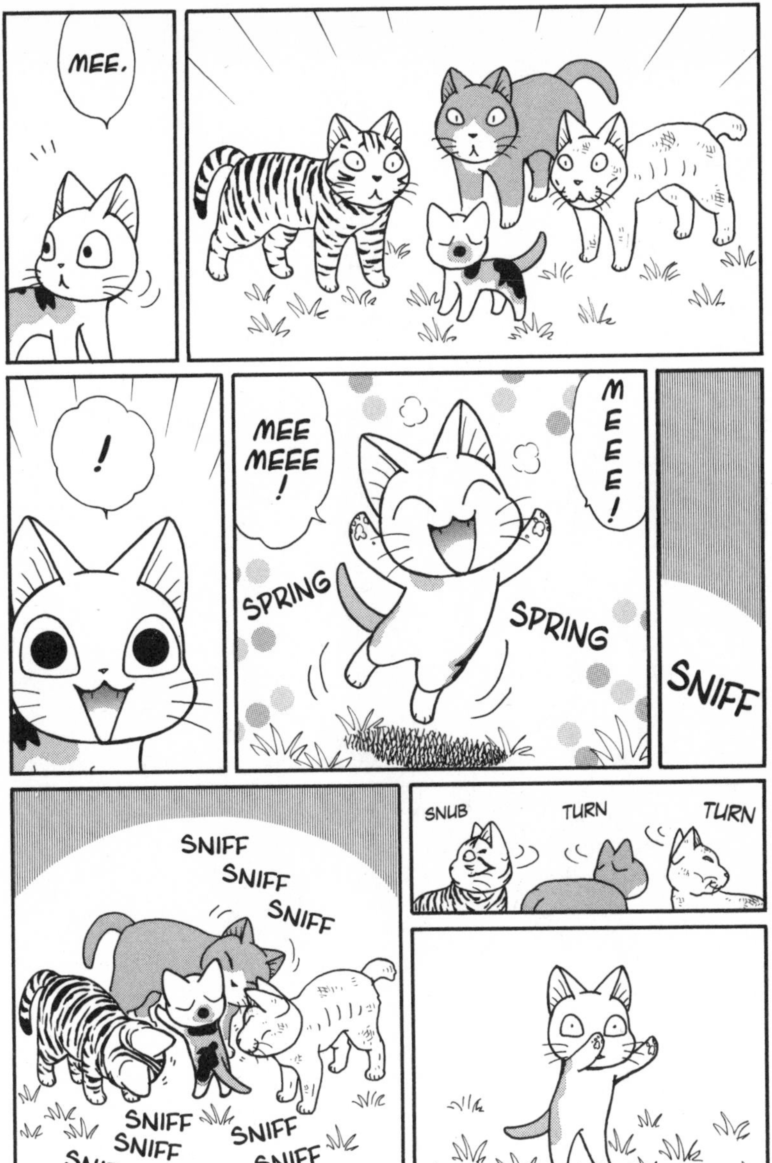
MEE.
!
MEE MEEE !
MEEE!
SPRING
SPRING
SNIFF
SNIFF
SNIFF
SNIFF
SNIFF
SNIFF
SNIFF
SNIFF
SNIFF
SNUB
TURN
TURN

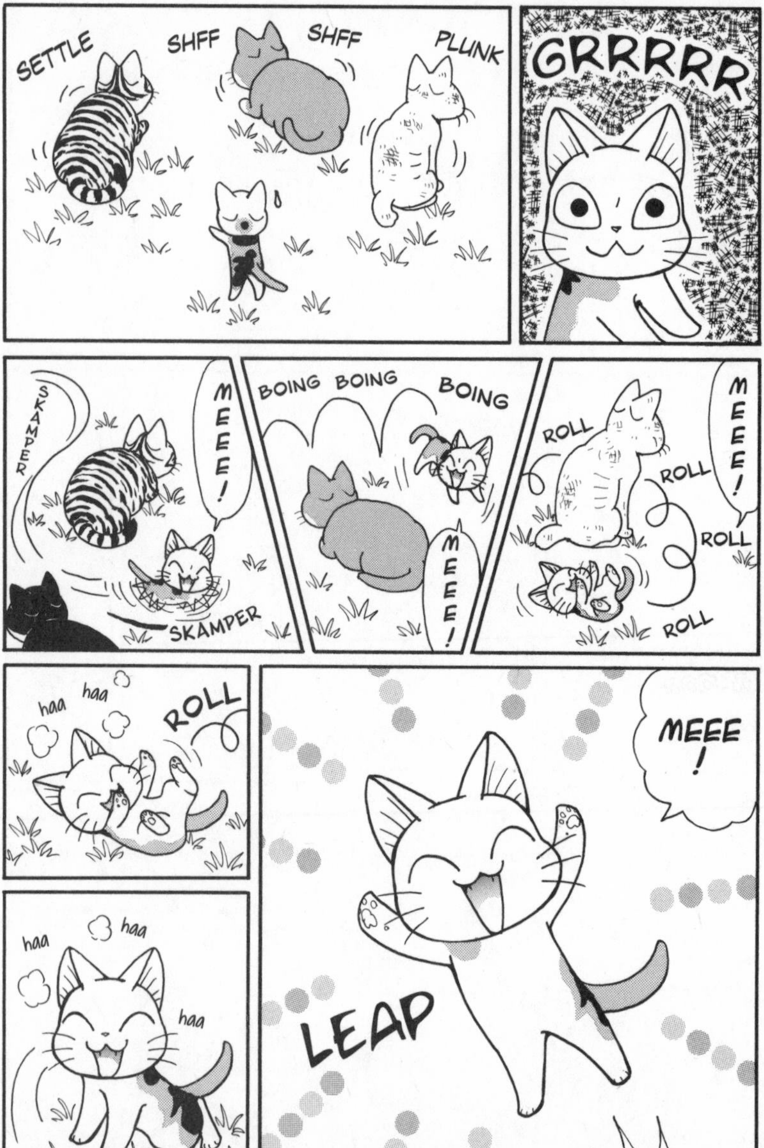
SETTLE
SHFF
SHFF
PLUNK
GRRRRR
SKAMPER
MEEE!
SKAMPER
BOING BOING
BOING
MEEE!
ROLL
ROLL
MEEE!
ROLL
ROLL
haa
haa
ROLL
haa
haa
haa
MEEE!
LEAP

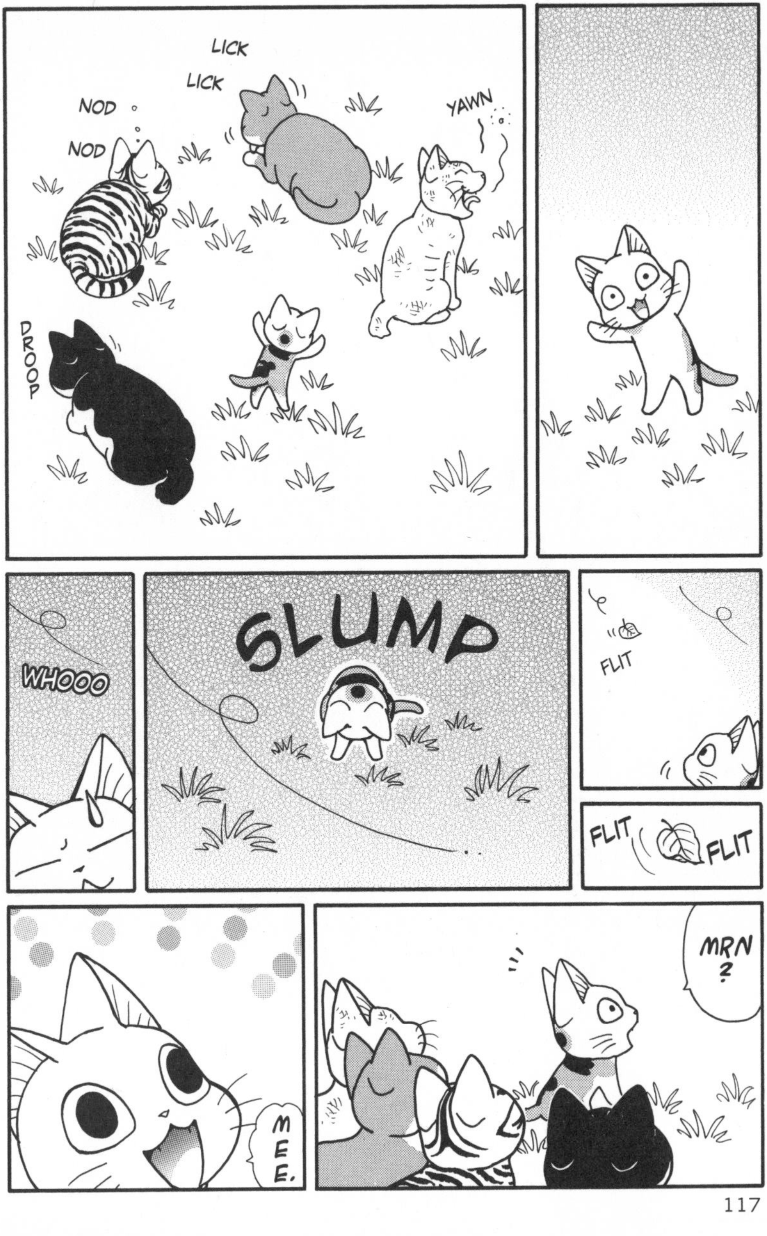
NOD
NOD
LICK
LICK
YAWN
DROOP
WHOOO
SLUMP
FLIT
FLIT
FLIT
MEE.
MRN?

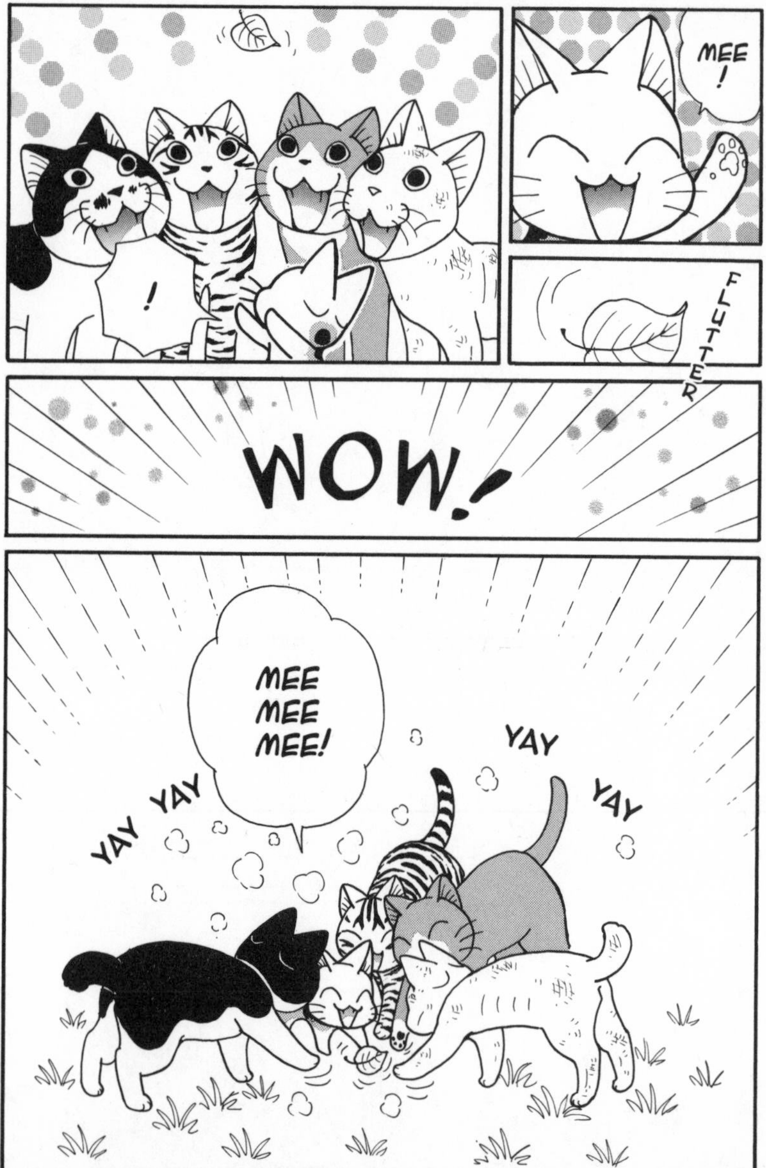
!
MEE!
FLUTTER
WOW!
YAY YAY
MEE MEE MEE!
YAY
YAY

the end

# First Snow

FUKU FUKU

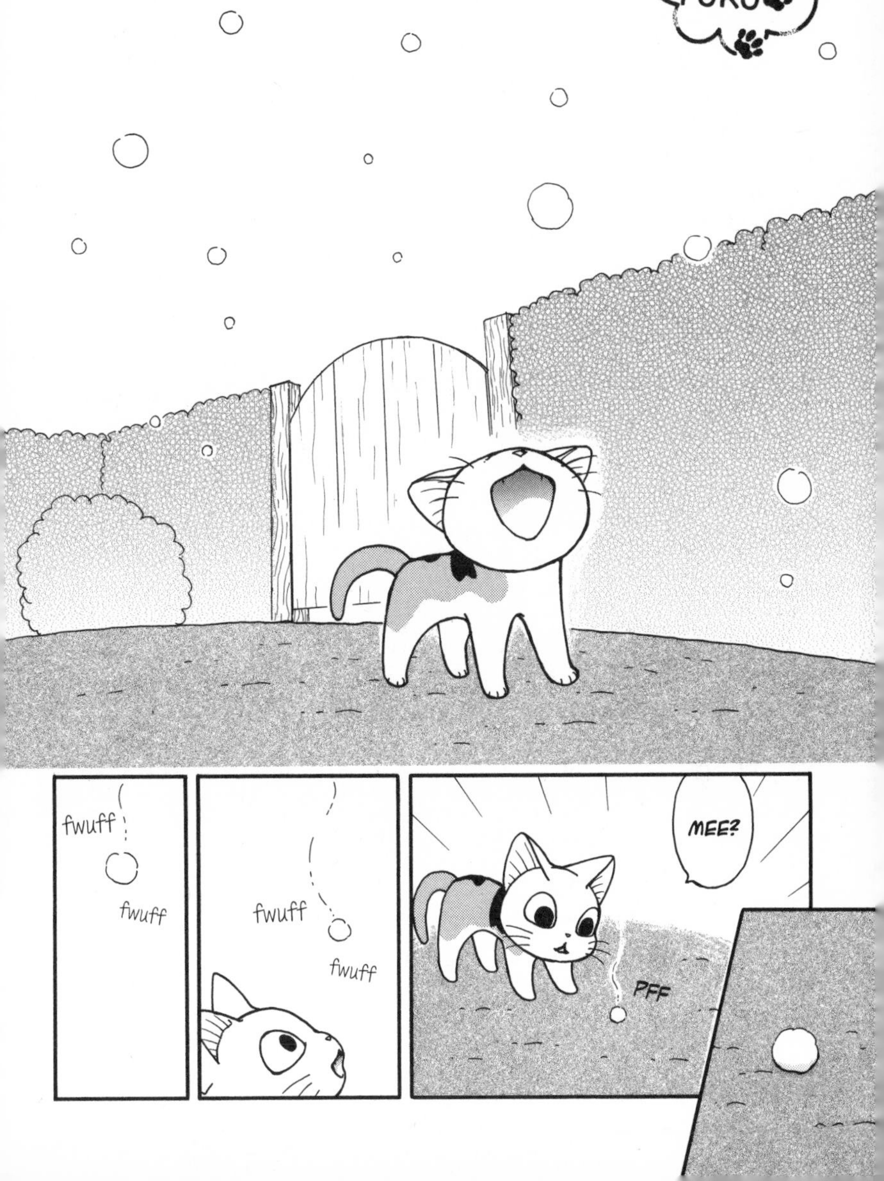
fwuff
fwuff
fwuff
fwuff
MEE?
PFF

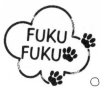

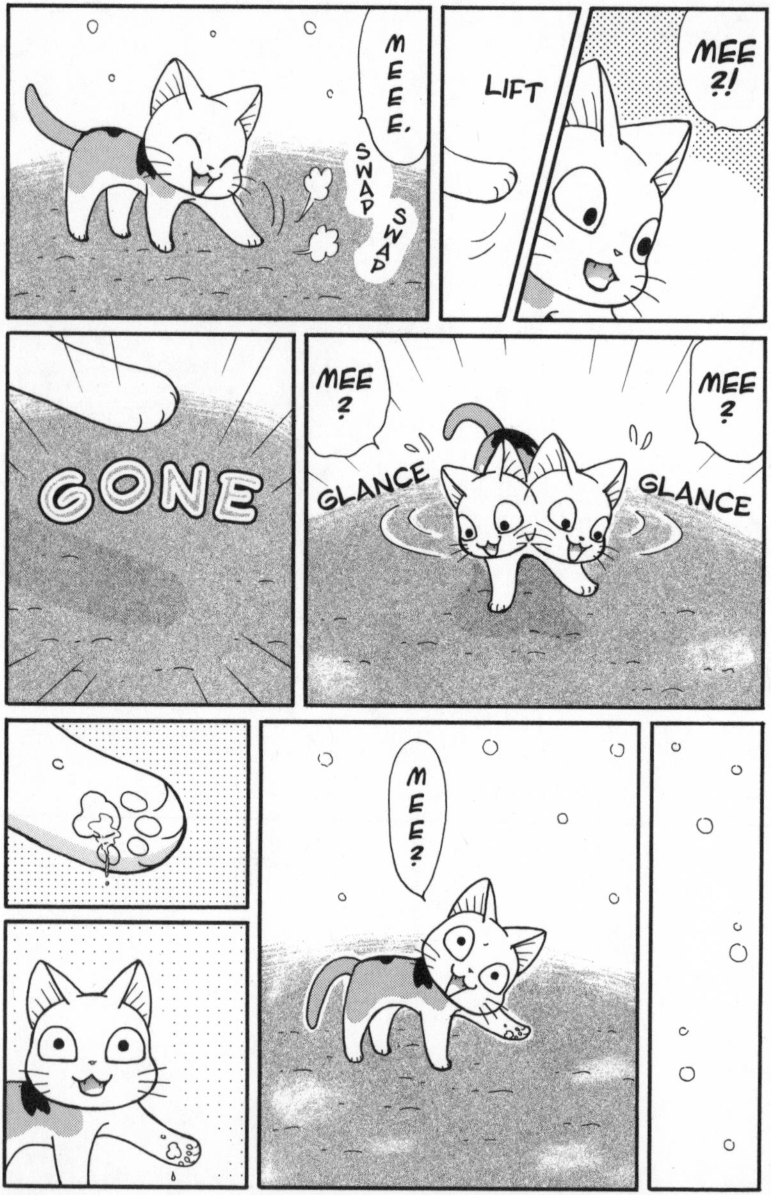
MEEE,
SWAP
SWAP
LIFT
MEE?!
GONE
MEE?
MEE?
GLANCE
GLANCE
MEE?

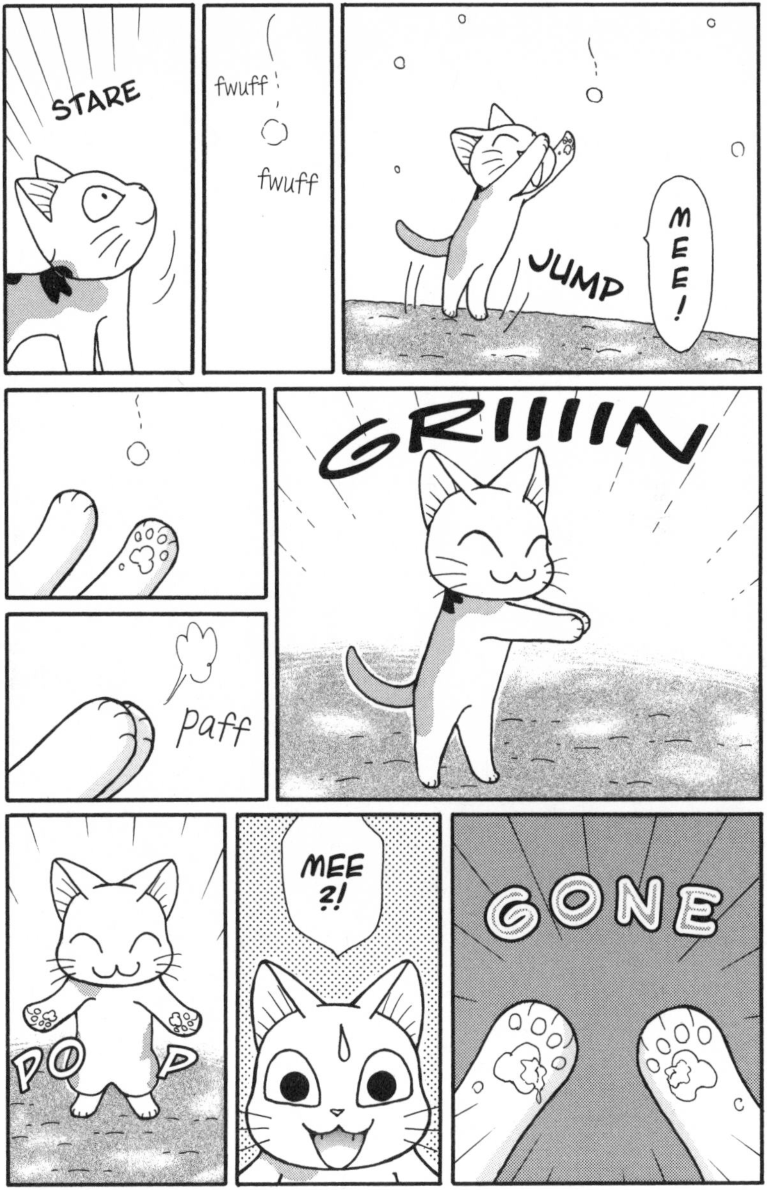
STARE
fwuff
fwuff
JUMP
MEE!
GRIIIIN
paff
POP
MEE ?!
GONE

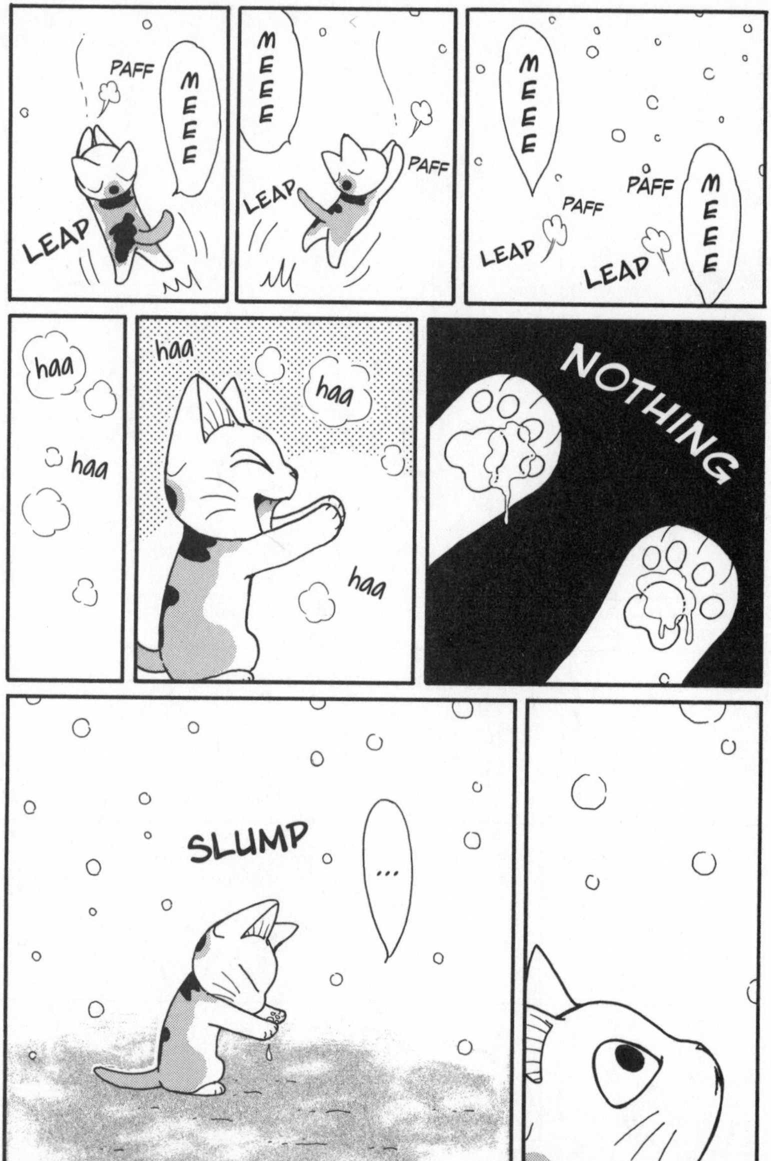

PAFF
MEEE
LEAP
MEEE
LEAP
PAFF
MEEE
PAFF
PAFF
LEAP
LEAP
MEEE
haa
haa
haa
haa
haa
NOTHING
SLUMP
...

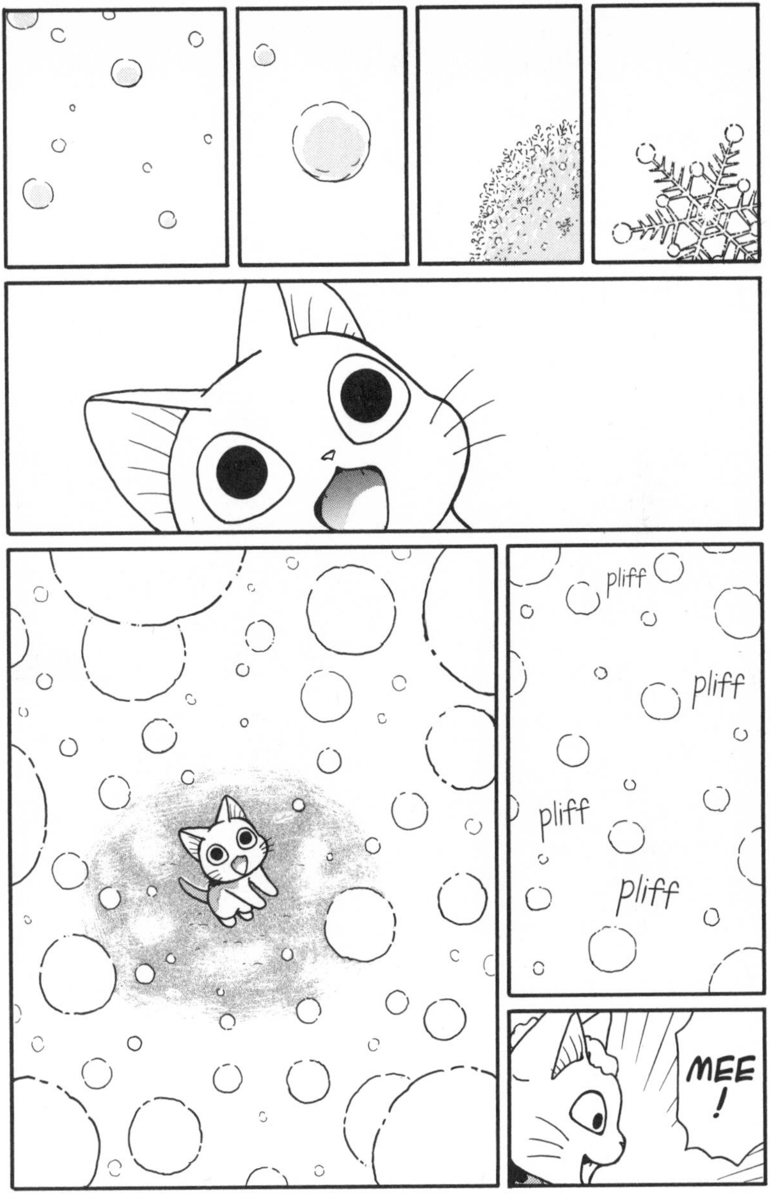
pliff
pliff
pliff
pliff
MEE !

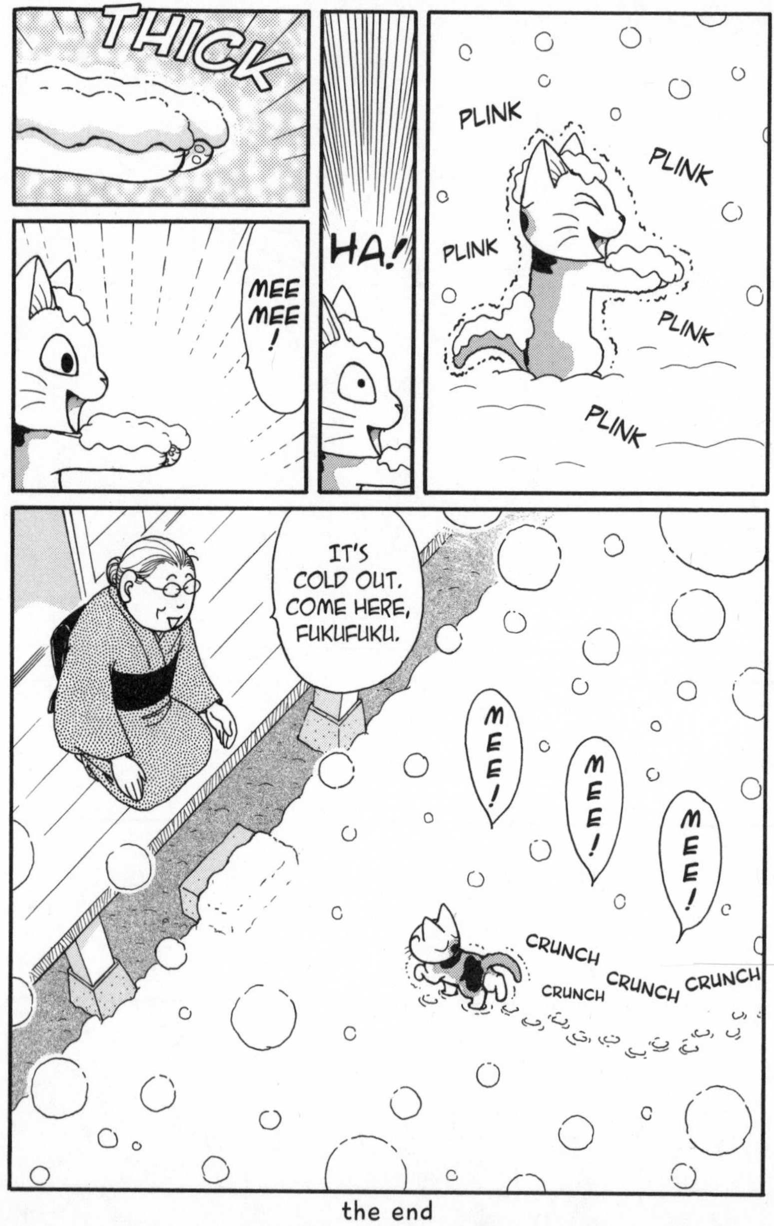
THICK
MEE MEE!
HA!
PLINK
PLINK
PLINK
PLINK
PLINK
IT'S COLD OUT. COME HERE, FUKUFUKU.
MEE!
MEE!
MEE!
CRUNCH
CRUNCH
CRUNCH
CRUNCH

the end

# FukuFuku in Wonderland

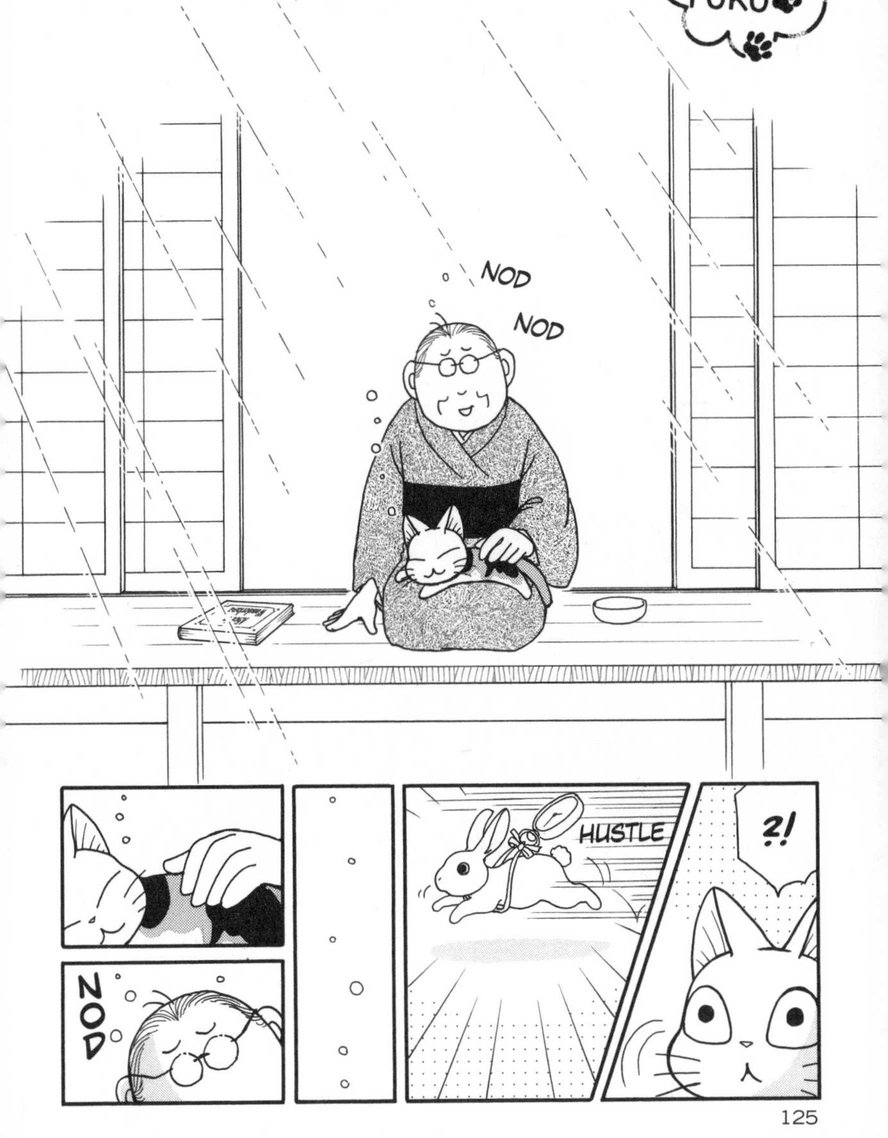
NOD
NOD
NOD
HUSTLE
?!

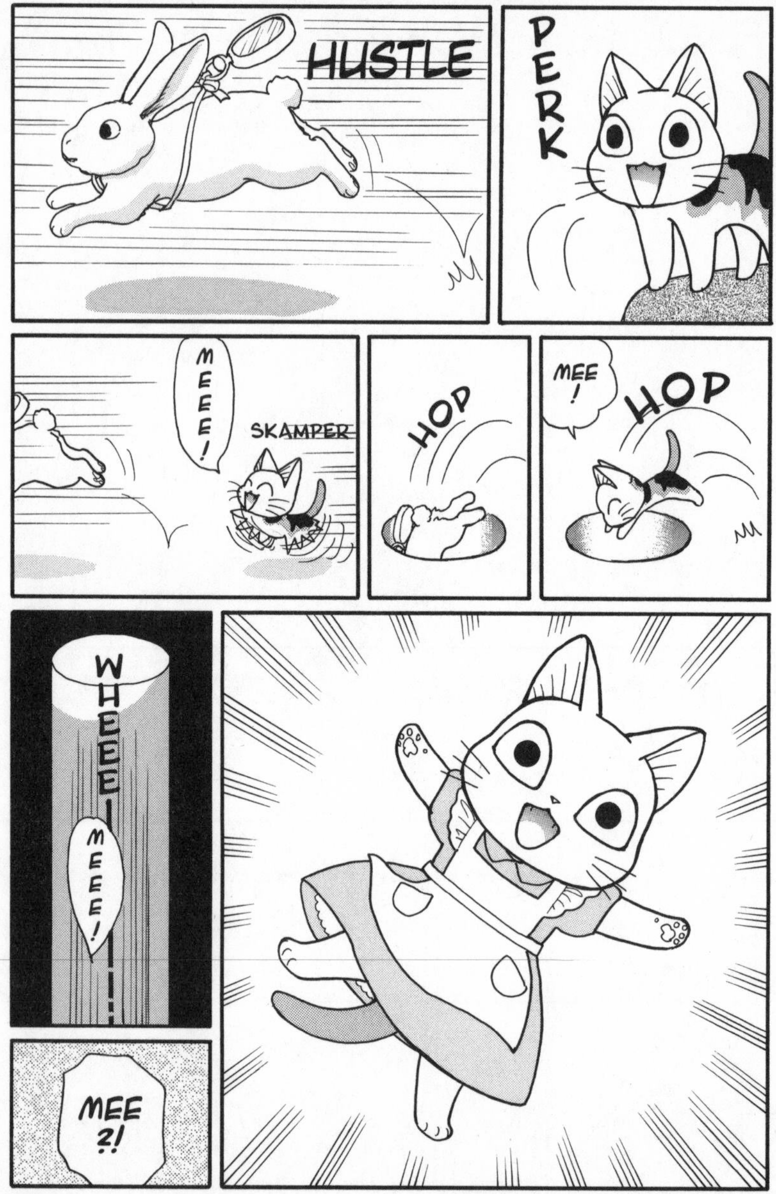
HUSTLE
PERK
MEEE!
SKAMPER
HOP
MEE!
HOP
WHEEE—
MEEE!
MEE?!

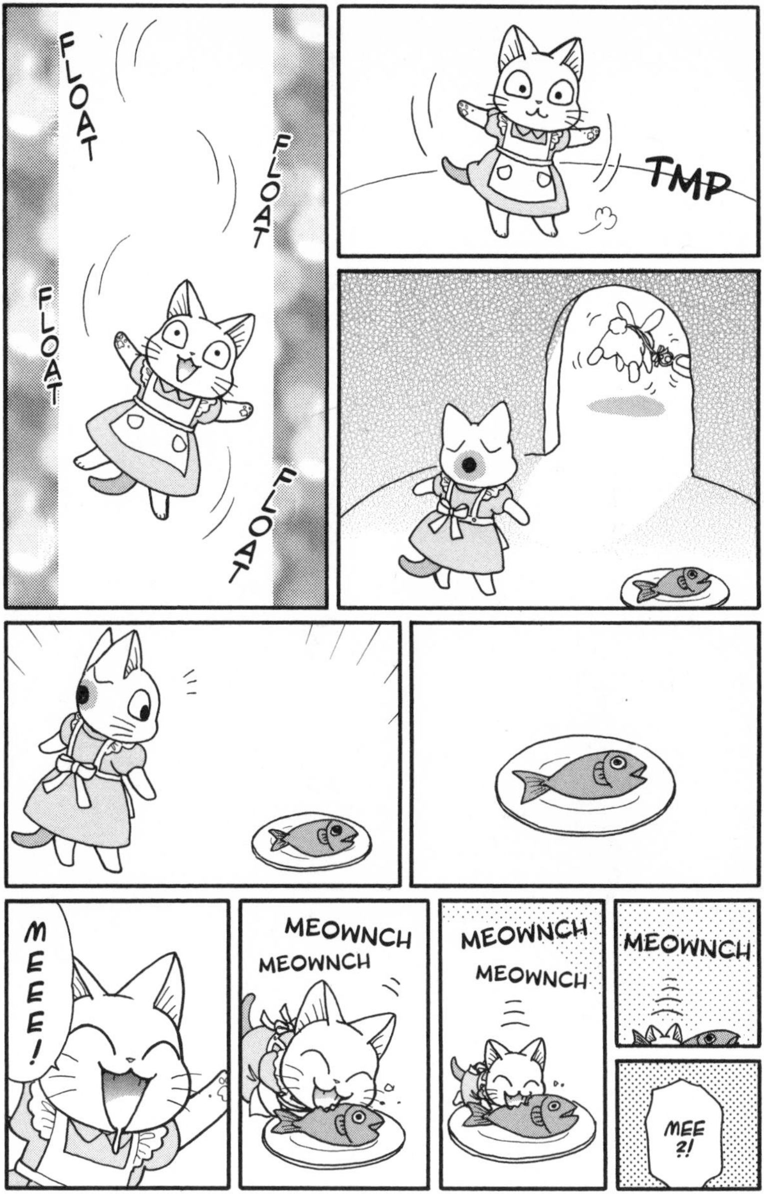
FLOAT
FLOAT
FLOAT
FLOAT
TMP
MEEEE!
MEOWNCH
MEOWNCH
MEOWNCH
MEOWNCH
MEOWNCH
MEE?!

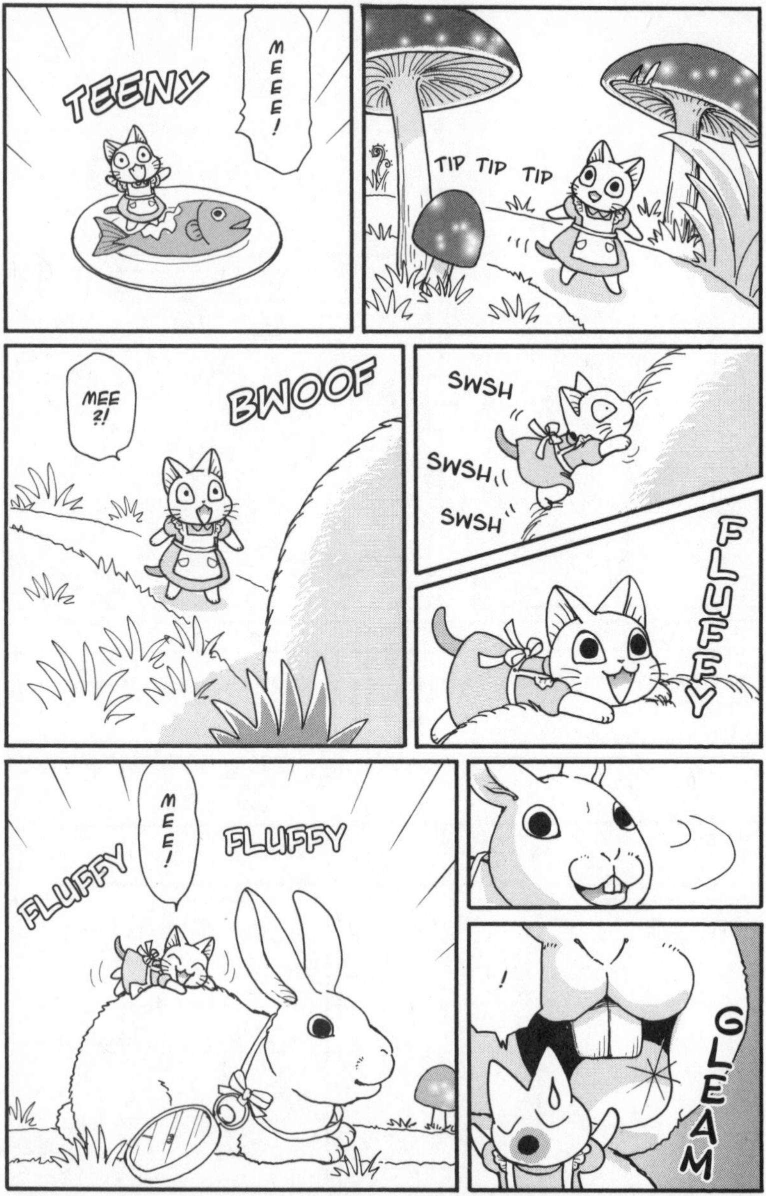
TEENY
MEEEE!
TIP TIP TIP
MEE ?!
BWOOF
SWSH
SWSH
SWSH
FLUFFY
FLUFFY
MEE!
FLUFFY
!
GLEAM

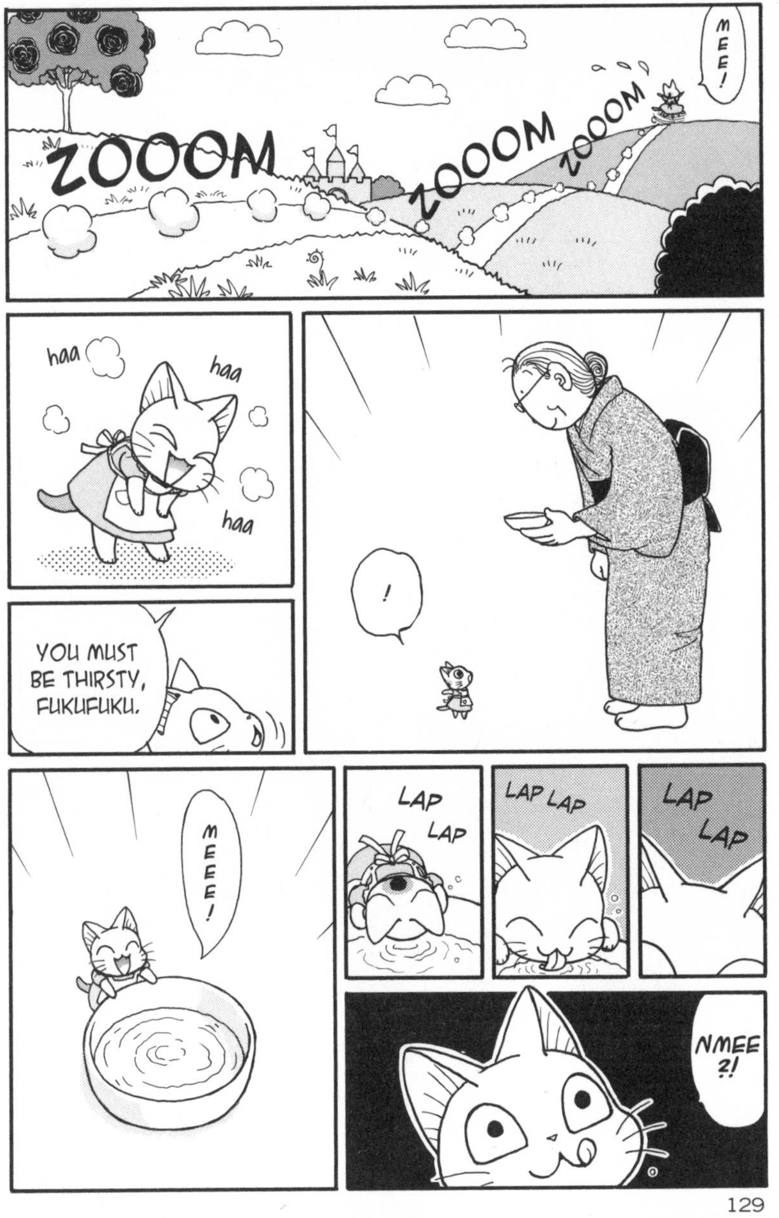
ZOOOM
ZOOOM
ZOOOM
MEE!
haa
haa
haa
YOU MUST BE THIRSTY, FUKUFUKU.
!
MEEE!
LAP
LAP
LAP LAP
LAP
LAP
NMEE ?!

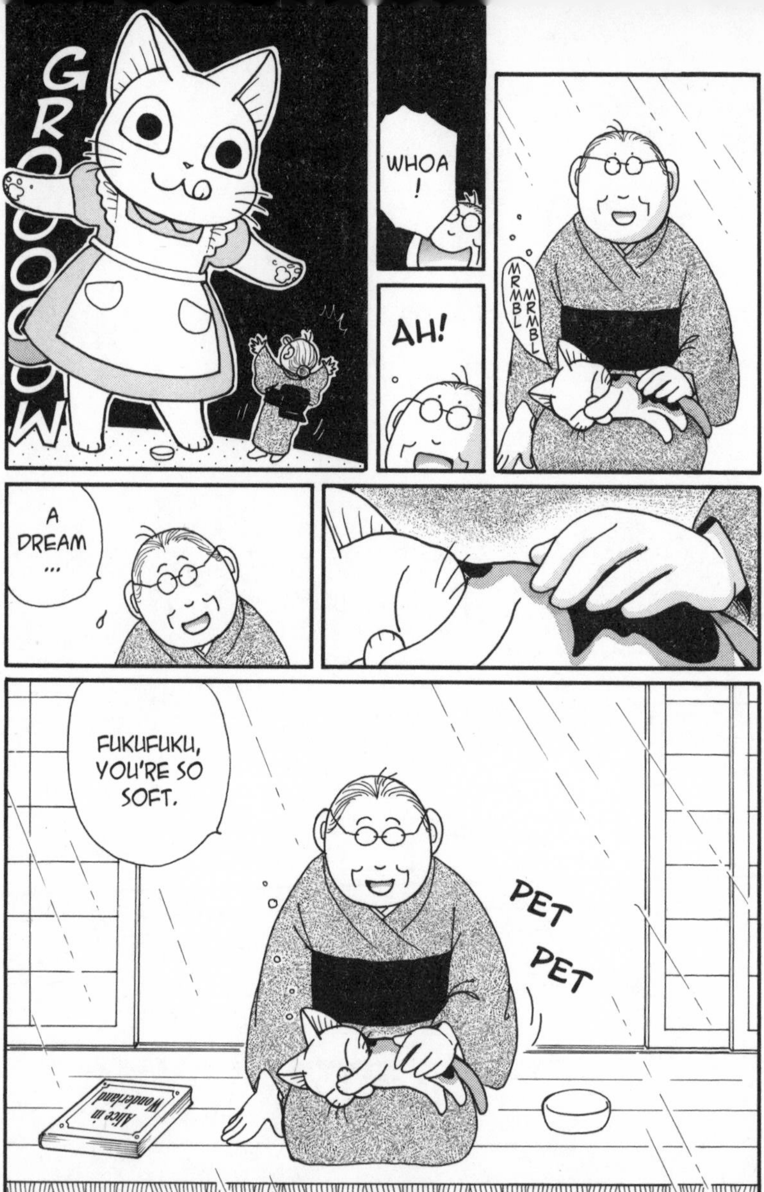
GROOOOOW
WHOA !
AH!
MRMBL MRMBL
A DREAM ...
FUKUFUKU, YOU'RE SO SOFT.
PET PET
Alice in Wonderland

the end

# Calling to Play

FUKU FUKU

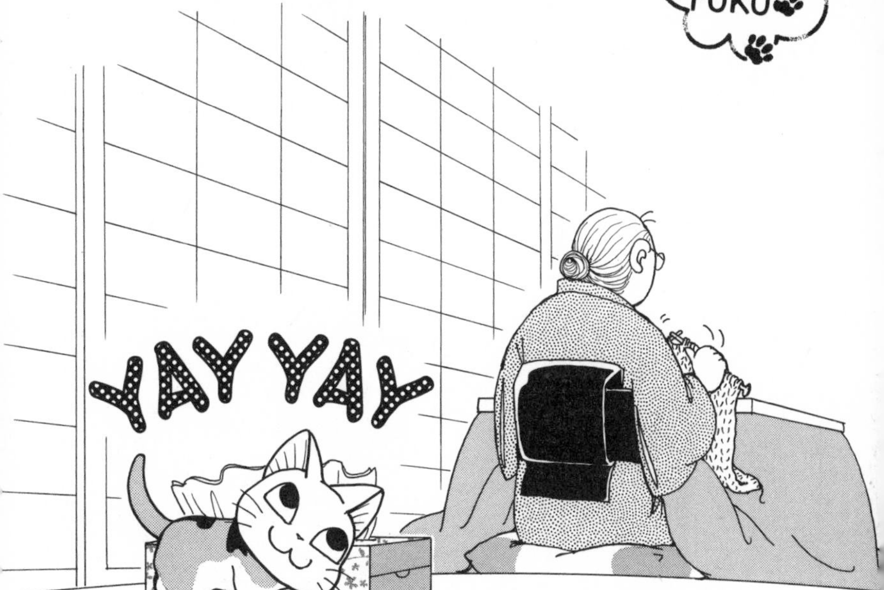
YAY YAY

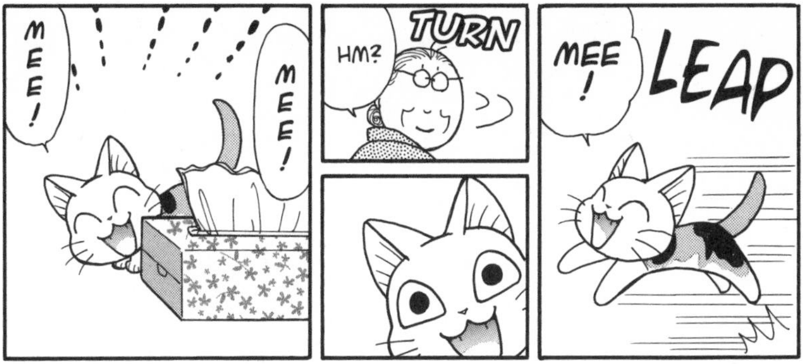
MEE!
MEE!
HM?
TURN
MEE!
LEAP

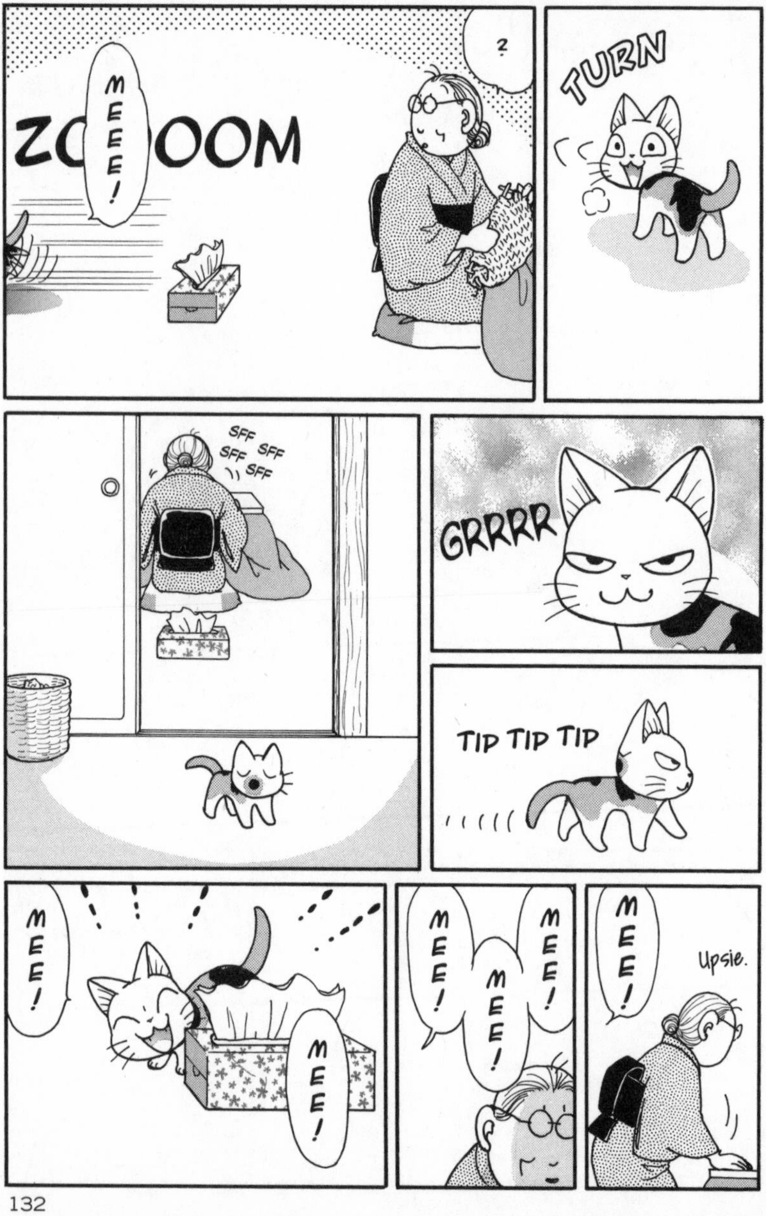

MEEE!
ZO OOM
?
TURN
SFF SFF SFF SFF
GRRRR
TIP TIP TIP
MEE!
MEE!
MEE!
MEE!
MEE!
MEE!
Upsie.

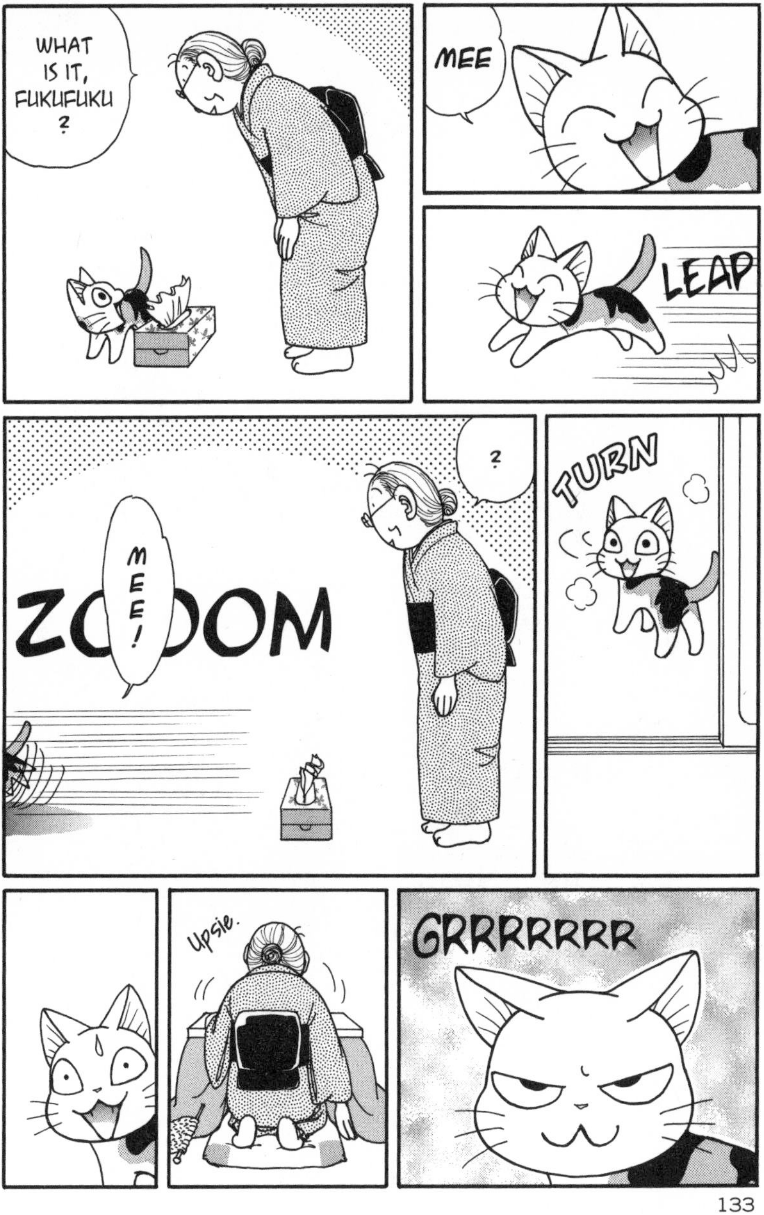
WHAT IS IT, FUKUFUKU?
MEE
LEAP
?
ZOOOM
MEE!
TURN
Upsie.
GRRRRRRR

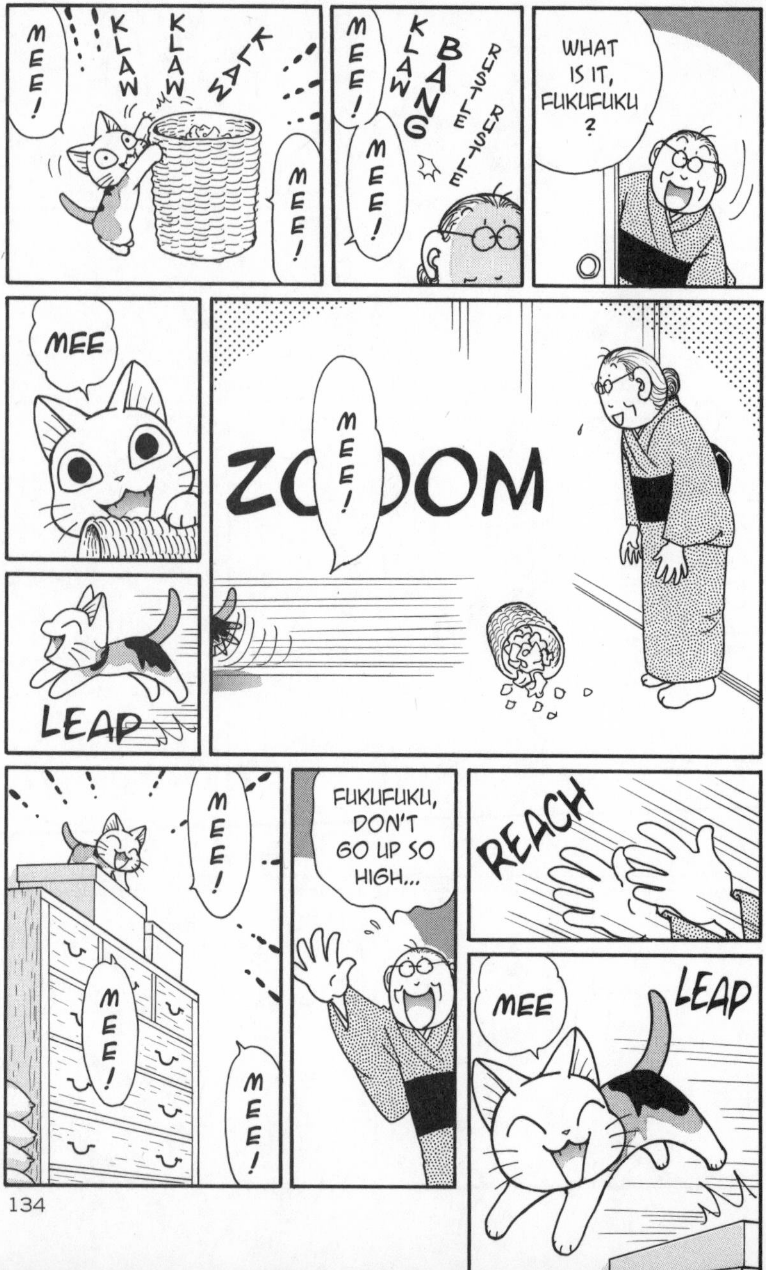
MEE!
KLAW
KLAW
WALK
MEE!
MEE!
KLAW
BANG
RUSTLE
RUSTLE
MEE!
WHAT IS IT, FUKUFUKU?
MEE
LEAP
MEE!
ZOOOM
MEE!
MEE!
MEE!
FUKUFUKU, DON'T GO UP SO HIGH...
REACH
MEE
LEAP

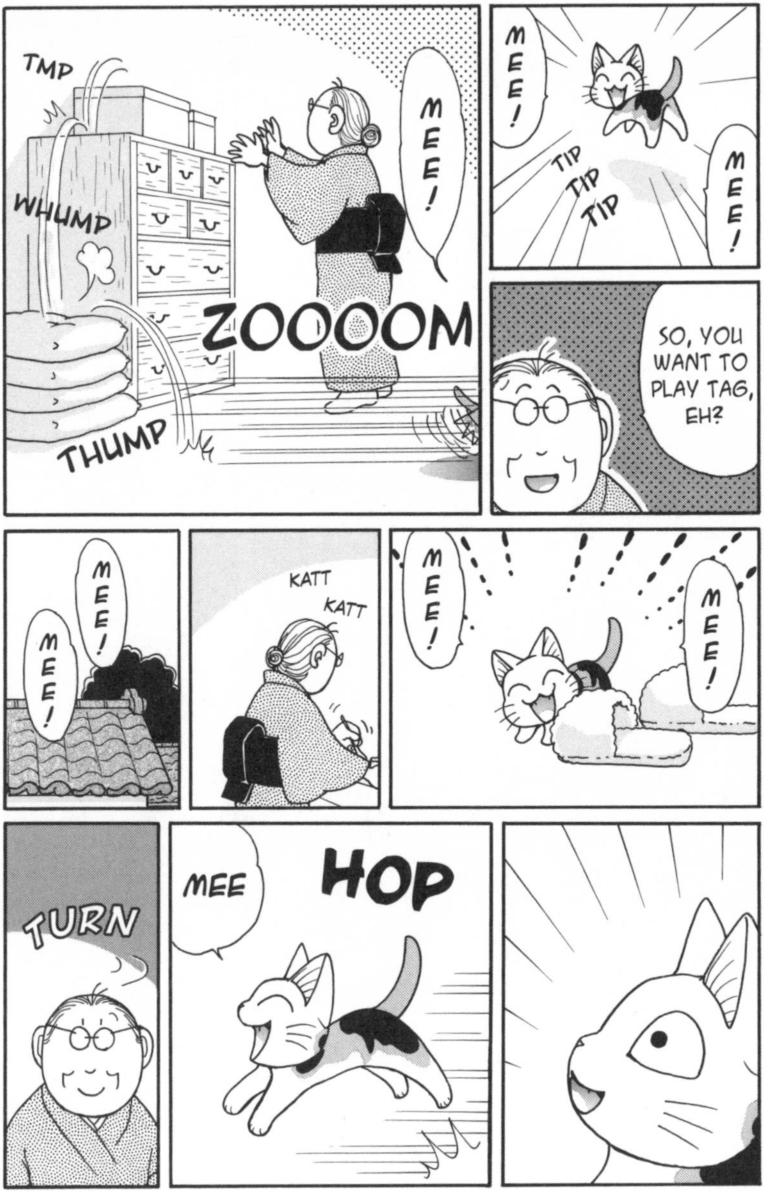

TMP
WHUMP
THUMP
MEE!
ZOOOOM
MEE!
TIP
TIP
TIP
MEE!
SO, YOU WANT TO PLAY TAG, EH?
MEE!
MEE!
KATT
KATT
MEE!
MEE!
TURN
MEE
HOP

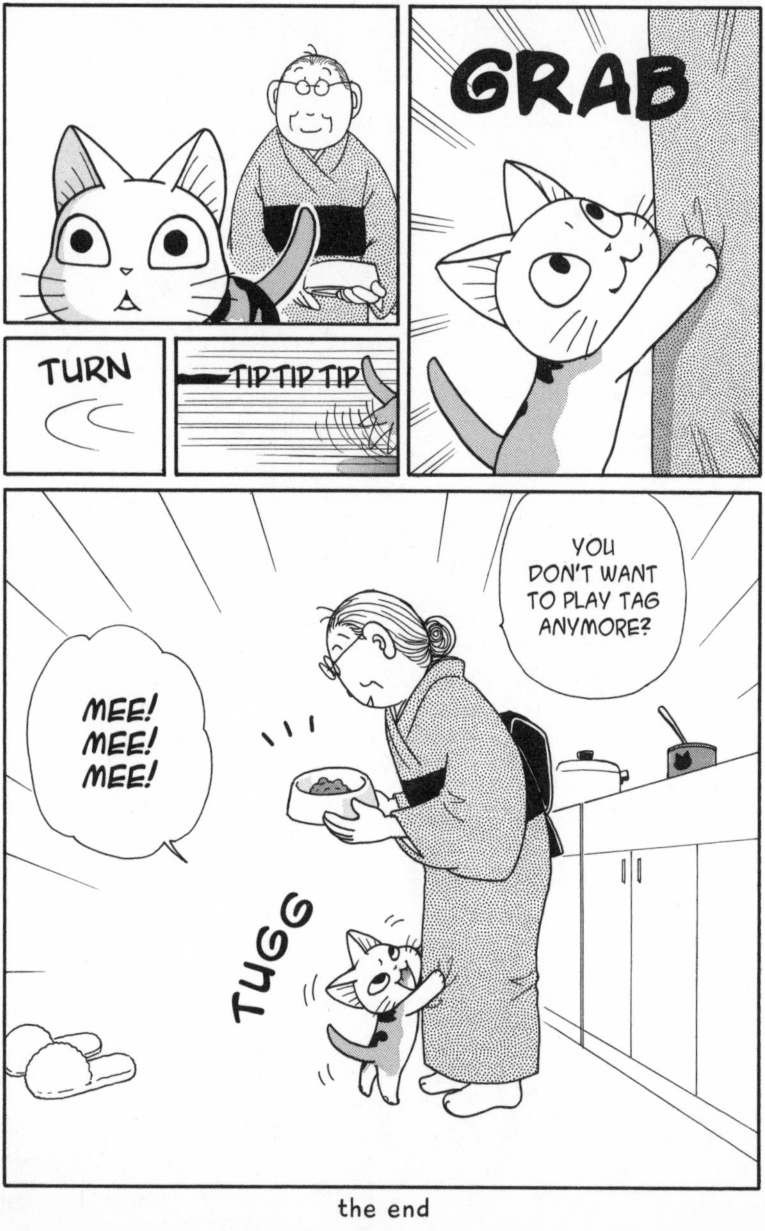
GRAB
TURN
TIP TIP TIP
MEE! MEE! MEE!
YOU DON'T WANT TO PLAY TAG ANYMORE?
TUGG

the end

# Benefit of the Kotatsu

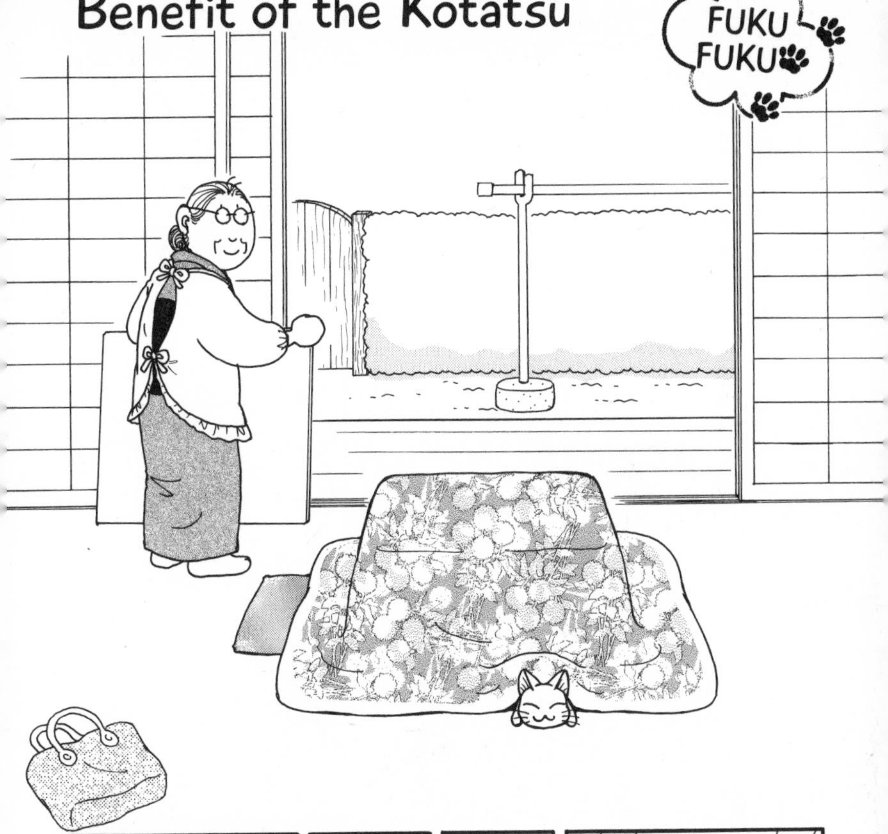
FUKU
FUKU

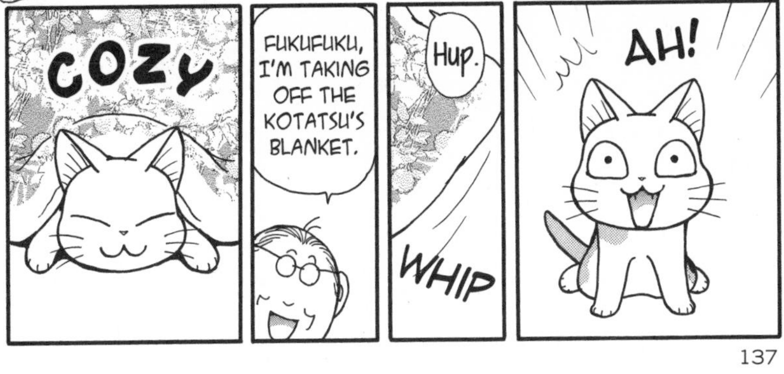
COZY
FUKUFUKU, I'M TAKING OFF THE KOTATSU'S BLANKET.
Hup.
WHIP
AH!

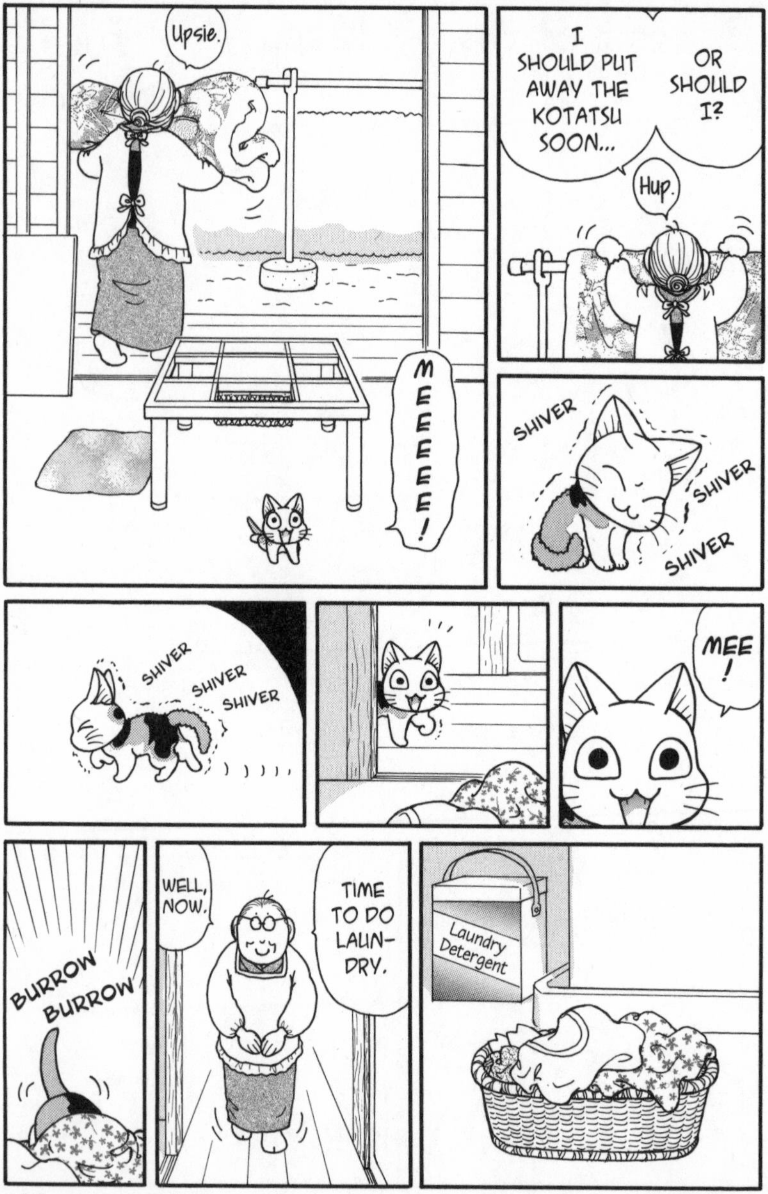
Upsie.
MEEEEEE!
I SHOULD PUT AWAY THE KOTATSU SOON...
OR SHOULD I?
Hup.
SHIVER
SHIVER
SHIVER
SHIVER
SHIVER
SHIVER
MEE!
BURROW BURROW
WELL, NOW.
TIME TO DO LAUN-DRY.
Laundry Detergent

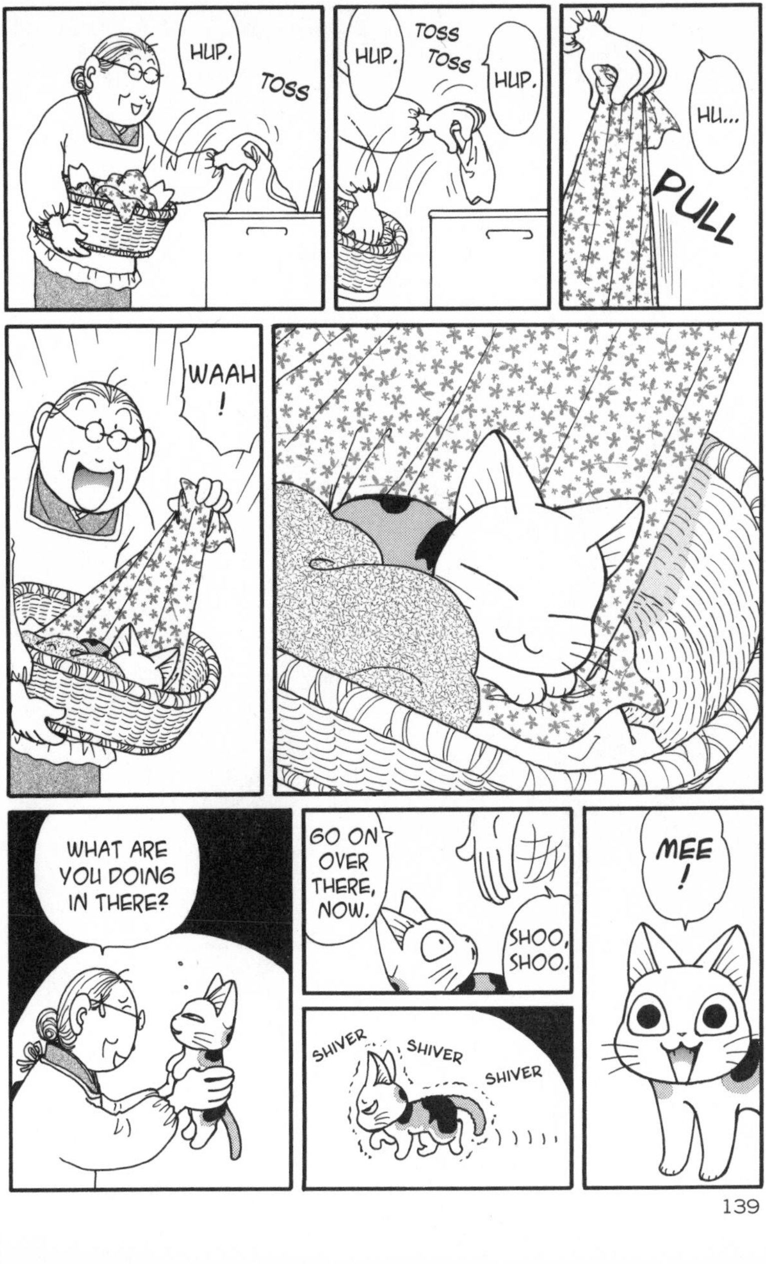
HUP.
TOSS
HUP.
TOSS TOSS
HUP.
HU...
PULL
WAAH!
WHAT ARE YOU DOING IN THERE?
GO ON OVER THERE, NOW.
SHOO, SHOO.
SHIVER
SHIVER
SHIVER
MEE!

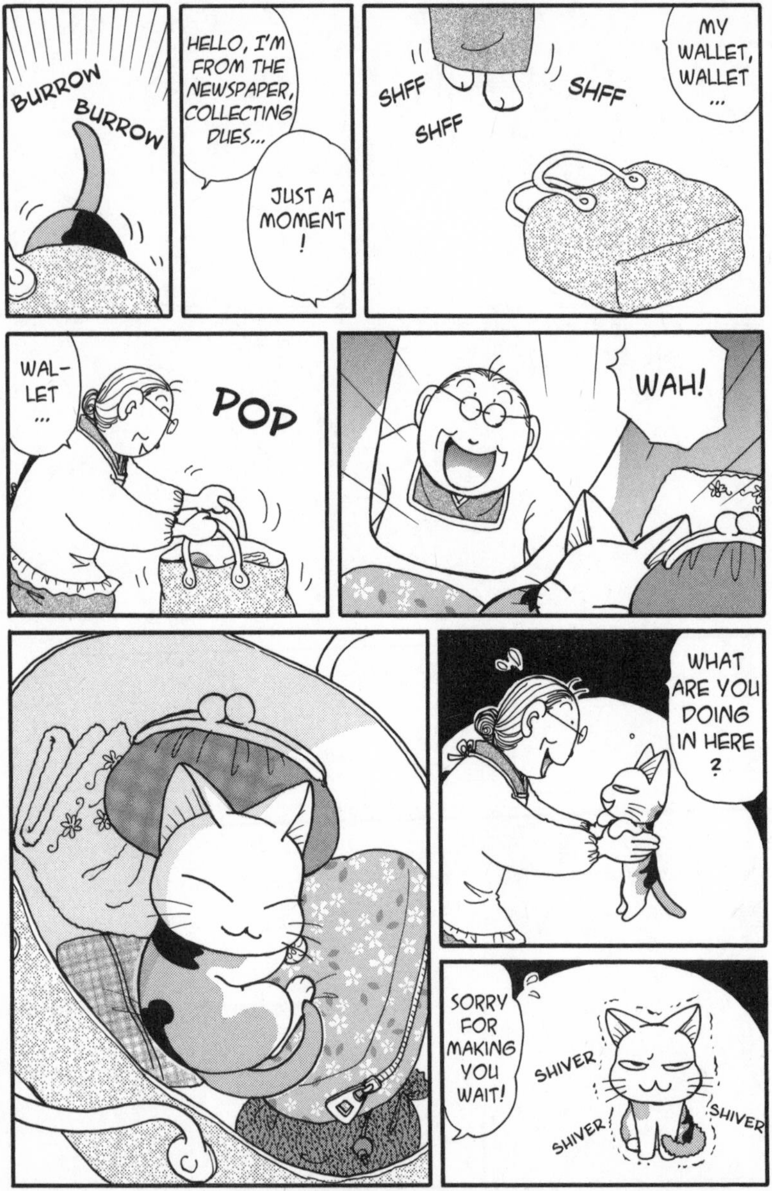
BURROW
BURROW
HELLO, I'M FROM THE NEWSPAPER, COLLECTING DUES...
JUST A MOMENT!
SHFF
SHFF
SHFF
MY WALLET, WALLET...
WAL-LET...
POP
WAH!
WHAT ARE YOU DOING IN HERE?
SORRY FOR MAKING YOU WAIT!
SHIVER
SHIVER
SHIVER

WHEW

FUKUFUKU SURE GAVE ME A SHOCK.

SHFF

SHFF

SHFF

SHOWING UP IN PLACES I NEVER EXPECTED ...

AH!

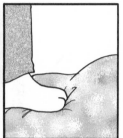

SOFFT..

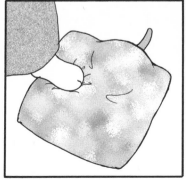

WAH!

141

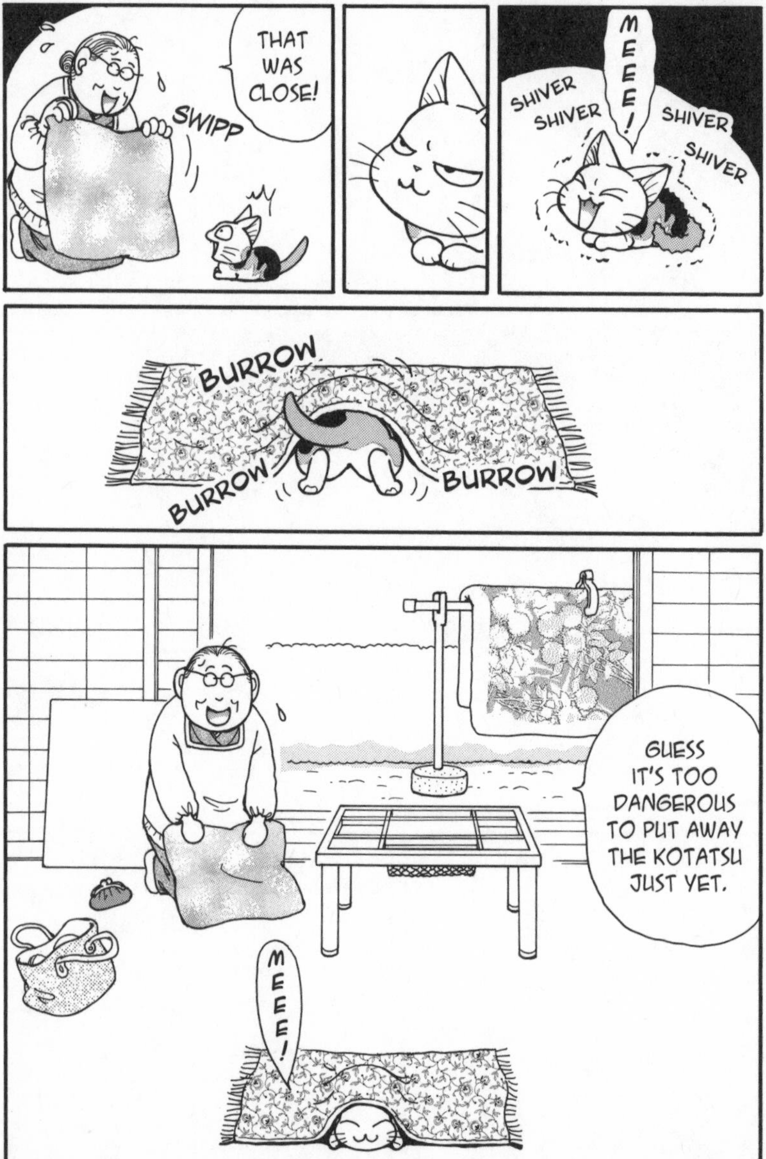
THAT WAS CLOSE!
SWIPP
MEEE!
SHIVER
SHIVER
SHIVER
SHIVER
BURROW
BURROW
BURROW
GUESS IT'S TOO DANGEROUS TO PUT AWAY THE KOTATSU JUST YET.
MEEE!

the end

# Flower Viewing Happiness

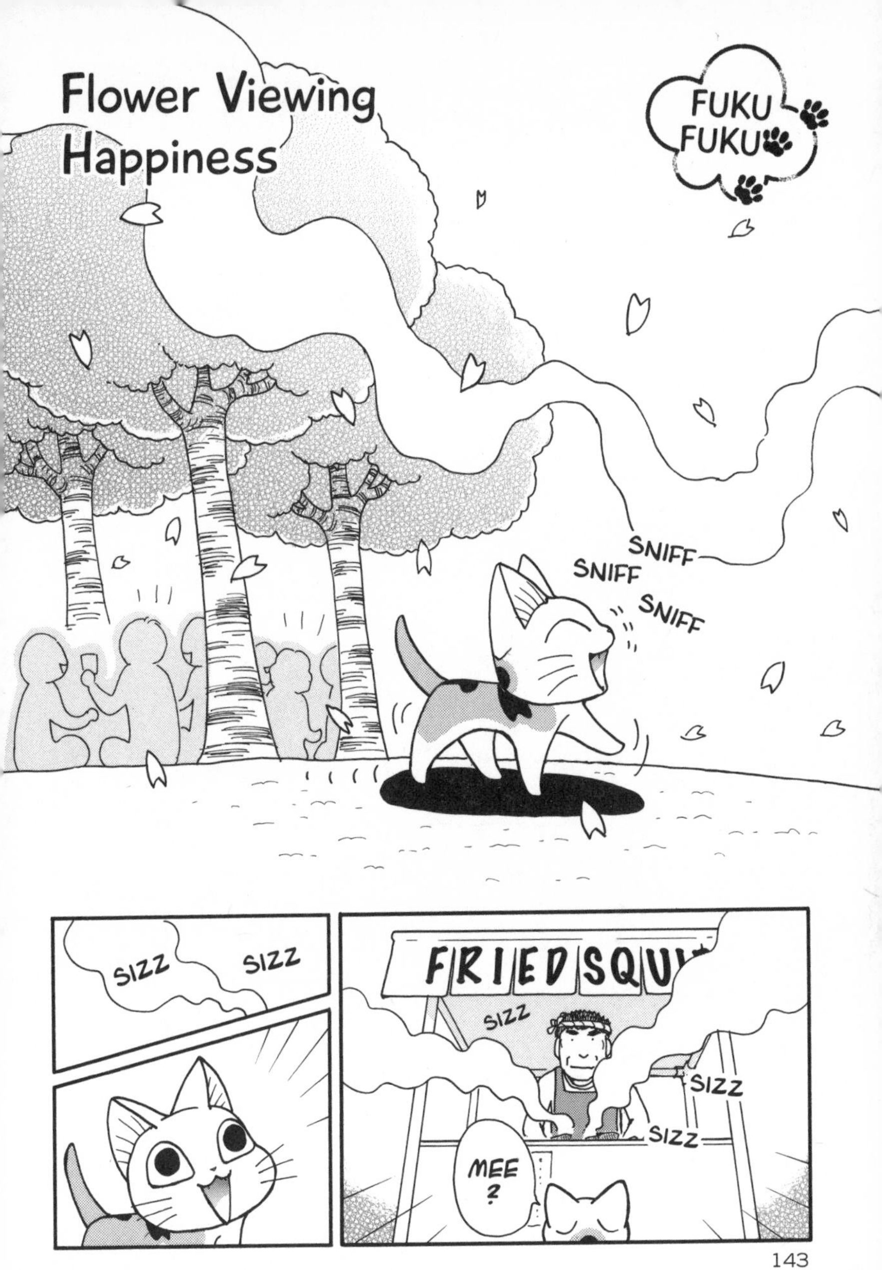
FUKU FUKU
SNIFF
SNIFF
SNIFF
SIZZ
SIZZ
FRIED SQU
SIZZ
SIZZ
SIZZ
MEE?

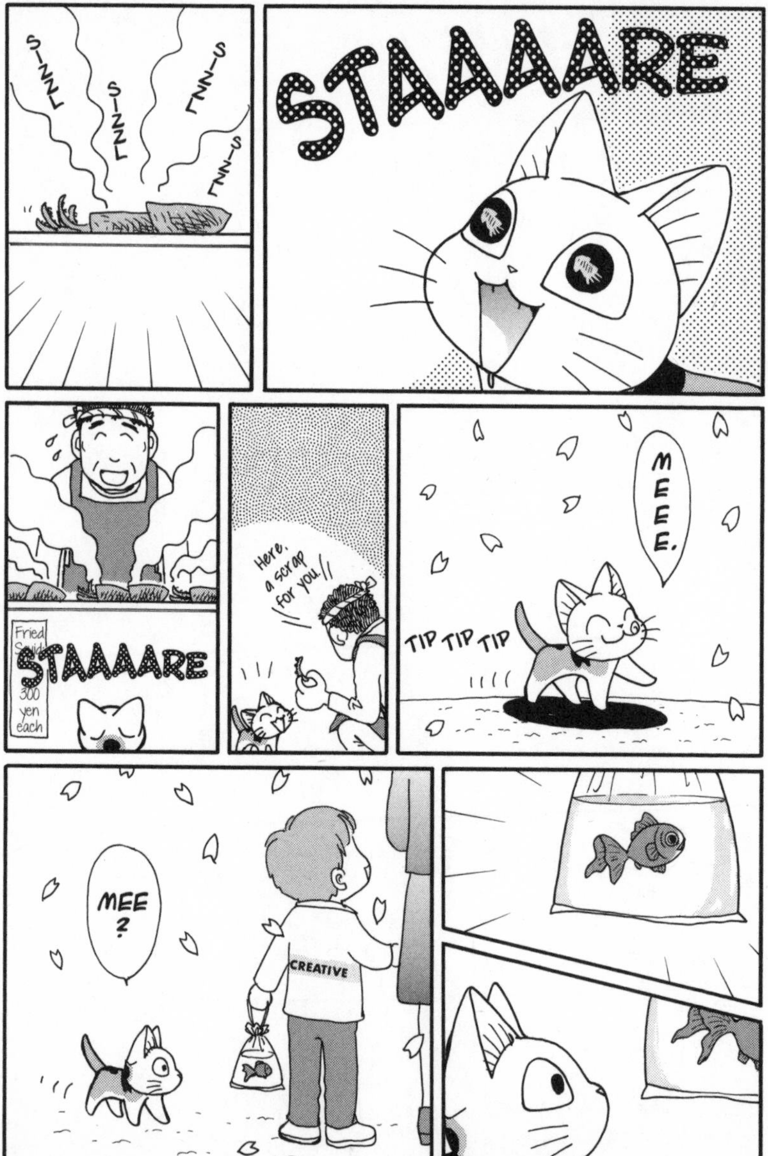
SIZZL
SIZZL
SIZZL
SIZZL
STAAAARE
Fried Squid 300 yen each
STAAAARE
Here, a scrap for you.
MEEE.
TIP TIP TIP
MEE?
CREATIVE

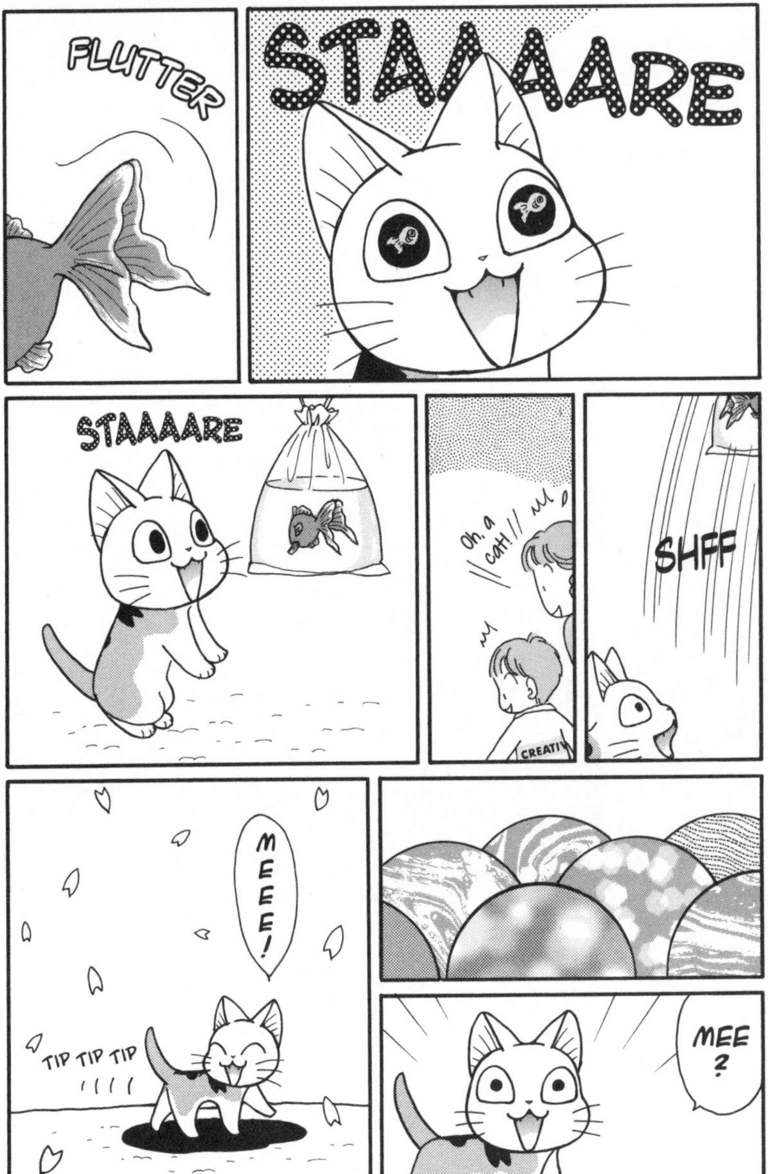
FLUTTER
STAAAARE
STAAAARE
Oh, a cat!
CREATIV
SHFF
MEEE!
TIP TIP TIP
MEE?

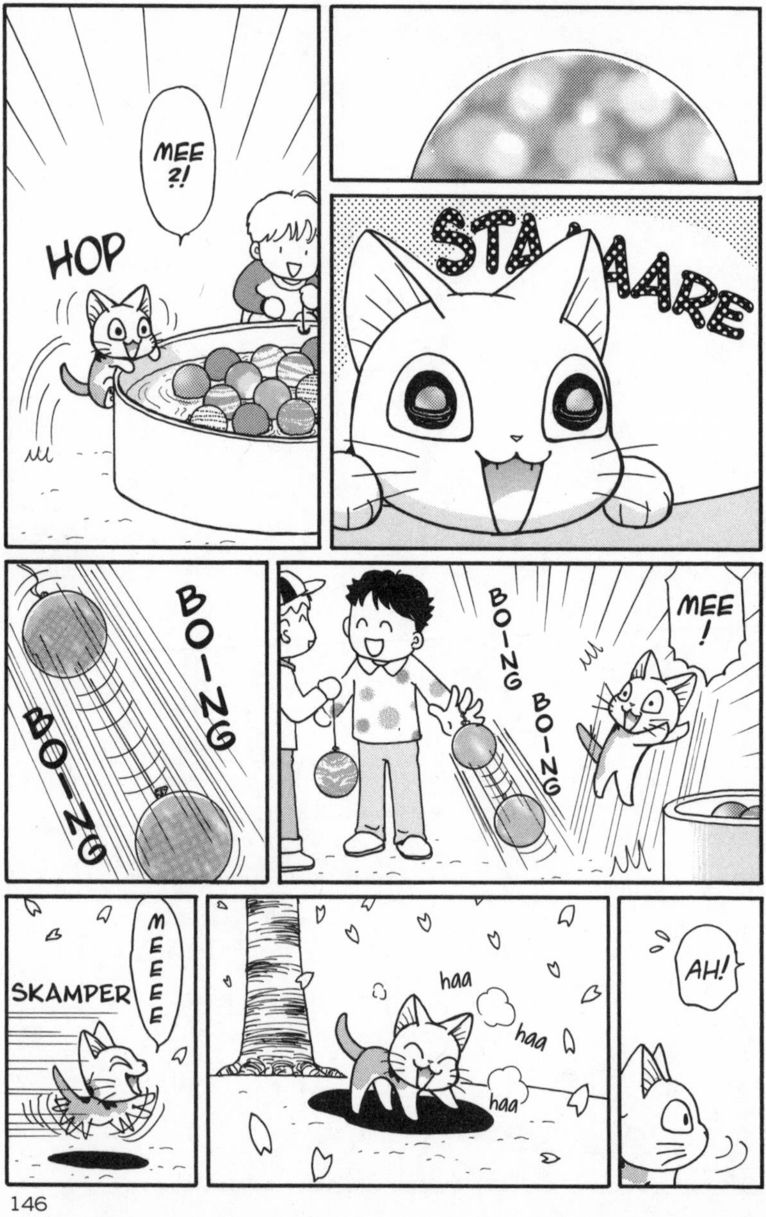
MEE ?!
HOP
STA AARE
BOING
BOING
BOING
BOING
MEE !
MEEEEE
SKAMPER
haa
haa
haa
AH!

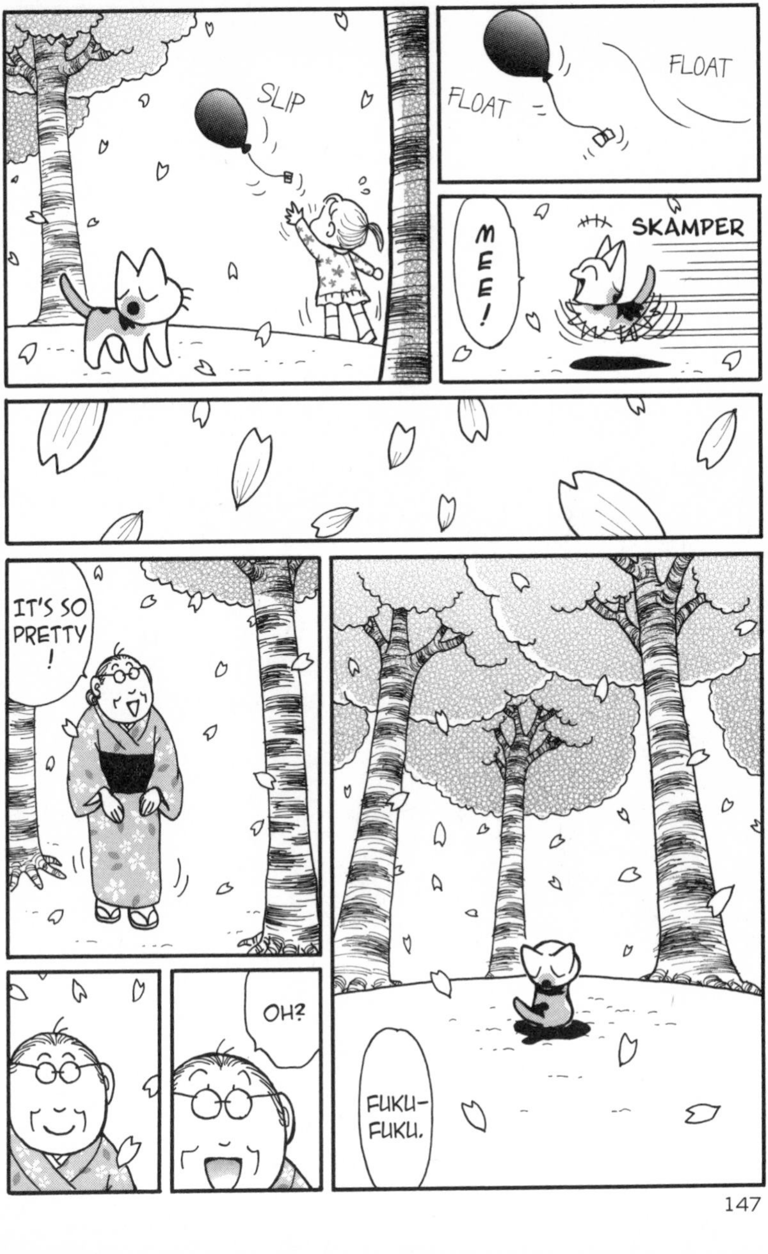
SLIP
FLOAT
FLOAT
MEE!
SKAMPER
IT'S SO PRETTY!
FUKU-FUKU.
OH?

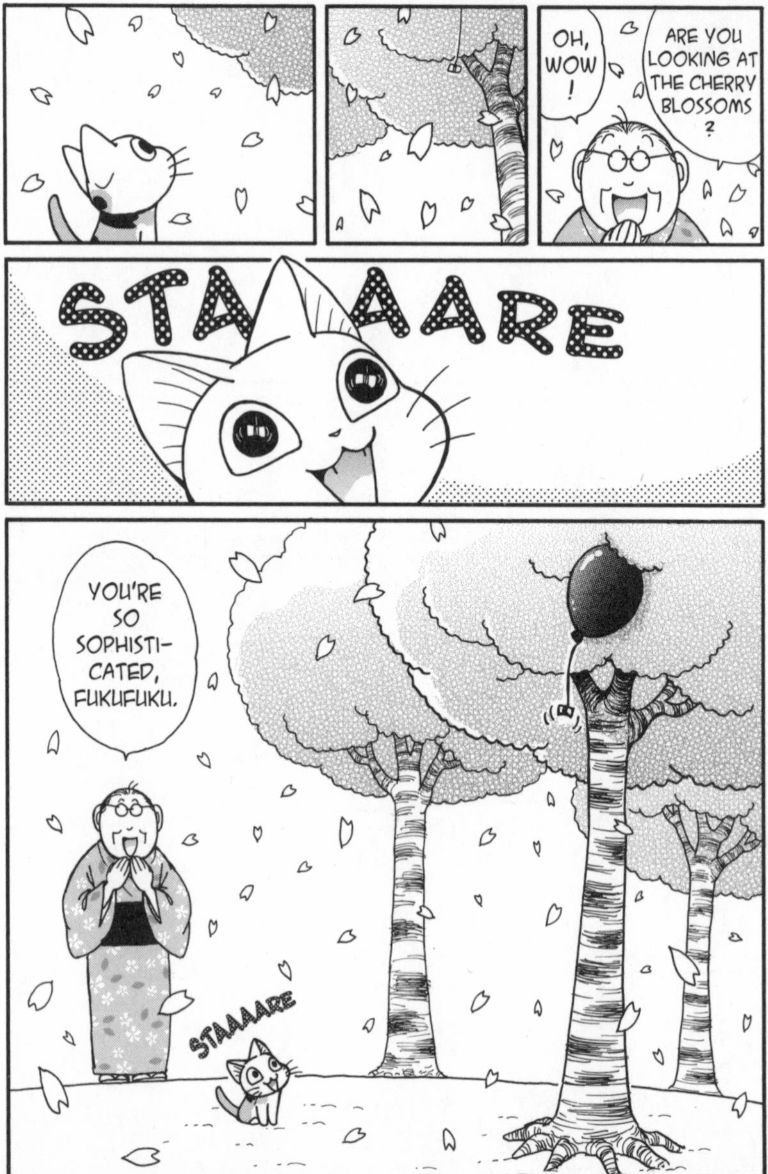
OH, WOW!
ARE YOU LOOKING AT THE CHERRY BLOSSOMS?
STAAARE
YOU'RE SO SOPHISTI-CATED, FUKUFUKU.
STAAAARE

the end

# The Puppy and the Kitten

FUKU FUKU

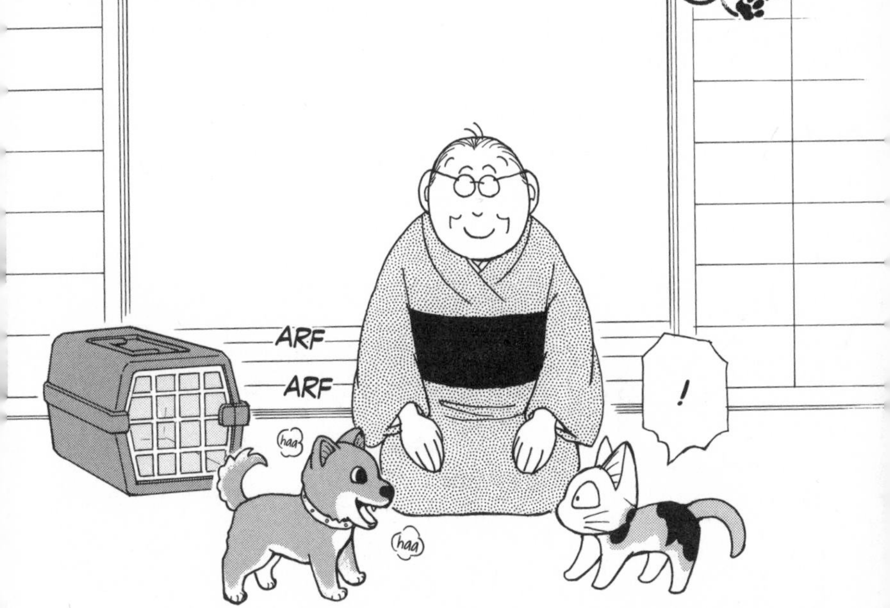
ARF
ARF
haa
haa
!

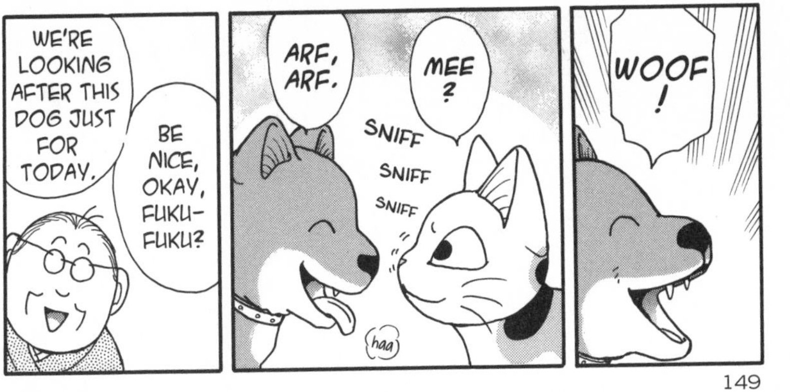
WE'RE LOOKING AFTER THIS DOG JUST FOR TODAY.
BE NICE, OKAY, FUKU-FUKU?
ARF, ARF.
MEE?
SNIFF
SNIFF
SNIFF
haa
WOOF!

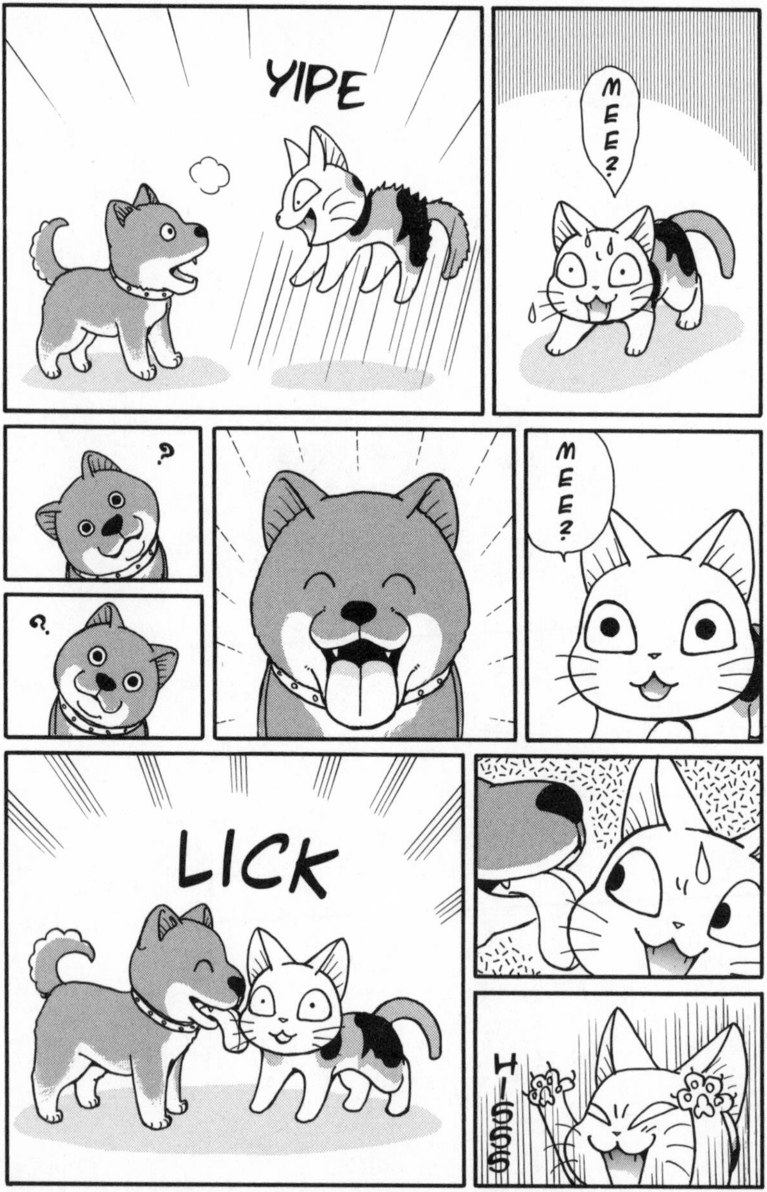
YIPE
MEE?
?
?
MEE?
LICK
HISSS

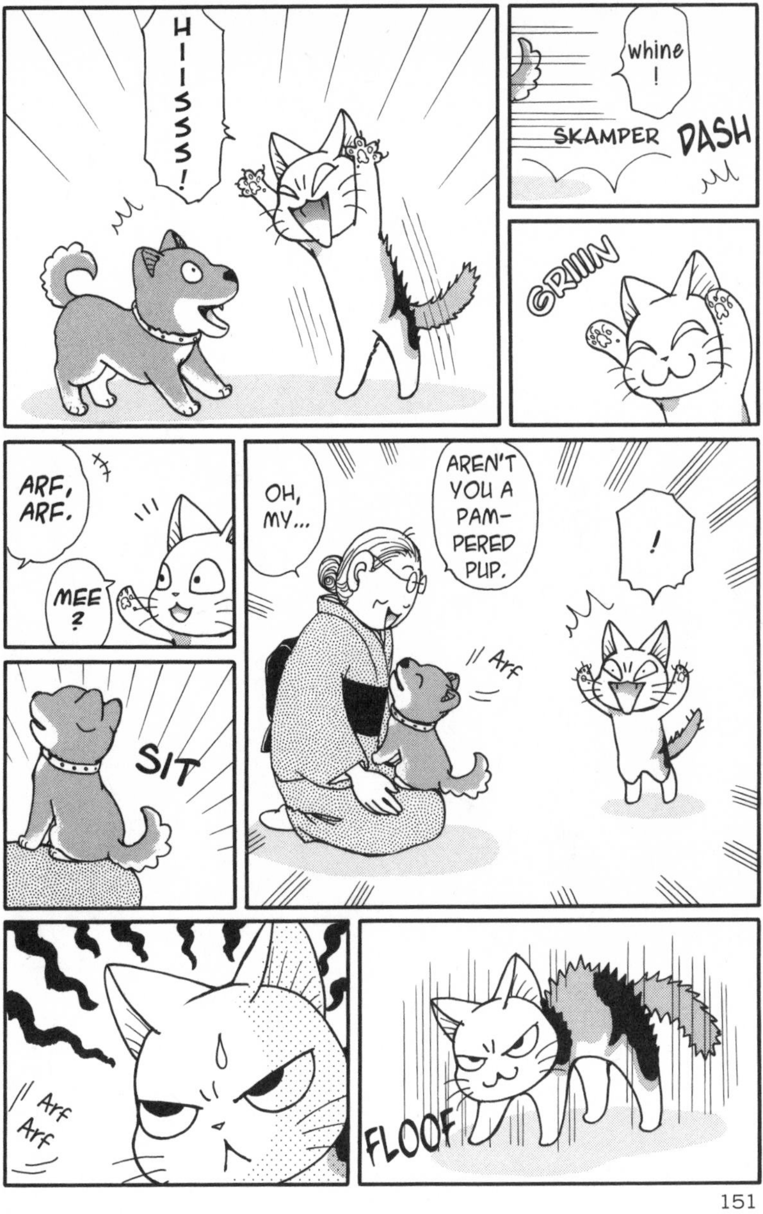
HIISSS!
whine!
SKAMPER
DASH
GRIIIN
ARF, ARF.
MEE?
SIT
OH, MY...
AREN'T YOU A PAMPERED PUP.
Arf
!
Arf
Arf
FLOOF

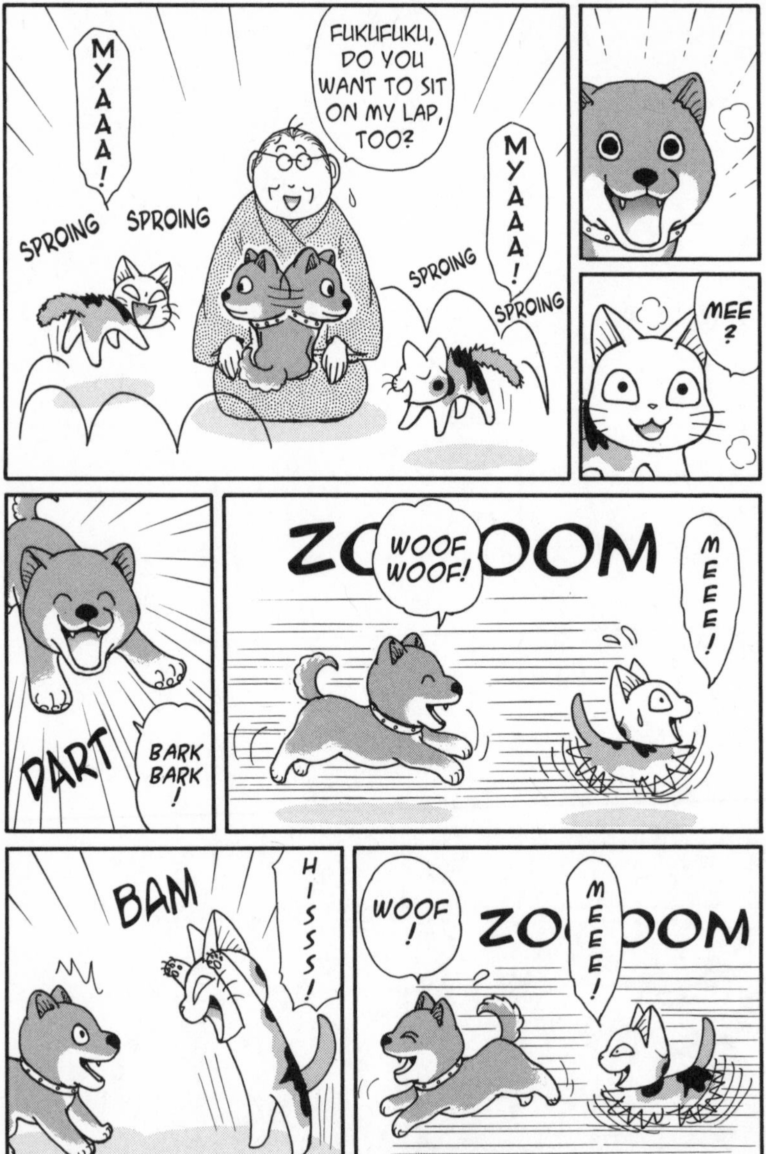
MYAAA!
FUKUFUKU, DO YOU WANT TO SIT ON MY LAP, TOO?
SPROING SPROING
MYAAA!
SPROING
SPROING
MEE?
DART
BARK BARK!
ZOOOOM
WOOF WOOF!
MEEE!
BAM
HISSS!
WOOF!
ZOOOOM
MEEE!

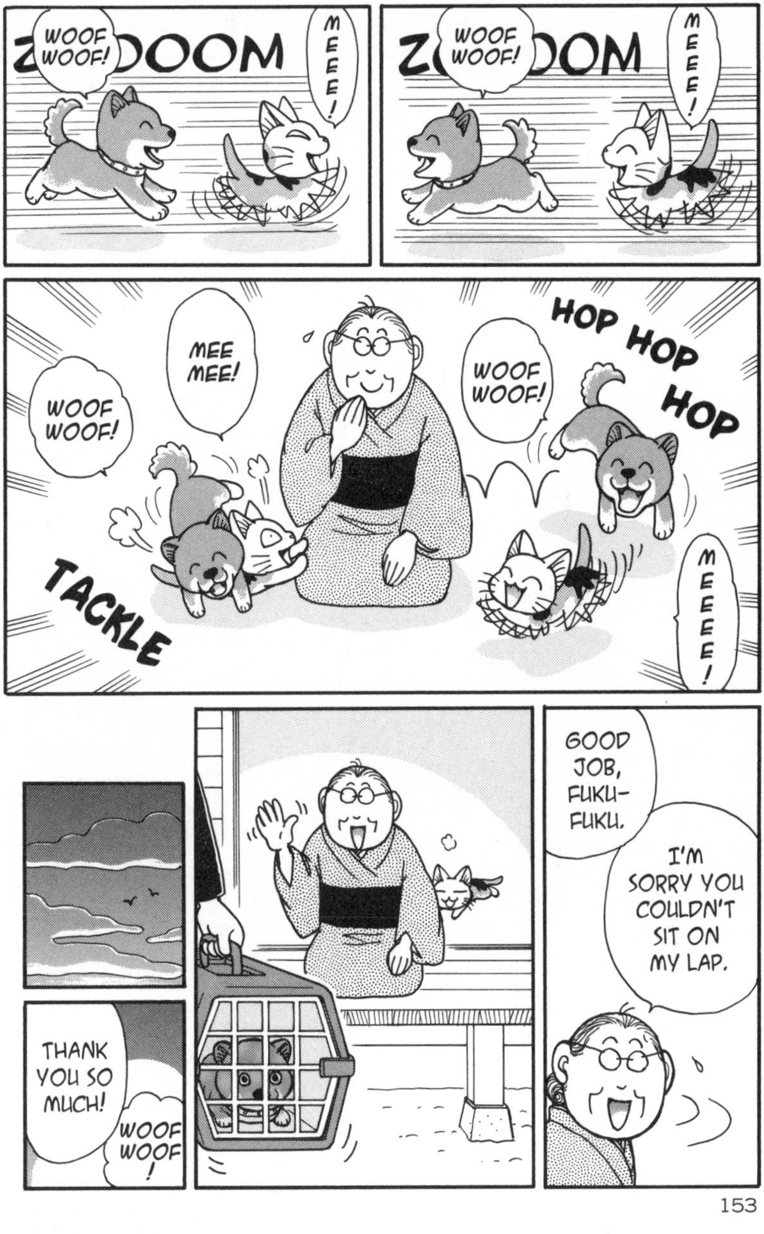
WOOF WOOF!
ZOOOOM
MEEE!
WOOF WOOF!
ZOOOOM
MEEE!
WOOF WOOF!
MEE MEE!
WOOF WOOF!
HOP HOP HOP
TACKLE
MEEEE!
THANK YOU SO MUCH!
WOOF WOOF!
GOOD JOB, FUKU-FUKU.
I'M SORRY YOU COULDN'T SIT ON MY LAP.

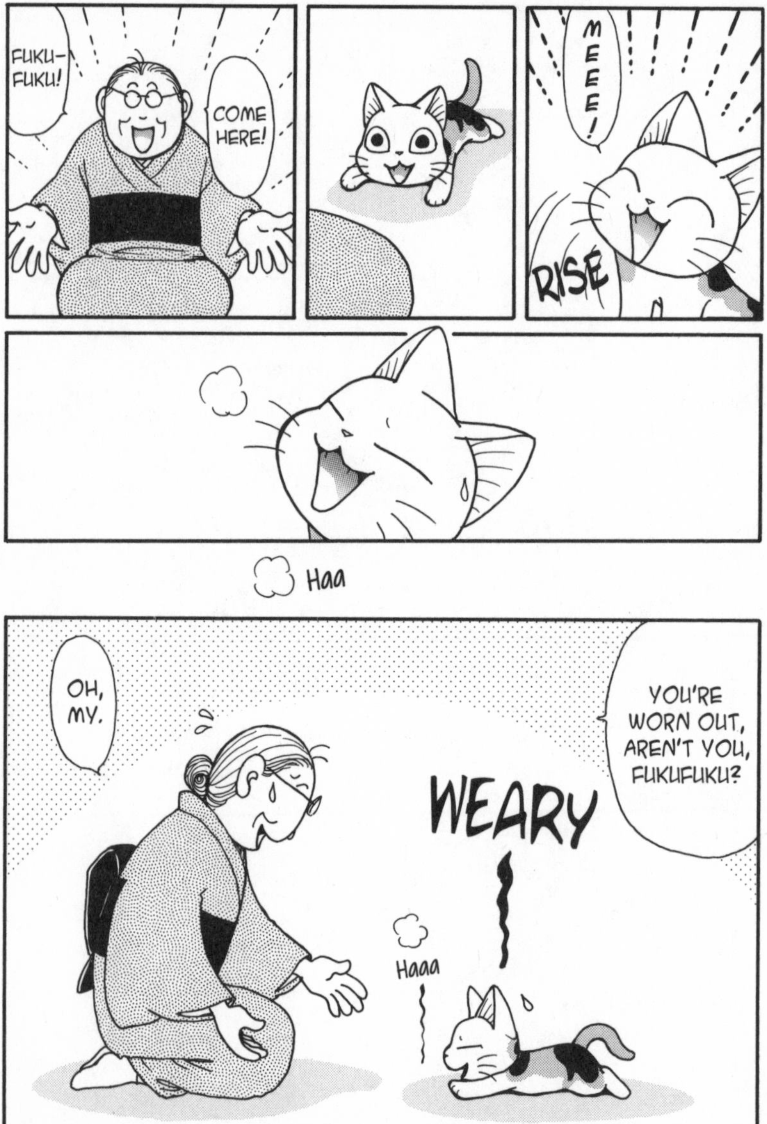
FUKU-FUKU!
COME HERE!
MEEE!
RISE
Haa
OH, MY.
YOU'RE WORN OUT, AREN'T YOU, FUKUFUKU?
WEARY
Haaa

the end

FUKU
FUKU

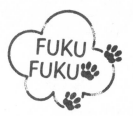

# This Book is the Cat's Meow

Celebrating the conclusion of Konami Kanata's international megahit *Chi's Sweet Home*, **The Complete Chi** is a new edition that honors some of the best Japan has ever offered in the field of cat comics. A multiple *New York Times* Best Seller and two-time winner of the *Manga.Ask.com* Awards for Best Children's Manga, Konami Kanata's tale of a lost kitten has been acclaimed by readers worldwide as an excellent example of a comic that has truly been accepted by readers of all ages.

Presented in a brand new larger omnibus format each edition compiles three volumes of kitty cartoon tales, including two bonus cat comics from Konami Kanata's **FukuFuku** franchise, making **The Complete Chi's Sweet Home** a must have for every cat lover out there.

"*Chi's Sweet Home* made me smile throughout... It's utterly endearing. This is the first manga I've read in several years where I'm looking forward to the [next] volume."

—Chris Beveridge, *Mania.com*

"Konami Kanata does some pretty things with watercolor, and paces each of the little vignettes chronicling Chi's new life to highlight just the right moments for maximum effect... This is truly a visual treat."
—*Comics and More*

## Part 1 contains volumes 1-2-3

## Part 2 contains volumes 4-5-6

# Parts 1 and 2 Available Now!

# The Complete

# Chi's
# Sweet Home

## Part 1

### Konami Kanata

# nichijou

## my ordinary life

## (1)

keiichi arawi

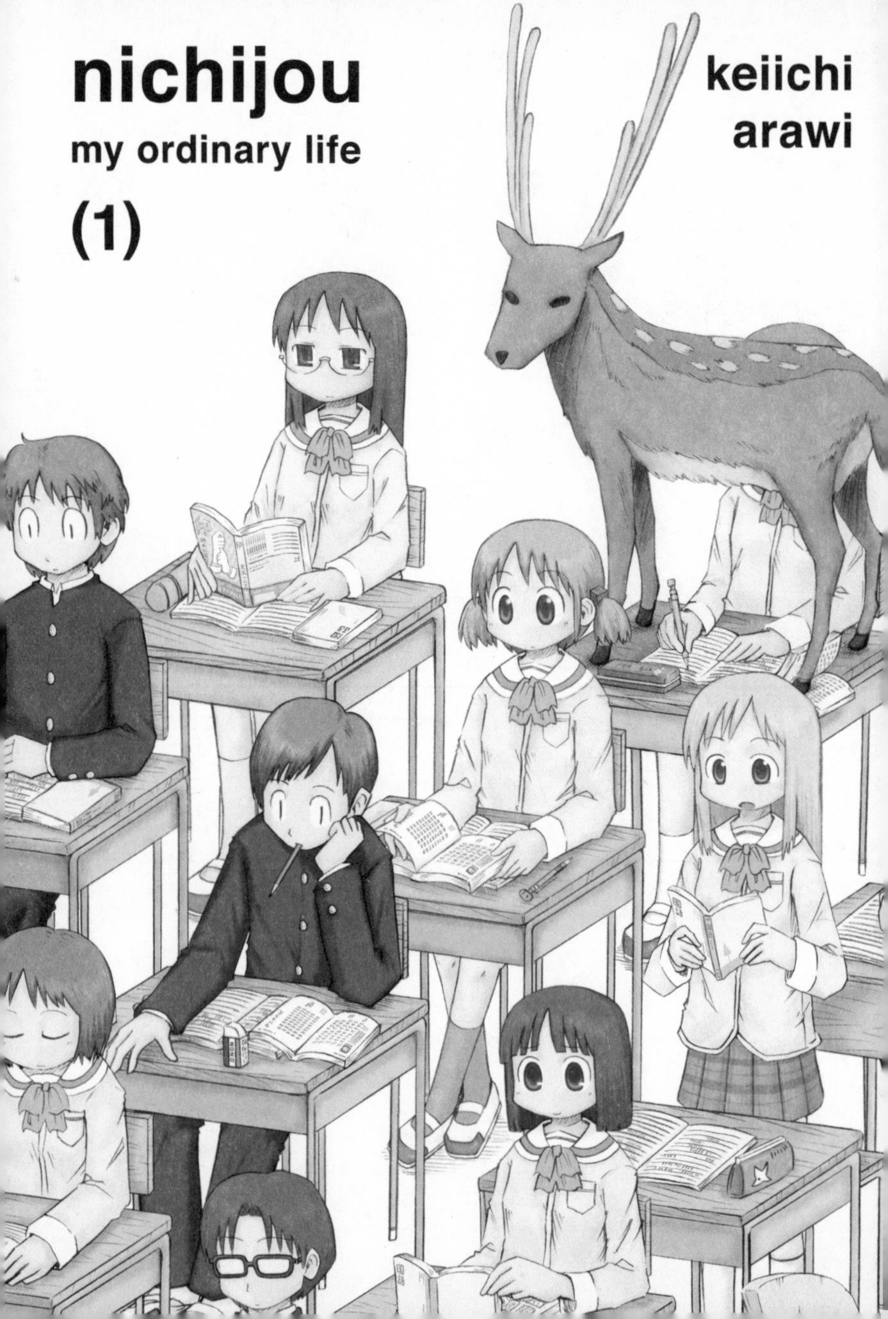

## define "ordinary"

in this just-surreal-enough take on the "school genre" of manga, a group of friends (which includes a robot built by a child professor) grapple with all sorts of unexpected situations in their daily lives as high schoolers.

the gags, jokes, puns and haiku keep this series off-kilter even as the characters grow and change. check out this new take on a storied genre and meet the new ordinary.

# on sale this march!

# My Neighbor Seki

Tonari no Seki-kun

Takuma Morishige

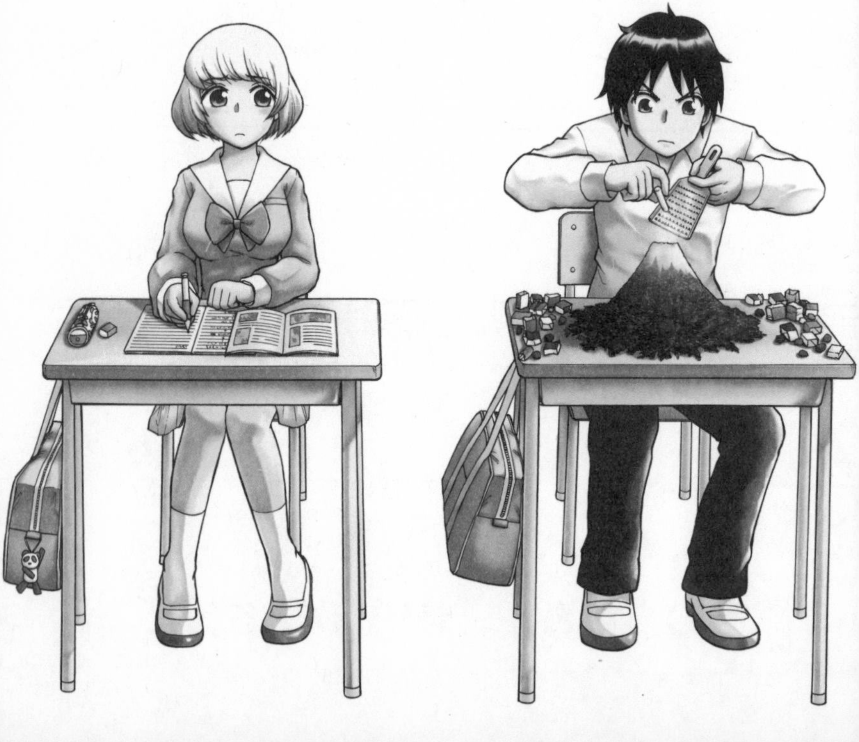

# The Master of Killing Time

Toshinari Seki takes goofing off to new heights. Every day, on or around his school desk, he masterfully creates his own little worlds of wonder, often hidden to most of his classmates. Unfortunately for Rumi Yokoi, his neighbor at the back of the room, his many games, dioramas, and projects are often way too interesting to ignore; even when they are hurting her grades.

## Volumes 1-6 available now!

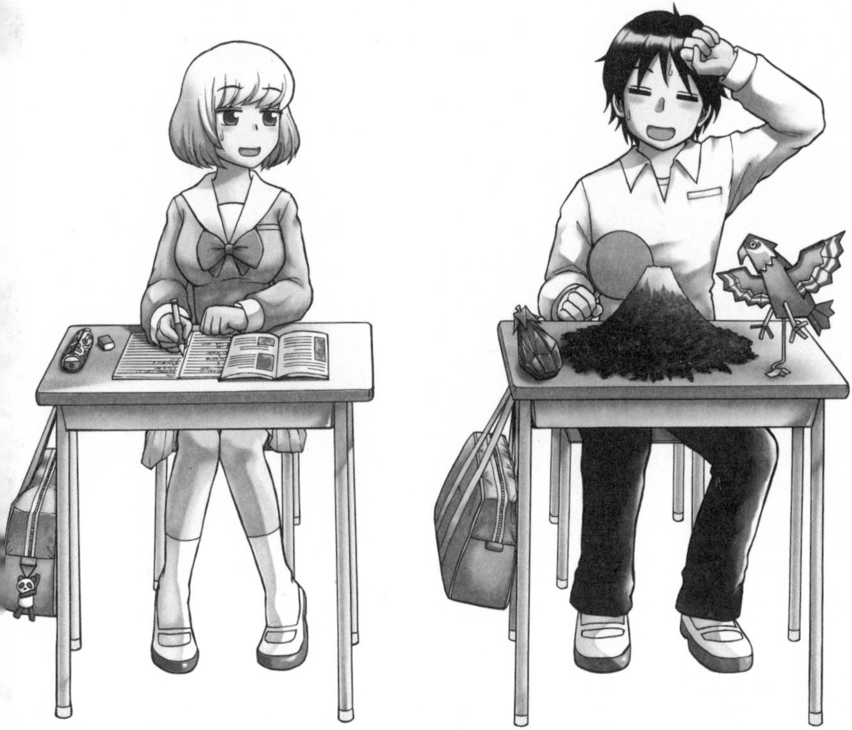

# FukuFuku: Kitten Tales

Translation - Marlaina McElheny
         Ed Chavez
Production - Grace Lu
         Anthony Quintessenza

First published in Japan in 2014 by Kodansha, Ltd., Tokyo
Publication for this English edition arranged through Kodansha, Ltd., Tokyo

Translation provided by Vertical Comics, 2016
Published by Vertical, Inc., New York

Originally published in Japanese as *FukuFuku Funya~n Ko-neko da Nyan* by Kodansha, Ltd., 2014
*FukuFuku Funya~n Ko-neko da Nyan* first serialized in *Be Love*, Kodansha, Ltd., 2013-

This is a work of fiction.

ISBN: 978-1-942993-43-8

Manufactured in Canada

First Edition

Vertical, Inc.
451 Park Avenue South, 7th Floor
New York, NY 10016
www.vertical-comics.com

Vertical books are distributed through Penguin-Random House Publisher Services.